With the Assist

A Boston Playmakers Novel

Nikki Reid

First Edition

ISBN: 979-8-234-05764-8

Cover design by Gisele G.

Published by Nikki Reid

For the women who never accept anything less than everything.

1

Wesley

I'm fighting with a dress.

It's black, expensive, and currently winning.

"You look hot," Avery says from my bathroom doorway, her mouth tilted into a smug grin as she admires her handiwork. Also known as me. "Headline-worthy hot. If the Boston City Athlete Awards had a Most Likely to Get Hit On category, you'd win."

"I look like I can't breathe." I tug at the fabric that's digging into my ribs. "And I don't need to get hit on. I need to survive three hours of forced mingling and get eight hours of sleep before training tomorrow."

Harper snorts from the edge of my bed, scrolling through her phone and eating the last of the Oreos. "Most people don't schedule early morning training after an awards banquet. Especially not after just winning the championship."

I don't have the luxury of being like most people.

"Most people aren't trying to get picked up for the U.S. Women's National Team."

Our season ended this week, but I have no plans to slow down. My off-season training starts tomorrow morning with cardio and weightlifting, followed by yoga in the afternoon, then ice baths and massages in the evening to help with recovery.

Not tonight. Tonight I have this stupid ceremony that probably won't even serve anything within my diet plan. It's not my figure I'm worried about. My grueling exercise regimen takes care of that, leaving me toned in all the right places. My concern is ensuring optimal performance. Everything in my life, down to what I eat, is centered around guaranteeing my excellence on the field.

This year, the National Team is within my reach, and I can almost feel that jersey on my skin. I want it more than I want to breathe. Events like tonight's are distractions I don't need.

In theory, one night off shouldn't matter. Except the last time I let myself forget my priorities, I'd almost blown everything. I won't make the same mistake twice.

Avery pushes off the doorway and saunters across the room. Her confidence is the perfect accessory for her backless emerald dress. She looks like she stepped out of a magazine, not off the same field as me, with her bright red hair pulled into a slicked-back bun. She's showstopping and knows it.

"Coach Bennett would be so proud of you," she says. "Captain of the team. Face of the franchise. Hates dresses."

Next to her, I feel like a troll. A well-dressed troll, but still a troll. She claims confidence will make my dress work. I claim confidence is impossible while wearing five-inch heels and a dress this tight.

"I don't hate dresses," I say. "I hate clothes designed to be uncomfortable while serving no real purpose."

"This dress serves a purpose," Harper mumbles around her mouthful of cookies. "It makes men forget how to think with their heads. At least the one on their shoulders."

Avery howls and high-fives her. They get sick enjoyment out of my misery. I need new friends.

"That's exactly what I want to avoid." I latch a bracelet around my pale wrist. "A room full of male athletes boasting about how big and strong they are."

Avery grins, sliding on her heels that are somehow even taller than mine. "You think that's all they talk about?"

"I think they'll take one look at us." I motion between Avery and me. "And think we're just girls, not professional athletes."

"I like being both." Avery turns to the mirror, fixing her cleavage as if it wasn't already impressive.

We're opposites in every sense of the word. She might be small, but her personality is huge, and she knows it. The girl takes outgoing to another level. We have a running joke, that it's why we work so well. When I go anywhere with her, I don't have to say a word.

I catch my reflection in the mirror and grimace. My brown hair is curled into large waves that end midway down my back, and my makeup is dark. Since I prefer my hair up and my face bare, it feels like I'm pretending to be someone else.

It's fitting considering that's exactly what I'll have to do to get through the night. Be someone friendlier. Be someone who enjoys the attention. Be someone less intimidating.

"I don't understand why I have to go. I already thanked them for the nomination. That should be enough."

"You're the team captain," Harper says, offering me the last Oreo. "You can't send a fruit basket and call it leadership."

"I could," I argue, taking it from her. "I should."

I crawl up onto my bed and rest my head on her shoulder, the way I have since we became friends. The Oreo crumbles as I take a bite, scattering crumbs across my dress. I don't care enough to swipe them away. Screw the diet plan, Oreos are delicious. Besides, tonight is shot to hell anyway. Now, at least I'm enjoying one thing about this day.

"Send the fruit basket after you win." Her hug is warm, and it calms the storm of anxiety brewing inside me. She's always believed in me more than I believe in myself.

My commitment to soccer has nothing to do with ego or believing I'm the best. It's necessity. It's been my life for so long that I don't know how to carve it out of me. I stopped trying to a long time ago.

Avery leans in, fixing a loose curl near my temple. "Coach Bennett would hunt you down if you skipped."

I sigh. "She already threatened an extra conditioning session."

Harper winces, tucking a piece of her blond hair behind her ear. "That's cruel."

"Ha. That's supposed to be a deterrent?" Avery jokes. "Extra training for you is like orgasms for me. Never enough."

Harper and I both choke on our cookies.

"You are so wrong." I slap her shoulder. "Even if you aren't actually wrong at all." I sigh. "She knows I wouldn't let the team down, even if I do hate this."

Avery rolls her eyes. "You hate social events. You secretly love winning awards."

"I love winning games," I correct. "Awards are for the ego."

Harper laughs. "God, you're exhausting."

"You'd think after seven years together, you'd be less averse to fun." Avery brushes more blush onto my cheeks.

She's been my glam expert since freshman year, back when we both played for Boston College. I wish I could say I had more fun back then, but I wasn't much better. Still, we fell in love with this city together.

After college, I managed to get a contract here, and after one season apart professionally, the soccer gods shone down on us, and Avery signed with Boston, too.

Now, as she touches up my makeup for the hundredth time, I realize it isn't the makeover that I hate. It's what the night represents. Shaking hands with people who don't even know what a center midfielder is while standing next to one.

As women in sports, we're expected to mix and mingle, always wearing a smile on our faces while people act like they know more about our sport than we do.

The mansplaining at these kinds of events is usually out of control. And while I prefer to stay quiet, I have a hard time biting my tongue when people deserve to be put in their place.

"I have fun."

"What's the last fun thing you did?" Avery challenges.

Shit. My mind actually comes up blank. Empty. That should be the only sign I need to know that they're right, but I refuse to acknowledge it.

"I ran that 10k for the animal shelter."

"You mean the one you took so seriously you trained for it?" Harper asks, standing and curling her shirt up to catch the falling cookie crumbs.

"Says the girl who married an accountant," I fire back.

Harper shoots me a look as she dumps the crumbs into the trash. "James is a very exciting accountant."

"Name one exciting thing he's done," Avery demands.

"He proposed to me at midfield, during my last collegiate soccer game."

Avery and I exchange a look, silently acknowledging how little we understand her choice to give up her dreams for a guy utterly undeserving of the sacrifice.

A brief silence settles over the room, and I regret prodding at her. Talking about her soccer career and early retirement makes her nostalgic. It's like when a song you haven't heard in years comes on, and you still know all the words.

She'd been more talented than Avery and I combined despite being three years younger. When James, her high school sweetheart, proposed, she gave it all up and married him the second she graduated this past summer.

Considering she would've been able to play anywhere she wanted, I'd be lying if I said her choice didn't bum me out. All three of us playing on the same team, kicking ass and owning the field together, would've been a dream.

But underneath it was a bite of jealousy because she could choose a lower-paying career as a teacher without consequences. I'd never tell her that, though. If she is happy, I'm happy for her.

I clear my throat, throwing myself back into the line of fire. "Okay. What about when we wrapped every single thing in Coach Bennett's office with Christmas wrapping paper?"

Harper's quiet demeanor is replaced with laughter. Mission accomplished.

Avery's face lights up. "Every single paperclip. It took her hours to unwrap it all."

"And it took us a week of suicides to pay for it."

"Worth it, but that was a year ago. If you're counting that as your most recent fun, we have a problem."

I don't want to unpack that. Not tonight. Maybe, not ever.

"You're twenty-five," Avery says. "Single and hot. The room will be filled with professional athletes who have stamina." She wiggles her eyebrows.

"I have stamina," I say, knowing that's not what she means.

"You know what you don't have?"

Harper cuts her off. "She means a partner who's not battery-operated."

"You know nothing about my vibrator."

"You mean the one over here?" Avery sprints toward my nightstand drawer, but I stop her by launching a pillow across the room.

"Leave him alone!" I squeal, cheeks flushing when I realize I gave it a gender.

They both turn their heads to me, eyebrows raising, before we dissolve into a fit of laughter. For a moment, all the pressure and expectations fade.

These two are the only people who somehow get me to let my guard down. They might tease me about being too serious and focused, but they know I have my reasons, and they accept them. They accept me.

My circle may be small, but I'd take two friends like them over anyone else every single time.

"Seriously, though, you need to put yourself out there. We're only this young once." Avery gives me her look. The one that says 'I'm right and you will not win this.'

"I've tried dating." I switch the contents of my everyday purse into my small clutch. "They all suck."

The real truth is more embarrassing. It's been four years without sex. Not because the opportunity hasn't been there, but because I refuse to waste time on building a connection that might not even last. My family needs my support, which means my career needs my attention. Connections and sex are just noise. They'll still be there when my athleticism fades.

Avery reapplies her red lipstick for a final time and offers it to me. I shake my head. It would inevitably end up all over my teeth. She shoves it into her purse. "Listen. You don't have to hook up with anyone. Appreciate the view. Live a little."

"I live plenty."

"You live on a training schedule," Harper says gently.

I shrug. There's no use pretending otherwise with them. "It works."

It has to.

My phone buzzes on the counter with a message from Coach Bennett.

Coach Bennett: Don't be late. Represent us well.

As if I need the reminder.

I groan. "She texts like my dad." The words slip out, and for a brief second, something twists inside me. My dad used to text that way before the hospital visits became more frequent. Before I started covering bills and pretending it didn't scare me. We stick to phone calls now.

It's just another reason why I'm working so hard to make the National Team. With him not working anymore, it falls on me to ensure that we're taken care of financially. It's the least I can do.

Harper grabs her glass of wine, finishing it in one gulp. "For what it's worth, I think it's good you're going."

"Why?"

"Because you deserve to be celebrated," she says. "Even if you hate the party."

I meet her eyes in the mirror. Harper has always been the soft one, human in a way Avery and I sometimes forget to be.

Avery claps her hands. "Okay. Final checks. Wesley, you look like sex in heels. In a good way. Harper, thank you for your emotional labor tonight. And me, I look incredible."

I take one last look at myself. Award nominee and reluctant attendee.

"Fine," I say. "Let's go get this over with."

"If either of you end up making out with a stranger, I want details," Harper calls from the entryway, halfway out the door.

The chilly October air stings my skin as people push past us. My apartment is small, but it's in the heart of the city. I like being in the thick of everything.

A limo waits at the curb.

"Avery. Please tell me you didn't."

"Think of it as a fancy bus."

I scoff, refusing to step closer.

"There's a red carpet," she reminds me. "We cannot pull up in your Hyundai."

I glare at her through the fake lashes that I already want to rip off. This was not the deal, and she knows it.

"You'd have refused or demanded to drive separately." Avery steps forward as the limo driver opens the door for her.

She isn't wrong. I groan inwardly at the amount of attention this is going to send our way.

"The winner of tonight's biggest award should arrive in style." She pulls me in next to her.

I roll my eyes at the car, but grin at the award. Sue me, I do like being nominated for this kind of thing. It shows the sacrifices are worth it. And as useless as I think this ceremony is, the award itself is just another achievement that can help propel my career forward.

It's only a fifteen-minute ride before the limo stops outside the event center. There is a red carpet leading to the doors, and the media crowd is huge.

The cameras click around us while the crowd leans forward to see who we are. The attention wanes once they realize I'm not someone they recognize.

My nomination does not equate to popularity. As is the case for most of the women athletes here tonight. Nobody really knows who we are. Occasionally, a couple of us might get some attention, but it always fades back out when the next story breaks.

It's not like I'm one of the players for the Blades, our city's professional hockey team. The general public is obsessed with them.

To be fair, it's not hard to see why. Every man on that team looks like he was built to be admired. You can't make it through the week without seeing something about one of their games or infamous nights out. I'm fairly certain that if the paparazzi could follow them into the bathroom, there'd be entire articles online outlining their shitting schedules. Yes, it really is that ridiculous.

If I were into conceited men, which I'm not, maybe I'd get the hype. But honestly, who wants to be Nathan Wilder's flavor of the week, just to be discarded when the novelty wears off? Not me.

I remind myself of that when my door opens, and I spot a cluster of Blades players by the entrance. I remind myself again when Nathan's deep brown eyes catch mine, and my breath hitches.

If arrogance had a face, it would smirk like that. He stands comfortably in his own body, shoulders relaxed as if nothing could stand against him. His black suit is tailored to a frame earned only through professional-level conditioning.

It's annoying and still, my eyes trail up his body anyway.

His dark hair falls messily over one eyebrow, and then…

He winks at me.

He fucking winks.

I force my eyes back to my feet, refusing to acknowledge him. Besides, I will not let myself trip in these stupid heels because I'm ogling someone I have no business ogling.

The flashes are blinding, and while the yelling may not be directed at me, it's loud enough to be distracting. When I finally make it through the crowd and onto the carpet, the Blades players are gone.

Nathan 'sin-in-a-suit' Wilder included.

Good.

2

Nathan

Awards shows are ninety percent small talk and ten percent pretending to enjoy it. I'd rather be at the bar, but our PR director insisted the Blades 'show face' tonight. That's code for smiling, shaking hands, and not starting a brawl on the dance floor.

Normally, I'd push back, but with my contract up at the end of the season, it's best to do what's asked of me.

It doesn't matter that I was drafted to the Blades at eighteen as their youngest player ever. It doesn't matter that after my two-year rookie deal ended, I'd snagged one of the best eight-year contracts in the league. It doesn't even matter that I want to start and end my career with the Blades. What matters is stats, and mine are shit.

After two years of decreasing goals and assists, it's hardly surprising that there's no talk of a contract extension. So, here I sit, ready to kiss the asses of the people who hold my future in their hands.

I fucking hate it.

The red carpet was brutal, full of reporters asking if the Blades are restructuring in the offseason. It was a nice way of asking if I'm going to be traded. I had smiled and given some bullshit responses that were sure to be painted in a bad light whenever they went public.

I've learned that it really doesn't matter what I say; someone will always find a way to poke holes in it. Once I figured that out, talking to reporters became easy.

Liam adjusts his tie for the tenth time, staring at his reflection in the champagne bucket. "Tell me I don't look like a GQ cover."

"You look like you're trying too hard," Wyatt mutters, his arms crossed. He's already drained his first drink, probably to numb the pain of being in public. Our goalie hates crowds and all things social.

Grayson pops a canapé into his mouth and grins at Liam. "You look great, man. Very tailored."

"That's not a compliment," I say.

Grayson shrugs. "Still true."

"So is the fact that I smoked you in our one-on-one drills this week." Liam grunts and sets the champagne bucket back up.

"Hey, I was trying to be nice." Grayson throws one of his mini pastries at Liam, who returns the favor.

"Fuck's sake. We're too old for a food fight. Grow up." Wyatt leans away as if that will make it less obvious that he's one of us.

I snort. At six-foot-five-inches with a permanent scowl etched onto his face, there is almost nothing Wyatt could do to make people forget he plays hockey.

I sip my champagne, letting the noise of the room fill my head. The banquet hall is packed with athletes, sponsors, reporters, and team staff. It's everything I should be good at navigating.

The right persona was hard to create: charming, confident, and only borderline cocky. The respectable bachelor. Someone seen out on the town as much as he's seen on the ice. It sells tickets and jerseys.

That persona is the only thing keeping me on the first line at the moment. It's hard to bench a crowd favorite and hometown hero, even if he's playing like trash.

Regardless, I'm dangerously close to getting pushed to the second line. Just the idea of playing on the wing with someone other than Liam at center pisses me off. It's starting to feel completely out of my control, especially considering nothing I do seems to help.

"Stop brooding." Liam claps a hand on my shoulder. "You look like someone told you the bar is closing."

"That would actually be tragic," Grayson adds, shoving a slider in his mouth. "Seriously, what's wrong with you? You love these things."

"That was before he pissed off Coach Rylan at practice by failing to score a single goal on me," Wyatt deadpans.

I glare at him. He's not wrong, just an ass.

Liam smirks. "Is contract year making you tense?"

"Oh, fuck off." I slap his hand away. "Where's your date? Teresa? Or is it Tina?" I rattle off more names I know he's hooked up with this month. I may be the team's eligible bachelor who doesn't take anything too seriously, but Liam is the playboy through and through. He couldn't keep it in his pants if he tried.

"Her name's Teagan," he huffs.

We're harsh, but that's our friendship in a nutshell: mild bullying and the unspoken willingness to take a puck to the face for each other. These idiots? They're family, and losing them if my contract tanks is what I'm most worried about.

I'm still good enough to go somewhere else, but I don't want to. Boston has been home for my entire life and leaving now? It wouldn't just be embarrassing, it'd be heartbreaking.

My eyes scan the room, checking who's here and which sponsors might need ego fluffing later. It's all the usual contenders, until I spot her.

The same long legs from the limo outside suddenly have my full attention. Most women here are soaking up the attention, but she looks like she'd rather be kicked in the shins.

I caught her checking me out when we were still outside. At least, I assume that's what she was doing, considering the way she blushed when I winked at her. Now, without the chaos of the media, I let my gaze trail over her.

Her brown hair is curled, trailing down her back. Her black dress hugs every delicious curve, cinching around her hips and showing off her figure. Damn it if she's not the sexiest woman here tonight.

Liam follows my gaze and whistles low. "Nice. Haven't seen her before. New reporter?"

"Publicist," Grayson guesses. "Or someone's plus one. Too put-together to be an intern."

Wyatt snorts. "She was dragged here against her will. Look at her jaw. She wants to murder someone."

He's not wrong. She's checking her phone, ignoring everyone, clearly wishing she were somewhere else. But even though she's miserable, she's turning heads. It's not an airbrushed influencer type of gorgeous, but the kind that's worked for if her toned legs are any indication.

I take note of the multiple men who watch her, but she doesn't seem to notice at all. She's either the most overconfident woman I've ever seen or utterly clueless. It doesn't really matter which one, I'm into it either way.

I don't date much, but one night with a woman who looks that good might be exactly what I need to get out of my head.

Liam elbows me. "If you're going over there, sprinkle in some charm and try not to scare her. She's obviously not from this scene."

"I'm always charming, and I'm not going over there." I am definitely going over there.

Wyatt snorts again. "Sure."

I hand my empty glass to a passing server. "Back in a minute."

Grayson smirks. "He's going to crash and burn."

"I am not. I'm just going to start a conversation."

"About what?" Liam's voice is a little too loud. "Her shoes? Her dress?"

My glare shuts him up. When I glance back at her, another woman is by her side, and they giggle with each other. On a whim, I grab Liam by the shoulder. "Let's hope Trisha doesn't mind you playing wingman."

"It's Teagan," Liam says dryly. "And what do you..."

I ignore him, pulling him along as I stride toward her. The crowd parts around me. I smile and nod when necessary, like I've done a thousand times before.

It's the same old shit, except for how my pulse picks up as I get closer to her.

She turns, unaware I'm approaching. Her high cheekbones catch the light, and her glossed lips are tempting.

I slow to a stop a few feet from her. For the first time tonight, maybe in my life, I don't have a line prepared.

She doesn't even notice me.

It does something annoying to my ego. People notice me. I'm Nathan Wilder, one of the best players in the NHL, or at least I was. I shake my head to rid myself of the doubt that's started creeping in.

I've never used my status to get a girl, but it never hurts. It saves time getting through the surface stuff like my name and job. Though, based on her indifference, it might not get me anywhere tonight.

Liam coughs, pushing me forward until her piercing eyes finally land on me. They're the blue of a cloudless summer sky.

My mouth goes dry. Fucking hell.

"Yes?" She asks, her voice soft and sure. Her hand fidgets at her side in a tiny, nervous motion. It's a small crack in the confidence she radiates. I take it as a sign that approaching her wasn't a mistake.

"I don't think we've met. I'm Nathan." I lift my hand slightly before realizing that it's a ridiculous thing to do. I'm not going to shake her hand like a business partner. Idiot.

She tilts her head ever so slightly, lips curving into the faintest smile. "Hello," she says, but she doesn't give me a name. Not yet. It becomes my personal mission to get it.

"I have to say, you seem to be surviving this circus better than most."

"You know what they say." Her laugh is brief. I wish it were longer. "If you can't beat them, join them."

"It's impressive. Most people here seem like they're trying too hard."

She raises an eyebrow, scanning my custom suit. "You mean, like you?"

Liam snorts into his drink, and I elbow him. Mystery girl watches me, amused, but not brushing me off entirely.

I let my eyes wander over her for a minute before pushing a little further. "So, are you here as an invitee, or has your date made a terrible mistake in leaving you alone?"

"Why do you want to know?" She asks, letting the challenge hang. Definitely not brushing me off.

I smile. Game on.

"Curiosity, mostly. Also, trying to toss my hat in the ring before the rest of the room does."

Her friend bumps her shoulder as if she's been saying the same thing all night. Interesting. If her friend has had to reiterate how good she looks, then the confidence oozing off her isn't related to her appearance, even if it should be.

"That's a bold assumption considering you're the only one who's approached me tonight."

"Trust me. Plenty of guys wish they'd beaten me over here, but they knew they didn't stand a chance." I take a sip of my drink.

"And you do?" She quirks an eyebrow.

"A guy has to have dreams." I shrug, dialing up the charm. "I'll definitely be dreaming about that dress."

Her friend snickers, but she shakes her head. "There are at least ten other people here in a similar dress. It's hardly impressive."

"I'd say managing to look that stunning in it, especially when you don't even want to be here, is impressive."

"I never said I don't want to be here."

"Do you?" My lips twitch as she pretends to consider my question.

"Nope." Her lips pop at the end of the word, forming an O that heats me from the inside out. I force my eyes away from her lips before I embarrass myself.

Liam steps toward her friend, grinning like a shark. "Hey there. I'm Liam."

Both girls exchange a look, and a silent conversation happens in front of us. Finally, the smoke show in the emerald green dress turns toward Liam. I swear she could cut glass with the look on her face.

"I don't fuck hockey players," she says flatly, no hesitation or mercy in sight.

Liam freezes mid-charm, lips parting in confusion. "Right. Got it," he stammers.

She saunters away, and Liam's eyes trail her across the room.

I feel a little sorry for him after dragging him over here. That being said, my mystery girl hasn't shut me down yet. I shove the ceremony program from the bar top into Liam's hands, so he can act distracted while I keep shooting my shot.

"Your friend's… fierce." I nod in the direction of the redhead, now surrounded by a group of girls across the room.

She smiles, taking a sip of what looks like water. "Avery's not a fan of athletes, especially hockey players."

"And you?" I ask.

Her eyes widen, and she shifts on her feet. I find myself focused on her red nails that are toying with the straw of her drink.

"To be determined." She bites her lip.

"Maybe we can exchange—"

I don't get to finish before Liam starts waving the program in front of me. "Did you see this shit?"

"Dude." I glare at him.

He rubs the back of his neck sheepishly. "Um, sorry to interrupt. But seriously, look at this."

He shoves the program into my hand. I lock eyes with my mystery girl and give her an apologetic smile. She nods as if understanding the pain of over-the-top friends. Considering Avery's exit a few minutes ago, she probably does.

"They have some fucking nobody winning athlete of the year. Who the hell is Wesley Miller?" Liam points to the center of the program.

Clear as day, it says: **2025 Athlete of the Year – Wesley Miller.**

"I've never heard of him," I say. After ten years of playing professional sports in this city, I know most teams and their players.

"The guy doesn't even sound like an athlete. More like a finance bro." Liam shakes his head in frustration.

She chuckles into her drink, letting us rant about our broken streak as the recipients of this award. Normally, I'd be as worked up as Liam, but I can't help grinning at her.

"We brought home the Stanley Cup," Liam mutters, face scrunched up. "And some random guy gets the nod?"

I try not to wince. To be fair, last year Wyatt won athlete of the year. The year before was Grayson. I was the year before him. I'm sure Liam had his hopes up.

"The Stanley Cup was four years ago," the girl says smoothly, taking a sip of her drink. "It's Athlete of the Year, not Athlete of Four Years Ago."

Ouch. But fair. I swallow my guilt, knowing our team's setbacks happen to correlate with my personal slump. My team deserves the cup. Knowing that I am a huge reason we keep missing the mark fucking sucks.

"She has a point," I concede, patting Liam on the back.

"Still, some unknown name getting it doesn't sit right."

"Definitely not," she adds, sympathizing with him. Something is glinting in her eye. "He's probably a loser with a name like that."

"Oh, he's definitely a nobody." Liam looks around the room as if the guy will have an arrow above his head, pointing him out.

Alright. Enough of this. I still need her number, and my chance of getting it is shrinking.

"Anyway, your name?" I ask, flashing my flirtiest smile.

She sucks on her bottom lip, eyes glinting mischievously. I'd do just about anything to know what she's thinking right now.

The program announcer's voice booms over the speakers, signaling the start.

Without answering me, she turns toward her table.

"What's your name?" I ask again, trying not to yell across the room like a desperate idiot, even if that's exactly how I feel.

At the last second, she glances back, lips curving enough to drive me insane.

"You'll see," she says, leaving me at the bar with my mouth half open, watching her walk away.

3

Wesley

By the time I reach my table, my pulse has finally stopped sprinting, and I'm ready to pretend the last ten minutes didn't happen. The ballroom lighting glitters off crystal chandeliers above, casting soft gold across the tables that are too elegant for the chaos in my head.

Avery is already seated, stirring her cocktail with a knowing smirk like she's been waiting her entire life to interrogate me.

"That little chat looked interesting." She arches her brow. "Anything you want to share?"

I focus on my water instead of her face. "Not particularly. A guy talked. I listened. End of story."

"A guy who happens to be Nathan Wilder. Boston Blade's forward. Future Hall of Famer. He's six foot two and the owner of cheekbones sharp enough to cut glass."

"I don't care who he is. I'm not interested."

The lie comes easily, practiced. It's what I'm supposed to say, but it shouldn't tremble at the edges the way it does.

Avery rests her chin on her hand, studying me. "You flirted."

"I'm blaming the dress. It's cut off my oxygen for far too long."

I force my face to remain neutral, but inside I'm spiraling. His voice replays, telling me I'm stunning even though I still don't believe it.

Surely, I don't stack up to the women who must constantly throw themselves at him. Everyone is obsessed with the hockey hometown hero. The man might as well have action figures made of himself.

There is no way that I'd catch his eye. He'd probably been heading for the bar to get another drink and hit on me out of convenience. Yeah, that was it.

One thing is for sure: the commercials and ads don't do him justice. They don't show how broad he is up close or the woodsy smell that lingers when he is close enough.

Flirting back was knee-jerk. A momentary lapse in sanity. I couldn't help the way my eyes tracked his hand rubbing at his freshly shaven jaw, or how I leaned toward him.

Avery taps my hand. "You know, it's fine to be interested in someone."

"I'm not that girl."

"But you can be tonight."

I swallow. The suggestion presses against the back of my neck, tempting in a way it's never been, but I push it away.

"Even if I were that girl, I wouldn't be that girl with a guy like that."

"What do you mean?"

I laugh, recalling the way Nathan and Liam ranted about me without realizing it.

"They saw that some guy named Wesley Miller won Athlete of the Year and were pissed."

Avery's eyes widen before she leans over, howling. "No way."

"Oh yes. The outrage was real. Apparently, some nobody stole their spotlight. They don't see how some guy no one's heard of could win over them."

"Did you correct them?"

I wiggle my eyebrows. "I figured the surprise would be more fun."

"This is why we're friends." Avery turns to glance at the Blades' table, her humor dimming. "The one shoveling appetizers down his throat is looking at me."

"Ignore him," I say, rubbing her shoulder. "But Avery, he's not Damon."

Her eyes go cold at the name. She dated Damon for a year before they broke up a couple of months ago, but she refuses to talk about why it ended. The ballroom isn't the place to unravel heartbreak, though, so I let it go.

The lights dim slightly, signaling the start of the ceremony. Presenters shuffle onto the stage as it begins with the usual lineup of awards: community impact, lifetime achievement, and youth coaching excellence. Names are called, and winners pose, smiling for the cameras.

My hands clap along, though my mind drifts in and out. Sitting here surrounded by the hum of the crowd, my nerves have me second-guessing my speech.

I risk a glance across the room, finding Nathan's brown eyes already on me. He's relaxed with one elbow propped casually on the table, watching me with quiet curiosity.

I turn back to the stage before the moment can become anything more. I'm only here for my team.

"And now, the Athlete of the Year Award." The presenter clears his throat.

My hand presses into my thigh to keep my foot from tapping.

"This honor recognizes outstanding performance, leadership, and sportsmanship at the highest level of competition. This year's recipient led their team to win the NWSL Championship, while serving as captain and center midfielder for the Boston Tempest."

The room fades until there's only his voice.

"She recorded the most assists in the league this season and maintained a ninety percent pass completion rate. Her commitment to her team sets a standard for excellence."

There is a beat of silence before my name is spoken.

"Congratulations to Wesley Miller."

My table erupts, chairs scraping back in a chaotic chorus. My teammates shout my name as if we scored in overtime.

When I reach the microphone on the stage, I find Nathan's eyes again and nod at him. This time, his surprise is unmistakable. Embarrassment flickers beneath it, coloring his cheeks. My lips twitch with amusement as he realizes they had unknowingly insulted me to my face.

The speech in my hand crinkles under my tightening grasp. The words written on it no longer seem appropriate. I set the paper on the podium, deciding to wing it.

"Being captain of the Boston Tempest is an honor I carry with pride, not just for the wins, but for the work behind them. The early mornings, the rehab days, and the sacrifices we all make to play the game we love."

"It reflects every teammate who trusts me, every coach who pushes me, and the young athletes who watch from the stands, dreaming of standing where we stand."

The faces in the crowd blur as silence grips the room. My eyes stay locked on Nathan for the next part, considering my experience with him tonight sums up the experience of most women in sports.

"This award has never been given to a woman before. I checked," I joke. "So tonight, I accept it on behalf of every female athlete in this room. Most of us don't get the fame, glory, or money our male counterparts do. The path we take to play the sport we love does not come easy, yet we commit our lives to it anyway. Because of that, we know better than to take a second of it for granted. Thank you for trusting me with this honor."

I step back as the applause picks up. The mayor takes the stage, saying something into the microphone that stops me cold only halfway back to my table.

"And now, our favorite tradition of the evening, the annual charity auction."

My stomach plummets.

No.

I forgot about this part.

A spotlight pins me in place. I smile, though I'm sure it looks half-crazed.

"Every year, our athlete of the year donates a day of their time for this auction. The highest bidding athletic team will receive a full day with Wesley, including a walkthrough of training, conditioning, and game preparation. Not only is this a fun way for our sports teams to see how another team excels, but all proceeds will go toward our city youth recreation programs."

I swallow hard. A whole day dedicated to this means more time away from my training schedule. Normally, I could choke that down, but the glint in Nathan's eyes causes my stomach to sink even further.

Bidding starts immediately. Our football team, then basketball.

I glare at Avery as if she can help me escape the literal spotlight on me. She tosses out a bid on my team's behalf, but it's immediately overtaken by softball. She shoots me a silent apology as the numbers climb higher than what she can afford to bid.

Eventually, the knot in my chest loosens when the bids slow with men's soccer in the lead. I was nervous about nothing. A ten-minute conversation at the bar doesn't justify spending over seventy-five thousand dollars on a day with me. Right?

Then a deeper voice carries over the crowd.

"One hundred thousand."

Every head swivels.

Nathan Wilder sits casually in his chair, hand raised like he's ordering appetizers instead of publicly buying a day of my time. His teammates exchange looks, a combination of amusement and confusion on their faces.

I glare at him.

He smiles back, looking far too entertained.

Another bidder counters. Nathan raises without hesitation.

Another team joins in.

Nathan matches, eyes never leaving mine.

I can feel the shift in the room as the playful charity tone turns into something else entirely. Reporters lean forward, and phones come out. My palms sweat, but I refuse to show it.

Avery whispers, "Oh my god, he's doing this on purpose."

Of course he is. I can't decide if I'm furious or flustered.

The bidding war escalates until it's only Nathan and the owner of the Boston Guardians, our baseball team.

When Nathan places the final bid over two hundred thousand dollars, the baseball team bows out. I hate that it makes my body start buzzing. It's the highest bid ever, according to the mayor.

"To the Blades, courtesy of our very own Nathan Wilder."

My team erupts. The Blades table claps loudly, already discussing cleats and cardio and 'whatever soccer people do.'

Meanwhile, I stand frozen with one horrifying realization. Next week, I'll lead a workout with an entire professional hockey team, Nathan included. I'll be running them through soccer drills and conditioning. The works.

I glance at Nathan on his feet, bowing and basking in the attention. Satisfaction is all over his face, smug with the glittering knowledge that he has rattled me more than any flirtation could.

My skin prickles when he crosses to me for photos of the award winner and the winner of the auction.

"Hi, Wesley." His voice dips, warm and teasing.

"Nathan," I mutter, crossing my arms.

"They want our photo."

I roll my eyes.

He grins wider. "Smile pretty."

Arrogant ass.

I want to smack the smile right off his perfect face. He should be groveling for insulting me, not teasing me. I'm about to tell him to shove it when I catch Avery mouthing Coach Bennett's name at me.

Right. Best behavior.

My jaw works. "Fine."

I run my tongue across my teeth to keep myself from saying what I'd really like to.

His gaze flicks to my mouth, trailing the motion. Something darkens in his eyes, and desire curls low before I can stop it. That's a problem. A big problem.

We pose, and his hand settles on my waist. It's normal contact, not illicit, but my skin lights on fire. His palm is firm against my hip, comfortable even, and it's distracting in the worst possible way.

The photos are endless, and I manage to smile through them, ignoring the way my body seems to react to him. When the flashes stop, though, I step away fast, desperate for space.

He catches my forearm gently enough to pause me.

"I didn't realize you were an athlete," he admits, rubbing his neck. "When we were talking, I mean."

At least he has the decency to look embarrassed now.

"Yeah, I figured."

"I wouldn't have let Liam drag you like that if I'd known."

"Just Liam?" I quirk my brow.

"Oh, c'mon, I mostly just listened. You could've said something."

"But where's the fun in that?" I shrug, coating my tone in ice. "Now I have my official answer to your question."

Confusion knits his brow.

"You asked what I thought of hockey players." I tap my chin as if I'm thinking it over. "I can confidently change my answer from 'to be determined' to 'not a fan'. A little too arrogant for my tastes."

"I'm not... we didn't..." He stammers.

I shouldn't enjoy it, but I do.

I'm not actually bothered by what they said. My name is unconventional for girls. They made an honest mistake. Besides, it was mostly Liam's jealousy doing the talking. Nathan really hadn't contributed much. He seemed more in his head, especially when I mentioned the lack of Stanley Cups recently.

But none of that matters. If I'm going to see him again, I need to set boundaries. I don't flirt. My stomach doesn't flutter. My skin doesn't prickle. I sure as hell don't think about the hand imprint that's burned into my hip.

I have more important things to do than flirt with a pretty hockey player who throws around hundreds of thousands of dollars for fun.

"See you next Saturday at seven a.m. sharp." I grab my purse, then pause, pretending I didn't notice his eye watching my ass. "And Nathan, don't be late."

"Don't be late?" He raises an eyebrow, not even bothering to hide the way his gaze rakes over me. "Careful, Miller. I might just get the idea that you're looking forward to seeing me."

"Don't flatter yourself." I turn to go, but then glance over my shoulder. "I'm looking forward to fixing your attitude."

I stride away from him and out into the cold. Only then does my heart begin to slow.

4

Nathan

I'm never late.

Not for practice or games. And definitely not to a charity commitment that I threw a small fortune at in front of half the city.

But here I am, five minutes past seven, as I sprint across the parking lot toward Harborlight Stadium, home of the Boston Tempest. The icy morning wind rips through my sweatshirt, and my breath fogs in one long stream as I fly through the doors.

Hopefully, Coach Rylan won't hear about this. He doesn't need any other reason to be disappointed in me, and I don't need any other reason to stress about my place on this team.

As if on cue, my phone buzzes again in my pocket. My sister, Delaney.

I should ignore it, but the message lights up the screen as I swing open the facility doors.

Delaney: Did you make it? Were you late?

Leaving her stranded with a dead battery on the side of the road wasn't an option. She refused to call Dad because 'he'd be dramatic' when he found out his nineteen-year-old daughter had been driving around with her maintenance light on for days. I refused to call him because, well, talking to him would be worse than being late.

Instead, I'd tracked her down and given her a jump so she could take it to a shop, wasting precious time I didn't have.

The moment I burst onto the turf, I know I'm screwed.

Wesley stands in the center of the field as if she owns it. Her hair is pulled back, with joggers hugging her strong and very distracting legs. She looks professional in her Tempest pullover with her clipboard in hand. But the look in her eyes?

Pure arctic frost.

My teammates are circled up, already stretching, but they quiet down as my footsteps echo across the turf.

"I'm sorry." I drop my bag, making my way to the group.

Wesley steps toward me, and the air outside drops ten degrees.

"You're late." Her voice is deadly calm.

"Yeah, I know. Look, my sister…"

"Drop the excuse. You owe us a lap for every minute."

"Eight laps?"

My insides twist as my hope for making a good impression vanishes. I spent over two hundred thousand dollars so that I could impress the woman in front of me, and not even ten minutes in, the money's wasted.

A few of my teammates wince on my behalf.

Wesley lifts a brow. "Did I stutter?"

"Nope." I swallow. Her tone has me terrified and turned on in ways that it shouldn't. "Isn't this supposed to be a fun charity day?"

"Actually," she says, glancing toward her clipboard as if she's reading the rules. "It's supposed to be an authentic training day."

"So, if you were eight minutes late…" I start.

She nods toward the path circling the turf. "I'd run."

I could ask her to be reasonable, but something in her expression tells me it won't matter. This isn't the same woman who flirted with me in a cocktail dress; this is the woman who led her team to a championship, and damn if the authority doesn't have me even more interested.

Does that bossiness carry over to the bedroom? My dick twitches at the prospect of Wesley in my bed on top of me. Apparently, I have a thing for women who are bossy. It just so happens that it's the same woman who is now committed to not giving me the time of day.

Wyatt pretends to cough, snapping me out of it. Wesley's glaring daggers at me, and considering the path my brain just traveled down, I deserve it.

I lower my head, tighten my shoelaces, and start my run.

The first four laps are a breeze. My cardio's good, elite, even. I hit my stride, and my muscles loosen.

By lap eight, the burn has set in. The soccer field is a lot larger than the rink. As I finish, my lungs ache, and my calves are on fire. The obvious disadvantage of hockey? Our bursts are short. We specialize in explosive and controlled movements, not marathons.

The way she watches me the entire time tells me she knows it, too. She's not smug exactly, but she is enjoying torturing me. The twinkle in her blue eyes gives her away.

I brace my hands on my hips and blow out a breath. Sweat is pouring down the back of my shirt, but Wesley doesn't give me a break.

"Since everyone is finally ready," she says, her gaze cutting to mine, "we can begin."

The team looks genuinely nervous, and for the first time in a long time, I empathize with our rookies on hell-day conditioning.

"We'll run through our Tempest warm-up first," she orders. "Two-mile run. Keep pace with me."

Liam shoots me a glare that reads, "What the fuck have you gotten us into?"

I deserve whatever she throws my way. I know that. I mean, we insulted her to her face, acting like egotistical assholes. My jaw had hit the floor when she stood for the award. But the embarrassment was nothing compared to the overwhelming curiosity that had taken root over the past week.

After the banquet, I'd done my research. Her accolades went pages deep on the internet, and I'd read every single one. At the time,

I thought it might help me get into her bed, or at least her good graces. Seeing her now, I know it had been nothing more than a fool's hope.

It's obvious that she plans to teach me a lesson today. Unfortunately for her, all I'm learning is that I'll gladly suffer through her barking if it means her eyes keep glancing in my direction.

She doesn't just set the pace; she sets a blistering one.

Within the first half mile, the team is winded. By the second mile, some of the guys start complaining. Wesley runs like she doesn't need oxygen. It's like the ground moves for her, not the other way around.

I knew she was an award-winning athlete.

I didn't know she was this.

When she notices my stare, her lips tilt up slightly as if she knows exactly what I'm thinking.

Next up, bleachers.

Up. Down. Up. Down. By the tenth cycle, my thighs are screaming. Grayson looks like he might actually cry. Wyatt seems to be the only one okay, probably because he spends the whole game squatting in the net.

"Don't get too comfortable," she says, her tone strict but playful as she lets us take a quick break. "I see Liam over there trying to convince his lungs that they matter more than I do."

Liam coughs, waving a hand in mock surrender. "I'm never assuming someone's gender for the rest of my life."

"What was it you said again?" Wesley asks, patting his head. "Oh, yes, 'some fucking nobody' won the award. Today, that nobody is your worst nightmare. Time for soccer drills."

The team groans, murmuring curses at Liam. But then she adds, "Don't forget to thank Nathan for bidding everyone. He's the reason you're here."

Then the curses are directed at me. I don't hear them, too focused on the intimidating woman jogging back out onto the field, as if she's just getting started. My eyes trail her, watching the way her hips sway as she goes. It isn't until Liam smacks me in the back of the head, his face alight with humor, that I realize I'm the only one not standing. Shit. I have got to stop doing that.

I don't fixate on women. Dating while traveling for most of the year is a gamble that I don't often feel like making. I am more of an occasional date with decent sex at the end kind of guy. And I never stay up half the night researching one of the women I'm seeing. So why the hell am I doing it with Wesley when I'm not even seeing her?

"Shooting drills!" She announces from outside the goalie box. "Wyatt, get in the goal. That's your position, right?"

"Uh, yeah, but it's a much smaller goal," Wyatt answers nervously.

He faces down terrifying men on the ice, but Wesley has him almost trembling.

She smiles and then points. He hangs his head and gets in the goal without argument.

"I'll walk you through the basics, then everyone will try it out. We'll go until everyone has scored a goal."

I try to focus on her demonstration. She shows us the spot on our feet that should connect with the ball and how to swing our legs. I really do try to pay attention, but my eyes keep drifting up to her face.

She was stunning at the ceremony, but here, like this, is better. She's in her element and completely at ease, even if she is being a hard-ass.

"Wilder," she says, everyone turning toward me. "You might actually learn something if you focus on the ball and not the pretty brunette schooling you."

The team bursts into laughter. I want to die. Then I notice the hint of amusement in her eyes, and it doesn't sting quite so bad.

Five minutes later, she stands there, one hand on her hip, ponytail whipping as she fires pass after pass with perfect accuracy. I have to force my mind to focus on the task at hand.

Really, the only place my mind should be focused is on hockey. We're almost fifteen games into the season, and while the team is doing well overall, my stats are bad. Like really fucking bad. I've spent almost all my free time stressing about it. Come to think of it, today, with Wesley kicking my ass, is one of the few times that I haven't been in my head about it.

Not a single person has scored yet, and the arrogance grows on Wyatt's face as he gets comfortable in the net.

As if sensing it too, Wesley steps forward to take a turn. She rolls the ball under her foot into placement, then takes a slight step away from it. Her eyes stay focused on Wyatt as she pulls back, firing the ball into the top corner from twenty yards out. Wyatt dives the complete wrong way, looking pissed once he realizes how easily she scored on him.

Determined to be the first hockey player to score, I try to mimic her action, running up and swinging hard, but the ball veers left and misses by a mile.

Wesley doesn't make fun of me as I anticipated. "You rely on power because you're used to it, but power without precision is wasted energy. Go again."

I bite my tongue and nod, waiting for her next pass.

This time, I score. It's fun. This whole workout is fun.

I can't remember the last time I worked out or played a sport without hockey and my contract at the forefront of my mind. It's almost like I've forgotten how enjoyable it is to test my body's limits without it being make or break.

"Maybe there's hope for you yet." She teases before working her way through the rest of my team.

By the time she calls it, most of the Blades look like corpses. Someone is lying flat on the turf, whispering, "Tell my family I love them."

I am exhausted.

She's everything I fear I'm losing about myself: strong, confident, and focused. Maybe that's why I decide to torture myself and stick around while the rest of my team files out.

She stands at the sideline checking her clipboard, mindlessly twirling her ponytail with one hand.

I clear my throat. "Hey."

Her eyes rise slowly. The playfulness that crept in during training is gone, replaced by something more guarded.

"Wilder."

"Good session," I say. "Brutal, but good."

"That was the point."

"Yeah. We deserved it after accidentally shit-talking you to your face." I use the bottom of my shirt to wipe the sweat off my forehead. "Listen, about earlier. I wasn't late because I overslept or anything. My sister…"

Her expression drops into impatience. "I said I didn't want excuses."

"It's not an excuse," I insist. "She was stranded, and I had to help."

For a moment, something softens in her gaze. Then it's gone.

"You still made the commitment. You still showed up late. Helping someone doesn't erase responsibility."

I blink. Ouch.

"Right," I mutter. "Got it."

Silence stretches. I can't help myself.

"I was wondering if maybe I could get your number?" I swallow, suddenly unsure. She has shown no interest other than a few flirty comments. Maybe I'm a masochist.

"No."

The blow hits harder than expected.

It shouldn't. I barely know her, but rejection is new territory. Territory I don't particularly like.

"You don't get to flirt with me at a gala, underestimate me in a conversation to my face, and then buy my time in some sort of grand gesture. I'm not interested in any games other than the one I play professionally."

She takes a sip of her water. "You might be hot shit to the whole city, but I don't date, and I don't have time to pretend otherwise."

Brutal and direct. After the past couple of hours of training with her, I know it's only partially personal.

I nod, understanding and respecting the answer. "To be clear, I don't date either, not seriously. We could still hang out." I eye her suggestively, wondering if she'll get the insinuation.

"Oh." She looks confused, and then, "Oh. Oh god. No. Absolutely not. I'm not interested in that either."

Her cheeks turn molten, and I can't help but smirk. Of course, she's not interested in hooking up. She doesn't seem like the type, even if I wish she were. A few rounds in bed with her would surely cure the fixation I've developed over the past week.

"You sure?" I tease, enjoying the way she's trying to act unbothered.

I can read her well enough to know that she's at least somewhat attracted to me, but it's not enough to act on. She takes soccer seriously in a way that I haven't taken hockey in a long time.

Is that my issue? Complacency. I fought my whole life to be in the NHL, then I made it. Next was fighting for the Cup, then I won it. Maybe somewhere along the way, I've started settling for good enough, lost in the monotony that comes with playing a sport for nearly my whole life.

"Not every woman wants to sleep with you, Wilder."

"I'm not propositioning every woman. I'm propositioning you." It's only after the words leave my mouth that I realize how bold they are.

I half expect Wesley to kick the ball at my head. Instead, she quirks an eyebrow like a disappointed teacher giving me a second chance to not be an idiot.

I grin wider, doubling down on what I said.

"Does that line actually work for you?"

She's trying desperately to keep a straight face, but I can see the corner of her mouth tilting up just slightly.

"What? Too forward?" I chuckle.

Contrary to what's published about me, I don't sleep around or hook up that often at all. I really only brought it up to fluster her. I like seeing her cheeks turn pink when I catch her off guard.

"Nope."

I pause, body thrumming with the possibility of her taking me up on my offer.

Then she adds, "Not too forward at all. Gives me the chance to make sure you know it's never going to happen."

I deflate.

"I need to get back to work. You should get going, Wilder." She walks right back into the middle of the field, lining up more shots on goal.

How she has the energy to keep going, after the workout we've already done, is a mystery to me. A pang of jealousy stabs between my ribs because she knows exactly who she is. And I'm not sure I know who I am anymore.

5

Nathan

I rip the gloves off in sharp, angry tugs, thinking about the shot I sent sailing into the stratosphere. It was a perfect setup and an open net, and I still managed to lift it like I was aiming for the nosebleeds instead of the twine.

The second my stick touched the puck, I knew I fucked up, but it was already too late. The disappointment on everyone's faces stung, but was expected. One thing about continuously playing like shit is that I'm becoming very used to letting people down.

The locker room buzzes with hissing showers and the clatter of sticks hitting the ground. The faint smell of sweat and disinfectant burns my nose. None of it cuts through the replay looping in my head. If I close my eyes, I swear I can still hear the crowd groan.

"Pretty sure that puck's still orbiting Earth," Liam calls from a few stalls down, voice dripping with sarcasm, a crooked grin cemented on his face. As my best friend, he's legally obligated to roast me first.

"NASA wants tracking rights," Grayson adds, a towel slung around his neck.

The guys laugh. It's the kind of ribbing only teammates who've bled beside you on the ice can throw without drawing blood. I toss my balled-up tape in Liam's direction, pretending to be unfazed.

He responds by squeezing his water bottle at me, a cold stream hitting me in the chest. If it were anyone else, I'd be annoyed, but Liam is like a brother to me.

We met at a hockey camp when we were ten, our friendship surviving living in different states and going to different colleges. We both ended up with the same agent, Ryan Elliott, and eventually on the same professional team, a couple of years ago. It was the first time we got to play together, and we clicked immediately, becoming the best duo in professional hockey. Until my slump, at least.

"Glad I could keep you all entertained," I say, bitter edges impossible to hide.

"You'll bury the next one." Grayson leans back on the bench without a care in the world. "Everybody has off nights."

Off night.

If only it were just one. Unfortunately, this was a pattern, not the exception.

Luckily, Wyatt crushed it between the pipes, so we managed to skate by with a slim victory.

I stare at my gear, the pads scuffed and battered. I'm not supposed to be this guy, the one who doubts every step. I'm a confident veteran with ten years of professional play and the skills to show for it. Except lately, those skills are nowhere to be found.

A week ago, after the training session with Wesley, I felt electric. Maybe it was her, or maybe it was training somewhere new, doing new things.

I've played hockey since I was five. I've been on skates even longer. That's over twenty-three years of doing the same drills and sprints. I still love the sport without question, but I'd be lying if I said my heart was in it the same way it used to be.

It makes me feel like an asshole. Guys all over the country would kill to be in my position, and I'm wasting it.

What the hell is wrong with me?

All it took was a day of training in a new way for me to think I was finally clawing my way out of this slump. For the first game this week, I was faster and hungrier. I could see it on the crowd's faces. The excitement for the Wilder they know and love.

Now? The spark burnt out as fast as it came, doubt flooding right back in.

"Hey," Liam says, nudging my shoulder. "You're not the first guy to choke on a gimme."

I don't have a chance to answer because a knock cuts through the room's noise. One of the assistant coaches sticks his head in.

"Wilder, Coach Rylan wants to see you."

There's a chorus of groans and drawn-out "oohs." Someone mutters, "Dead man walking." I pretend to laugh, but my heart dips hard.

I peel off the last of my gear, shove it into my bag, and head down the hallway. Each step feels heavier, like gravity doubled. Coach Rylan's office waits at the end, the door cracked open with fluorescent light spilling out.

I remind myself that nothing he says to me can be worse than the thoughts already running through my head. I'm not playing great, sure, but it isn't bad enough to ship me off to a farm team. At least I fucking hope not.

I knock once.

"Come in."

I step inside. Coach Rylan sits behind his desk, his face set in the kind of seriousness that leaves no room for misinterpretation.

"Sit."

I do, pulse thudding in my ears.

"You know I believe in you," he starts, voice even. "Always have. You've got the kind of talent guys dream of."

For a moment, hope flickers. Then he crushes it.

"But talent and showing up aren't translating into results."

I swallow. "I know. I'm…"

He cuts me off. "Being here isn't enough right now. Not with where we are in the standings. Not with your contract expiring at the end of the season."

The words hit with the weight of a cross-check to the ribs.

"If you don't turn this around, we're going to have to make some tough decisions," he says, firm but not cruel. "And as much as I like you, that includes your extension."

My lungs seize up.

"You've got some time," Coach continues. "Figure it out. Because the way you're playing is not sustainable, and it's not enough."

The chair creaks as I push up. "I'll figure it out."

"I want to keep you here, but the league won't wait for you to get your head right."

I nod once and walk out, the door shutting behind me with a soft click that feels like a gunshot.

The locker room is quieter when I push the door open again. Most of the guys have cleared out, leaving behind the lingering smell of sweat. I don't say a word, heading straight for the showers.

I'm not the captain, but the team still looks to me as a leader. That's what happens when you play in one place longer than most. The Nathan Wilder they know is confident, if not a little cocky. He doesn't feel lost. He doesn't feel weak. So, I take ten minutes in the shower, shaking it all off.

Hot water pounds onto my skin, but it doesn't do a damn thing to loosen the coil in my shoulders. Coach Rylan's words replay, circling like vultures.

I brace my hand against the tile and let the steam blur everything. For a few minutes, I let myself feel the disappointment and fear that's been building for months before cracking open tonight.

Then, I shut off the water, ready to plaster a fake-ass smile on my face. When I step out, only three guys remain.

Liam is sprawled on the bench, still shirtless, scrolling on his phone. Grayson is perched on top of a stall like some kind of gremlin because he has zero regard for normal etiquette. And Wyatt is leaning against his locker with his arms crossed.

All three look up when they hear me.

Liam whistles low. "Well? Are you dead? Do we need to plan a memorial?"

I toss my towel at him, sliding my suit back on. It smacks him in the face, and he pretends to gag.

Wyatt's gaze is steady. "It's bad, isn't it?"

I sit on the bench and drag a hand through my hair. "Yeah."

"What'd he say?" Grayson asks, sliding down to sit properly for once.

"He likes me," I mutter with a humorless laugh. "He thinks I've got talent, but if I don't turn this around, my contract's gone."

Silence fills the room like smoke.

Liam's joking expression falls completely, the reality setting in. "Damn. He actually said that?"

"Word for word."

Wyatt curses under his breath. "Shit."

I shrug even though every muscle in me is knotted. At least my friends agree that it's bad news, because my parents would be thrilled.

"He's not wrong." I sigh, shoving stuff into my bag.

"You were getting it back," Grayson says. "After that charity thing, you looked different for a couple of days. Like the old you."

"You did play well against Tampa." That's Wyatt practically writing me a sonnet.

I laugh despite myself. "Thanks, man. Inspirational."

Liam nods. "Whatever clicked for you with that soccer girl…"

"Wesley," I correct.

He raises his eyebrows. "Right. Whatever clicked for you with Wesley seemed to work."

"Yeah," I admit quietly. "It did."

The workout was brutal. Humiliating. And the most alive I've felt in months.

"She challenged you," Wyatt says.

It really was as simple as that. She didn't care that I was Nathan Wilder. She didn't care that I played hockey. She only cared that I showed up and busted my ass to keep up with her. Being pushed like that, without it being tied to the Blades, my teammates who count on me, or my contract, was freeing.

Grayson nods. "Maybe you should ask her to help you again. Like… privately. Extra training and conditioning."

"Cross-training in a new sport helps people get their groove back all the time," Liam adds.

I cringe. "She turned me down, and not gently. Like a very intense rejection."

Liam finally pulls on the rest of his suit. "That girl scares the shit out of me. But I also saw the way she looked at you. Like she wanted to break you in half and then maybe ride you into the sunset."

Wyatt groans. "Jesus, man."

Grayson leans forward. "She doesn't have to want to fuck you. Just help you. Athlete to athlete."

"And if something else happens…" Liam waggles his brows.

Wyatt, ever the realist, says, "You need to fix your game. If she's the spark, what choice do you have?"

I let their words settle.

The idea of spending more time with her ignites something in my chest. Not just desire, but drive and competition. The urge to be pushed and challenged in a new way. Maybe I could prove something to myself in the process.

"I don't think she'll go for it," I admit.

"But you like the idea," Liam says knowingly.

I meet his gaze. "Yeah, I do."

"Then ask," Wyatt orders. "The worst she can say is no."

I remember the sting of her last rejection. There are definitely worse things she can say. But as I sit here, surrounded by three of the only people who still believe in me, one thing becomes clear: doing nothing is no longer an option.

And for the first time in far too long, a sliver of hope cuts through the doubt.

Maybe she won't do it. Maybe she'll laugh in my face.

But maybe, just maybe, she'll say yes.

6

Wesley

Harborlight Stadium is quiet except for the rhythmic thump of the ball against my cleats. Cold air bites at my cheeks, and my breath fogs in pale clouds, but I barely notice. I'm in the zone, my mind and body syncing in that rare place beyond fatigue.

Shot after shot, I fire with precision, replaying techniques in my head. The ball responds like it's a living thing, obedient to my movements. This is why I love the sport. The control.

My muscles burn, but I feel sharper than I have in weeks. Another medical bill for my dad arrived this morning, and the weight of it pushes me harder.

If I make the National Team, it changes everything.

I love playing professionally, I really do, but women's salaries are minuscule compared to men's despite the same effort and travel. I'm lucky to be paid as much as I am, but I can't play soccer forever. I have to think ahead to make sure I'm set for life. But Dad's medical bills and Emma's tuition add up fast these days.

Men like Nathan Wilder don't have this problem. His salary alone dwarfs mine, never mind the endorsement deals. He gets to live luxuriously and show up late to things with no repercussions.

My mind circles back to this field one week ago. Nathan had looked good in a suit, but in his teal Blades sweatshirt, dripping with sweat, he was completely distracting. I'd watched him far more than I was comfortable with. It was infuriating.

I ran them into the ground that day. To his credit, Nathan held up better than most. He was the first to score, even with his legs shaking. It was a decent shot too, not that I'd admit it. And that smile he wore afterward? Damn.

Then he had to open his mouth and ruin it. I mean, asking for my number was one thing, but implying that all he wanted was a hookup? It was confusing, then insulting, and maybe flattering?

A hookup with Boston's most well-known and sexiest athlete would be a dream for most girls. It's exactly why I refused to give him my number. He's the kind of distraction that would be fun in the moment and a disaster afterward. I need focus, not flirtation.

The crunch of shoes on half-frozen turf catches my attention.

"Careful, Wesley. Don't want the turf to miss you too much."

I turn sharply to find Nathan Wilder with his sweatshirt half-zipped and his hockey bag slung over one shoulder. It's as if my thoughts conjured him.

He's interrupting my flow, but that does nothing to stop my insides from somersaulting. Especially not when he's wearing one of his infuriatingly confident grins.

"Wilder," I say, rolling my eyes. "Shouldn't you be anywhere else?"

He shrugs, hands sliding into his pockets. "Thought I'd check in on my favorite soccer captain. Make sure she's still finding the back of the net."

I raise a brow. "Only one of us seems to have that issue. And it's not me."

"You watched my game."

"I like watching games with or without you in them." I kick the ball back and forth between my feet. "Nice deflection from the fact that you missed an easy goal."

I'm teasing, but a shadow passes over his face. Interesting. He's still upset over it. I'd pegged him for the type of guy who skates by on minimal effort and raw talent.

"You got me." He holds his hands up in mock surrender. "But you have to admit games are much better when I'm in them."

"I'll admit nothing." I pop the ball up, juggling it back and forth between my feet in the air. "Except that you have an incredible ability to show up when I'm most focused and ruin it with your voice."

"I call that good timing."

"Or unrelenting arrogance?"

"Maybe both. Throw in a little delusion, too."

A laugh escapes before I can stop it.

"I'm still not giving you my number." I pop the ball in his direction, and he catches it.

"That's not why I'm here." He runs his palm down his jaw, suddenly serious. "Well, I guess I am, but not the way you think. It's something else."

"Spit it out." I snag the ball out of his hands, careful not to touch him. The last time we touched, it was days before I stopped feeling it.

"Right. I was hoping that maybe you could help me with some cross-training? Stuff like we did last time?"

I pause before unrestrained laughter bursts free from my mouth. Except he doesn't even crack a smile. In fact, he looks like he wants to crawl into the nearest hole and never show his face again.

"No one's ever hit on me before by asking me to exercise with them," I say, catching my breath.

At that, his lips tilt up. "Not hitting on you, promise. It's a serious question."

This guy makes millions. He has coaches, trainers, regimens, and a million other things at his disposal. Why would he need me?

"Why?"

He exhales slowly. "It's a contract year, and my stats suck. I'm at risk of losing my contract altogether if I don't turn it around."

It seems like he is playing fine, by the way ESPN raves about him. You'd think he is God's gift to earth the way they talk about him.

"What does that have to do with me?" I let my hair down before pulling it into a tighter ponytail.

"The first couple of practices and games after I worked out with you, I performed better."

"That could be a fluke," I argue, because surely he can't actually think one practice with me is responsible for his hat trick the next day.

Yes, I know he had a hat trick. Professional interest. That's all.

"Maybe, but it felt good. I haven't been challenged that way without all the pressure in a long time. I've been doing the same drills and exercises for so long, but training with you was different. It helped."

My pulse stutters at the implication that I inspired something in him. I tell myself he's only referring to the workout, but my heart beats faster anyway.

"Will you help me out?" His voice drops, quieter now. "Just a couple of days a week. Nothing crazy." Hope shines in his eyes as if I'm his only chance.

I feel for him. I know what burnout and complacency look like, even if you still love what you do. I've watched teammates struggle with those issues at every level. I want to help.

But…

The last time I let myself be talked into something, back in college, I almost lost my scholarship.

My family needs me to concentrate on one thing, and it's not him. If I say yes, it might help him, but it could hurt me. Besides, spending too much time with him feels dangerous in a way I can't afford.

"I can't," I say finally.

He deflates. "It was probably a stupid idea."

"It's not stupid. I just don't have time to commit to that. I'm chasing the National Team, and I can't risk messing up my own progress."

He nods, but his jaw twitches.

I know he gets it. Athletes understand sacrifice better than most. His own commitment to his sport is the only reason he'd swallow his pride and ask for my help in the first place.

"In case you change your mind." He pulls out a piece of paper with his number on it.

"I won't." I don't toss it aside, instead tucking it into my pocket. The lone butterfly in my stomach is impossible to ignore.

His crooked grin appears, but this time it's layered with a resignation that cuts into me. "You're brutal, you know that?"

"I don't have a choice but to be." It's not snappy, just honest.

In my life, there's only one thing that gets me where I need to go: unwavering dedication to soccer. Anything else is wasted energy.

His head tilts, smugness blending with earnest curiosity. "What if you did have a choice?"

I swallow, refusing to answer. I don't consider it for more than a second because it's hypothetical anyway.

"Anyway," He motions to the pocket I've slipped his number into. "Give me a call when you change your mind."

Then, he turns and walks away.

"I told you I don't have time to train with you." My voice echoes across the field.

"That time, Miller," he calls without turning back, "I wasn't talking about training."

My cheeks flush as I watch him walk away with a confident swagger that screams of a man who's used to getting what he wants.

I'm about to force myself back into drills when a voice drifts down from the bleachers.

"Interesting visitor you had."

I stiffen.

Coach Bennett stands halfway down the bleachers. Her blond hair is pulled back in a tight braid. She looks like she came straight from a meeting, but could start into a sprint without warning. Most people assume she's a player heading to drills, not the coach who spends the afternoon in meetings.

I drag my bag over and meet her halfway up. There's no point in pretending my session isn't over now.

"He seemed friendly," she says, her eyebrows raised while she watches me carefully. "Nathan Wilder, right?"

"We met at the award gala," I say quickly. "Nothing to talk about."

Her brows lift. "Nothing? He looked very interested, and you didn't exactly chase him off the field with a broom."

"It's not like that."

"Shame."

I blink. "Shame?"

"A little distraction would be good for you."

My frown deepens.

She softens her stance, voice gentle but firm. "Wesley, you're twenty-five. You have more talent than most of this league, but you're going to burn yourself out."

"I'm not…"

"You're here six days a week. Sometimes seven. We aren't even in season. You train harder than my entire roster combined. That dedication is admirable, but it's not sustainable." She looks me dead in the eye. "Frankly, it's putting your captaincy at risk."

I toy with the sleeves of the jacket in my lap.

"Being captain is about more than stats. It's leadership and relationships. It's about balance. Your teammates respect you, but they don't know you. They barely see you outside practice. You avoid team dinners and bonding nights. I asked you to go to Paige's birthday, and you skipped it to watch game tape."

I flinch. She isn't wrong, but the team doesn't need me to be their friend. They need me to win us games.

"I'm trying to make the National Team."

"And I want you to, but if you want to be at that level, you need more than talent. You need balance. You need a life. Off the pitch."

I stare at the turf, resisting the urge to argue. She doesn't get it. Every day not spent training is a day someone else gets better.

"I don't think you're hearing me," Coach says. "If this doesn't change, I'm going to be reconsidering who wears the captain's band next season."

The words hit like a sucker punch.

Captain isn't a title. It's a purpose. It's proof I deserve to be here. It's also my financial security.

Panic surges.

The lie leaves my mouth before I can stop it.

"I've thought the same thing. That's why Nathan was here a little while ago. He's been begging me to spend more time with him. He's actually my boyfriend. We were making plans."

Silence falls. Holy shit. I really said that.

Coach blinks. "Your boyfriend is Nathan Wilder."

"Yes." Shit. I said it again.

She studies me for a long moment. I hold my breath, praying she can't see the tremor in my hands.

Then, she smiles. "That's wonderful to hear."

Guilt knots in my throat, but I nod stiffly, having no idea how to walk back the lie.

"You've been so isolated," she continues. "It's good to see you letting someone in. I want you to bring him to the team party in January."

My eyes widen. "The team party…"

"Yes. It'll be good for the team to see you with someone. They can see that their captain has the work-life balance everyone deserves."

It was nearly two months away.

Fucking perfect.

Enough time for this lie to explode spectacularly in my face.

I force a smile that feels more like a grimace. "Of course. I'll… tell him."

Coach squeezes my shoulder. "I'm proud of you, Wesley. Truly. You deserve to have something outside this sport."

Then she walks off, leaving me alone in the stands. My fingers brush the slip of paper in my pocket.

My captaincy is on the line. My National Team dream is at risk. And now I have a fake boyfriend I absolutely didn't ask for.

So much for no distractions.

7

Wesley

I might have lied to Coach Bennett and told her Nathan Wilder is my boyfriend."

Avery freezes mid-chip dip, and Harper nearly drops her wine bottle. I shove a throw pillow over my face as if I can smother the words back into my mouth.

This is how our emergency girls' night begins.

We're at Harper's townhouse, curled up in her living room, where everything is soft tones and candlelight. A diffuser hums in the corner, pushing out vanilla and lavender like we're supposed to be meditating, not spiraling. The coffee table is a battlefield of snacks, including cheese, chocolate, and a bowl of chips that Avery is single-handedly annihilating.

"You told her he's your what?" Harper asks from her place on the rug next to me. Her legs are curled up under her with a blanket wrapped around her shoulders.

"My boyfriend," I mumble through the pillow pathetically.

Avery shrieks. Actually shrieks. "Wesley, really? Oh my god, our little captain has finally cracked." She rolls from her back onto her stomach on the couch so that she can look at me.

"It was an accident." I throw the pillow at her, knocking her twisted bun of red hair into something messier.

"You accidentally gave yourself a famous hockey player as a boyfriend?" Avery arches a brow. "That's not an accident, it's a manifestation."

"I panicked. She was lecturing me about balance and how, as captain, I need to have a life. I told her I did. She saw him leaving, and I went with it."

"Wait." Harper pauses mid-glass refill. "What do you mean she saw him leaving?"

Heat crawls into my cheeks. Damn it.

"He came to the field and asked me to do more training sessions with him." I try to sound indifferent, like my pulse wasn't sprinting when it happened.

Avery snorts. "More like, he wanted to see all the different ways you can make him sweat."

"Don't start." I shift, leaning my back against the couch and straightening my legs out in front of me. "Anyways, now she expects me to bring said boyfriend to the team party."

"In January?" Avery brushes at the chip crumbs she's dropping onto the couch.

"That's the one." I pat my hands against my thighs.

Harper sets the wine bottle down and pinches the bridge of her nose. "Wes, sweetheart, you could've said you go to trivia night, or take pottery, or volunteer at a shelter. Something normal. But a fake boyfriend? And a famous one? That's... bold."

Avery smirks. "Honestly? I love it. Finally, you're using that brain for chaos instead of memorizing film."

I groan, pulling my hair out of its sweaty ponytail and redoing it. My usual anxious tick. "You weren't there. She looked so disappointed. She was already demoting me in her mind."

"And instead of accepting constructive leadership feedback," Avery says, swinging her legs off the couch and sitting forward, "you conjured a romance."

I glare at her. "Shut up."

Harper hands me a sparkling water, her eyes warm with concern. "Coach Bennett cares about you. She's not trying to ruin your life.

She's worried you train too hard and isolate yourself. She wants more for you."

"I know."

"But also," Avery interrupts, "I'm thrilled you lied."

"You would be."

"You're always the responsible one, the structured one, the girl who eats protein bars for dessert and schedules her emotional breakdowns."

"I don't…"

Avery lifts a brow.

"Fine. Once. But it was during finals."

She grins victoriously. "See? Iconic."

Harper rests a gentle hand on my arm. "What now? Tell her you broke up before the party?"

"I'm pretty sure she already thinks I lied. If I show up without him, it'll confirm it."

"So take him," Avery says simply, as though recruiting a famous athlete to go on a fake date with me is as casual as adding almond milk to coffee.

I laugh, a borderline hysterical sound. "Yeah, I'll take the famous hockey player who has no idea I've lied and said he's my boyfriend. I look like a fan girl."

Avery shrugs. "Some guys are into that."

Harper swats her. "You're going to have to tell him if you want his help."

"I don't want his help."

"Yeah, but it doesn't sound like you have a lot of options."

She's right. I don't. If I show up without my very fake boyfriend on my arm, then I'll look like a liar. Which I am, but Coach can't know that. The only choice is getting Nathan to agree to helping me out.

Avery interrupts my train of thought. "You could use the distraction. A short-term, no-strings type of distraction."

"You are encouraging her to use and lose him," Harper says, unimpressed.

"Precisely. She needs to loosen up."

I shake my head. They don't even know that he propositioned me for exactly that last week. If they did, they'd never let it go.

"It needs to be a purely professional arrangement. I keep working out with him as he asked, and he gets seen in public with me enough times to look convincing."

As I fiddle with his phone number in my pocket, Harper's husband wanders through the living room hunting for his keys. He glances at the three of us and offers a strained smile. Harper walks over to him, and they have a brief conversation, all mumbled words and biting edges.

They trade a look I can't decipher. I nod at Avery, and she widens her eyes as if sensing it too. The silence he leaves behind is awkward, but Harper smooths it with a practiced smile.

"Sorry. He's been swamped at work."

We nod, pretending we believe that's all it is. Married couples probably argue all the time. As someone who has avoided a relationship for five years and hasn't had sex in four, I'm in no place to assume anything.

Avery senses the tension and, bless her chaotic heart, changes the subject instantly. "Back to our fearless, lying captain. How are you going to get a hold of him? Show up at a game with a sign? Barge into the locker room wearing nothing but a coat?"

I laugh despite myself. It's ridiculous. This whole thing is ridiculous.

"You need to get your mind out of the gutter," I tease.

"I need to get laid. Unfortunately, my only prospect is your fake boyfriend's teammate."

After dropping that bomb, Avery hops up off the couch and darts to the kitchen.

"Who?" I yell, trailing after her with Harper following closely behind.

"Grayson Shaw followed me on Instagram after the award ceremony. He tried to slide into my DMs that have been otherwise empty as of late."

Harper crowds Avery, peeking at her phone on the kitchen island. "The Grayson Shaw?"

"He's hot," I admit, flanking her other side.

Avery smirks, pulling a tub of ice cream out of the freezer. "Interesting how you can admit Grayson is hot, but not Nathan."

"I never said Nathan wasn't attractive," I argue weakly, mind jumping to how he looked this morning. My pulse betrays me. That's going to be a problem.

"Grayson liked an old post." Harper motions to the screen. "That's deliberate."

"It's stalking," Avery counters.

"Why haven't you responded to him?" Harper pulls out spoons for us all, but I leave mine on the counter.

Avery waves a manicured hand. "I don't like hockey players."

"And?" I press, knowing damn well there's more to it.

"And nothing. I'm not interested."

Harper asks the question we're both wondering, "Is this about Damon?"

Too many emotions ripple in Avery's eyes, from hurt and anger to something like fear. "Please drop it."

Harper nods, and I don't push. Avery has always been more of a closed book when it comes to her feelings. Besides, some wounds are never healed enough to poke.

We lean back. The room crackles with quiet, and the only sound is their spoons clanking together in the tub of ice cream.

My heart beats an anxious, stubborn rhythm.

Finally, I whisper, "I'll text him."

Harper gasps. "You have his number?"

"Why didn't you start there?" Avery locks her phone screen, tossing it away and giving me her full attention.

I pull out my phone, which feels heavier than it should. Am I really going to do this? This morning, I told him no. My heart stutters and then plunges at the idea of spending time with him. Training is bad enough, but pretending to date him?

It's ridiculous.

We'd have to seem together in a way that I hadn't let myself be in a long time. I can't tell if I'm twisted from the lie, the distraction of working out with someone else, or if it's because of Nathan himself. Probably a combination of all of the above.

I blow out a breath. "What do I even say?"

"Be hot," Avery says.

I try typing out everything, but when I get to the fake boyfriend part, I chicken out. Typing out that I told my coach we were dating is an embarrassment I'm not sure I'd ever recover from. So, I split the difference. My thumbs shake while I type.

Me: Hey. About helping you train… I'll do it. But on one condition.

I don't bother letting him know it's me.

Avery fans herself. "That could be interpreted in so many ways."

"It's not even flirtatious." Harper reads over my shoulder.

"I can't say it in the message, it's too embarrassing," I groan.

"Right, get him in front of you, then flirt your way into a yes," Avery says.

I hit send before I lose courage. "No one is flirting here. Not him. Not me."

He replies immediately.

Of course he does.

Nathan: One condition? Should I be worried?

Me: Probably.

Three dots blink.

Nathan: And here I thought you were the reasonable one.

My pulse stutters. I hate that it does.

Nathan: Tell me the condition.

Me: Meet me at the field again on Tuesday at 7am.

There's a beat.

Nathan: Bossy. I like it. I'll be there.

 A flush crawls up my neck. God help me.
"Right, no flirting," Avery squeals. "He's so into you."

Me: And this time? Don't be late.

Nathan: I'll be good. Promise. Winky face.

I drop my phone like it's on fire. Nathan always seems to know exactly what to say to fluster me.

My skin seems to have caught flame as my entire body heats up in response to his text. I need to set boundaries as soon as I see him. Whatever he's thinking will happen, won't.

Avery nearly levitates. "That's basically second base."

"It is not."

Harper nudges me. "How do you feel?"

"Like I'm in deep shit."

Avery grins. "Correction: deep, sexy shit with brown, messy hair that begs to have your fingers running through it."

I shake my head. "It's only until the party. Then I can say we broke up and figure out other ways to show the balance coach wants."

Harper studies me. "Are you trying to convince yourself or us?"

"I'm not trying to convince anyone."

"There are worse things than fake dating the hottest man in this city," Avery chimes in.

She's right. There are worse things. Things like being too tired after training with Nathan, causing me to practice like shit with my team. Or straining a muscle while I work out with Nathan and having to sit out of a scrimmage. Or missing a meeting with Coach because Nathan won't stop flirting with me while we pretend to date. Getting too caught up to remember who I am. Who I have to be.

Am I being dramatic? Probably. Knowing that does nothing to stop the anxiety swirling in my gut.

"I'm doomed." I rub my forehead.

They laugh.

I try to reassure myself that I can do this. I can help him save his career and show up to some social events with him to save my captaincy. I am disciplined and focused. Someone like Nathan Wilder, who is seen with girls all the time, is not going to knock me off center.

Even if a whiff of his cedar soap sends my heart spiraling. Even if he's made it clear that knocking me off center is his new favorite hobby. I'm the one in control.

8

Nathan

I'm half an hour early, which is ridiculous, even for me, but there's no ignoring the pit in my stomach that formed when I pulled into the parking lot. The stadium lights are off, but the soft gray morning light spills over the turf, making the painted lines look bright.

Coffee in hand, I pace along the edge of the field, my shoes crunching against the frost that the sun hasn't had a chance to melt. The crisp air bites at my cheeks, but sweat forms at my hairline regardless.

I keep my hands wrapped around the cup, a flimsy barrier between me and the chaos of my thoughts.

I replay her text over and over: *I'll do it, but on one condition.*

My skin was buzzing with frantic energy. That one condition is still a question mark, but I don't care. I'll do whatever it is. I can't afford not to.

Ever since Wesley texted me, I've been a wreck. Sure, hanging out with an attractive, confident woman is half of it. The other half is because I'm watching my future on the Blades slip away. I'm terrified that cross-training won't do anything, and then it'll be too little too late.

I check my watch again. Five minutes have passed. Only five.

My phone buzzes with texts from the group chat.

Grayson: First day of school vibes, man?

Wyatt: Don't tell me you're nervous about a soccer player.

Liam: He's had the jitters worse than a rookie at camp for days now.

Normally, I'd fire back something cocky. Today, the usual bravado isn't there. It's hard to pretend when everything feels like it's dependent on the next hour.

Me: How about you all shut the hell up?

Liam: Uh-oh. Somebody is a little touchy this morning.

I cram my phone into my bag, trying to ignore the fact that they are right. I'm really fucking nervous.

And then she appears, twenty minutes early.

Wesley moves across the frost-kissed grass with a confidence that would make everyone else look like they're moving through molasses. Her stride is smooth and athletic in a way that's effortless. The few pieces of snow drifting through the air catch at the ends of her hair, turning a few brown strands white.

My nerves spike, but this time they twist into something warmer; an anticipation I have no right to feel. She's made it clear that there will be nothing going on off the field. I'd be lying if I said I wasn't disappointed. Our chemistry is there. At the end of the day, though, I respect it. Her boundaries matter, even if they rain on my parade.

Flirting, though? I won't be giving that up. I'm not sure I could if I tried.

Her eyes meet mine before darting to the ground. A flush rises in her cheeks, and I can't help but wonder what's going on in her head.

"Morning," she says, sounding more collected than I feel.

I give her the cup of coffee I brought for her. Not knowing what she liked, I completely guessed. She lifts it to her mouth and lets out a soft groan when the warmth hits her tongue. The sound rips straight through me, and I swallow hard, willing my thoughts to behave.

"How'd I do?" I ask, trying to ignore the spark lit low inside me.

"Coffee black?" she asks, narrowing her eyes.

"You didn't seem like a sugar and frills kind of girl."

"You'd be right."

I mentally curse myself for the hundred sugar and creamer packets in my bag just in case. Pathetic.

"You said you wouldn't change your mind."

"Yeah, well. I may have put my foot in my mouth."

"You?" I tease. "Seems out of character."

She huffs, and a cloud of breath swirls in the cold. "Very."

"Are you going to explain or keep me guessing?"

"I told my coach you were my boyfriend."

I nearly spit out my coffee.

"What am I supposed to say to that?" My mouth feels like sand. Because seriously. What the fuck?

Sure, hitting on her is quickly becoming my favorite pastime, but I haven't thought of being in an actual relationship in years.

She's pacing now, sleeves tugged past her fingers. "I know you're not, nor do I want you to be."

Ouch. Talk about emotional whiplash.

"Did you call me here to shut me down again? Because I got the message the first three times."

"No. Shit—" She runs a hand through her hair. "God, this is so embarrassing."

I laugh. I've seen her cocky, ruthless, and laser-focused. I've even seen her flirty and unguarded, but I've never seen her this rattled.

"Maybe start over," I nudge.

She drops onto the bench. I sit down, too, careful not to touch her. Even still, every inch of me is aware of how close she is. I'd only need to tilt my leg slightly for our knees to brush. It's tempting, considering the heat radiating from underneath her dark purple Tempest jacket.

"My coach saw you here and assumed something was going on. Which it's not."

Her eyes flick to mine, daring me to argue. I raise my hands in surrender playfully.

She takes her hair down and redoes it up into a ponytail. I've noticed she does this when she's nervous. "She says I need to show balance. Be an example of a captain who's not all soccer, all the time."

"You? Too focused?" I smirk. "Shocking."

She rolls her eyes, but her lips twitch.

"She threatened my captaincy. And you had just left. Bam. Boyfriend created."

I sip my coffee, letting the bitterness and warmth settle my nerves. I should be more annoyed. Should be. Instead, my skin tingles with excitement.

"It was harmless, until she said I have to bring you to the team party."

My mind instantly flashes to the night we met. Wesley, all dressed up for a party, would be reason enough for me to say yes. "When is it?"

"Second week of January." She bites her lip. "I know it's kind of a long time away."

I nudge her with my shoulder, unable to stop myself. "Are you asking me on a date?"

"A very fake date."

"All I'm hearing is date."

"You're impossible."

She swats me. I grin.

"Is that the condition?"

"You don't think I'm crazy?"

"I think you're dedicated and willing to do what it takes to succeed. Even if it's embarrassing."

We're the same that way. We're both leaning on each other to help prove something to the people doubting us.

She stands, kicking her ball between her feet.

"I don't usually have girlfriends," I say.

Her face softens, vulnerability peaking through. "If you don't want to…"

"That's not what I'm saying," I start, her eyes lighting back up. "I'm saying that I'm not like Liam, who goes through women like candy, but I'm also not like Grayson, who is perpetually in a relationship. I date, but not seriously. It's usually highly publicized. People aren't going to believe that we're in some multiple-month relationship if we're only seen at your party."

"Right." She nods. "Unless maybe we have a couple of dates before the party."

Yes.

Instant yes.

The idea of spending time with Wesley sends a spark racing through me. I manage to tone down my response out loud.

"I'm in."

"Really? Thank God."

She launches herself at me. I wrap my arms around her way too eagerly without thinking. It's like she's made to fit right here, and it feels way too good. She pulls back when she realizes what she just did, smoothing her jacket back into place. She puts space between us. I let her. Because professionalism.

My body hates me for it.

"Strictly professional. I'll help you cross-train, and you'll help me prove I have a life outside of soccer." Her eyes flash in a way that's equal parts warning and challenge, and I wink.

"Of course. Professional," I echo.

"Are you ready to work out, then?" She asks, shedding her anxiety and stepping into sport mode.

It's the first time she's been comfortable since getting here.

"I thought you'd never ask."

She rolls her shoulders, adjusts her stance, and we fall into the rhythm of exercise.

We stretch, mostly familiar ones with a couple that pull on muscles I've never thought of. Then, we run three miles instead of two like last time, but her pace is just as aggressive.

Our breaths fog the air in synchronized bursts. Muscles I never use for this length of time burn. She moves with relentless purpose, and I try to keep up.

If anyone thinks women aren't as athletic as men, they need to meet Wesley. She's an endless well of energy and effort. The fact that I didn't know who she was until a couple of weeks ago is a damn shame. I make a mental note to watch more women's sports.

An hour in, I'm less eager when we do agility drills. She says they're soccer-specific, but they seem more like foreign torture tactics. I follow her through them anyway. More than once, I feel her eyes on me, but every time I glance, they're focused on her feet.

I'd rather do the Gauntlet and let my team slam me into the boards repeatedly than do this multiple times every week, but I asked for this. I'm not a quitter, but I am a complainer. So even though Wesley's quiet, I chirp away, coming up with different ways to describe the hell she's putting me through.

After what feels like hours, she finally calls a pause, wiping her brow. "Alright. That's enough for today."

I shake my head, still buzzing with energy. "We can keep going."

"You've been bitching the entire time."

I gasp. "I don't bitch."

"Yes, you do. And whine. And moan. And groan."

I smirk, sweat dripping down my cheek. "You're right, I do do that."

"Fuck off, Wilder." She sighs, exasperated with my antics.

I shake my hair, sending a few stray drops of sweat in her direction.

Like she always does, she steers the conversation back within our boundaries. "Let's not push it. You were dead on your feet last time."

"I'm a little more motivated now." I sigh, taking a sip of my water.

"Do you really think this is going to help with your game?"

"I have to think that," I admit. "I'm out of ideas otherwise."

She hauls her bag over her shoulder and nods for me to follow. "I hope it does."

I can tell she means it. It's nice to have someone new in my corner, rooting for me, even if it is only because of an arrangement.

"When's our first date?"

She glares at me.

"Oh, come on. I'm not going to specify that it's fake every single time." I switch into my casual shoes and shoulder my bag.

"Maybe Saturday. We can grab lunch or something?" She doesn't look at me.

"Can't. We have an away game stretch, starting tonight, until then. What about Sunday?"

"Fine."

"You do know that the fake-date part of this arrangement is to help you, right?"

"Yes." She looks at me warily.

"So, I think you meant to say: Thank you, Nathan."

She huffs a laugh, lips twitching up despite the annoyed look on her face. "Nope. Definitely didn't mean to say that."

We walk wordlessly through the hall, our footsteps the only sound. Eventually, we make it to the parking lot, where only two cars sit. My Range Rover and a Hyundai Santa Fe that looks almost ten years old. Why would a professional athlete be driving that?

"Is that your car?" I point to the grey clunker.

She clicks the button on her keys, unlocking the car. "Yes. What about it?"

"Why are you driving that?"

"Not everyone wants something flashy like you."

My Range Rover is pretty tricked out, but compared to my teammates, like Liam, for example, it could be worse.

"No, but everyone wants something that can pass an inspection."

She doesn't answer, and I know that I've crossed one of her lines. Her privacy is clearly sacred to her, and I just keep pushing right through her boundaries anyway.

"Look, I'm sorry. I just… I don't get it. You're a professional athlete."

Her laugh is loud and condescending. "I'm a woman. My entire team makes a fraction of what you alone make in a year."

Oh. Fuck. I didn't think about that. It never even crossed my mind. She's clearly an elite athlete. I figured she got paid somewhere in my ballpark. I should've known better.

"I didn't know." I rub the five o'clock shadow on my jaw.

"No worries," she says, but I can tell she's embarrassed.

My foot practically lives in my mouth around this girl.

"Text me your address."

"Why?" Her brows furrow.

The hesitancy is rolling off her in waves, but I ignore it.

"Because we have a date on Sunday."

"I'll meet you there."

"My girlfriend would never meet me there," I argue. This is not debatable.

"I'm not your…"

"Until your team party, you're my girlfriend. At least in appearances, which means you're getting treated as such."

Either she thinks I'd be an awful boyfriend in real life, the kind who wouldn't even pick her up for a date, or she hasn't dated anyone in far too long. The way her foot is tapping a mile a minute leads me to believe the latter.

She shakes her head. "You don't have to."

"I'm picking you up. End of story. Text me your address. Now, Wesley."

"I can later."

I wave my phone at her, and she sighs. "I'm not leaving until your address is in my phone."

There is no way I'm letting her leave without it. Not when she could make up some excuse later to keep it from me. If we are doing this, we're doing it right.

"Fine." She sets her bag down in front of me, dropping to her knee to pull out her phone. "Here. See? Address sent," she says while typing.

I should be paying attention to her words and the text dinging through my phone, but instead I'm acutely aware of her proximity, the way her scent is mixed with sweat, the taut line of muscle in her calves, and the curve of her neck. The realization hits me like a jolt: she's on her knees in front of me, and I'm getting hard.

I take a sharp breath, forcing myself to step back and shake out my shoulders. My mind struggles to refocus, but the tension lingers, delicious and maddening. She doesn't notice, or at least she doesn't comment, and I shove my awareness into checking my phone.

Maybe I find her attractive. Okay, I definitely find her attractive, but that doesn't matter. Just like it doesn't matter how much I enjoy teasing her, or how she taps her hands against her legs when she's flustered. None of these things matter because I don't want it to go anywhere, and neither does she.

It would complicate everything. Besides, just because we have physical chemistry doesn't mean we should hop into bed, even if it would be so fucking good.

My sole priority is using these workout sessions to my advantage. Risking my contract over a girl would be next-level stupid. Two months of fake dating and working out together, then we go our separate ways.

Now, if I could get my body to remember that and keep my head in the game.

9

Wesley

Avery is the only person I know who treats getting ready like a competitive sport. In fact, she might take it more seriously than she takes soccer.

At the moment, she's tearing through my closet like a natural disaster, sending clothes flying in every direction as she hums under her breath. Her perfectly manicured nails flick hangers aside with ruthless efficiency.

I sit on the edge of my bed in the outfit I'd selected earlier, picking my cuticles and watching the destruction unfold. It's jeans and a t-shirt. After all, it's lunch, not the Oscars.

"No. No. Absolutely not," Avery declares, spinning toward me mid-rampage. "You're not wearing black."

Before I can protest, she's already tugging my shirt over my head with a concerning amount of force, and I don't bother resisting. I don't have the mental bandwidth. My thoughts are spiraling too fast, looping back on themselves in a way that feels dangerously close to nerves. Instead, I let her manhandle me while I stare at the floor.

"I like black," I mutter.

"Yes, and today you need to look like a woman going on a date," she says, already reaching for another hanger, "with her very new and very hot boyfriend."

"It's not a real date," I remind her, the words have a permanent place in my brain.

She pauses to level me with a look that could peel paint. "Fake or not, you're going to a restaurant with a hot hockey player who agreed to spend his free time helping save your captaincy. Humor me and put in a bare minimum of effort."

"This is business," I insist, though even to my own ears it sounds thin, like I'm trying to convince myself as much as her. "We're saving each other's asses with our coaches. Today is part of the strategy."

Avery snorts, "And I only watch Love is Blind for sociological research."

I bite down on the smile threatening to give me away.

She holds up a soft blue sweater dress. It's cut simply, but flattering, with long sleeves and a hem that falls right above the knee. It's feminine without trying too hard, which somehow makes my nerves pick up.

"No," I say immediately, even as my stomach flips with pesky butterflies that won't die no matter how hard I try to kill them.

"Yes," she replies, tossing it at me. "Try it on."

I sigh but comply, pulling the fabric over my head and stepping back into the room. Avery's reaction tells me everything before I even glance at the mirror.

"You look adorable."

"I look—" I stop short, finally meeting my own reflection. I look good. Me, but softer somehow. My hair is freed from its usual ponytail, falling around my shoulders in loose waves.

Avery steps behind me, fastening a pair of earrings that I haven't worn in years. She insists that they bring out the blue in my eyes.

"You look approachable," she says, her tone gentler now.

It's a nicer way of saying I look like someone who doesn't spend every waking moment thinking about soccer. Someone who remembers how to exist outside of obligation and pressure. The realization sits strangely behind my ribs.

I drop onto the bed to pull on my boots, focusing on the zippers as Avery's expression shifts to reveal concern.

"You okay?"

I nod, a little too quickly. "Just thinking."

"About him?"

I hesitate, fingers stilling. About a lot of things, actually. About the way Nathan hadn't hesitated when I asked for his help. About the focus in his eyes when he worked, not showy or performative, just locked in. About how I'm afraid I was completely wrong about him. I'm worried that fake-dating him will derail the entire future I've dreamt of since I was a kid.

"I didn't expect him to agree so fast," I admit quietly. "Or to actually follow through on it."

It was true. I'd texted Nathan on and off throughout the week to see if he would show up today. He liked it a little too much, taking it as a sign to tell me about his practices or days as if this wasn't only a strategic arrangement.

I had to hand it to him; he was charming, even if that charm didn't work on me. Not visibly, anyway. I'd kept my messages short and focused, ignoring him every time he tried to flirt with me. Eventually he got the message long enough for me to double check that he'd be here. Getting stood up for a fake date would be too mortifying.

Avery leans against my dresser. "That's because most men suck."

She makes a face, and I laugh.

"We're figuring out how to exist around each other outside of workouts, so this doesn't fall apart the second someone asks about us."

"Is that all it is?"

"Yes," I say it confidently enough to convince us both.

Avery steps forward and pulls me into a quick hug. She understands the pressure I'm under better than anyone. My family. My captaincy. The National Team. All of it balanced on a knife's edge.

"Didn't the Blades lose last night?" she asks, deliberately changing topics.

I glance up. "How do you know that?"

She shrugs, suddenly very interested in smoothing my hair. "I saw it somewhere."

I don't miss the deflection.

"Think your *boyfriend* will be in a mood?"

I almost correct her, but that's what she wants me to do, so I ignore it.

"A couple of weeks ago, I would've said no." I swipe on lip balm. "He acts like none of it matters, at least in front of the cameras. Now? I'm pretty sure he cares more than he lets on."

"Desperation will do that."

"It sounds like his contract is actually at risk." I surprise myself with my own empathy.

"That has got to be tough."

"Yeah, especially because it seems like hockey may be one of the few things he's serious about."

A knock sounds at the door.

My entire body freezes while my pulse picks up to a frantic pace.

Avery steps behind me and physically shoves me down the hall before disappearing entirely. I take a breath and pull the door open, finding Nathan on the other side with his hands tucked into his coat pockets.

He's dressed simply in dark jeans and a black Henley, somehow still oozing sex appeal. Everything about him, from his perfectly messy hair and confident stance, screams effortless.

His gaze sweeps over me, lingering a fraction of a second, something shifting there before he schools it away.

"You look nice," he says easily. "Really nice."

"Thanks." I'm carefully neutral, ignoring the warmth flickering low in my gut.

The car smells faintly of clean laundry from an air freshener, the windows fogging from the heater to blur the city as we pull away. For a few quiet seconds, neither of us tries to fill the space. The silence stretches, more curious than uncomfortable.

"This is weird." He's drumming his fingers against the steering wheel while we sit at a red light.

I bite the inside of my cheek. "Very."

"I don't know how to act on a date that isn't a date."

I watch the traffic crawl past us, headlights reflecting off damp pavement. "Friends get lunch all the time." The word friend settles oddly in my mouth.

His eyes search my face. "Is that what we are?"

"Yes," I answer, then tease, "Just out of order."

The sound of his laugh eases something in the car and in me. "Friends works for me."

I can be friends with Nathan. Honestly, he isn't as bad as I'd thought he'd be. His jokes are even sort of funny, not that I'd ever let him know that. So yes, we can be friends. Just friends.

We merge onto the highway with the skyline rising ahead. The glass and steel catch the pale winter sun, making the city look tired and busy in a way that steadies me.

"So," I say after a moment, mostly to break the silence, "rough game last night?"

He shrugs, eyes focused on the road. "Lost in overtime, which sucks. Houston's fans are pretty brutal when we play there, too. But this time the loss wasn't fully on me, so I'm calling it a personal win."

"Your stats aren't that bad."

He smiles, brief but real. "They pay me too much for me to have average stats." His thumb taps along to the music, then stills. "How would you know my stats?"

"I told you I watch games." I smooth the hem of my dress, my hair sliding over my shoulder and falling into my face, giving me a convenient excuse not to look at him.

"That's a little more than just watching."

My heart kicks up, betraying me. I told myself it was necessary research, but we both know that no one is going to quiz me on his scoring average.

"Hey," he says, gentle enough that I look up despite myself. His hand lifts without urgency, brushing my hair behind my ear so he can see me, his fingers linger long enough to feel intentional. "It's okay. I looked you up, too."

"Really?" My hands go still in my lap as something in my chest loosens, then tightens again when his hand drops away.

"Yeah. I needed to know how badass my girlfriend is. Turns out, very."

I laugh, a little breathless, my gaze staying on him a beat while he focuses on the road. Every time I think I have a grasp on him, I realize I'm only scratching the surface.

The restaurant parking lot comes up quickly, and I blink. It's the kind of place with warm lighting and polished wood and no ambiguity about its purpose. A date place. Fake date, I internally reiterate. Chosen for appearances. Nothing else.

He's already out of the car by the time I reach for my door, holding it open with an expression that suggests this is simply how things are done. I swallow my instinctive protest and let it go.

Inside, we're guided to a booth by the window with sunlight spilling across the table. The low hum of conversation wraps around us.

Once our drinks arrive, his beer and my sparkling water, I lift my menu like a shield. "We should probably come up with our story."

He arches a brow, still scanning the menu. "Story?"

"You know, how we met. How long. The basics."

He pauses, then sets the menu down, thoughtful. "Probably best to keep it close to the truth. We met at the awards ceremony and started dating right after."

"Where was our first date?" I ask, the word date catching in my throat despite myself. "And who asked who?"

"I asked you. No one would buy it the other way around." His smile widens as I order the salmon and rice, like my entree proves his point. "And our first date was here."

I choke on my water as logic and something softer collide beneath my ribs. It makes sense to stick close to the truth, but it also makes today feel more real than I expected.

He watches me with careful attention, amusement tucked beneath the surface.

"Aren't you worried this will mess up your image?" The question slips out before I can stop it.

He leans back, crossing his arms. "No."

"Ladies' man Wilder. The city's most eligible bachelor." I gesture vaguely, quoting headlines I've read too many times. "A girlfriend doesn't exactly fit the narrative."

His shoulders drop. "I know what they say."

"I'm just saying," I add when the waiter passes, refilling glasses, "it doesn't seem on brand."

"I'm not a brand," he cuts in, sharper now. "I'm a person. Even if everyone forgets that."

The frustration in his voice makes my heart sink.

"Most of those photos are of Liam," he continues, calmer but no less honest. "I play wingman more than anything. Most nights end with me calling someone an Uber and going home alone."

"I didn't mean to assume."

He exhales. "I know."

But it still sits wrong, the ease with which I let someone else define him.

"So," I ask after a moment, "you don't actually hook up with that many women?"

He shakes his head. "Not even close. Occasionally, I date, sure, but nothing serious. My travel schedule scares most people off, and the ones who aren't scared usually want something other than just me."

"Oh."

It sounds kind of sad. I might not open myself up to relationships, but if I wanted to, I'd never have to wonder if they were in it for the right reasons. Never quite knowing if someone wants you or just your fame or money would be exhausting.

Nathan leans back in his chair, arms resting on the table casually. Anyone walking by would think it's normal, but I can see the hint of sadness behind the glint in his eyes. I can see the way his jaw twitches as he thinks about the women who have walked into his life only to use him and then walk back out.

Am I doing the same thing? I might be honest about my intentions with this charade, but that doesn't mean I'm not just another person using him.

"I always thought it was bullshit that I work as hard as other professional athletes only to get a fraction of the recognition," I explain, smiling despite myself. "But that kind of attention actually sounds awful."

He grins, the tension easing. "It is. There's this version of me everyone expects all the time. My team. The media. My parents. No one's ever happy."

"Will this," I say, gesturing subtly between us, "mess anything up?"

"No," he answers without hesitation as his food arrives. "But even if it did, I'd still do it."

That shouldn't cause a slow warmth to pool low in my stomach. But it absolutely does.

10

Nathan

By the time the food hits the table, I've already catalogued at least a dozen ways this could go sideways if I stop paying attention.

I'd asked Grayson if he knew of a good date place, considering he's known for having long-term, stable relationships. Well, that and the man is literally always eating. Constantly. If there is a restaurant worth going to, he knows about it.

I'd kept things vague, telling Grayson I wanted to go somewhere new. He was suspicious, but luckily didn't pry. His recommendation turned out great. Maybe even too great.

I haven't told the guys about this whole fake-dating arrangement yet. Mostly because I don't want to hear about it, but also because I know Wesley's embarrassed.

A woman like her doesn't ask for help often, and right now, she needs mine. The last thing I want to do is blast her panicked declaration to my entire hockey team and make this harder for her.

Wesley sits across from me with the sunlight catching in her hair. Her posture is relaxed in a way that still reads disciplined, like even her ease has been practiced.

When she'd answered the door in that dress, I practically had to pick my jaw up off the floor. I know for a fact that Avery probably dressed her, not because Wesley couldn't pick something like this out herself, but because she wouldn't.

Nothing about Wesley's personality screams 'I love to wear dresses on a Sunday afternoon'.

I thought about teasing her about it, but decided to let it slide. The last thing I want is to minimize how beautiful she looks today. And God, does she look gorgeous.

For the third time since we sat down, I remind myself that this is professional. I agreed to this because I need help trying some new workouts.

It has nothing to do with the way her mouth curves when she's trying not to smile or how her eyes sharpen when she's thinking three steps ahead of a question I'm still forming.

Her plate arrives first. She ordered salmon, probably operating off some sort of meal plan that she doesn't need. I'd contemplated following suit, but the burger looked too damn good. Now that it's in front of me, I have zero regrets.

"Okay," she says, lifting her fork. "Now, we eat like normal people."

I laugh under my breath. This lunch is somehow extremely awkward and comfortable at the same time. "I'm capable of that, you know."

"I've seen how hockey players inhale food."

"That's fueling," I counter, taking my first bite. "Very different."

She hums, unconvinced, but smiles anyway.

We eat for a few minutes in silence, the kind that doesn't feel like a test, just space to exist. It's rare for me. Every interaction lately feels like a performance with someone expecting something, reading into how much I drink, who I leave with, and if it all might impact my game.

I can hardly escape a conversation without someone giving me their two cents about how I choose to live my life. My parents. My coach. Everyone has an opinion that I'm supposed to hear out. It's exhausting. Here, no one is paying us any real attention, and if they are, it's exactly what we want them to see. And Wesley, she doesn't seem to expect me to fit into some predetermined mold. It's nice.

I wipe my hands on my napkin, keeping my tone light. "Baseline lunch assessment. How am I doing?"

Her eyes flick up, amused. "You haven't said anything wildly incriminating yet."

"Yet."

"That's promising."

I notice her shoulders are more relaxed. "You seem less tense than earlier."

"That's because we're not talking about contracts or captaincies or coaches right now." She takes a sip of her sparkling water. "This feels easier."

"You're saying there's more to Wesley than soccer?"

The question hangs a beat longer than intended, and I shift in my chair, rolling my shoulders as if I can physically shake off the awareness of her watching me.

"Much more." She tilts her head. "What about you? Other than hockey and apparently being tragically misunderstood by the media."

I snort. "That's my whole personality, actually."

"I don't buy it."

"Hockey, hiking, and exploring whatever city I'm in that week."

Her eyebrows lift. "You hike."

"I do."

"Where?"

"Well, it's more like I enjoy walking near nature."

Her laugh comes quick and unguarded, and I file that sound away immediately. "Of course it is. Hiking and exploring? I figured you were a city boy."

"I am," I say, setting my fork down. "I grew up here and don't ever want to leave. But we're surrounded by a lot of sights, and I like seeing what else is out there."

"But no scaling mountains?"

"Hell no. I use the word hiking loosely."

She laughs again, and I catch myself wondering how often I can get her to do that.

"You have to be careful when saying 'hiking'. The next thing you know, you're three miles into climbing Mount Monadnock, scrambling for your life."

The memory flashes across her face.

"Speaking from experience?" I ask.

"Unfortunately." Her cheeks flush. "There was no second date."

"He sounds horrible. Who the hell takes someone on that kind of hike on a first date? You dodged a bullet."

"A twenty-one-year-old guy trying to show off how cool he was, that's who."

"I'm definitely doing better than that guy."

"If you say so." She takes a sip of her water, wiggling her eyebrows.

"What about you? What does Wesley Miller do outside of soccer?"

She shifts uncomfortably as if I'd asked a hard question and not just about her other hobbies. Except...

"No," I say, shaking my head. "You can't seriously mean you have literally nothing you enjoy outside of soccer."

There's serious and then fixated. Clearly, she's the latter.

"I don't have time for much else. When there's room in my schedule, I like to run in charity runs or try different local yoga classes."

"That doesn't count," I argue, knowing that she only does those things to help with soccer.

"They count." Her jaw works.

"I'll give you half credit. Maybe."

She scoffs. "I did not agree to be graded on my hobbies."

I take a bite of my burger, eyeing her while she squirms under my gaze. "Too bad. Give me something else. Anything else."

She toys with the straw in her water longer than she should have to. My heart tugs.

"Girls' nights with Avery and my friend Harper." Her smile is triumphant.

"Do you talk about soccer at these girls' nights?"

"Yes," she says, holding up a finger to stop me from interrupting. "But we talk about other things more."

Her cheeks turn scarlet. She's probably thinking about their recent conversations. Whatever they were, she doesn't want me to know. My grin widens because I'm about ninety percent sure my name was involved.

Knowing that she's talking about me with her friends does something to me.

"Fine. I'll accept it."

Her eyes roll, but her grin stays in place.

She relaxes more after that, leaning forward onto the table as the conversation becomes a rhythm of shared stories. She tells me about pregame rituals, insisting she's not superstitious even though she dresses in the same order before every game. I tell her about junior leagues and how a prank involving a puppy in the locker room turned into Wyatt owning a dog against his will.

"I'd never be able to handle the shit you guys throw at each other." She shakes her head.

"I like the surprises."

Surprises like how well the conversation is flowing with Wesley. Surprises like how much I want to keep talking to her.

"I like control. Knowing what's coming. Planning for it."

I watch her neatly align her cutlery when she finishes. "This whole thing must feel like chaos."

"You have no idea."

"For what it's worth, I'm going to try to make things as easy as possible for you. I know we're both walking a line."

She meets my gaze and nods. Something unspoken settles between us, a tension neither of us is ready to acknowledge.

When we're finished, I pay the bill before she can argue. She looks like she might, but then lets it go. I take it as a small victory.

Outside, winter bites at the air, and the pale sky stretches overhead. She tucks her hands into her coat pockets while we walk to the car.

As I pull out of the parking lot, I ask, "Do I get a second date?"

"And a third and a fourth," she says easily. "If you behave."

It's a joke, but my body reacts to her bossiness anyway. Not now. Not now. Not now.

"I've been a perfect gentleman."

It's true. I haven't pushed the boundaries, even though the longer lunch went on, the more I wanted to.

"You have." She says slowly, as if it surprises her.

My grip tightens on the wheel. The fact that being a gentleman is a surprise shows how fake this all is. If it were real, she'd already know it's the least she could expect from me.

Between the name misunderstanding and my being late, we had a rockier start than I'd like. I hope she is at least starting to believe better of me. Though I can't quite figure out why her approval matters at all to me.

"We've already agreed on training twice a week when we're not on an away series. In the mornings," I add reluctantly, hating getting up before eight when I don't have to.

"At seven." She smiles as if my pain brings her joy.

"Yes, seven." I glare at her. "What about on your end? How often do we need to be seen in public?"

"As often as we can spare until the party." Then, as if realizing the implication, she adds, "without cramping your style, obviously. No formal statement or anything."

"It doesn't cramp my style." I turn the heat down a little. Being this close to her is more than enough heat without the car warming me up further.

"We should probably go out a couple of nights with the girls on my team."

"You've thought about this."

"I think about everything," she says dryly.

"When's the next night out?"

Her street comes into view, and I'm tempted to circle the block.

"Next weekend. We have a home scrimmage on Friday. Win or lose, the girls always go out after." She fidgets in her seat, fingers tapping on the center console.

"Do you usually go?

"No. That's why I'm in this mess."

"Why not?" I know she's dedicated, but it's not like she doesn't have friends.

She glances up at me, chewing on her lip while contemplating her answer.

"I try to keep it all as a job. My family needs me to succeed in this to support them. I don't want to get involved with the team personally and offset the balance. It's better to stay focused."

I understand that weight instantly, even if our lives look different on paper, we both have something to prove. Before I think better of it, I take her hand, stopping its restless movement. Her head jolts up, eyes locking with mine.

"You can succeed in soccer and still let yourself live a little." My voice is gentle as I pull up to her place.

"No. I can't."

There's more to that answer, but her tone makes it clear that she doesn't plan to tell me.

For a few aching seconds, I get caught up in the feel of her fingers against mine. I should let go. Hell, I should've never grabbed her in the first place. Instead, my fingers trail up her wrist. I drag them up her arm, relishing in the way her breath hitches.

She's not looking at me. Instead, she's watching my hand with determined focus.

"What about touching?" I force myself to pull back, returning my hand to my lap.

She coughs, my question catching her off guard like I hoped it would. "Huh?"

"Well, if we're dating, then people will expect touching." I tilt my head, forcing a professional expression onto my face even though my heart is beating out of my chest at the thought of getting my hands on her.

"Holding hands, arms around each other, and hugging. That's all okay by me." A red tint takes over her cheeks.

"And kissing?" I'm pushing the boundaries, and I know it.

She folds her arms as if she knows it too. So, I give her a second, rounding the car to open her door. Her eyes burn into my skin, watching me with curiosity.

As I open the door, I lean in using my arms to brace myself against it, caging her in. "Well?" I ask.

"If the moment calls for it." Her eyes dart to my lips as she slowly climbs out, bringing us eye level.

"And now? Someone could be lurking, wondering if this is fake." I lean closer to her, feeling her breath against my lips.

We pause, lips only inches from each other. Then, right before I do something extremely stupid, she turns.

Her lips brush against my ear. "Then let them talk."

And then she's gone, pushing past me and smiling like she knows exactly what she's done to me.

"Don't be late Tuesday," she calls.

"I wouldn't dream of it." I groan, watching her walk away and forcing myself not to chase after her.

Once she's inside, I toss my head back against my car, letting out the breath I'd been holding. Fuck.

Friday.

Only a few days until I can pretend she's mine again.

Spending two months with her platonically is going to be a test of my willpower. A test I'm not sure I'll pass.

11

Nathan

The rink is quieter than it will be in an hour. It's the kind of quiet that only exists before a game, when blades have yet to cut the ice, and the air still feels clean. Last night we managed a win, so hopefully, we'll pull through again tonight. But for now, everything is still untouched by expectation.

I like this part best.

My headphones are in, and the music is low enough that I can still hear the scrape of my skates and the echo of voices somewhere down the tunnel. I move through my warmup more out of habit than intention, stretching muscles that already know what's coming and loosening joints that don't need the reminder. My body's locked into routine while my mind refuses to stay where it belongs.

Because it keeps drifting back to her.

Wesley.

At lunch, we'd been casual and familiar, but our workout sessions were different.

We'd convened at seven a.m. sharp on Tuesday and Thursday. She'd been exactly what she promised. Professional and focused. There were no lingering touches or teasing glances, just quiet instruction delivered with the same calm authority she brings to everything else. It was as if Sunday's lunch never happened.

I matched her energy because I said I would, because I told her I'd make this easy, and because I don't want to be the guy who proves her caution right.

Still, it wasn't easy at all.

Not when I caught myself noticing how she shifts her weight when she demonstrates a drill, or how her voice changes slightly when she pushes me harder. I left each session feeling wrung out in ways that have nothing to do with the muscles I don't normally use.

She never once let her gaze linger anywhere it shouldn't. It's like there are infinite Wesleys and every single one is tempting in a different way. I'm hooked on trying to figure out which version I have in front of me every time we're together.

It's becoming a problem. I don't do this. I don't like women who are completely uninterested in me. As a matter of fact, I can't remember the last time I really liked a woman at all. At least not enough to be thinking about them when my mind should be focused on my game in a couple of hours.

I check my phone again, even though I already know there won't be anything new.

Our text thread is short and painfully well-behaved.

I tried flirting, lightly at first, then bolder, but backed off when she responded with scheduling confirmations and eventually nothing at all. Rationally, I know that she ignored me today because she has her own scrimmage tonight that she's warming up for. Focus, for her, is sacred, and she doesn't break it lightly.

Even with the less-than-promising text chain, I'm looking forward to tonight.

We're going out with her team. We're supposed to be seen together as a couple. I get to be less careful and pretend she's mine. That thought alone sends a restless spark through me that I can't quite shake.

I skate a slow lap, then another, keeping my breath steady as I fight the urge to pull my phone back out.

Liam appears right as I am about to climb off the ice.

"Waiting for an important call?" He asks, already wearing a shit-eating grin.

I flip him off without breaking stride.

Grayson follows close behind him, smiling like this is the best part of his day. His stick is slung over one shoulder, and he looks like a captain in every way that counts. Wyatt, of course, brings up the rear with his mask dangling from one hand and his expression permanently unimpressed.

"You've checked it twelve times." Grayson points at my phone in my hand. "We counted."

"I was stretching." Had I really checked it that much?

Wyatt snorts. "Your thumbs don't stretch."

Liam peers at my screen like he might be able to see through it. "So," he says, voice dripping with interest, "Wesley?"

"Fuck off."

"That's not a no."

Grayson raises a brow. "You went on a date."

"No," I say, even though my palms sweat as I try to figure out if that's a lie or not.

Liam's grin widens. "You've got that look."

"What look?"

"The one that says you're pretending you don't care while caring a lot."

I push past him toward the bench. "Mind your own fucking business."

Sometimes it's really annoying that Liam has known me for so long. He can see right through my bullshit.

"That's a yes," Grayson says, amused.

"You guys are worse than middle-aged women with your damn gossiping."

"Call me Karen, I don't care as long as you tell me what's going on with the scary soccer captain." Liam blocks my path, preventing me from fleeing, even though that's exactly what I want to do.

Luckily, just as I'm about to try to make a break for it, a familiar face from our PR team appears at the tunnel entrance, tablet tucked under her arm.

"Nathan," she calls. "We're doing pregame media in five."

"We're not finished here," Liam calls as I walk off.

The media corner is already crowded by the time I'm waved over, with cameras angled and microphones clustered like I'm talking about something groundbreaking instead of hockey. I pull my headphones down around my neck and school my face into the neutrality needed when facing the sharks.

This is familiar territory. Safe, even. Hockey questions are predictable. I answer cleanly, saying nothing interesting and giving them enough to chew on without causing problems.

The first few come exactly as expected.

A question about the upcoming matchup against Dallas. Another about line combinations. Someone asks about the pace of play we're trying to establish early. I answer on autopilot, nodding where it's appropriate, using the right phrases, and keeping my voice even while my mind drifts elsewhere.

Then one of them clears his throat.

"Nathan," he says, tone casual but sharpened enough to put me on alert, "your numbers this season have been steady, but not exactly what people expect from you."

There it is.

My shoulders stiffen with the instinctive urge to retreat inward, to clamp down before my thoughts spiral somewhere I don't want them to go.

"How do you respond to criticism that your performance has been mediocre by your standards?"

Mediocre.

The word sinks like a stone in my gut because it's not entirely wrong. I've been trying like hell not to let that thought take root, though.

I exhale slowly through my nose, buying myself half a second.

"Hockey's a long season. There are stretches where things click and stretches where you're grinding, and right now my focus is on consistency and contributing where I'm needed."

A couple of heads nod. Pens move.

Another voice cuts in. "Do you feel pressure to prove something tonight?"

Pressure. Prove. Perform.

I keep my gaze forward. "Pressure comes with the job. If you let it get in your head, that's when you make mistakes. I'm trying to stay present and play my game."

It's the right answer. I know that. Still, the truth underneath it hums uncomfortably. Staying present has been harder lately because a part of me knows exactly what they're seeing, and that part of me is terrified they're right.

Sure, last night was the best game I've played in a while, but one game's not enough to secure my contract.

The questions shift again, mercifully, toward the team, strategy, and other topics I can discuss without feeling exposed. I relax slightly, the edge dulling as I fall back into rhythm.

And then someone at the front raises a phone.

"So," she says, her tone bright, almost amused, "care to explain this?"

She turns the screen toward me.

It's a photo from my lunch date. I'm opening Wesley's car door. She's mid-laugh, head tipped back so the light catches her face. It's harmless.

And it hits me harder than any hockey question they could've asked.

"Is this the same woman you donated two hundred thousand dollars to spend the day with?" Another reporter adds quickly. "The soccer captain?"

There's roaring in my ears.

I hadn't planned on this. I hadn't planned on saying anything, on making it real outside of our carefully constructed bubble.

Commenting formally seemed pointless when it was all a temporary arrangement.

We should've known better. Privacy is not a luxury I'm afforded.

My instinct is to deflect and downplay it until it disappears. But if I do that, if I shrug it off like it's nothing, I don't just protect myself. I undercut her. Her plan. And potentially her captaincy.

That's not an option.

"Yes," I say, jaw tightening.

A ripple goes through the group. Someone murmurs her name. Someone else leans forward.

"Who is she to you?" the first reporter presses.

I don't hesitate this time, even as my heart starts to pound.

"She's my girlfriend."

For half a second, everything goes quiet. Then the room explodes.

Questions overlap, cameras shift, and someone whistles under their breath. I catch fragments as they come at me from every direction.

"How long has this been going on?"

"Is this serious?"

"Does this affect your focus?"

I hold my ground the way I do on the ice when chaos hits, creating too much noise with no space to breathe.

"We're private," I say simply. "And no, it doesn't affect my focus. If anything, having the right support makes it easier to do my job."

It's true. Knowing that she's fully in my corner, hoping I get my contract renewed is a breath of fresh air. Having support outside of my teammates isn't something I'm used to. My sister tries, but considering my parents vehemently disagree with me playing hockey at all, her hands are tied.

As the questions keep coming, the shift settles in, the moment where something private becomes public, whether you're ready or not. Somewhere across town, Wesley is probably taping her ankles or lacing her cleats, completely unaware I've changed the narrative.

I hope she understands why.

My fingers curl around my phone as I head for the locker room. Do I warn her, or does that risk throwing her off before her game?

I decide to hold off. I'll see her in a couple of hours and can explain then.

As I'm about to slide my phone into my pocket, it lights up. Mom.

I decline it. I'm sure she saw the interview and wants more details. That's not the problem. The problem is that the conversation will inevitably shift to what she'd rather I be doing with my life. I don't have time for that when I need to be on the ice in an hour.

The locker room doors barely close before the guys descend.

"You absolute bastard," Liam says, clapping me on the back. "Girlfriend?"

I drop my gear onto the bench harder than necessary. "Don't start."

Grayson doesn't laugh. He studies me with his head tipped slightly to the side like he's assessing a play unfolding in real time. "You good?"

Wyatt shakes his head.

I strip off my aqua practice jersey, muscles tight, aware of all three of them watching me now. They've seen me through slumps, streaks, and things I don't talk about, but probably should. They know when I'm lying. They definitely know when I'm dodging.

"What's going on here?" Grayson asks, sitting down on the bench.

I contemplate lying, not wanting to out Wesley's situation. But it's not like her coach knows my teammates. "Fake dating," I explain, turning to see all three guys staring at me like I've lost my mind.

"She said no to working out with me at first." I left that detail out when I first told them she was going to help.

"I like her more already," Wyatt grunts, adding tape to his stick.

"Then her coach told her she needs to have more balance outside of soccer. She assumed something was going on between us. Wesley ran with it."

"She lied?" Liam asks, grin growing. "Wouldn't have thought she had it in her. Maybe her friend, that girl, is a different breed."

"Avery?" Grayson asks, head darting up at the mention of her.

Liam's eyes narrow, and we all exchange a glance at his sudden interest. Before we can dig in, he shifts back to me.

"Do you really need her help training with you?" Grayson asks, sliding on his game-time skates as the locker room fills with the rest of the team.

"Have you noticed how he's played this week?" Liam asks. "It's the best he's looked in months."

I lace my skates, letting them talk. He's right. This week has been my best in a long time. Whether I want to admit it or not, something in me knows she's part of that.

"She challenges me, not only physically, but mentally. It's different than working out with you guys. It's less pressure, even though she pushes me just as hard. She doesn't care who I am or what my numbers look like."

"That's hot," Liam mutters.

"Shut up." I shoot him a look.

Grayson's gaze stays steady. "You're enjoying the work again."

It's not a question.

"Yeah. I am."

For a moment, no one jokes. The weight of it settles in the space between us. Hockey isn't a job for us, no matter how much money gets thrown at it. The sport is ingrained into who we are, but when it stops feeling like yours, something breaks that's hard to name and harder to fix.

Liam, of course, ruins the moment.

"Sex has been known to improve performance. Endorphins. Stress relief. I'm just saying." He leans back on the bench.

"It's not like that," I snap.

Even as I say it, my throat burns with the truth I don't voice. That I want it to be like that. That I fantasize about her hands on me more than I should. That I'd like nothing more than to see what she looks like when she finally lets go of her super-human restraint.

It's irrelevant.

Wyatt snorts softly. "You're in trouble."

Grayson smiles, clapping a hand on my shoulder. "Yeah, you are."

Liam slams his locker closed. "Damn. And here I was hoping for a scandal."

"Don't worry," I mutter, grabbing my stick. "I'm sure you'll find a way to make one of your own."

"How does the fake date thing work?" Grayson asks.

"Just a few public outings. I'll go to her team party in January. And I'm going out with her friends tonight."

Liam's eyes pop out of his head, and I swear there might be drool falling down his chin.

I glare. "No. Hell no. Liam, do not sleep with one of her teammates. For the love of god, leave that team alone."

Wyatt's head is down, shaking with quiet laughter, and Grayson is not much better, cheeks full of air as he holds it in. Liam, though, looks like a kid in a fucking candy store.

"So, what time are we going out tonight?" Liam asks, shit-eating grin spreading across his face.

"We're not going out," I argue, clenching my jaw. "I am."

"He'll just stalk you all the way to the bar if you don't tell him." Wyatt points out.

I curse under my breath.

"We're going to the Blue Line. But Liam, don't be a jackass, please."

He huffs, "The ladies love me."

Grayson chuckles. "*The ladies* would get the ick if they heard you say that."

"Fine. I'll do my best to behave, but it's not my fault if one of them hits on me."

I whip my towel at him, "It's never your fault when you wind up in someone's bed."

He quirks a brow. "What's a man to do, really?"

Wyatt decides to jump on Liam's train. "Yeah, Wilder, not everyone just stumbles into fake relationships."

I flip them both off, turning toward the tunnel. As I file into the cluster of players waiting for our coach's speech, one thought loops relentlessly through my head.

My friends are crashing my second fake date tonight. The date with the woman who is now publicly mine.

I told the world she's my girlfriend.

And the woman who likes control and planning is about to be blindsided.

12

Wesley

The locker room hums with post-scrimmage energy. Adrenaline crackles, and every voice sounds loud and bright, the way it only does after a win. The excitement is earned. It may have been a friendly match, but we kicked ass. It's good to know that even though the season is over, we're still sharp.

Sweat cools on my skin as I sit on the bench, sliding my shin guards free. My legs are heavy, and my muscles are buzzing with the satisfying ache of a night well played.

The final score was three to one, and I put up a goal and an assist. It was the kind of performance that lingers, quieting the part of my brain that always seems to race toward what's next.

Avery drops onto the bench beside me, tugging the braid from her fiery hair. Her eyes are lit with the adrenaline she thrives on. "You were on fire," she says, nudging my shoulder. "That breakaway in the second half, straight through the center? I don't think they even saw you until it was over."

"It was the opening," I say, bending to unlace my cleats. "They overcommitted."

Becca laughs from two lockers down, a towel slung around her neck. "As if you didn't absolutely cook their back line."

"I did not cook anyone," I argue, even as my mouth curves.

"You even smiled when you scored," Haley adds from across the room, stuffing gear back into her locker. "That's a celebration for you."

The room erupts into overlapping voices.

I lean back against the cool metal, letting the noise wash over me, the weight of the week loosening its grip. I played well. I know I did. There's comfort in that, especially after the last few days, which have felt anything but comfortable.

I had two training sessions with Nathan. He'd been early both times with two coffees in hand, focused in a way that made it clear he was taking this seriously. No flirting. No boundary testing. Just effort, attention, and a willingness to be corrected without ego.

I matched him step for step because I said I would, and because working out with someone stronger, faster, and as driven as I was felt electric. It pushed me to be better.

I refused to let him see me tired, even when I soaked in ice baths afterward to stop my legs from shaking. These workouts were helping me just as much, if not more than, they were helping him.

Still, no matter how hard I tried to stay focused, I couldn't stop noticing things I shouldn't have. Like the way he locks in when I challenge him or how he absorbs feedback as if he actually wants it. Conditioning with him was feeling less like an obligation and more like something to look forward to.

And then there was last Sunday.

Lunch that slipped past polite and into friendly, in a way I hadn't expected. The laughter surprised me. I didn't check my watch once.

If Avery asked me right now, when I'd last had actual fun, I wouldn't have to think, because the answer would be that day. Nathan might be the hockey player, but I'm the one skating on thin ice.

I shower, taking my time to rinse the sweat from my skin, my nerves buzzing with anticipation for the night ahead.

When I finally return to my locker, I catch Avery watching me from the corner of her eye, a knowing smile already forming. "Does a certain hockey player have anything to do with why you've brushed your hair for five minutes?" She asks.

My eyes narrow, but Haley beats me to it.

"Yeah," she says. "When were you planning on telling us you have a boyfriend?"

My head snaps up. Tonight was supposed to be a soft launch. She shouldn't know anything about it.

"Well, um…" My heart starts racing. "It's early and not exactly official."

I glance at Avery, trying to figure out how the team seems to already know, but she looks just as surprised.

Haley pulls out her phone, scrolls, then turns the screen toward me. "Seems pretty official. At least for him."

The video is already playing.

Nathan sits beneath bright arena lights, answering questions with the calm confidence he brings to everything. The angle shifts, and I'm on the screen, mid-laugh, caught in a moment I thought belonged only to us.

Then his voice fills the room.

"She's my girlfriend."

The words echo far louder than the phone should allow.

My breath catches, sharp and involuntary, the post-game high shattering as anticipation gives way to spiraling anxiety.

What the fuck?

Avery's head snaps up. "Oh my god. He didn't."

Becca whistles low. "Damn. Nathan Wilder claimed you on ESPN."

Haley drops her head back. "I need a boyfriend to drop two hundred thousand dollars on a day with me. It's so hot."

I scan the room and catch sight of Coach standing in the corner. I can't deny it or minimize it. I'm cornered.

Why would he say that? I asked him to help sell it, sure, but I assumed that would be discreet dating, not a national announcement. Not this.

Avery nudges me. "Panic later. They're watching."

I take a steadying breath and force a laugh. "He was planning to announce us next week after we met each other's friends and teams, but I guess he couldn't wait." I lie, smiling as if it's charming and not my worst nightmare.

"Wait," a rookie yells. "He's meeting us?"

"Tonight, I'm coming out with you guys." I nod.

My team erupts in excited chatter, highlighting how right Coach Bennett is about the way I've isolated myself.

Coach flashes me a smile before she exits, and I drop mine the second she's gone.

I pull out my phone to check for a message explaining why he'd jump the gun like this, without at least talking to me. There's nothing new, just his good luck text from this morning. The one I left on read when I should've at least said it back. But I didn't, my mind screaming that it would blur lines I didn't want blurred.

I open my Instagram and watch the numbers climb. Thousands of new followers, all adding me after his announcement. My direct messages are clustered with girls either wishing to be me or saying the cruelest things they can think of.

I swallow, realizing my expectations for this entire charade have been tossed into the wind.

Avery waits until the locker room clears before gripping my shoulders. "Hey, are you okay?"

My eyes water against my will. "When I told Coach we were dating, I didn't think it would turn into this. Now, people are watching me. Not for soccer. And this is fake, but now it has to look so real, and—"

"Wes," she cuts in. "Breathe. You're fine."

"How is any of this fine?" My voice cracks.

"Because you're Wesley fucking Miller. There is literally nothing you can't pull off when you want to." She takes my phone from me, shoving it into my jacket pocket. "You slide on your shoes, go to the bar, and lie flawlessly to the whole city."

I snort, but nod furiously to everything she says. I only get thirty more seconds of panic. Then, I shove the lump of anxiety down, slip my bag over my shoulder, and force myself into action. This is just performing, nothing emotional about it. I can do that.

Except the moment I step outside, I know that everything has changed.

Lights flare, popping in rapid succession. For half a second, I think I've wandered out of the wrong exit or into someone else's event. Then voices start layering over one another, and I realize, with a sickening drop in my stomach, that they're saying my name.

"Wesley, over here."

"Wesley, is it true?"

"Can you confirm the relationship?"

I slow, drawing my jacket tighter around myself, scanning the lot for Avery or anyone familiar, but there's no space. They're already closing into a semicircle that's tightening with every step I don't take.

"How long have you and Nathan been together?"

"How does it feel to land the most eligible bachelor in the city?"

"Did this start before or after his massive donation?"

Cameras are raised. Microphones appear in my peripheral vision. Someone's shoulder bumps my arm, and I flinch, heart slamming so hard it feels like it might bruise.

I stop walking, and they close the gap instantly.

My breath comes in short bursts, anxiety spiraling out of control. On the field, chaos is expected. Here, it's invasive and unpredictable, crawling under my skin.

"Are you worried about how dating Nathan could affect his focus?"

My mouth opens to answer, but then the questions collide, words blurring into noise. Their faces are indistinct behind lenses and flashes. My pulse roars in my ears.

This isn't about me at all. It's about him. A shiver runs up my spine as I realize that he lives this way all the time.

I take a step back, trying to get back inside, but the crowd moves with me, tightening until I smell cologne and hot camera equipment.

My hands curl into fists as I try to stop them from sweating.

I don't know how long it lasts. Thirty seconds. A minute. Long enough for panic to sink its claws in.

Finally, cutting cleanly through the noise like a blade through ice, his voice echoes around me.

"That's enough."

The words are sharp, carrying with them a command that turns heads before I even see him.

"Back up," Nathan says, louder now, already pushing into the space between me and the nearest camera. "Give her some room."

The crowd hesitates, surprise rippling through them, but it gives him room to get to me. His hand slides around my waist, pulling me to his side and grounding me back in the parking lot. A tendril of wet hair is stuck to his forehead, but he somehow makes it work for him. He's wearing his gameday suit, but the top of the shirt is unbuttoned, making it look more casual.

"I've got you," he says, low, meant only for me, before raising his voice again. "She played ninety minutes of incredible soccer. If you are going to show up at her game, maybe try asking her about that."

He doesn't slow, just keeps moving, guiding me through the bodies. His presence is a shield I didn't realize I needed until it was here, solid and unyielding.

"She had a goal and an assist tonight," he continues, eyes flashing as he glares at the nearest reporter. "Though it doesn't seem like any of you bothered to watch the game you showed up to."

Flashes go off again, faster now. Frantic.

"Nathan, is this serious?"

"Is she the one?"

He ignores them, getting me to his car in a few quick strides and ushering me inside with one hand at my back, blocking the cameras with his body. I slide into the seat, heart still racing and hands trembling despite my best efforts to still them.

The door shuts with a solid click.

Silence. Or at least, as close as possible with a crowd of people outside the car.

He rounds the hood, shoulders squared as he says something sharp to the nearest cameraman before getting into the driver's seat, shutting them out.

For a moment, neither of us moves.

The world narrows to the inside of his car, the sound of my own breathing, and the warmth still lingering where his hand touched my waist.

Then he turns toward me.

"Hey," Nathan says, voice softer now, careful.

13

Wesley

"Can you please take me home now?" I ask, desperate to get away from the crowd lingering around the car.

Nathan's hands are tight on the steering wheel.

I notice that first, before anything else. Not the speed, not the way the city blurs past the windows, but the tension in his grip. His knuckles are pale, and his jaw is set like he's bracing for impact.

I stare out the passenger-side window, trying to process what the hell just happened.

"How are you doing?" He asks, breaking the silence.

I shrug, because I don't know how I'm doing. "Fine."

The word sounds small even to me.

He nods as if he believes me, but it looks more like he knows better and is letting it go for now. The city lights reflect off the windshield, streaking gold and white across his face. He looks different like this. An ordinary guy who looks like he might be regretting a dozen choices at once.

"We can reschedule." His fingers tap on the wheel.

I realize then that he's nervous. How many relationships of his have broken down under the type of scrutiny that just ambushed me outside the stadium? Is that what he's worried about? That I'll call the whole thing off.

Lucky for him, I don't scare easily. I also don't back out of promises. We both need this to keep going. Cameras be damned.

"We're going," I clarify. "But I need to change."

Another nod. A beat of silence.

Finally, I glance over at him. "Why were you at the stadium?"

His eyes flick to mine, then back to the road. "Our game ended an hour ago. I was going to try to warn you."

I blink. "Did you win?"

He huffs out a disbelieving laugh. "That's what you want to ask me? If we won?"

"Yeah." It's a start at least.

"Yes, Wesley, we won." The corner of his lip tilts up in a smirk.

We pull onto my street, which is quieter and darker than the rest of downtown. The familiarity settles me further. My unit comes into view, the porch light glowing softly in the night.

"And you? Did you play better?" I ask, knot forming as the question leaves my lips. He only agreed to this ridiculous arrangement to improve his game and rediscover his love for the sport. I've been trying to challenge him in new ways during our sessions, but the workouts aren't groundbreaking. He could easily decide to do them alone without having to play into this charade.

"Yes. I did. I have been all week." He pulls into the space outside my apartment. "Can I explain?"

I know he wants to talk about what happened. We should talk about it, but I don't know what to say. So, instead of doing what's reasonable, I burst out of the car and into my apartment. I'm a coward.

Inside, I pull on the outfit I'd laid out this morning when I was excited for tonight and not hesitant. Dark jeans and a black crop top. I'm ready in two minutes, but I hesitate in my bedroom.

My phone buzzes with a text from my sister.

Emma: Streamed your scrimmage tonight. Nice win! Are you coming home for Thanksgiving next week?

Me: Thanks, but I'm not sure I can make it.

Emma: Why?

Because going home hurts. Because I'm teetering on the line between responsibility and recklessness, and going home might push me over the edge. All things I wish I could say, but can't.

Me: A lot of team responsibilities. Sorry.

Emma: So, it has nothing to do with THE Nathan Wilder telling everyone you're his girlfriend.

Emma: I'm your sister! ESPN is not the place for me to find this out!!!

Fuck. The last thing I need is to explain this arrangement to my little sister.

Me: It's not what it looks like. Please don't tell Dad. And pretend you never saw that.

Three dots show up, but I've already been inside too long. I click my phone shut and slide it into my jeans. Emma's guilt-trip can wait until I know what the hell to say.

As I head down the steps to the car, I realize I still don't know how to act around him.

I didn't want this kind of publicity. Maybe I should've expected it considering who he is, but I didn't. I didn't anticipate it at all, but none of it is his fault. I'm the one who came up with this whole story. He's the one playing along.

A bubble of nerves rises in my chest when he's in the same spot waiting for me.

"I'm sorry." He says as I climb in. Then, his eyes focus on me, darkening. "Wow, you look great. Like really great."

"Jaw off the floor, Wilder." I tease, trying to lighten the mood. "And you have nothing to be sorry for. I'm the one who lied about us dating in the first place."

The car pulls away from the curb as he plugs in the address for The Blue Line, the bar my team frequents. I notice that it's only a twenty-minute walk from my apartment. For years, I've been sitting at home while my team hangs out only a mile and a half from my apartment. Coach Bennett really is right.

"Yeah, but going on a couple of fake dates is different from announcing publicly that you're my girlfriend."

"It is." I turn toward him, raising my eyebrows. "You could've said it wasn't what it looked like."

"I know."

"You could have said it was just a date."

"I know."

"You could have said nothing at all."

"I know," he repeats, softer now. "But none of those answers make this believable or help you."

The car slows as we hit a red light. For a second, the city feels suspended around us. I study his profile, noticing the faint bruise along his cheekbone from a rough hit last night. My heart jumped into my throat when I watched it happen.

He looks like he's waiting for me to end our agreement.

"I'm not mad." I'm not entirely sure that's true. I'm not mad at him, at least.

His shoulders loosen a fraction. "Okay."

"I'm just overwhelmed."

"That's fair."

The light turns green, and he eases forward. He seems so steady; meanwhile, I'm anything but.

"I didn't mean for it to get like that," he says. "The attention tonight. All of it."

"I know." And I do. That attention is unavoidable for him. It's his life. This was always part of the deal, even if I pretended it wouldn't be. "I can't believe they're that concerned with your life. It's kind of awful."

"Yeah, my parents think the same thing. It's not ideal, but hockey is worth it."

I don't like the way his eyes drop when he mentions his parents, but I know my place, and it's not in his business.

He parks at the curb and cuts the engine.

Neither of us moves.

"My teammates are excited to meet you," I say, reaching for the door handle.

"About that," He starts, reaching across me to pull my door closed again. He climbs out and walks around to reopen my door for me. He did the same thing last Sunday, and it still makes my heart beat faster.

"In the spirit of not blindsiding you again, some of the guys invited themselves tonight. They know this isn't real." He rubs the back of his neck. "But they know how to keep their mouths shut."

"Fuck," I say, climbing out. "Okay, Avery and Harper know too, so I get it."

He laces his fingers through mine, grip tightening when I go to pull away.

I don't like the way his hand feels in mine. Well, I do like it, but that's the problem.

"Ready, girlfriend?" He asks, his grin widening.

"As I'll ever be." I can't help but smile back.

Luckily, there is no press outside the bar, and they're banned inside. We make our way through the doors without any other confrontations.

The noise hits us immediately. The music is low enough to talk over but loud enough to feel the speakers vibrate. The Blue Line looks exactly as I expected, with dark wood and exposed brick. TVs are lining the walls, replaying highlights from earlier games.

Nathan's hand stays in mine as we move through the clusters of people. His thumb brushes the side of my knuckle once, absentmindedly, and I tell myself not to read into it.

My teammates are easy to spot. Becca is perched on a barstool as if she owns it, and Haley is leaning against the high-top beside her, mid-laugh. Avery notices me first, her eyes immediately dropping to our joined hands.

"Oh," she says, winking at me. "This is happening."

I laugh, nerves loosening a fraction as we weave through the crowd. "You're acting like he's a party trick."

Avery's grin widens.

Becca chimes in, "Actually, she's acting like our captain, who has never come out with us before, showed up with the entire hockey team in tow."

I glance behind us to see Nathan's friends pushing their way inside. The idea of them mingling with my team makes me jittery, but it's too late to do anything about it.

I turn to Nathan, motioning to my friends. "You've already met Avery."

"Right around the time, you trash-talked my girl to her face," Avery says, eyes gleaming and hand extended. "Nice to meet you again."

"Ouch," Nathan replies, chuckling.

"We've already paid our penance for that." Liam strolls over, saddling up next to us. "In the form of hours of cardio torture."

The rest of Nathan's friends follow behind. We take turns introducing everyone while I try to ignore his hand sliding from mine and shifting to my lower back. His palm is flush against me, but the contact is casual. Normal for anyone dating. Except, it sparks under my skin in a way that's anything but casual.

Grayson's eyes flick to Avery, who has gone completely still beside me. His smile sharpens, like he's been handed an unexpected puzzle.

"Well," he says, resting an elbow against the table. "If this isn't fate."

Avery doesn't miss a beat. "If by fate you mean you've stalked me on social media before, then sure."

"I never stalked."

"The picture was from a year ago."

Grayson's lips tilt up as he leans forward, eyes laser-focused on Avery. "Well, you looked good."

There's a beat of silence that hums with something unfinished. I glance between them, curiosity sparking. Avery has always been friendly, flirtatious even, but there's a wall there now that I've never seen before. Unlike most men, Grayson doesn't seem put off by it.

Nathan clears his throat. "Okay, drinks."

We turn toward the bar, catching the eye of one of the waiters.

"Finally," Liam says. "What're you having, Wilder?"

Nathan looks down at me, his thumb tracing a lazy circle against my back. "What do you want?"

"Water," I say without thinking. It's my default. The smart athlete choice.

He nods immediately. "Water for Miller and me."

I stare at him, knowing he's only getting water because I am. The confused expression that passes across Wyatt's face says as much.

His willingness to follow my lead causes something warm to spread throughout my body. So much so that when the waiter arrives, I change my order.

"I'll take a beer."

Nathan's head turns toward me, eyes searching my face. "You sure?"

"Yeah, I want one." I can't remember the last time I had a drink, but with tonight being one big performance, now seems as good a time as any to break the dry spell.

His lips twitch, and he squints his eyes, trying to read my face. "Then I'll have one too."

The bartender slides them over. I take a sip, the cold bitterness washing away the spark tingling beneath my skin. Nathan lifts his bottle a second later, our eyes meeting over the rims. He doesn't say anything, but his hand finds my hip again, resting there as if he's done it forever.

Conversation loosens after that. Liam tells a story about getting lost downtown after a road game. Haley chimes in with one about

Becca nearly missing a flight because she refused to leave a coffee shop. Laughter weaves between us, and I order another beer.

Then Harper appears, sliding in beside me.

"You made it." I lean over to hug her.

She grins. "Wouldn't miss this."

Nathan turns, eyes lighting up. "You must be Harper."

"That obvious?" She asks.

He laughs. "You're exactly how she described you."

I'd only mentioned Harper briefly last Sunday on our date. I was telling him about a time when Avery, Harper, and I missed the bus home from our game because we got lost. Our coach warned everyone she wouldn't wait, and left us to Uber the two hours back to campus.

He'd not only remembered her name, but how I described her. I beam, leaning into his side without thinking. His arm tightens slightly around me, subtle but deliberate, and my heart does something stupid.

Whether his hand settles on my back, his fingers brush mine, or his knee presses lightly against mine when we sit, his touch never seems to leave me entirely.

I'm aware of all of it.

When I look up at him, catching his gaze as the room buzzes around us, he smiles like he is exactly where he wants to be. God, he's good at this. At pretending.

I pinch my arm as if to wake me from the dream I feel like I'm in. This isn't my life. But pretend or not, I find myself wanting the night to drag on. For the second time in a week, I'm having the kind of fun that I haven't allowed myself in years. And again, it's because of him.

14

Nathan

It would be impossible not to notice the way Wesley looks tonight. Her jeans fit like they were designed with her in mind, and her top is simple, but tempting when it reveals a thin line of her belly. It makes her feel untouchable in the way women who know exactly who they are tend to be.

What's really driving me crazy is the way she moves once we're inside the bar. Her shoulders have loosened, her smile comes easier, and her laugh is freer. The version of Wesley, with walls higher than her passing completion percentage, isn't here tonight.

I add this mental picture to my running list of different versions of her.

I can't seem to keep my hands off her.

Luckily, I don't have to.

Dating, even fake-dating, comes with certain expectations. It's why I can casually put my hand on her lower back when we walk, or lace our fingers when someone looks our way too long. My palm settles on her hip when I lean in to hear what she's saying over the music. All of it looks natural. All of it feels dangerous.

She notices. I know she does.

Every time my thumb brushes bare skin or I guide her through a cluster of people, there's a split second where her breath changes.

It makes my chest feel tight.

I've dated women who cling to attention and push for more, faster. Every single girl I've been with in recent memory liked the media attention. In fact, I'm pretty sure some have even leaked our dates to the press to get more of it.

Wesley would never do that. The attention from the press at her game really rattled her. Maybe that's why I haven't been able to talk myself into hooking up with anyone since I met her.

No, Wesley doesn't like the attention at all, but she's willing to tolerate it. That makes two of us.

She's surprising the hell out of me tonight.

I planned to stick with water, willing to follow her lead, but then she ordered a beer. My friends all take note of the way my order changes when hers does. I know I'll get shit for it when we're at morning skate tomorrow. I just don't care.

I catch Wesley watching me as I lift the bottle to my lips. There's something playful in her expression, like she's proud of herself for catching me off guard. When her eyes stay focused on me as she wraps her lips around the bottle, my mind pictures unholy things. I look away to keep from getting a boner in front of the entire bar.

God, this fucking woman might kill me.

This version of her reminds me of the woman I met at the awards ceremony. The one who'd teased me without hesitation. The one who had leaned into conversation instead of away from it. Seeing her like this feels like being let in on a secret.

The night settles into something easy. Stories are shared. Teammates clash in playful ways. Grayson keeps poking at Avery, who's acting annoyed, but not walking away. Liam's hitting on the entire soccer team with no shame, and Wyatt's somewhere off to the side, watching the night unfold.

Wesley stays close to me, even when she doesn't have to. Her shoulder brushes mine. Her hand finds my wrist when she laughs too hard. It feels intentional, even if it's not. Fake, I remind myself. This is fake.

Only when she finishes her beer does she pull away. My eyes track her as she moves easily through the crowd, gaining confidence the longer we're here. When she reaches the counter, she leans in to get the bartender's attention.

"Water," she says.

Of course. After two beers, she's still as responsible as ever.

The bartender smiles, the kind that lingers. He looks her over like he's assessing a situation rather than taking an order. I don't like it.

"Just water?" He asks. "You sure?"

She smiles politely, the professional kind. "I'm sure."

He doesn't take the hint.

"Come on," he says, leaning an elbow on the bar. "First one's on me."

I step in behind her, close enough that my chest brushes her back. My hand settles at her waist, instinctive and steady, thumb pressing lightly into the space between her hip and ribs, where her shirt doesn't reach.

"She said she's good with water," I say.

The bartender's eyes drop to my hand, then back up to my face.

I don't move it.

In fact, I pull her back slightly. Mine, at least for tonight.

"And I'll have one too," I add easily.

Wesley tilts her head, glancing back at me. I can feel the pause in her body, registering my presence and then deciding not to pull away.

The bartender's smile tightens, professionalism snapping back into place. "Coming right up."

When he turns away, Wesley looks up at me, her brows raised.

"I can order my own drink," she says quietly.

The bar is loud enough that she has to lean in slightly, her shoulder brushing mine as she speaks. Music pulses through the floor relentlessly, while laughter and overlapping conversations fill every inch of space around us.

"I know." My hand stays where it is.

"Well, thank you, boyfriend." Her voice stays even, but her pulse betrays her. It flutters fast beneath my fingers, a rhythm that doesn't match her composure.

The bartender slides the drinks across the counter, glass clinking against wood this time without the earlier commentary. Condensation gathers instantly, dripping down the sides.

Wesley shifts her weight, just slightly, and my hand adjusts without thinking, fingers flexing to keep contact like it's instinct instead of choice.

When she turns fully toward me, her eyes flick down to where I'm touching her.

"You looked a little jealous."

I huff out a quiet laugh. "Did I?"

"A little."

I consider that for half a second, leaning one shoulder against the bar. "Guess I'm committed to the role."

Her lips twitch. "You're very convincing."

Something about that makes my pulse kick harder.

"Why'd you change your order before?"

She reaches for her water, fingers wrapping around the glass as she stares at it for a second longer than necessary. Her teeth catch her bottom lip, worrying it slightly.

"Being out like this feels different," she says finally. "The pretending, the teams, the noise… all of it. It's nice not being me for a night."

The words land more heavily than they should.

Wesley Miller, the most fascinating person I've ever met, wanting to step outside of herself, even for a few hours, feels like an injustice.

"But this is still you," I say, quieter now. "Just a different part. You don't have to shut one off to be the other."

She has to know that she's perfect as she is. Ordering a beer and hanging out with friends doesn't have to be some mask she pulls on.

She glances up at me, really looking this time, like she's trying to decide how much of that she believes.

"I'm not really good at juggling."

Her gaze sharpens, focus narrowing, and I can practically see the calculation happening. Deciding what to say and what to keep to herself. Finally, she sighs.

"In college, junior year, I let loose a little." She huffs out a small laugh. "Hardly at all really, but enough that I got busted at a party the night before a game."

Her fingers trace the rim of the glass as she talks, slowly.

"I wasn't even drinking. I was the DD. But I wasn't twenty-one and was holding a beer in the images that floated around. I was on a full-ride scholarship. It looked bad."

I nod, hoping she'll keep talking.

"I almost lost my scholarship," she continues. "It didn't matter that I was sober. It didn't matter that it wasn't mine."

The lights above us flash, casting her face in brief shadows, and for a second, she looks younger. Less untouchable.

"What happened?" I ask.

"Nothing." She shrugs.

My face twists with confusion.

"When I thought they were going to pull my scholarship, there was this split second of just full body relief."

That surprises me.

"No more pressure. No more expectations." Her voice softens. "I had an out."

Okay, yeah. That I get. More than most people would.

"It makes sense. You've spent your whole life committed to one thing."

"Yeah." She nods faintly. "I felt like shit about it after."

She takes a sip of her water, then adds, "A week later, my dad got laid off. My sister's college fund went into holding us over for the next year."

I nod, the versions of Wesley all blending together into the one in front of me.

Her mouth curves into a small, almost disbelieving smile.

"The next year, I got my rookie contract. Helped pay off the house and get Emma's college fund back." She glances at me. "If I'd lost that scholarship, I don't know what would've happened to my family."

The weight of it settles between us, heavier than the music, heavier than the crowd.

"Do you even like it?" I ask, my voice low enough that it barely carries past her.

"Soccer?"

I nod.

"I love it," she says instantly without an ounce of hesitation. "I love it so fucking much."

"That whole thing sounds small," she adds, "but it showed me exactly what I have to lose." Her eyes meet mine. "And how careful I have to be not to lose it."

"It doesn't sound small," I say.

My hand slides down from her back to her hand, fingers threading with hers. It's all in the name of our fake date, but honestly, I just want to touch her.

Behind us, a familiar voice cuts through the noise, breaking the tension.

"So," Liam says loudly, climbing out of his chair. "Who wants to dance?"

One of the girls from Wesley's team stands, luring Liam onto the floor. Eventually, the empty dance floor is completely full of teammates and strangers dancing to whatever pop song pounds through the speakers.

Wesley stiffens almost imperceptibly.

I turn to her, keeping my voice low. "Dance with me."

She opens her mouth to say no. I can read it on her face.

Harper nudges her side, smiling like she knows exactly what Wesley's thinking.

Wesley hesitates, then sighs. "Fine."

I don't let her obvious distaste for the idea stop me from trying my luck. When I take her hand and lead her toward the floor, she doesn't pull away.

The first song is upbeat. She turns her back to me, moving easily and laughing when Avery says something to her from across the floor while dancing with some guy I don't recognize.

We move to the beat. I keep my hands respectful, light on her waist, more for show than anything else.

I'm actively willing myself to behave and not press against her more firmly.

She smells good, like citrus and cinnamon. Her hair brushes my chin when she tilts her head back, and I close my eyes, letting myself pretend this isn't for show.

The song changes, and the lights dim, setting the tone for something slower.

My hands adjust as she turns to face me, toying with the bottom of her shirt, letting my fingers trail across her bare skin. Her arms come up, resting loosely around my neck. We sway more than dance now, bodies close in a way that feels different than before.

I look down at her. Her lashes cast shadows against her cheeks, and there's a crease between her brows like she's thinking too hard about this.

I want to kiss her.

I don't want to scare her off.

Before I can decide what to do, Liam's voice cuts through the moment.

"Your teammates are watching pretty closely."

Ever the wingman, he nods his head across the room to a cluster of girls who're watching Wesley, as if her being here is too strange to be real.

"You really never come to this kind of thing?" I ask, trying to understand why she refuses to let herself have fun.

"No, not really. That's probably why they're looking at me like I have three heads."

"Do you think they'll report back to your coach?"

"No, I don't think so. We get along fine. I'm just nervous they'll see through this charade. It's embarrassing."

I lean in, my forehead resting briefly against hers. "Go with me here," I murmur.

My head lowers until our breath is mixing. Her breathing hitches when she realizes what I'm about to do, but she doesn't back away.

I close the distance, letting my lips brush against hers. It's brief and controlled. It's not nearly enough to sate the need for her that's screaming through my body. But this is fake, so one brush against her soft lips is all I can take.

Until her hands slide into my hair, fingers curling as she kisses me again, deeper this time. It's the kind of kiss that makes my brain short-circuit. My grip tightens reflexively at her waist as I sink into the feeling.

I pull her to my body, every curve of her fitting perfectly against me in a way that drives me crazier. It's heat and want, shooting straight through the resolve I've been carefully holding onto.

She breaks away first. My heart is pounding, and my hands feel like they don't belong to me anymore. She grins easily up at me, but there's something guarded behind it.

"That should sell it."

I lift my lips in a small smile even though my head is spinning. "For sure."

She bumps her hip into mine before stepping back, reclaiming enough space to remind us both what this is.

The rest of the night is unbearable.

All I want to do is taste her lip balm again. Instead, I mix and mingle, half-heartedly listening to conversations.

If Wesley feels even a hint of what I am, she hides it easily. It's like the kiss didn't affect her at all. She laughs when she should and adds to the conversation with ease. Meanwhile, my eyes keep finding their way to her.

I remind myself that it's okay to stare. I'm supposed to be her boyfriend. We want people to think we want each other. So, I let myself want her openly.

I sit closer. My hand laces with hers while my thumb traces shapes onto her knee at the booth. Except no one can see that.

When the bar starts to thin out and people begin to gather their things, Wesley leans into me, head resting briefly against my shoulder.

I freeze, pulse stuttering.

Eventually, she offers me a small smile. "Ready?"

"Yeah," I say, even though I'm not sure I am.

At some point throughout the night, my location was leaked to the media. Paparazzi line the sidewalk, and the cameras start going off the second we walk out.

We rush onto the sidewalk, both focusing on my car parked a couple of spots down the road. My grip tightens on her hand, and she leans into my shoulder, letting me guide her through the crowd. Their voices get louder the longer we ignore them, but neither of us takes the bait.

Once I get her safely into the car, as a good boyfriend would, I head for my side. In the ten seconds it takes for me to walk around the car and climb in, I replay the feel of her lips, the sound of her laugh, and the way she leaned into me when we sat at the booth.

Either she's phenomenal at acting, or this is turning into something I'm not prepared for.

15

Wesley

Airports are designed to make people feel anonymous. Everyone is in motion, everyone is looking somewhere else, and everyone has somewhere to be that is not here. I booked my flight less than twelve hours ago, standing in my kitchen with my phone in one hand and my keys in the other, heart still racing from a kiss that had no right to undo me the way it did.

A couple of days at home for the holiday is the practical excuse. It's a family obligation. No one questions that.

Even if it is unplanned and completely out of character.

My knees press against the seat in front of me, and my backpack barely fits under my feet. The woman beside me is already asleep, leaning toward the window with her headphones in. I envy her ability to shut the world out so easily. The man on my other side is eating chips that smell like feet. Right now, I wish I were a male athlete who could charter a private jet or some shit because the next three hours sandwiched between two total strangers is going to suck.

I pull my phone from my bag, thumb hovering over messages I haven't opened.

Nathan messaged first thing this morning to coordinate schedules for our next training session. A session I'm utterly unprepared for.

My fingers fly over the keyboard with a half-baked excuse about how I'm heading home for an early Thanksgiving, and we'll have to push it to mid-week.

This is what I need. Distance. A hard reset. Whatever happened Friday night did not fit neatly into my life, and I don't have room for things that don't fit.

The plane begins to taxi as my phone vibrates. I can't help but look, but it's not Nathan who messaged me. It's the girls.

Avery: Are you alive, or did that kiss actually kill you?

I snort softly before I can stop myself, earning a glare from the man next to me. I type back before I can overthink it.

Me: Flying home for a couple of days.

Three dots appear immediately, and I already know what's coming. There is no way either of them lets me off the hook with this.

Harper: Cue emotional breakdown.

Avery: You couldn't flee the country, so you decided to cross two time zones.

Me: I hate you both.

Avery: No, you don't.

Harper: You kissed him.

I close my eyes, one hand rubbing at my temple as the plane heads away from the gate. This morning, I woke up with one hell of a stress headache, and their goading isn't helping.

Me: It was for show.

Avery: Someone needs to give you two an Oscar.

She's right. Anyone with eyes would've believed that kiss. Hell, I was a participant, and even I almost believed it.

Me: Not so sure I can keep this up.

Avery: So, the kiss was good.

Good does not even begin to cover it.

The problem is not that I kissed Nathan. The problem is that I liked it. The problem is that my body responded like it had been waiting for permission. It's like my instincts recognized something my brain is still refusing to acknowledge.

Me: It was fine.

Harper: Liar.

My palms start sweating. If I'm this transparent over text, how the hell am I going to face Nathan again?

Me: I don't have time for this kind of thing. It could mess everything up.

Harper: Or it could make it all better.

Me: I'll see you when I get back.

Avery: We love you, our little bolter.

Bolter. I hated the nickname, but I can't say I haven't earned it. Not just with relationships, but with anything that has created a complication in my life. A college course that conflicted with soccer? Dropped. A friend who didn't understand why I'd miss their get together for soccer practice? Friendship ended. Anyone who tried to connect over losing a parent? Hell no.

If it might distract or complicate my life, then it was gone. And yet, I'm the one who came up with this whole fake-dating charade. I'm the one who kissed him back and harder last night. I told him about the scholarship scare when not even my closest friends knew some of those details. I'm the one complicating things.

I turn my phone on airplane mode, shoving it into my pocket as the plane races down the runway and lifts into the air. The truth is, what scares me most is not the kiss itself. It's how easily it slid under my skin. Meanwhile, Nathan went back to normal, chatting with friends. It's obvious that he hadn't felt it the way I had.

The rest of the flight is spent oscillating between staring out the window and the back of my eyelids. Every time my mind tries to drift into forbidden territory, I yank it somewhere else.

Bills. Schedules. Training plans.

By the time we land, my jaw aches from clenching it.

My dad is waiting at baggage claim with his hands shoved into the pockets of his jacket. His posture is stiff in a way that has nothing to do with the cold. His arthritis has been bad lately. It's obvious in the careful way he shifts his weight and how he favors one knee without realizing it.

"Hey, kiddo," he says, smiling when he spots me.

I wrap him in a hug, mindful of his joints. He smells like coffee and the aftershave he's worn my entire life.

"Happy early Thanksgiving," I say.

"It's the best kind," he replies. "The kind where you surprise me."

My little sister, Emma, barrels into me from the side a second later, nearly knocking my bag from my shoulder.

"You said you weren't coming home." She squeezes me tightly, eyes bright with excitement. "I raced home just for this."

"I'm honored." I wrap my arms around her, laughing despite myself. "It must be such a sacrifice."

She rolls her eyes, and I keep my arm around her as we start to head for the car. We're seven years apart in age. She's eighteen in her freshman year of college, but I still feel protective of her anyway.

It's like no matter how much time goes by, she is still the seven-year-old who didn't understand when the police showed up at midnight to tell us that our mother had been killed in a hit and run. I was fourteen. I'd held Emma for hours, unable to explain what had happened and unable to offer consolation I didn't have myself. I'd wondered in private what my lack of tears said about me. I still do.

The funeral had been a blur of red-rimmed, tear-filled eyes. My mascara stayed perfect, as if appearances could hold everything together. After, Dad buried himself in work, always providing through the chaos. But it fell to me to fill the gaps. I still do.

They need me, and I refuse to let them down. Coming home is the reminder I need to remember why I stay focused.

The house is smaller than I remember it, or maybe I'm numb to moving through spaces that don't belong to me. It's been a while since I've come home. It hurts to be here. I've tried to talk them into moving to Boston, but until recently, my dad's work has kept him here.

The couch still sags in the middle. The kitchen light still flickers if you don't jiggle the switch just right. There's a stack of unopened mail on the counter. It's all silent reminders of things I need to fix and responsibilities one kiss cannot make me forget.

For dinner, we have pasta with sauce from a jar and garlic bread that's slightly overdone. It's our version of home cooking. Emma tells us about her classes, roommate drama, and a professor who has it out for her. Dad listens, nodding along, asking questions when he can. I do too, though it feels like I'm looking through a window instead of sitting at the table with them.

I watch Dad's hands as he eats. He pauses between bites, fingers curling stiffly around his fork. Whatever the doctors are doing is not enough to stop the pain he's in. Not for the first time, I wish I could do something other than help financially.

After dinner, he gathers the mail.

"We can look at this later," he says, shoving it out of the way.

"We can look at it now." I pull it back in front of me.

He hesitates, then nods.

The bills are worse than I expected. Specialist visits. Imaging. Physical therapy that insurance barely touches. A tuition bill is folded twice and shoved into an envelope as if hiding it in there will make it go away.

I do the math in my head automatically.

"Another one from the hospital," Dad mutters, rubbing at his knuckles. He tries to flex them, but they crack painfully. "They keep sending statements. I can't keep up."

My chest tightens, guilt twisting in a knot. "Dad, it's okay. I'll handle it. I have plenty for this and can get them all paid this weekend."

It's true. I do have enough for this, but it's the future I'm worried about. If these bills are any indication, it could be just the start.

He gives me a small, tired smile, but I know he feels like a failure. I've seen it in his eyes every time a new bill arrives or a doctor shakes his head. My dad's worked hard his whole life, and now, when he needs stability the most, his body is betraying him. After a lifetime of physical jobs, he can't do them anymore. That's why they had to let him go.

I lean my head on his shoulder, like I have since I was a kid.

"You've always been so reliable for us, Wesley." He wraps his arm around me, kissing my forehead.

It's meant as a compliment, but the words fall like lead inside me. He's right, I've been reliable. I need to be reliable, despite the parts of me that might want to throw caution to the wind.

I organize the envelopes into two piles: bills that accept online payment and those that require a phone call. It's after seven, so I can tackle the online payments tonight. I go through, checking them off one by one. My debit card is getting a hell of a workout, but by the end, there are only a few bills that have to wait until business hours on Monday.

"Is everything okay?" Emma asks, breezing into the room.

"Totally fine," I lie, plastering a smile on my face. Maybe I do deserve an Oscar.

Dad stands a little taller. "I'm looking into contract work. Consulting. It'd be easier on my body."

"You can't," Emma argues. "You need to rest."

"I need to contribute."

"You already did," I say, softer. "You raised us alone."

The room goes quiet.

We don't talk about Mom. We don't ever talk about the hole she left behind when she died. Instead, we let her ghost hover over all of us like a shadow we can't shake.

It's just another reason why coming home is suffocating.

I love my dad and my sister, but I hate it here.

Being in this house is horrible, but avoiding it just makes me feel worse. It's a vicious cycle that I've concluded can only be broken by getting them out of this house.

My dad won't consider it, though. At least, not yet.

Later, in my childhood bedroom, I lie on my back staring at the ceiling, the glow-in-the-dark stars Emma stuck up there when she was twelve are still faintly visible.

It's past midnight, and I should be asleep, but I haven't been able to get my mind to slow down.

My phone sits on the nightstand, screen dark.

I almost pick it up to message him. For what? I don't know. Comfort. Explanation. I manage to resist the urge.

Days pass, and I force all my focus into the house. I stock up on groceries, refilling the pantry to an indulgent standard. An electrician is scheduled to fix the light switch on Wednesday. The rest of the bills have been taken care of over the phone. Doctor appointments are scheduled. Virtual meetings with Coach Bennett to discuss next season take place in my childhood bedroom. It's been busy to say the least.

It all should take up the full capacity of my mind. Somehow, though, when Tuesday rolls around, my mind makes space to remember what I should be doing: training with Nathan.

I wake up early out of habit, body already anticipating a workout it's not going to get. My muscles feel restless, like they're waiting for direction. My brain follows, reaching automatically for the familiar. We've only been working out together for two weeks, and it feels like a staple in my routine.

The absence is uncomfortable.

I make coffee, pacing the kitchen while Dad reads the paper and Emma sleeps in.

My eyes focus on my phone for a full thirty seconds before I pick it up.

Me: Hey.

He responds immediately, and my body warms. He never hesitates to get back to me, as if the thought of playing it cool doesn't even occur to him. I secretly love knowing he drops whatever he's doing to text me back.

Nathan: Morning.

Me: You're up early.

It's 6:30am here, which means 8:30 am in Boston. To me, it's not early at all, but he hates mornings. It's partially why I pushed for them.

Nathan: I figure I should get used to the mornings for when you come back and run me into the ground.

I smile, taking a sip from my mug. He doesn't shy away from my athleticism like other men have. It doesn't intimidate him in the slightest. In fact, he seems to actually like it.

Me: Smart man.

Nathan: When will that be?

No pressure. No accusation.
I swallow.

Me: I head back tonight.

I contemplate pushing our next session to next week, but a deal is a deal. I need to hold up my end.

Me: We can pick back up tomorrow since Thursday is Thanksgiving.

There is a pause this time. It's long enough for me to imagine him reading it. My foot starts tapping faster against the floor.

Nathan: Yeah, sure. Might be extra tired though.

Me: Why?

Before I can wonder, a photo appears on my screen.

It's him at my stadium.

The field is empty behind him with lights turned half on. The turf's gleaming with frost. He's in workout gear, his hair damp with sweat, wearing a focused, slightly sheepish expression.

Nathan: The groundskeeper let me inside in exchange for tickets to a game.

Nathan: I wanted to keep the routine.

My heart gives a strange tug.

He went to the field and worked out anyway. If I hadn't texted him, I wouldn't have even known. He did it because it matters to him, not for show or for me. The media has this man all wrong, and so did I.

He is focused. He puts in the effort. The man getting up early on his own with no witnesses, just to sneak in an extra workout, is not the man I thought he'd be.

My throat tightens, and I set the phone down, pressing my hands flat against the counter like that will ground me.

This is what I'm afraid of.

Me: That's proof you don't even need me.

Nathan: Wrong. I'm not nearly as tired as I am when we do it together. Besides, I like you yelling at me.

I snort into my coffee, but quickly recover when my dad turns to me over the newspaper.

Me: I do like being in charge on the field.

Nathan: Where else do you like being in charge?

And there he is. Overly confident, flirty Nathan is back. Good. I can deal with the teasing and being hit on. I cannot deal with the rest of it.

Me: Wouldn't you like to know...

Nathan: Yes, actually. I really fucking would.

Me: Not a chance, Wilder.

There is another pause, and I can picture him contemplating whether he wants to push my boundaries further. My stomach sinks just a little when he doesn't.

Nathan: See you tomorrow at seven.

Me: I'll be there.

I had come home to clear my head, but it's more jumbled than ever. I can't hide here forever, though. Besides, we have another friendly match coming up, and I need to be there for my team.

Who cares if staying professional with Nathan is harder than expected? Difficulty has never stopped me before, and it won't now.

I make it through the rest of the day without thinking about him. Sure, it's only because I decided to kill myself, scrubbing the house from top to bottom. The floorboards won't clean themselves.

By the time Emma drives me to the airport, I'm exhausted. My joints ache from being hunched over and scrubbing so badly that I decide to count it as my workout for the day.

It's only once I get on my flight home that I let myself think about him. Thirty seconds to let my reckless thoughts run wild before I pack them up for good.

My mind flashes to the way he had looked at me across the bar like he was seeing something he didn't want to look away from. His kiss had felt like an answer to a question I've avoided asking.

Thirty more seconds, I promise myself. Thirty seconds to get it together. Thirty seconds to remember who I am and what's important.

But those thirty seconds end, and I can't shut it down the way I usually do.

16

Nathan

I've counted the days. Five. Five days since the bar and the night that was supposed to be 'fake', but somehow wasn't. Five days since I kissed her, her lips pressing into mine, making my brain go entirely offline. And five days since she retreated into the kind of silence that makes me wonder if she's going to call it all off.

Her trip home seemed conveniently scheduled, but maybe that's my high hopes talking. She's good at boundaries and compartmentalizing, so it's probably a coincidence. There's no way she's affected the way I am.

It shouldn't have affected me at all. I've been kissed plenty. Yet, here I am, pacing in front of the stadium before seven in the morning, the frost biting at my nose and my heart lodged somewhere in my throat.

I hadn't planned to come here yesterday by myself, but when I woke up before my alarm, staying away seemed useless. Our workouts over the past couple of weeks are some of the only times my mind quiets. And so, without Wesley, I ran through the drills she's had me practicing.

It wasn't the same, and I didn't enjoy it nearly enough, but it was better than nothing. Plus, it distracted me from the endless calls from my parents.

I'm avoiding them, especially considering they're only reaching out because they think I have a girlfriend. It grates on my nerves that they have the audacity to call me nonstop about this, when they haven't reached out once since the season started. They live twenty minutes away and haven't once come to a game. So yeah, explaining my nonrelationship with Wesley to them isn't going to happen. Ever.

If they aren't willing to hear about hockey, then they don't need to hear about anything else as far as I'm concerned.

Unfortunately for them, I kicked ass on Monday night. It was like I was my old self on the ice, making all the right moves at exactly the right times.

Actually, I've played well in all my recent games. They'd been fun. I wasn't feeling the pressure or the same going-through-the-motion pangs I'd been battling for a while. Instead, I was feeling alive, like every push of my blades was new and exciting.

The same way I feel here with her.

My feet create an obvious path in the wet turf as I start getting anxious for her to show up. Every part of my body screams that I'm in too deep. When she finally appears, moving through the gate with slow, measured steps, I know that it's not just my body that's in too deep.

Still, I can't help noticing every detail. The braided ponytail that swings with each step, the tightness of her sweatshirt clinging to her shape, and her eyes flicking to me while pretending to scan the field.

I take a couple of steps in her direction before forcing my feet to stop. What the hell am I doing? Five days of absence, and I'm unraveling as if I can't function without seeing her. I am Nathan Wilder. I am not desperate. Especially not after a single kiss.

A fake kiss. It was fake.

"Morning," I say, leaning against the bench.

She nods quickly, glancing past me. Her posture is rigid, shoulders slightly raised, and I can tell that today is all business. That's fine, maybe even for the best.

We start with stretches. I try to keep my distance, but it only lasts a minute before my mind drifts into dangerous territory. It's impossible for it not to when she's moving so gracefully through our warm-up.

And that night… God, that night.

Seeing her like that and seeing her like this is confusing. The Wesley who let me hold her on the dance floor and the Wesley who won't quite meet my eyes during this workout are polar opposites. My mind doesn't know how to process that she's the same person. Even still, I haven't seen a version of her that I don't like.

I know she's cautious for a reason. She's never laid it all out, but there's an obvious pressure to be perfect for her family. Considering she just spent multiple days with them, it shouldn't surprise me that she's trying to keep it strictly professional today.

It's her way of resetting the boundaries.

I decide to make it my mission not to let her.

"Careful," I say finally, sick of the silence between us. "You've taken some days off. You might actually break a sweat before I do."

She snorts, a sound I've missed more than I realized. "Doubtful. You hockey boys don't stand a chance against my cardio. You'll be panting before me."

The corner of my mouth lifts because she doesn't realize I already am. "We'll see about that."

We move to sprints after the warm-ups. I stay a stride behind her, letting her set the pace. She runs like she's wary of falling too far into my rhythm or letting me get too close. I mirror her, nudging her subtly when our paths cross on the track, letting my hands brush hers 'accidentally'. The touch is electric. She shivers. I can feel it.

"Trying to get me to trip?" She asks lightly, glancing back.

"Maybe," I say with mock innocence. "But I'd catch you before you fell."

She laughs, and it's real this time, the tension in her shoulders releasing until it's all but gone.

After the sprints, I suggest a long run into the woods behind the stadium. She hesitates for a heartbeat before giving a small, reluctant nod and falling in step beside me.

The crunch of pebbles beneath our sneakers is the only sound at first. She keeps her pace slightly behind me, letting me lead. My peripheral vision is full of her, every curve of her shoulders and swish of her braid. I fight the urge to close the distance and pull her closer. I'd do anything to remind her how much I want her. She has to know by now, though.

"You're awfully quiet," I say finally.

"I'm pacing myself," she replies between careful breaths.

"Or avoiding talking to me." My tone is light, but she doesn't shoot back with a witty remark, so I know I'm close to the truth.

Eventually, she admits, "Maybe a little of both."

That's all I need. That's all the invitation I need to push a little further.

"Why?" I pick up the pace slightly as we round a turn. "Because I'm full of questions. Starting with, how do you always make running in the freezing cold look like a stroll in the park?"

She swats my shoulder, but there is a twitch of a smile tugging at the corner of her mouth. "Practice." She ups the pace further.

"You know where you don't need practice?" I arch an eyebrow, glancing back at her. "Kissing."

Her stride falters for a fraction of a second. Her face warms, and I know exactly what I've done. I'm not ready to back off yet.

"I mean, seriously, who knew that the ice queen herself could melt an entire bar with her fake kissing abilities. It's impressive, really."

"You're impossible," she mutters, half annoyed and half amused.

"I prefer insufferable."

The woods open up to a larger path, the stadium coming back into view.

She moves up next to me, the silence between us brimming with tension. I notice the subtle things: the way her fingers flex with each stride, the quick inhale when I adjust my pace beside hers, and the almost imperceptible glances she casts in my direction when she thinks I'm not watching.

Once we're back at the field, we run through some agility drills that she seems comfortable with. I trip up on them more than I'd like. It's further evidence that even as a professional athlete, with ten years of experience and championships under my belt, there's still room for improvement. Wesley's constant pursuit of perfection brings out the drive in me, too.

Eventually, we cool down, walking laps around the field, stretching as we go. After a mostly quiet workout, I'm damn near desperate to get her to open up to me about anything.

"How was your family?" I ask gently, curiosity creeping into my voice.

She hesitates, tucking a loose strand of hair behind her ear. "It's hard, being back there. Comforting in some ways, but it reminds me how much everyone counts on me. Sometimes I just want to escape it all, you know? I wish I could completely ignore the responsibility on my shoulders."

I nod, understanding more than I should. "Yeah," I say quietly. "I get that. My agent, my coach, hell, the whole city has pretty high expectations for me, and I've failed at meeting them for a while. I know it's different, but…" I trail off.

"Yeah, it's different, but pressure is pressure." She looks at me then, a small spark of connection lighting her eyes. "You know, I've always been jealous of you. Well, not you, but like the Blades in general. We put in a lot of the same effort, and you all seem to reap a lot more of the benefits."

"'The path we take to play the sport we love does not come easily.' You were right, it's about time women athletes get more recognition."

I smile, remembering how impactful I thought her speech was. Bidding on her training day hadn't crossed my mind until she'd given her speech. Her looks may have been why I'd flirted, but it was her words that made me want more time with her.

She scrunches her eyebrows. "You remember my speech." We're both silent for a second. "I still mean most of it, but I'm starting to learn that just because there's money and notoriety, it doesn't mean it comes easily for you either. Sometimes it might make it harder."

I plop into the grass, moving into stationary stretches. "The media can be a real bitch."

"I've figured that out." She slides down next to me, not bothering to create as much distance. "I had to shut down my messages because girls started attacking me for taking you off the market."

"Oh damn," I say, laughing only when I realize she is too. "I'm sorry about that."

I mean it. She may have gotten us into this mess originally, but I poured gasoline on the fire. Though I'd be lying if I said I minded. It's nice having a little more peace and a little less of the eligible bachelor narrative following me around.

"It's not your fault." She unlaces her cleats and slides back into her tennis shoes. "Besides, I get it. You are one hell of a fake kisser."

My pulse skips, her words catching me completely off guard in the best way imaginable. "We make quite the pair."

"For two people who are living out their dreams, we complain too much." Wesley hops up, tossing her bag onto her shoulder.

I consider it for a second. It's the dream, but the sacrifices and the pressure sucks. I know I wouldn't give it up for a second, though. When my blades hit the ice, everything makes sense. It's all worth it.

"Even living the dream comes with its downsides."

"Yeah, it does." Her voice is quiet.

I watch something like sadness cloud Wesley's eyes before she chases it away.

I hate her tone. I hate that she won't let me all the way in.

"Are you busy right now?" The words slip out.

Her eyes flick to mine, and she chews on her bottom lip. "It depends."

I'll take it.

"C'mon, you've kicked my ass enough for today." I scoop up my bag and grab her hand, pulling her behind me as we head to the tunnel. "Let me show you what you're helping me save."

17

Wesley

The arena is dark when we walk in. The quiet doesn't feel eerie, but I move with caution. I don't belong here.

The overhead lights flick on as Nathan leads me through the tunnel, the hum of electricity echoing up into the rafters. The sound travels through the empty space, bouncing off thousands of empty seats that would normally be filled with screaming fans.

The Revere Center is bigger than I thought. Having only seen it on TV or from the street, I wasn't expecting to feel so small walking through it completely empty. It's like I've stepped into something not meant for outsiders.

"This is insane," I whisper.

Nathan grins over his shoulder like he's been waiting for that reaction. "Wait until you see it with the ice lit."

After spending time at home, I had planned to keep our workout today strictly professional. Keeping my distance from him was the only choice. The kiss had played on repeat far too often for me to let it happen again.

We were going to work out, make small talk, and then go our separate ways. Instead, I found myself wanting to open up to him about my family and drag the workout on longer. It's stupid.

And because I'm stupid, now I'm here. Spending time with Nathan outside of the arrangement. This isn't training, and it's not fake dating. So, what the hell is it?

A man pushing a wide mop bucket looks up as we pass.

"Morning, Nate."

"Morning, Cal," Nathan says easily. "How's your knee?"

Cal snorts. "Still attached."

Nathan laughs, claps him on the shoulder like they've known each other forever, and keeps walking.

I glance back. "You know his name."

"He's been here longer than I have."

That's not the Nathan most people see. The one who knows the custodial staff well enough to ask about their knee. No, that Nathan is reserved only for the people who really know him. Warmth spreads through me as I realize I'm becoming one of them.

He moves through this place as if it belongs to him, not in an entitled way, but in a familiar way. It makes sense that he'd know this arena like the back of his hand, but it's also kind of endearing.

A heavy door swings open, and he gestures for me to go inside. The rink opens up in front of us, smooth and untouched, the surface glowing faintly under the lights. There is no music or fans, just the faint hum of the refrigeration system beneath the ice.

It's beautiful.

Nathan studies my face instead of the rink. "Told you."

Before I can say anything else, he disappears down the hallway toward the locker rooms. I fold my arms and try not to look like I'm trespassing. Without Nathan by my side, I'm even more convinced I shouldn't be here.

This place must sound crazy when it's packed with fans. Every sound echoes, and there's nowhere for it to escape. I spin in a circle, taking it all in until a noise in the corner makes me jump. Nathan reappears with two pairs of skates slung over his shoulder.

I blink. My gaze flicks from his shy smile to the extra pair of skates in his hand.

He tosses them gently toward me. "They should fit."

I stare down at them. They're clean, maybe even brand new.

Suspicion creeps in. "When did you get these?"

He drops onto the bench, already unlacing his shoes. "After our lunch date."

"You're kidding."

He shakes his head, focused on threading the laces through his fingers. "Figured if I asked enough times, you might eventually say yes."

I like the idea of that far too much.

"You bought me skates," I say, sitting down across from him.

"I bought a size that might fit you," he corrects. "Very different."

"We'd only just agreed to do this."

He glances up at me. "Yeah. I thought ice skating would be a good fake date sometime, given what I do."

"There's no one here." I gesture vaguely to the empty arena around us. "It doesn't count as a fake date."

"Caught red-handed." He shrugs.

I narrow my eyes.

His smile is unbothered. "We're just friends. Friends can skate."

"I'm not going out there." I point to the ice as if it's insulted me.

"Oh, come on, Miller. You run circles around me regularly. It's my turn."

"You asked me to train with you. It's not my fault you're slow." I unlace my shoes, realizing that I've started a competition I won't back down from.

He scoffs. "You think I'm slow?"

"On your feet?" I glance up, sliding the skates onto my feet. "You're the one who said I run circles around you, not me."

The skates fit. Of course they do. Nathan pays attention more than anyone gives him credit for.

He stands up, now multiple inches taller than normal with his skates on, towering over me.

"Out there, I'm the fastest there is." He points to the rink, flashing a cocky smile and determined eyes. That look, the one that says he's the best and knows it. That's the Nathan that Boston sees. The one who might only actually feel that way on the ice. The one who doesn't seem to truly feel that confident at all anymore.

Something about his competitiveness has me spurring him on. "That's only because I haven't had a chance to kick your ass out there yet, too."

I pull the laces tight and stand up. Even standing, I'm forced to look up to him.

Before stepping toward the ice, I test my balance on the rubber mat. Nathan is completely at ease, like the blades are extensions of his body. Leaning forward, I reach out as if I might grab his hand, but instead, I push open the door and skate past him onto the ice.

Only once I reach the middle do I turn back to face him. He hasn't moved, still standing at the bench, but his arrogant grin is replaced with something far more dangerous. It's the same look he had after we kissed. The look that's been circling my mind for days. Warmth spreads low in my stomach as his eyes trail me.

I shouldn't be here.

"What, Wilder? Afraid that you can't keep up?" My voice echoes against the boards, spurring him into action as he steps onto the ice with a gracefulness I hadn't expected.

I'm utterly unprepared for the image of Nathan Wilder gliding toward me as if skating were as easy as walking.

"You can skate." His voice is low as he reaches me in the middle.

"You don't grow up in Colorado and not know how to skate." I glide backwards to create space.

The action breaks the tension that's been building between us. Nathan's easy smile returns as if it never left. I should feel relieved.

He pulls back, skating a slow circle around the ice, letting his hands hang loose at his sides.

I might know how to skate, but Nathan is another story. I can easily see why he'd fight to keep this. It's a part of him.

"You move like the ice is your home."

Nathan circles back toward me, skating backward like it's the most natural thing in the world. "It's more of a home than anything else I have."

"What about your actual home?"

"My apartment is just a place to sleep." He pauses as if he might stop there, but then continues, "I don't go home to my parents' house very often. We don't really get along."

I let it drop, sensing that he doesn't want to say more. My feet follow the path that his blades have left behind, and he slows to match my pace.

The arena feels impossibly big and impossibly small at the same time with him standing right next to me.

"Okay, let's see how fast you really are." I stop at the end of the ice, nodding toward the length of the arena.

"You want to race?" He lifts a brow.

"Yeah, I want to fucking race." I nod enthusiastically.

This is where I thrive. Competition.

"I don't know." He rubs the back of his neck, clearly worried about blowing me out of the water.

He will. I know he will, but also one day, when this is all over, I want to be able to say I raced one of the best hockey players of all time, and he barely beat me. That's my goal. Barely lose.

"It's a win-win for me," I tease. "Either I win, and I get to say I beat an NHL player in a race. Or I lose, which is what's expected anyway."

He laughs, tossing his head back. The way it echoes around me scratches a part of my brain that I hadn't realized needed it.

"You really want to race me?" He skates back against the wall, crossing his arms.

"Unless you're scared."

"God, that smart mouth of yours." His eyes darken, focusing on my mouth.

My heart skips involuntarily. I can't seem to keep my senses around him, so I settle for turning away and getting into position.

"What'll it be, Wilder?"

"If I win, you have to admit that this was a good idea."

"What do I get if I win?" I raise my eyebrows.

He meets my eyes and holds them. "Anything you want."

18

Nathan

My lungs burn.

I glide in a slow arc, hands over my head, chest heaving. The scrape of my blades echoes in the empty rink. Sweat is trickling down my spine under my sweatshirt.

Across the ice, Wesley bends at the waist, palms braced on her knees. Her ponytail has half-fallen out, strands plastered to her cheek. She's breathing as hard as I am.

For a second, neither of us says anything.

Then she straightens and calls across the ice. "Alright. I'll admit it. This was a good idea!"

My hands drop to my hips as I huff out a laugh.

Before turning toward her, I coast backward for a few strides. I didn't realize how hard I'd pushed until now.

She wasn't supposed to be that close.

Halfway down the rink, I'd expected space. I wasn't going full out, figuring that she'd be so far behind I could take it easy. Instead, I felt her there, close enough that I could hear her edges dig in when she took the corner too tight.

I underestimated her.

Again.

I slow as I reach center ice, studying her while she skates toward me. She's flushed, eyes bright, with her competitive spark still flickering even in defeat.

God, she's good at everything.

For a split second during the backstretch, I thought about letting her win. Not because I wanted to go easy on her, but because I wanted to see what she'd ask for.

I meant it when I said anything. There is nothing she could dream up that I wouldn't try to make happen. The thought surprises me, but I chalk it up to being friends. I'd do almost anything for most of my close friends. It doesn't have to mean anything more.

Instead, I picked up my pace, creating a gap, so that I could slide through the finish with my pride intact. If I had let her win, she would've known.

Wesley misses nothing. Whether it was in my stride or the way I coasted a turn, she would've seen it. Then, she would've razzed me about it for the rest of my life.

She stops a few feet away from me now, hands on her hips, still catching her breath.

"You were sandbagging," she accuses between inhales.

I grin. "You wish."

She narrows her eyes, studying me like she's trying to solve something. There's color high on her cheeks. A strand of hair sticks to her lip, and without thinking, I reach out and brush it away.

My fingers graze her skin.

She goes still.

So do I.

Up close, I can see the way her pulse jumps at her throat. Mine's not exactly calm either.

"You almost had me," I say, because it feels safer than whatever else I could say.

Her brow lifts as she pulls out her hair tie, just to gather her hair and pull it up again. "Almost?"

I shrug. "Corner three. You cut it tight. I thought you were going to try to pass on the inside."

"I was."

"Yeah. I know."

A smile curves her mouth, slow and satisfied. "Were you worried?"

"Not even a little."

She just looks at me.

I shake my head. "Although you were faster than I expected. You might be in the wrong sport."

"Small confession," she says, rolling her lips together, "I may have played hockey until high school. Then I had to commit to one sport. Soccer was the only choice."

A grin tugs at the corner of my lips. Of course she did. It makes me even happier that I brought her here. Every time she opens up, telling me something personal about herself, it's like getting a new piece to my favorite puzzle.

I haven't had fun like this in a while. Even with my friends, there's always looming pressure. This kind of fun adrenaline, without cameras or stress, is addictive.

She steps closer, the toe of her skate nudging mine. The contact is small, but deliberate.

"You don't let people win, do you?" she asks.

"No."

"Not even me?"

I glance down at our skates touching, then back up at her. "Especially not you."

Her exhale is shaky this time, and not from the race.

"You're competitive," I add, softer. "You'd rather lose for real than win because I feel bad."

At that, her chin tips up. "I don't need you to take it easy on me."

"I know."

That's the thing. She doesn't need anything, and for some reason, that makes me want to give her everything.

"Do you do this often?" She slides back from me.

"Sometimes." I let her glide away. It's safer with the space between us. "When I was eight, my dad snagged tickets to this open skate event that was hosted here."

Memories flash back to that day and the way my hands shook as we arrived. She watches me carefully, letting the silence spur me along.

"I'd been playing hockey for years at that point, but to come here? It was a dream. I wore my Boston Blades jersey, which was way too big."

She laughs. We both start skating slowly, side by side.

"I was the first kid on the ice, and I remember thinking this was it. This ice. This arena. That day, it all became my dream. I like coming out here by myself."

"I'm sure eight-year-old Nathan would be proud of where you are." She spins a quick circle, motioning throughout the arena.

"With all of the shit going on with my contract and how I'm playing, he'd probably be disappointed."

The words are honest, but saying them out loud cuts deep. It's a confession that I've never let myself voice. I've gotten used to disappointing everyone around me, but it's disappointing myself that I'm not sure how to live with.

"Bullshit." She shoves my shoulder. "You just said it. This ice was your dream. You did that. You've done it for ten years. Whatever happens next with your contract, you have to know that eight-year-old Nathan would do it all again if he knew it would get him to where you are right now."

I swallow hard. She makes it sound so simple. So obvious. Something inside me aches a little less. She watches me while I try to regain my composure.

We take the turn slowly, but with her eyes trained on me, her skate bumps into mine. She wobbles, instinctively grabbing my arm. The sudden movement catches me off guard, and we go tumbling down. I'm careful to catch her so that she doesn't hit the ice.

Instead, she lands half in my lap, our faces only inches apart. We're both silent for a second, my hands lingering on her waist. Then, we break out into a fit of laughter.

She bites the inside of her lip as she shifts, an unconscious motion. A nervous tic. I've noticed it before. I notice everything about her.

The laughter dies in my throat as my gaze drifts to her mouth and lingers there.

My brain betrays me immediately, replaying our kiss in full color. Her hands in my hair. The way she'd surged forward, not hesitant in the slightest.

Last time we were this close, we were surrounded by a crowd. An entire bar full of people considered us a couple. It was the reason and the excuse. Now, there's no one here but us. The space between us is charged.

She's close enough that I can feel the heat from her body pressing against me, close enough that if I leaned in a little…

My entire body comes alive at the thought.

It's not until she clears her throat sharply and springs to her feet that I realize my mistake. I hadn't just been thinking of leaning in, but actually doing it.

"Oh," she says, gliding toward the bench, looking anywhere but at me. The wall between us slams back into place so fast it almost makes my head spin.

Fuck.

I straighten, silently cursing myself. There's no way to play that off. No way to pretend I wasn't about to kiss her. I catch the flicker of questions in her eyes.

We unlace our skates in near silence.

She slings her bag over her shoulder and starts toward the tunnel without looking back. The distance she creates feels deliberate, as if putting us back where we belong.

I let her take three steps.

Then, "Hey," I say.

She stops, turning halfway toward me.

"We should probably figure out when we need to be seen together again." I try to meet her eyes, but she won't let me. "You know, another public date."

She hesitates. "Not this week."

The answer shouldn't sting, but it does.

"Okay," I say, even though every part of me wants to argue. It hasn't even been a week since our last one, but it already feels like too long. "That works."

Fake dating is her domain. I'm only there to help her sell it when she needs to.

She nods, relief flashing across her face. "I know you have leave for an away trip Saturday, and since tomorrow's Thanksgiving, we can plan to meet when you get back?"

"When we get back," I confirm.

She gives me a small smile, then turns and walks away.

I watch her go, shoving my hands into my pockets. My head is spinning with everything I didn't say and almost did.

But standing there alone, I know the truth. She's said it from the beginning.

She might find me attractive, and there might be tension, but she doesn't want me the way I'm starting to want her. I have to figure out how to stop wanting her anyway.

19

Wesley

You're late," Avery says, though the accusation lacks any real frustration.

She's already claimed her seat when Harper and I arrive. Her leather jacket is draped over the back of the booth, and a half-empty basket of chips sits between two sweating margarita glasses. It's clear evidence that she did not wait patiently.

"You said seven-ish." I shrug out of my jacket. "This is still ish."

Girls' night is always a reminder of who I am when no one is watching my performance metrics or dissecting my choices, when the only expectations for me are the ones I place on myself. Tonight, tucked into a corner booth at a loud Mexican restaurant with chipped tile floors and walls painted in sun-faded reds and yellows, it feels especially necessary.

Harper laughs as she settles beside me. "Must be serious if you're anxious, Ave."

Avery wipes her hands on a napkin. "I have things to discuss."

"That feels ominous." I reach for a chip.

Avery takes another sip of her drink, sliding the second margarita to Harper. "Did you see the article about the friendly match in Lisbon?"

Harper groans.

I have seen it. The headline alone was enough to make my knee hurt. As soon as I saw the title, I closed the app and shoved my phone face down onto the counter, as if avoiding the details would protect me from the harsh reality that comes with being a professional athlete.

"It was her third ACL," Avery continues, her voice lowering as if volume alone might soften the blow. "Same knee. Non-contact injury."

The table goes quiet in that way only athletes can really understand. It's the collective pause that comes when you realize how quickly the sport we love can be taken away.

I swallow, suddenly hyper-aware of my legs stretching beneath the table. The strength in my quads. The stability in my knees. Things I never think about unless something goes wrong.

"I couldn't bring myself to watch the clip," I admit, my gaze drifting to the condensation sliding down my water glass.

"She's done," Harper says, adding more salt to her chips. "There is no way she comes back from that again. Not at that level."

Retirement. The word hovers unspoken but heavy, a looming specter that follows every professional athlete whether we acknowledge it or not. Careers don't always end when we're ready in sports. Sometimes, they end when our bodies decide they're finished cooperating.

"I can't imagine," I murmur. "Training your whole life just to have it taken away because something snaps at the wrong moment."

Harper lifts her glass, swirling the lime wedge thoughtfully. "Soccer isn't everything."

Avery glances up sharply. "It was for you."

Just like that, we've stepped into our unspeakable territory. We may never fully understand Harper's choice, but she's made it clear we don't need to. Avery tends to forget how to tread lightly.

Harper smiles, but it's a little distant. "It was. And now it isn't."

I watch her for a second longer than necessary, thinking of the move she made for James, and the opportunity she walked away from. Regret is complicated. It doesn't always mean you made the wrong choice. Sometimes, it means the cost was higher than you expected.

The server appears, mercifully, and we order drinks and enough food to feed a small army. As the conversation shifts to tactics and formations, I relax.

This is familiar ground. Safe ground.

We fill Harper in on the new athletic trainer interning with the team, and she fills us in on her school's latest teacher drama.

"So, the new history teacher is hooking up with the science teacher who's married?" I ask, trying to keep up with what feels like a soap opera.

Avery snorts into her drink.

"Yup," Harper says, popping the 'p' and nodding vigorously like she can't believe it herself.

"There is nothing wrong with a workplace romance. Everything is wrong with an affair." Avery shakes her head. "That, my friends, is why I don't believe in love."

We laugh, but I can't help pushing her.

"You used to."

"I used to be blinded by lust. Now, I can separate the two." She cuts into her burrito as it's set down in front of her.

And then, as if reading my mind, Avery's eyes flick to my phone.

"So," she says. "How's Boston's King of the Ice?"

I roll my eyes. "Dinner was going so well."

Harper leans forward, interest piqued. "Oh no. You do not get to dodge that."

"I am dodging it." I take a bite of my chicken taco. "Successfully."

Avery snorts. "You almost kissed him."

I nearly choke. In a moment of weakness, I told Avery what happened with Nathan. I blame the extended period of stim treatment we were both doing post-lift this morning.

"That is not what happened."

Harper's eyebrows shoot up. "Almost kissed him?"

I fire daggers in Avery's direction. "You promised not to say anything."

"We both know that doesn't apply to Harper."

She's right. I sigh, sinking back into the booth. "He almost kissed me."

"Wait," Harper says. "Who almost kissed who? I need details."

"There are no details," I insist. "We were ice-skating."

"Why were you ice-skating?" Harper's confusion laces her tone.

"Because I am stupid." I squint my eyes at her as if it's obvious. "Anyway, he leaned in. I left."

Avery stares at me as if I've admitted to a felony. "You didn't tell me you left."

"Well, I did."

"You panicked."

"Yes."

Harper crosses her arms. "Why? You kissed at the bar."

Avery mumbles under her breath, "Yeah, and then she fled the state."

There's a bang, and Avery flinches. Harper must've kicked her. Good.

"Wes," Harper tries again. "Please tell me you didn't literally run away."

"Not exactly." I think back to being with him, how I let my guard down and flirted, how cute he looked when I called him a good kisser. How attractive it was when he kicked my ass in the race instead of letting me win. "I slowly made for the bench, took off my skates, and then left. We still made plans to train again after their away trip."

They both exhale, like that's better than expected.

If my best friends are this shocked that I didn't physically run away from him, what does that say about me?

"I still want to know why you were ice skating. That is not part of the arrangement." Avery wiggles her brows.

"We're friends. Friends skate." I echo Nathan's words to them, but they sounded infinitely more believable when he'd said them.

"Why did you panic?" Harper asks gently, like I'm a caged bird.

Because it scared me. Because no one was there and it would've been real. Because I'm not sure I'd be able to stop him.

Not sure I'd want to.

I pick at the edge of a napkin. "I can't afford distractions right now."

Avery groans. "You're already distracted."

"That's different."

"No, it isn't," Harper says. "You're already thinking about him. Training with him. Pretending to date him in public. And apparently, hanging out in private. Somehow, you think kissing him is where the line is."

The idea settles uncomfortably in my head, too close to something true.

"It changes things," I say quietly.

"How?" Avery presses.

"It makes it harder to walk away."

There it is. The truth, sitting between us like a fourth person at the table.

Harper softens. "Wes."

"I have worked too hard to get here," I continue. "I finally feel close to achieving everything I've ever wanted. I'm playing the best I have in years. I will not lose sight of that."

Avery reaches across the table, her hand covering mine. "You really think having fun with a guy will change that?"

I trace the rim of my glass, my head throbbing. "At the bar, it was like I forgot soccer altogether."

I seem to forget it every time I'm with him, which further proves it's an awful idea. Soccer needs to be the first thing on my mind right now.

"That isn't necessarily a bad thing." Harper takes a sip of her drink. "You could tear your ACL tomorrow in a friendly match."

I flinch.

"Sorry," she adds quickly. "Bad example, but you get my point. You can't only live for soccer. It's not healthy."

I stare at my phone again. Still face down. Still silent.

"What are you really afraid of?" Avery asks.

I don't answer right away.

"I'm afraid," I say finally, "that if I let myself want him, I won't know how to stop. And this has an expiration date right after the new year. I mean, do we seriously think Nathan Wilder would actually want something serious with anyone, let alone me?"

Harper smiles gently. "If he had half a brain, he would."

The idea shoots straight through my chest, equal parts terror and something dangerously close to excitement.

Avery's lips curl. "You know I hate hockey players, but I say go get him."

I laugh it off. He's already said he doesn't date. Besides, I don't either. I don't have the time to spare, not with the Futures Camp coming up at the end of January. If I want to make the National Team, I still need to fight for an invite to that camp.

"Anyway, how's your thriving dating life?" I shift the topic.

"A disaster."

"Shocking," Harper deadpans.

"I went on a date last week with a guy who spent thirty minutes explaining my own position to me. Incorrectly."

We all giggle, listening to her recount the whole date. For Avery, it makes complete sense. Her taste in men is interesting to say the least.

"Nice try deflecting, but I won't let this go until you text Nathan." Avery pops a chip into her mouth.

"Text him," Harper echoes.

"What would I even say?"

Avery shrugs. "Wanna bang?"

I slap her shoulder.

My phone buzzes suddenly, like it's listening.

I freeze.

Avery squeals. "Is that him?"

"No," I say quickly, flipping the screen over. It's a group chat notification. I relax, then feel foolish for doing so.

"Text him," Harper says again. "You don't have to make a move. Just open the door a little."

I stare at the screen, thinking of the way he looked at me on the ice. His attention had felt hot against my skin.

I type before I can overthink it.

Me: How was Thanksgiving?

Wanting to talk to him doesn't have to mean anything. I text my friends all of the time.

Nathan: Not much of a holiday since we're in season. You?

My heart kicks when he responds right away like he always does. Just friendly excitement.

Me: I celebrated with my family last weekend. Celebrating with the girls tonight.

Nathan: What're you thankful for?

It's a loaded question. I've been teetering on the line between flirty and serious since we met, and it feels like I'm about to fall off one side of it.

Me: Still thinking about it. You?

Nathan: You messaging me. I'm stuck watching game tape, and fuck, it's boring.

I smile despite myself. He wants to talk to me, too. That knowledge makes me feel a bit too giddy.

Me: I love watching film. It helps you get better.

Nathan: Of course you do.

Me: Maybe if you paid attention, you'd fix your backhand.

Nathan: Seriously, you can't talk dirty to me like that.

I roll my eyes. This man can't go five seconds without flirting with me.

Me: That's what you call talking dirty?

Nathan: Not even fucking close, Miller. Why? Thinking about finding out for yourself?

Me: No

Yes.

Nathan: We'll stick with your kind of dirty talk then.

Nathan: You would love watching hockey tape. So. Much. Pausing.

Avery leans over to read. "He's flirting."
"I know," I say.
Harper clicks her tongue.
I hesitate, then type.

Me: Lucky you that I messaged then.

Nathan: Seems that way. I was just hoping for a distraction.

My pulse jumps.
I think of how close he'd been. Our breath had mixed in the chilled air. There had been no crowd or excuse. He'd wanted to kiss me, for real.
The fear is still there, crawling up my spine. But beneath it is something else.

Me: Careful what you wish for.

Three dots appear. Disappear. Appear again. I slide forward in my seat, watching my screen in anticipation.

Nathan: I always am.

The words sit on the screen longer than they should, confident in a way that causes a slow burn to start under my skin. I don't reply.

Instead, I let the noise of the restaurant wash over me, my mind heading in directions that I don't usually allow.

I'm a professional athlete. The captain. The default mother to my sister. The budgeter and bill payer for my father. I'm the person everyone looks to when something needs to be handled, when pressure spikes, and there's no margin for error. I pull off the impossible not because it's easy, but because it's required.

I love soccer. I do. But loving it doesn't erase the weight of it. I play because I need to, because people need me to.

What scares me isn't Nathan. It's wanting something that doesn't serve a purpose beyond me. Letting myself want him doesn't pay the bills or further my career.

But maybe, letting myself have a little fun wouldn't derail everything I've worked for.

It's not like it would be serious. Nathan Wilder, Boston's golden boy, doesn't do serious. He has fun. He has flings.

Maybe that's what I need. Fun that can be filed away when everything goes back to normal.

I glance down at my phone again, my thumb hovering over the screen.

For the first time, instead of shutting the thought down entirely, I let it sit there.

I wonder what would happen if, just this once, I leaned in.

20

Nathan

Friendsgiving is a generous term for what's happening in my apartment.

There's takeout spread across the counter in mismatched containers, a grocery store pumpkin pie that no one bothered to eat, and Wyatt has already claimed the couch like he's guarding it in the crease.

Liam and Wyatt are deep into some hockey video game, Liam yelling at his on-screen player while Wyatt critiques every missed save as if it's actually him between the posts. Meanwhile, Grayson sits across from me at the kitchen island. My laptop is open between us with our game tape paused mid-play.

It's loud, but comfortable and exactly the kind of night I needed.

"Run it back," Grayson says, leaning closer to the screen.

I hit the spacebar and the clip rewinds. Tomorrow's opponent cycles the puck along the boards, with their defense pinching aggressively.

"That's where you'll be," Grayson says, tapping the screen with his knuckle. "Left side instead of right. You come down earlier. Don't wait for the lane to open."

Wyatt snorts from the couch. "Listen to Captain Sunshine. He's already planning the Cup parade."

Grayson grins without missing a beat. "If you're invited, you can bring your bad attitude."

Liam pauses the game long enough to glance over his shoulder at me. "It's still kind of wild that Coach is moving you, though."

I shrug. "Someone got hurt. It's temporary."

Wyatt snorts. "Temporary until you score twice and he pretends it was the plan all along."

"He's not wrong," Liam adds cheerfully. "You've been unreal on the ice lately."

Grayson nods. "The way you've been playing the past two weeks is what got you the contract in the first place."

I don't say anything. Acknowledging it feels like tempting fate.

They're right. I've been playing better, feeling more myself, and the stats show it. I'm still waiting for the other shoe to drop. Sure, I'm more excited to get on the ice, and my body feels more challenged and ready, but it needs to last.

Grayson notices, lifting an eyebrow. "You good?"

"Yeah," I say automatically. "Just thinking."

About Wesley. About how my game improvement seems directly tied to the guarded brunette who enjoys kicking my ass in our workouts.

Her breath caught when I leaned in. I'd come so close to kissing her, but she stood up and bolted as fast as she could. I've replayed that moment more times than I should in the two days since it happened. Every version ends the same way, with me certain that I've misread everything.

Until my phone buzzed earlier tonight.

I hadn't expected her to text me, and definitely not first. The relief coursed through me, settling low in my gut the second I saw her name.

"What's with the face?" Liam asks.

"I don't have a face."

Wyatt mutters, "You always have a face. It's annoying."

Grayson clears his throat. "Alright. Back to the tape before Wyatt finds new ways to insult us."

I lean in, refocusing on the screen as the play restarts. The players shift across the ice, and I track it, imagining myself on the left instead of the right.

It's probably overkill at this point. The game's tomorrow, and I've practiced on the left all week, but Wesley's obsessive nature seems to be contagious. I don't want to let the team down. More importantly, I don't want Coach to have another reason not to renew my contract.

"Here," Grayson says, pointing at the person in the tape who's playing my position. "You read the ice better from the left anyway. We should've done this ages ago."

"Call Coach up," Wyatt interrupts. "I'm sure he'd love to know you think he sucks at his job."

Grayson shrugs. "Fuck off, Knox."

"I don't care who plays where as long as we win. I need to get laid, but it looks bad after a loss." Liam laughs.

I snort. "It looks bad regardless."

Liam's hookups land him in the tabloids more than most celebrities. Hell, they've landed me in the crosshairs more times than I can count. Playboy by association.

I've never minded, not until Wesley thought it was true.

Wyatt adds, "Why girls still willingly hook up with you is a mystery I never want to understand."

"I'm charming." Liam kisses the air in Wyatt's direction.

He grunts and hits play on the game, scoring on Liam before he has a chance to pick up his controller.

"I'm grabbing a drink." I head into the kitchen, open the fridge, and stare inside far longer than necessary.

The noise from the living room fades slightly, replaced by the hum of the refrigerator and my own thoughts.

Wesley's texts replay in my head. She was flirting. At least I think so. Does that mean I have a chance?

Do I want to have a chance?

Flirting is one thing. It's harmless. Anything else is a bad idea, even if I do find myself thinking about her too much to be casual.

Liam wanders in a second later, interrupting my spiraling thoughts. "So."

I glance at him. "So."

He smirks. "You going to tell me what's going on with you?"

"Nothing."

"You haven't partied with me in weeks. You're not forcing shots on the ice. You stopped doing whatever the hell that thing was, where you tried to dangle through three guys every shift."

"Just development," I say dryly.

"Uh-huh." He watches me for a beat. "And?"

"You know how serious I am about getting my contract renewed."

"Yes. You always have been. What's changed now?" He pulls water out of the fridge, taking a long swig. "We've been friends since we were kids. Do you think I'm an idiot?"

I don't answer.

Liam laughs quietly. "You know that silence is an answer."

"I almost kissed her." I cringe when the words burst out against my will.

His eyebrows lift. "You mean you did. At the bar. We all saw it."

"No. A different time."

"For real?"

"Yeah. But then, she left."

"Did she sprint? Or exit like a normal person?"

I exhale. "She exited the ice immediately and then left. Like nothing happened."

"But she's still texting you."

I look at him, eyebrows scrunching.

He grins. "You check your phone like every five minutes. I'm not blind."

"Shut up."

He sobers slightly. "You like her."

It's not a question.

"I don't do serious," I say automatically.

"Did she propose or something?"

I flip him off, but he just smiles. "I mean it."

"You can mean it and still like her." Liam shrugs.

I don't respond.

"Why is this a problem?" He asks.

"I don't want to complicate things," I say. "My game's finally clicking. Coach is talking contract stuff after the holidays, and this whole fake relationship ends then."

I think about her and the way she carries pressure as if it's second nature. Then I think about how she looks at me when she forgets to guard herself.

"She has shit too," I add. "Her own reasons for staying focused, for not letting anyone get too close."

"You're inventing problems."

I hate that he's not entirely wrong.

"Spending time with her, training and stuff, it's all platonic, and it's helping my game. If we cross the line from fake to real, we both have a lot to lose. Also, I don't think she's interested in anything more, considering she literally ran away."

A knock sounds at the door. Loud enough to cut through the noise of the game and the low murmur of the game tape still playing behind us.

Wyatt pauses the controller. "That's got to be the pizza."

"It's too soon," Liam yells back, pushing off the counter.

Wyatt's already on his feet. "I'll get it. If it's cold, I'm complaining."

I take another sip of water, trying to refocus on literally anything else.

Grayson rewinds the tape again, mumbling something about neutral zone pressure, but my attention's split now, stretched thin between the knock and the conversation I was having with Liam. Between contracts and lines and Wesley's lips.

It's one and a half more months. I can ignore my desire for that long, especially with our long away stretch coming up. Easy. Then, I can move on.

Liam glances back at me. "You good?"

"Yeah," I say.

Another knock, but slower this time.

Wyatt groans. "Jesus, relax. I'm coming."

"So," Liam says, judgment bleeding into his tone. "You're going to make yourself miserable until you guys call it?"

Yes.

Wyatt's voice cuts in, louder now. "Uh. It's not the pizza!"

Liam shakes his head disapprovingly and heads for the door.

"It's…" Liam trails off. "Dude. Wilder. It's for you."

I turn the corner and stop.

Wesley is standing in my doorway.

For half a second, my brain refuses to catch up to what my eyes are seeing. It's like she's a trick of the light, or I've somehow carried her with me from the earlier texts and delivered her to my doorstep.

She's wearing jeans, sneakers, and a sweater that clings in a way that feels unfair. Her hair is pulled back, but loose strands have escaped, framing her face in a way that is a little messy and a lot sexy. Her cheeks are pink, not from cold alone, and she looks nervous.

Really nervous.

Attraction crashes in, curling low in my gut as I take her in slowly, helplessly.

Her eyes meet mine and widen slightly, like she didn't expect me to be standing in my own hallway.

She's here, at my place, unexpectedly and utterly by choice. Regardless of the hesitancy written all over her face, I choose to cling to the fact that she sought me out.

I'm aware of Liam beside me and Wyatt hovering awkwardly near the door, but I'd blink them away if I could. Hell, I'd shove them out the door. Maybe I will.

All I can think is that she came here.

Wesley swallows. "Hi."

My mouth opens, but nothing comes out.

I've faced sold-out arenas, contract negotiations, pressure that crushes people, and none of it compares to standing three feet from her, in my apartment, unsure of what comes next.

21

Wesley

I should be in an Uber.

That's the thought that keeps repeating in my head as I stand outside a penthouse door that definitely does not belong to me, clutching my phone as if it might still save me from whatever impulsive spiral led me here.

Twenty minutes ago, I was laughing over cocktails with the girls, swearing I was done making questionable decisions for at least the rest of the week.

Ten minutes ago, I told myself it was fine to walk home alone, that I needed the air and was just thinking.

Five minutes ago, I looked up the address of this building and realized it was within walking distance.

Now I am here.

I stare at the door, half-expecting it to reject me outright, like a bouncer who knows I shouldn't be here. My heart is beating faster than it does during a game, which is irritating considering I pride myself on being in control of my body and choices. This is not a controlled choice. This is me losing my mind because I can't stop thinking about the way Nathan looked at me earlier this week.

I can still leave. No one knows I'm here. No one would know if I left.

I knock.

There's a sound on the other side of the door, but it stays closed. Now. Now I should leave.

I knock again because apparently I hate myself.

This time, the door opens almost immediately.

The man standing there is tall, broad, and not Nathan.

He has dark hair, a sharp jaw, and an expression that suggests he would rather be doing literally anything else. He looks at me like I'm an unexpected maintenance issue.

I blink once. I was certain this was Nathan's penthouse. Hell, the tabloids have practically published that it is.

"I'm sorry," I say quickly, already mortified. "I must have the wrong place."

He squints at me, then looks past me, as if checking whether I brought a problem with me, then yells back into the apartment. "Uh. It's not the pizza!"

I step back, fumbling for dignity, when a voice carries from inside.

Before I can escape, a blond man rounds the corner into view, wearing a grin that belongs on a billboard. The air leaves my lungs.

The realization hits me all at once, pieces snapping together in a way I don't appreciate. Of course, this is Nathan's place. Of course, there are other people here. Liam and Wyatt, whom I now recognize. I'm standing here unannounced like a fucking stalker.

Liam's eyebrows lift when he sees me, surprise flashing across his face before something distinctly entertained replaces it.

"It's…" Liam trails off. "Dude. Wilder. It's for you."

My mouth opens and closes. "I was just, I mean, I didn't realize."

Behind him, the apartment is loud with the faint sound of a video game's theme music carrying down the hall. Every instinct in me screams retreat.

Footsteps sound, heavier than Liam's, more deliberate.

Then he appears.

Grey sweatpants are slung low on his hips, and a white cut-off shows off his muscles beneath it. Nathan's hair looks like he's run his hands through it one too many times, leaving it messy. He looks nothing like he does at our workouts, or the gala, or even our two fake dates. He looks casual and comfortable, and so fucking attractive that my chest actually clenches.

"Hi." My brain short-circuits long enough that I forget how to breathe.

He stops when he sees me, his expression unreadable but intent, eyes locking onto mine like everything else in the room has ceased to exist.

I'm painfully aware of the people behind him and their attention. My coming here was already a bad idea, but now it feels inappropriate. I'm an idiot.

"I shouldn't have come," I say too fast, words tumbling over each other. "I didn't realize you had people over, and this was a mistake."

Nathan doesn't look away from me.

"Get out," he says quietly.

Liam snorts. "Wow, you aren't actually kicking us out? Right?"

Nathan's jaw tightens, but his eyes stay on me. "I said get the fuck out."

The room stirs behind him, protests and laughter mixing together.

"Relax, man." Grayson appears from the other room.

"Don't do anything I wouldn't do," Liam says with a wink, clearly enjoying my suffering.

"Dude." Grayson slaps Liam in the back of the head as they push through the door.

Wyatt looks at me, then at Nathan, and shakes his head like a disappointed dad.

I stand frozen in the doorway, my cheeks burning, suddenly very aware that the hallway feels larger without their presence.

The silence presses in.

I swallow, nerves buzzing under my skin as the reality of being alone with him settles heavily in my chest. Why am I here?

He clears his throat and gestures toward the apartment, the movement subtle but deliberate.

"Come in."

The words hit me like a starter pistol, and instead of moving, I panic.

"I really shouldn't," I say immediately, the sentence tripping over itself. "I mean, I don't normally show up at people's homes, especially not unannounced, and I swear I'm not a stalker even though this absolutely makes me look like one, and that sounds worse when I say it out loud, but I promise I'm not unhinged."

Nathan doesn't interrupt me.

He just watches.

His expression is unreadable, but his attention is absolute, as if he's letting me burn through all the nervous energy I brought with me. The silence stretches, my rambling finally running out of oxygen as I realize I'm talking to fill the space I'm too afraid to step into.

When I stop, he speaks again.

"Wesley, just come in."

There's no edge to it this time, only certainty.

"Okay." My feet move before my brain catches up, and suddenly I'm inside his apartment.

It's simple and modern with plain white walls that seem to stretch on forever. I'm not sure what I expected, but this wasn't it. He's so friendly and charming. This apartment is impersonal in a way that bothers me.

Nathan lives here. He lives here, but it looks like anyone could.

He steps toward me, our bodies close enough that the heat of him burns into me, close enough that my pulse starts doing something reckless.

"You always act like you've got everything under control, but you always look at me like you're about to lose it."

I hate the way he sees me. Despite my best efforts at blocking him out, he always manages to see right past my walls. And he's right, I'm about to lose it entirely.

For a second, we just stand here.

Then he reaches behind me to shut the door fully, the click of the lock breaking whatever trance I've fallen into. He pulls back, giving me space, and I suck in a breath I didn't realize I was holding.

"I'm sorry," I say again, quieter this time. "For interrupting your night."

He shakes his head. "I'm not."

I look up at him, searching his face for signs that he's only being polite, but there are none. Instead, he looks pleased and maybe relieved.

"Do you want some pumpkin pie?" he asks, nodding toward the kitchen. "I can't promise it's safe."

I follow his gaze and spot a sad-looking pie on the counter, still in its plastic container, untouched.

My face twists before I can stop it. "That looks like a crime."

He laughs, the sound loosening the tension in my chest. "That's what I said. They insisted."

"I respect your survival instincts." My gaze scans the space. "So, when you said you were watching film?"

"Yeah, it was with the guys," he admits sheepishly.

I walk down the hall, entering the larger living area, only to find more impersonal decor.

"Your apartment is—"

"Nice?" He finishes.

"No." I drag my hand across the painting on the far wall, it's nothing but black and grey, like everything else. "It's not very you." I glance in his direction, only to find him trailing behind me.

"Oh." He looks around as if seeing his own place with new eyes. "It's not really. I wanted something bigger, so I sold my old place last fall. I was in the process of buying a new one." He pauses, his jaw working. "But my agent got wind that my contract might not renew, so I decided to rent this place for the year."

There's pain in his eyes as he speaks. His shoulders are tight as he forces the words out. Seeing him so insecure does something to my heart that I don't like.

The Blades would have to be insane not to want this man on their team. Nathan playing average is better than most guys could ever hope for. Besides, I'd come to learn that his dedication to that team was second to none. Looking around this apartment, I realize that Nathan doesn't quite believe that anymore.

"Renting doesn't mean you have to keep it impersonal." I glance around, noting that there's not a single personal picture frame. "Besides, you want to stay, right?"

"Well, yeah. That's kind of the whole point." He motions to me as if he has made his intentions perfectly clear.

"If you want to stay, then you need to act like you're going to." I turn to face him fully.

"What do you mean?" He leans against the back of the couch, one leg crossed in front of the other.

"I mean." I motion around the room. "This is not good for your mental game, Wilder. No wonder you're playing off. You're living in an impersonal, personally created jail cell that reminds you that your contract's up, constantly. It's a mind fuck."

I walk past him and around the couch.

He's silent for a minute, and I wonder if I've said too much. I'm pushy. I know it. But I want to help, and that means pointing out that this place sucks. If he can't convince himself that he's going to get his contract renewed, there's no way he's going to convince management of it.

After making my way around the room again, sufficiently convinced that there's not an ounce of Nathan in this place, I stop my pacing in front of him.

When I do, his stoic expression breaks into a full-on belly laugh. He throws his head back laughing so loud, it practically echoes in this makeshift mausoleum. It goes on for minutes, and I'm too confused to join in.

"I've brought girls here. I've brought my teammates here. No one has ever said a fucking thing about it," he finally says between gasps.

"I'm sorry." And I am.

"Don't apologize." He stands upright, uncrossing his legs. "I just mean, you're right. I hate this place, and it does make me feel like every day is a day closer to me leaving. No one has ever noticed before, though."

He finishes, eyes shifting from amused to something more earnest.

It makes my mouth dry.

"Wesley, why are you here?"

I open my mouth, then close it again. "I don't know."

He tilts his head slightly, studying me. "Yes, you do."

The air shifts, the weight of his attention sharpening.

"You were going to kiss me on Wednesday."

I swallow. I don't know why I say it. Maybe I just need to hear him confirm it before I make a fool out of myself.

He heads to the kitchen, grabs his drink, and then takes a long pull, never breaking eye contact with me. The pause feels intentional, like he's choosing his honesty instead of defaulting to charm.

"Yes," he says simply.

Well, shit. I knew in my gut what he'd been doing, but hearing him say it out loud is different. Heat pools low in my belly because hearing him own it without trying to minimize it is so damn attractive.

"Why?"

"It should be obvious."

I cross my arms, more to give my hands something to do than out of defensiveness. "Well, it's not. There are a lot of attractive girls in Boston you could kiss."

"I know," he says easily. "That's not the point."

He sets the cup down on the counter and leans back, still watching me.

"There aren't many who insult my apartment," he continues. "Not many take being an athlete as seriously as I do. Not many remind me what it feels like to love the grind instead of surviving it."

My heart stumbles for a second as he goes on.

"You remind me not to take this for granted," he says. "You remind me why I play." He pauses, then adds, "You said it yourself. We earn every moment we get to do this."

"That's the second time you've quoted my speech back to me." My lips curve into a smile before I can stop them. "Do you have it memorized?"

He shrugs. "Most of it."

I break eye contact first, grabbing a glass from the drying mat by the sink to buy myself time. I fill it with water, hands steady even though my pulse isn't, and take a small sip as I lean back against the counter, watching him carefully over the rim.

"So, yes, there are many attractive women in Boston that I could kiss, but why would I kiss them when all I want is to be kissing you?"

His eyes dart to my lips as I reflexively curl my bottom lip into my mouth, wetting it. I can't help but think about how his lips felt on mine at the bar.

The silence between us feels different now.

Heavier. Expectant.

"I don't date." I set the glass down a little harder than necessary, the quiet clink cutting through the room.

Nathan doesn't look surprised. If anything, he looks relieved. "I don't either."

"Right." I know he doesn't. He's told me that already. I gesture vaguely between us. "You've been a really good fake boyfriend, you know."

A sharp noise escapes him as if it were dragged out of his chest against his will. "Yeah. Thrilled to hear it."

I wince despite myself and take a step toward him. "I mean that in a good way. I really am grateful. You stepped in when you didn't need to. You saved my ass."

His jaw tightens slightly.

"I'm just saying," I continue, softer now, "you didn't have to do any of that."

"I wanted to," he says immediately. "Let's not pretend my intentions aren't selfish." He stays where he is, hands loose at his sides, deliberately not closing the distance between us. He's giving me space even though everything in the room feels like it's pulling us together.

The restraint does something to me.

"I don't date," I say again.

Annoyance flashes in his eyes. "I get it."

"I don't go out."

"I know." He's no longer looking at me.

"Nathan."

His eyes shift back to me, so much frustration they're burning like a wildfire.

"I don't drink beer. I don't kiss boys on the dance floor. I don't do any of this."

At least I never have. I've never wanted to. The click happens so suddenly it's almost physical.

I step forward, closing this distance between us.

His breath hitches, barely perceptible, but enough.

I reach him before my nerves can talk me out of it, before logic can remind me of consequences. My hand curls into the fabric of his shirt, and I rise up to bridge the last inch between us.

I kiss him.

It's not tentative. It's decisive, like I've made up my mind and my body knows it before the rest of me does. He freezes for half a heartbeat, and then he's kissing me back, slow and devastatingly careful.

The world narrows to heat and the quiet sound he makes when I pull away to breathe.

"I've been thinking about doing that," I murmur, my mouth still close to his, "since Wednesday."

His eyes are dark, focused entirely on me. "Yeah?"

"I figured," I say softly, "I'm already breaking all my rules, I might as well go all in."

Then I kiss him again.

Harder this time. Hungrier. His hands finally come up, settling at my waist like he's been fighting the instinct, and the way he exhales against my mouth feels like relief.

22

Nathan

The kiss hits me before I'm ready for it.

Her mouth is warm and sure against mine, and her hand is fisted in my shirt like she's anchoring herself. For half a second, my brain blanks entirely. All I can register is the softness of her lips and the way the counter is digging into my back.

Then everything comes rushing in at once.

Wesley. Here. Kissing me.

Shock flares first, sharp and disorienting, followed immediately by want so intense it makes my entire body thrum. I stay still for a heartbeat longer, every instinct screaming to slow down so that I don't fuck this up.

She pulls back to breathe, her lips still brushing mine, but I lean forward, my lips searching for hers instinctively.

This is a bad idea. I don't date. She doesn't date. She's made that painfully clear. She's disciplined and focused and allergic to anything messy, and I'm very much a complication.

If I hesitate, even for a second, she might decide this was a mistake and walk out the same way she walked in, leaving me standing here replaying it.

I'm a selfish bastard because I'm not willing to risk it.

I kiss her back, slow at first, like I'm asking instead of taking, and the sound she makes when she melts into me wrecks whatever restraint I have left. My hands come up, sliding to her waist, feeling the curve of her, grounding myself in the fact that she's here and kissing me for real.

There is nothing on this planet that feels better than Wesley's lips. I'd bet my contract on it. At this moment, I'd bet everything on it. Hell, that might be exactly what I'm doing by allowing this to happen. Because when we both have a moment to remember ourselves and our responsibilities, this will only complicate everything, putting it all at risk.

I can't bring myself to care.

I spin her without thinking, turning us so she's the one against the counter now, her breath hitching when she realizes what I'm doing. I crowd into her space, trailing my lips along her jaw before I find her mouth again. The way she tilts her head back for me feels like permission I'm not going to waste.

Her hands tighten in my shirt as I lift her, setting her on the counter. Her legs fall open instinctively, my body settling between them, and for one dizzying moment, I forget everything outside of her body against mine.

Something clatters over the counter.

We both freeze.

Then she laughs breathlessly, forehead dropping to my shoulder. I start laughing too, the sound ripped out of me by pure disbelief.

"That was my water glass," she says.

"RIP," I reply, still grinning like an idiot.

The laughter fades, the space between us charging all over again, quieter now but no less intense. My hands are still on her hips. Hers are still in my shirt. Neither of us moves away.

I swallow.

"So," I say, voice rougher than I want it to be. "What does this mean?"

She looks at me, calculating her next words before she says them. Not regret. Just control reasserting itself.

"I don't date," she says again, gentler this time but no less firm.

I nod. "So you've said."

She studies my face like she's checking for cracks. "But if we're already pretending, if we're already fake dating, we might as well reap some of the benefits." Her lips twitch.

My pulse kicks.

"Benefits," I repeat.

Wesley Miller is standing in my kitchen after kissing me senseless and offering benefits. My mind flashes through a dozen inappropriate images of what those benefits will be.

"Strictly temporary. Until my team party. When we fake break up, this ends too."

Every smart part of me knows I should be thrilled.

This having an expiration date means I can keep my focus on my game and saving my contract.

But there's something in my chest that sinks. The idea that this is a fling, that she'd categorize what's happening as a matter of convenience, stings more than I would expect it to. Every relationship I've had in recent years has been a matter of convenience, and yet, now, when that's what I should want, it doesn't feel like enough.

Still, I nod.

"Yeah," I say. "I can do that."

I mean it. I've never wanted more from anyone, and I'm not going to start now.

She smiles, biting her lower lip in the process.

"Good," she says.

I kiss her again.

This one is different. It's hungrier and less careful. My hands slide along her sides, holding her there like I'm afraid she'll disappear if I let go. She kisses me back just as hard, her fingers threading into my hair, pulling me closer until there's no space left between us.

Right now, with her mouth on mine and her body warm under my hands, I'll take whatever she's willing to give me, even if it is temporary. There's not a person alive who would be able to resist giving Wesley exactly what she wants.

My mouth stays on hers until water spreads across the counter, seeping under my hands, from the glass we knocked over in our carelessness. She notices it at the same time I do, her body shifting as she breaks the kiss to glance down.

"I should probably get down before I end up soaked."

"You'd look good wet." I flash my cocky grin, the one that riles her up.

"I can't believe you just said that." Her cheeks flush, and she starts to slide off the counter, but I don't let her.

"By now, you should know I'd say just about anything to throw you off balance." My hands tighten, one at her waist, the other under her thigh. I lift her like she weighs nothing. She gasps and instinctively wraps her arms around my neck.

"Nathan," she breathes, half laughing, half something else entirely.

"I've got you," I murmur, kissing her again before she can argue.

Her mouth opens under mine as I carry her away from the counter. My focus is narrowed to the heat of her body and the way she clings to me. Her legs hook around my hips without thinking, and their grip sends a jolt straight through me.

The couch comes up behind my knees.

I lower us down, until I'm sitting and she's straddling me. Her breath is uneven, and her eyes are dark with desire and her signature restraint. The restraint that I love finding ways to break.

Then, as if making another decision, her hands latch onto the bottom of her shirt, sliding it up her body before tossing it onto the floor. My eyes search hers, filled with the desperate desire to touch her, to explore her body the way I've longed to.

She kisses me first this time, hands sliding into my hair, her mouth demanding and unrestrained. I groan, my fingers digging into her hips, pulling her closer until there's no question about how much I want her.

I can't believe she wants me, too.

Her hands slide on top of my own as she moves them slowly up her body, her bare skin soft and tempting in my grasp. I let her lead my hands up her stomach and across the outside of her bra. It's a light blue, lacy bra that will forever be burned into my memory.

My control snaps, and I take it upon myself to continue my exploration.

"This is pretty." I run my fingertips across the light blue material, savoring the way her skin prickles at the teasing touch. "If I'd known you wear lacy things like this, I'd have had you strip for me sooner."

"What makes you think I would've let…"

Her words die in her throat as I lean forward, dragging my mouth over the fabric.

I grin against her chest, teeth grazing across her skin as I slide my hands around her back, unlatching her bra. "What were you saying?"

She starts to talk, but curses under her breath, eyes darkening when she sees me close my teeth around the front of her bra, dragging it away from her body and down her arms. My mouth waters at the sight of her bare breasts only inches from my face.

"Where'd all that attitude go, Wesley?" I lean forward, my tongue brushing across her nipple. She moans as I suck it into my mouth.

Her hips wiggle in my lap as she throws her head back. My body responds on its own, hips pressing more firmly against her, desperate for the drag of her jeans to create more friction against my cock.

I force myself to slow down, dragging my mouth up along her collarbone and against her neck. Her skin is warm under my lips, and I breathe her in, grounding myself in her scent. I plan to spend all night seeing how I can get the most controlled woman I've ever met to let go for me.

She shivers. "God, Nathan, I…" I cut her off, kissing her again, deeper this time, my hands sliding up her back, feeling every inch of tension and heat between us.

She rocks forward, her fingers creeping under my shirt, tracing their way up my spine, and setting my skin on fire. When they trail back down, she reaches for the hem and pulls it over my head.

Her eyes darken with desire. "Your body is unfair," she says, voice breathless.

I smile against her skin. "As if every part of you isn't fucking perfection."

Her back presses into the couch as I roll on top of her, letting my weight press against her. A groan slips free from somewhere deep in my throat when her hips rise to meet me. The sound spurs her on, and she starts grinding against me, my cock straining against my sweatpants.

She's clumsy now, fumbling with my waistband before sliding it down my thighs so that she can palm me through the thin fabric of my boxers.

Fuck. I can't believe this is happening. I can't believe it feels this good. I don't let myself think about what that might mean, instead opting to lose myself in her. In the way her eyes roam my body and the way her breath feels against my skin.

Her hand grips me and tugs, drawing a curse from my lips. I force myself to pull out of her grasp. Standing just long enough to get my sweatpants the rest of the way off.

I take a breath, pausing. I'm already too close to coming in my boxers at just the feel of her hand wrapped around me.

She watches me with her mouth parted as she lies across the couch. A vision of her on her knees in front of me with those lips parted for my cock flashes vividly, but right now, I have different ideas.

"Up." My fingers tug on the button of her pants. My voice is husky and demanding, and I half expect her to argue.

Instead, she does as I ask, raising her hips enough that I can slide her pants past her ass. I smirk. "Wesley Miller, following my orders, for once."

"I'm very coachable," she murmurs, hips still raised while I take my time pulling her pants off, dropping kisses on the small bruises that scatter across her legs from her practices and games.

I slide back onto the couch by her feet, grabbing each of her legs. "Prove it by being a good girl and putting your legs on my shoulders."

Her eyes widen with surprise, but she spreads her legs anyway, letting me slide up the couch while she drapes them over me. I finally have the view I've been aching for.

Her panties match her bra, with the same lace frills at the top. My focus, though, is on the obvious damp circle her arousal already created on the fabric. I can't resist placing a tantalizing open-mouth kiss against it, sucking it into my mouth.

My first taste of her is better than anything I could've hoped for. Without even taking her panties off, she's responsive and desperate.

She combs her fingers into my hair, gripping it tightly as if to hold me in place. I'd stay right here forever if she wanted, breathing in the scent of her wetness. I pull the fabric down her legs, then slide a finger up her slit.

"Fuck, your pretty little pussy is weeping for me." I dip my finger into her, and she moans. "You're so tight around me, too."

I grind my cock into the couch as her legs tighten around me.

"Nathan, please," She cries when I pull it out.

I slide two fingers back into her, feeling her stretch for me as I push them deeper.

"I like you like this," I tease, leaning down and gliding my tongue along her center. "Losing control for me."

I'm starting to think I like her anyway I can have her.

I close my lips around her clit, sucking it into my mouth, relishing in the taste and the moan it pulls from her. My fingers keep up their steady rhythm, pumping into her pussy as I flick my tongue across her clit in a repetitive motion. Her hips start to work against my face, her grip tightening in my hair.

"That's it, Wes, ride my face."

The sharp bite of her nails against my scalp has me feral for her. I'd gladly walk around wearing her nail marks all over my body if I get to have her like this.

I glance up, meeting her hooded eyes before sucking my fingers into my mouth slowly. My cock twitches at the way she sucks on her own lip in response. I can't resist moving up her body and crashing my mouth onto hers. The kiss is rushed, the taste of her arousal on both of our tongues. Somehow, it's not enough. I'm not sure I'll ever get enough. My finger moves in gentle circles against her clit, slow and steady.

Her breath comes shorter against my mouth as she bites my lip. She might just fucking ruin me.

I move back down her body and join my hand between her legs. With my finger still working her, I slide my tongue inside her pussy. She clenches around me. There's nothing I want more in this moment than to be the one she comes undone for.

I drive her closer to the edge.

"Wesley, I'm fucking begging you." I drag my thumb across her clit. "Come on my tongue."

It sends her toppling over. She cries out my name as the orgasm courses through her, and I almost come in my boxers at the sight of it.

Wesley Miller shattering for me, because of me, might be the most amazing thing I've ever seen. I mentally memorize the version of her lying below me with her eyes closed, utterly relaxed. It's my favorite version so far.

"You've got a dirty mouth," she says, still breathing heavily.

I flash an arrogant smile.

Then there's a knock at the door, loud and persistent as if whoever it is has been knocking for a while. It's loud enough to jolt us both out of whatever trance we were in.

It's insistent, echoing through the apartment like whoever is on the other side has decided subtlety is no longer an option.

"What the hell," Wesley breathes, already scrambling upright.

My heart slams into my ribs as another knock follows, harder this time, the sound bouncing off the walls. We move at the same time, bodies colliding in a mess of limbs and whispered curses.

"Shit," I mutter, grabbing for my sweatpants where they're tangled on the floor. I shove one leg in, then the other, hopping as I yank them up while the knocking gets louder.

"Who is that?" She whispers, wide-eyed.

"I don't know," I say, even though part of me already does. My brain catches up as I'm pulling the waistband into place.

The pizza.

Ordered before the guys left and completely forgotten. Of course, this would be how the universe chose to remind me that I shouldn't have been doing what I was just doing.

"I'll get it," I say quickly, already moving.

Another knock lands as I reach the door. I yank it open to find a delivery guy holding a stack of boxes, irritation written all over his face.

"Finally," he says. "I've been knocking forever. Oh shit. You're Nathan Wilder."

"Yeah, I am. Uh, sorry." I pull my wallet out, tipping him more than necessary to make him go away faster.

Hopefully, he'll keep his mouth shut about what he might have heard. Once I have the boxes, I shut the door with my foot. The silence now feels deafening.

I hesitate in the hallway, not knowing what version of Wesley will exist when I walk back to her. Will she regret this? Will she want more? Will I be able to play it cool? I don't feel cool. I feel confused. Stressed.

I don't like her. I can't. At least, not as anything more than a fling.

Reentering the living room, my heart slams against my ribs. I freeze.

Wesley is sitting on the couch, knees pulled up slightly, with my white cut-off hanging off one shoulder. Her hair is twisted up into a messy bun with loose strands framing her face.

The girl who always seems to have it all figured out looks vulnerable. Like the weight of what we did is settling in for her, too. As the heat dissipates, reality sinks back in.

I'm at a loss for words, part of me wanting to take my clothes back off her and repeat everything we've just done, while the other part is waiting for the other shoe to drop.

"We, uh, ordered this earlier," I say quietly, raising the pizza in front of me.

She nods, fingers worrying at the hem of my shirt. For the first time since she showed up tonight, neither of us seems to know exactly what to say.

"I like pizza." A shy smile ghosts across her lips.

I smile, setting the stack of pizzas down and grabbing a box from the top. I make my way over to her and sit down, close enough that our legs brush.

The knocking is gone. The panic has faded. What's left is the reality of us, half-dressed, sharing pizza, pretending this hasn't changed everything.

23

Nathan

The gym is quiet in that early-morning way that always feels a little sacred. There's no music yet, only the soft clank of plates and the low hum of the HVAC. It's exactly how game days are supposed to start.

The lights are still dimmed to half power, casting long shadows across the rubber floors and the rows of racks. Chalk dust lingers faintly in the air, mixing with the familiar scent of metal and sweat. I've always liked this hour best. Before reporters. Before fans. Before the noise.

I'm halfway through my first set when I catch myself smiling at nothing.

It's been two fucking weeks since I've seen Wesley, and we're finally back in town.

There has to be some kind of cosmic joke behind the fact that our longest road trip of the year started the day after she showed up on my doorstep. Seven games, a ridiculous number of red-eye flights, and more hotel beds than I care to count later, and the trip is finally over.

My muscles buzz with restless energy as I move through my set. Some of it is the usual game-day adrenaline. Some of it is the relief of playing on home ice again after weeks on the road. Most of it, though, is because Wesley's coming tonight.

We texted almost every day while I was gone. Sometimes it was about the workouts she's been putting together for me, and other times about my games. She actually knows hockey, which makes talking to her about it different from talking to most people. When I asked for her opinion, she gave real critiques. When I didn't, she just listened.

My favorite moments were when I managed to coax a little flirting out of her. It didn't happen often, and it took a hell of a lot of effort on my end, but damn if it wasn't cute when she slipped and let it happen.

Flirting might be teetering on the boundaries we've set, but it's far less concerning than the way she understands me so perfectly.

She somehow knows when I want to break down a shift or when I just need someone to remind me that I'm not playing like shit. Even when I'm hard on myself, she balances it out. It's as if she believes in me in a way I haven't believed in myself for a long time. Aside from my teammates, I haven't had anyone support me this way in years.

It has alarm sirens ringing in my head.

But it still didn't stop me from asking her to come to the game tonight.

After weeks on the road, I told her it would look good to have my supportive girlfriend in the stands on my first night back. Technically, that's true.

But really, I just want to see her. Touch her. Taste her.

Since our night together, I've been surviving on my hand and the memory of her underneath me.

Hopefully, tonight I won't have to settle for that.

I'm desperate for her. Call it benefits, or lust, or something a little more pathetic, but I can't seem to shake it. Especially not when she mentioned wanting to hang out after the game. I have no idea what hanging out actually means. It could be exactly that: just hanging out.

My body has already decided it means something else entirely.

But even if it doesn't, I'm more than okay with only hanging out.

It had been surprisingly fun to eat pizza and watch an international soccer match while Wesley ranted about the bad officiating. I hadn't understood a damn thing, but watching Wesley get animated about it was more than enough.

I've spent the past two weeks watching every soccer game I could find on TV to hold me over until I'd see her again. By now, I'm even starting to understand it.

So yeah, whether tonight includes benefits or not doesn't really matter to me, as long as it includes Wesley.

I shake my head and step back under the bar for my next set, grounding myself in routine. Lift. Breathe. Control the descent. Explode upward. This is what I should be focusing on.

"Hat trick hero."

I glance up to find Liam grinning at me from the next rack over. He's already sweating, towel draped over his shoulder and water in tow.

"Thursday night," he continues. "Three goals against the defending conference champs. You're playing the best hockey I've seen out of you in years."

"Stats don't lie," Grayson adds, coming up behind him. "You're on fire."

I shrug, but can't stop the smile. "Just doing my job."

Wyatt snorts. "Yeah, sure. And I'm the Pope."

I rack the bar and sit down, grabbing my water. "What's that supposed to mean?"

Liam lowers his voice, leaning closer like he's about to share state secrets. "Means you're getting laid."

I shake my head and point at him. "You don't know anything."

"Oh, we know," Liam says easily. "We all got kicked out of your apartment. That's not exactly subtle."

"That was unrelated," I say flatly, even as heat creeps up the back of my neck. The mention of that night drags every sensation back to the surface. Her breath. Her hands. The way she sounded when she came with my name on her lips.

I step back under the bar before they can push further.

"Sure it was," Wyatt mutters.

I don't take the bait. I've learned better. Instead, I focus on my next set, jaw tight, refusing to give them anything. They can speculate all they want. Wesley is not up for group discussion.

Still, I can feel my grin creeping back in, uninvited.

"Who've we got tonight again?" Wyatt asks, loading plates onto his bar.

"Chicago," Liam answers without looking up. "It's the second half of their road swing."

I grimace. "They've been chippy lately."

"Chippy is generous," Grayson says. "They're pissed after losing three straight."

Chicago plays heavy. Every shift against them feels like a tax you pay with your body, especially along the boards. They walk the line between physical and reckless. When they're frustrated, their sticks get lazy, and they'll be frustrated tonight.

Liam nods toward me. "You still on the left?"

"Yeah. Coach wants to keep the line intact."

"And you're killing it there," Grayson adds. "Took you long enough to admit it fits."

I roll my shoulders again, stretching out lingering tension. I fought the switch at first. Left wing isn't where I've built my instincts, but after seven games, it feels natural with more time to read the play instead of forcing it.

"Feels good," I admit. "Opens up the ice a bit."

"Also makes you harder to read," Liam says. "Defense doesn't know what to do with you right now."

I like hearing that.

Playing the left changes everything against a team like Chicago. The angles come faster, and the pressure hits from the blind side instead of straight on. On the right, I used to drive wide and cut in on instinct. On the left, I have to think half a second earlier about where the puck will be, not where it is.

We move through another set, the rhythm familiar. The room fills slowly as more guys trickle in, the quiet giving way to low conversation and the occasional laugh. The clatter of weights, the scrape of shoes on rubber mats, and the distant beep of timers all blend into a soundtrack that reminds me why I love this chaos as much as the calm from earlier.

"So, any word on your contract?" Liam asks, a little quieter now.

I hesitate, fingers tightening around the bar. The question lands heavier than any weight I've lifted today. My agent, Ryan Elliot, has been cautiously optimistic, but nothing is final. The switch to left wing, the extra goals, the increased ice time; it all counts, sure, but until the ink is on paper, it's all hope and strategy.

"Ryan's been more upbeat," I say carefully. "Nothing concrete yet, but he thinks the switch and the production are helping."

"That's huge," Grayson says. "Told you. You needed a little shake-up."

The past couple of weeks, it feels like everything is clicking when it needs to. Every successful shift feels like a tiny piece of proof that I still have value. Anxiety still gnaws at the edges. One bad game or careless move against a team like Chicago, and it can all evaporate overnight.

I can't seem to think about my success on the ice lately without thinking about the brunette who seems at least partly responsible for it. A heavy pull settles in my chest at the thought that wanting her might be misplaced gratitude.

Wesley circles my mind until I'm thinking about her in my apartment. On my couch. Wearing my shirt as if it belonged to her.

I fight my way back to the present. "I'm not counting on anything until it's signed, but it's better than it was a month ago."

Grayson claps my shoulder. "If you keep playing like this, they'll have no choice."

"Yeah, so don't fuck up." Wyatt takes a swig from his water bottle.

"Fuck you, Knox." I throw my towel at him.

The pressure is there tonight. Not only because of the contract, but because Wesley will be in the stands. I know she's watched our games on TV, but she's never come to a game before. I want to impress her.

She drew the line at wearing my name on her back, but her being here is enough. I got her last-minute tickets in the stands since she refuses to sit in the box. She claims to want to be in the thick of things, but I think she's worried about the attention she'd inevitably get with the WAGs.

I've already scoped out her section, so I know where to look tonight.

"Is she coming tonight?" Wyatt asks as if reading my mind.

We're in the final stretch now, wiping down benches and re-racking plates. Sweat clings to my skin, and my muscles feel loose in the good way, worked but ready. Game-day lifts are always like this. We lift only enough to wake everything up without taking anything away.

"If he has anything to say about it, I'm sure she is," Liam says, waggling his eyebrows.

Grayson smacks the back of his head without breaking stride as he reaches for his towel.

"Don't go there," I warn, voice flat. "Yes. She'll be at the game tonight."

That gets their attention.

Liam pauses mid-stretch. The looks they exchange are quiet but loaded, the kind of shared skepticism you only earn after years of being forced together for hours on end every day.

"How deep are you in?" Liam asks.

I don't think about it, denial ringing as the answer flies out of my mouth.

"I'm not. We're fake-dating to get her coach off her back, and she's helping me with some cross-training. That's it."

Wyatt snorts, grabbing his water bottle. "I didn't realize her coach was at your house at almost midnight two weeks ago when she showed up looking like she wanted to rip your clothes off."

Grayson chokes on his water, and heat creeps up my neck. I open my mouth to argue, already lining up the words, but Liam cuts in first.

"You could train without her now," he says, more careful than before. "She's already taught you everything to do."

I don't answer.

Technically, he's right.

I shouldn't need her anymore. The thought of calling it all off, though, leaves me hollow. Besides, I can't bail on her when she's counting on me to sell this fake relationship. It means too much to her.

I hook my towel over my shoulder and start toward the lockers, the rubber floor giving way to cool tile under my shoes. The silence stretches, saying everything I'm not ready to.

"Look," Grayson says, catching up to me. "We like her. She's great. But she's also intense and maybe a tad unavailable."

"Intense?" Liam's eyes widen as we pass the doorway into the locker room. Steam drifts out from the showers. The hum of the vents is louder in here, echoing slightly. "She ran circles around all of us without breaking a sweat. She's discipline wrapped in a sexy body."

"Shut up," I snap.

I'm louder than intended. A couple of guys down the row glance over, then look away.

Wyatt smirks, clearly enjoying this far too much. "Yeah, there's nothing going on at all."

I drop onto the bench in front of my stall and lean forward, forearms resting on my thighs. My pulse is still elevated, but not from the lift anymore. Now, it's from them poking at something I've been avoiding naming.

"We're having some fun. Nothing serious." The words scrape on the way out, but I shove the feeling down before I can think about why.

"You've got momentum. Real momentum." Grayson rubs at the back of his neck, eyes on the floor. "I don't want your game to slip when this ends."

"And it will end," Liam adds, meeting my gaze this time. "We both know that once her coach is off her back, she goes right back to being focused on whatever the soccer equivalent of the Stanley Cup is."

I nod, even though it feels like swallowing glass.

They're not wrong.

I reach down, untying my shoes and sliding them off, mostly to keep my hands busy.

They're right to remind me what this is. Temporary. Fake. An arrangement.

But she'll be in the stands tonight. For me. In mere weeks, this will all be over, but right now she's mine. Publicly and privately.

I'm not going to let the future steal this from me.

If I happen to catch her eye when I score, if I see her lean forward, focused and intent, eyes glinting with excitement the way they do on the field or on my couch, well, that's just a bonus.

24

Wesley

I can't believe you dragged me to a hockey game. I hate hockey. Hate it," Avery groans beside me, slumping into her seat.

Harper snorts. "What could you possibly hate about hot, athletic men roughing each other up all night for our entertainment?"

"Everything." Avery grabs a fistful of her stale popcorn and stuffs it into her mouth.

It's early. The stands are still mostly empty, with only the smell of concession food and the chill of ice in the air. I tug at the hem of my cropped Blades sweatshirt, pulling it a little lower over my midriff. When people start filling up the arena, I know I'll be hot, but right now the cold is getting to me.

"You dated a hockey player." I steal a kernel of popcorn. "You went to his games all the time."

"Don't remind me," Avery mumbles through her mouthful. "That's why I hate hockey now."

Her words are clipped, making me want to push her harder to understand what happened. I don't get the chance, though, because Avery is an expert at shifting the attention to me.

"Seriously, why are we here? A fake boyfriend is one thing, but coming to his game feels real."

"No." I blurt out, cheeks flushing. "Not real, but an easy way to make it look real without actually having to put on much of an act. I like hockey. I watch it at home. I can watch it here while giving the reporters something to talk about."

It's the same reasoning that Nathan gave me for the two weeks he's pestered me about coming. I couldn't argue the logic, so here I sit, almost an hour before gametime, wondering what the rest of the night will entail.

We're going out with his team after the game, knowing that pictures will be published to give our relationship more credibility. Who knew dating a famous athlete would be so easy to fake? We pose for a couple of viral photos and then can go our separate ways. Except tonight, I'm hoping we don't go our separate ways at all.

It's a bad idea, but one I've committed to. So with any luck, the plan for the night will include finishing what we started before the pizza interrupted us. I've been a ball of nerves thinking about it since he's been gone. It felt so good, letting my guard down and letting him touch me the way I've been wanting but fighting.

But I haven't been able to shake the nagging feeling that it felt too good. Too real.

I push those concerns down because, regardless of how danger-ous this tension between us feels, I need to see it through. My friends are right, I deserve to have some noncommittal fun, and Nathan seems more than willing to help with that.

My mind flashes to his head between my legs, and my skin heats. The media has publicized so much of his romantic life, but even with the knowledge that he has an extensive dating background, I hadn't expected him to be that good. Good enough that I've lain in bed every night thinking about it. It's never been clearer how inadequate my vibrator really is.

I exhale slowly, letting my gaze wander to the rink to distract my-self from the lack of control I have when I think about him.

The Blades' colors gleam under the arena lights, the ice reflecting streaks of both shades of teal and gray like a frozen mirror. Players are starting to warm up, their skates scraping lightly against the ice while their mascot, Razor the Raccoon, circles the outer edges, exciting the kids who run to the glass.

I catch a glimpse of Nathan exiting the tunnel wearing his number seventeen jersey. His hair is already wet with sweat, pushed out of his face, while he fidgets with something on his helmet. Something about seeing him here after being down there on the ice with him feels surreal.

My heart stops. What the hell am I doing here? Why can't I get these feelings under control?

"Uh, Wes?" Harper eyes me carefully. "Are you okay?"

Her question breaks me out of my trance, but doesn't stop my anxiety spiraling faster by the second. I bolt out of my seat and make for the aisle. "Yeah. Just got to pee."

It's a lie. We all know it, but they don't stop me. I fight the flow of traffic up the stairs and into the concourse, trying to calm my heart that's picking up speed.

My feet guide me in circles around the concourse, passing the same concessions three times before I'm calm enough to stop moving. Stress is no stranger to me. It constantly lingers right over my shoulder, waiting for me to feel too comfortable before making a reappearance. No matter how under control I might have things, the anxiety always finds a way to crash back into me at the most inconvenient times.

I talked to a doctor about it once, but she tried to get me to go to therapy. As if I needed someone to tell me what my issue is. I know my issue. I don't allow myself to feel things. I block it all out until it sends my walls tumbling down and floods my nervous system. I know that.

Unless a therapist can pay the bills, lead a professional athletic team, or bring my mom back from the dead, there's not much they can do about it. So, I cope. I run faster. I keep moving, pushing my walls back into place until my will is stronger than the anxiety trying to tear me down.

It usually works. But tonight, everything feels fragile, as if I'm balancing on the edge of a tightrope and falling is inevitable.

I watch the concourse flood with people before thinning back out as people make their way to their seats.

I should leave and take back my insane suggestion that we fool around for the duration of our fake fling. Clearly, it's weighing on me enough to send me spiraling. It's one of many signs that the whole thing is a bad idea.

I pull out my phone to cancel, scrolling to Nathan's number.

"Wesley," a voice calls out from behind me, and I turn to see Coach Bennett approaching.

Seeing her outside of soccer feels like seeing a teacher during summer break as a kid. Uncomfortable. She's wearing Blades gear, and her husband trails behind her.

"Hey, Coach." I fake an easy smile. "I didn't know you were a Blades fan."

It's true. Other than knowing she's one hell of a coach, I know next to nothing about her.

"Runs in the family," She answers, gesturing to her husband, who might be more decked out than she is. "I would've thought you'd be in the family box, with the rest of the players' girlfriends."

It's not a question, but the skepticism written on her face is clear as day. I hate lying to her, but not enough to back down now.

"Nathan really wanted me to, but I love being in the thick of things. A part of the crowd. Avery's down in the stands with me, too." I nod generally toward my seat.

Her lips form a thin smile, one that says she thinks I'm full of shit. Anyone who has met me knows the last place I want to be is in the thick of things. Well, second to last place. The last place is in a box designed for very real, very significant wives and girlfriends.

"It's good to see you out having fun with your friends and supporting your boyfriend."

"Yeah, it's been really good for me." I nod, eyes darting back toward the entrance I'm desperate to escape to. "Well, I should get back in there, don't want to miss Nathan's official entrance."

"Of course, see you at practice." She nods, brushing past me with her husband trailing behind.

I move toward the entrance, taking the steps one at a time. It's ironic that everyone says this is all good for me. If only Coach knew that the 'life' she wanted me to have is making me a spiraling, stressed-out mess. What a fucking joke. If anything, this entire thing is complicating my life far more than I can handle.

"You were gone for a while." Avery eyes me, standing up so I can squeeze by her.

"Ran into Coach." I sigh as I take my seat.

"I swear she might be stalking you or something."

"Apparently, she's a big Blades fan." I smile, picturing how ridiculous she looked with her foam finger and face paint. "I need to cancel tonight."

Both of their heads snap to me, confusion and concern flitting across their faces.

Harper speaks first. "Why? Don't you need to convince everyone you're dating?"

Avery's face shifts from concern to a knowing smile. "You fooled around, didn't you?"

Damn it.

"What? No way, she would've told us." Harper looks between us, before seeing the guilt on my face and jabbing her finger at me. "You totally did, and you didn't tell us? Spill it."

"It doesn't mean anything. We both figured if we're going to pretend to date, we may as well reap some of the benefits." I shrug, clicking my tongue against my teeth. "It's just until we fake break up after the party."

"Oh my god." Avery's eyes widen, like a shark circling its prey. "How good was the sex? I bet it was so good. He looks like the kind of guy who would bang you into oblivion. You know?"

"Shut up." I slap her arm, but she smiles wider. The idea of telling them everything has the pressure in my chest dissipating, so I do. "We didn't have sex. I mean, it was heading there, but then a pizza arrived after he'd gotten me off. It kind of killed the vibe."

"So, he got you off, then you left right away?" Harper scrunches her eyebrows.

"Well, no. We ate some pizza and watched the Brazil game. Then I left." They exchange a look.

"He didn't get any *benefits* for himself? He got you off and gave you pizza. You watched soccer, then you left. He didn't even ask if you'd help him out?"

"No," I admit sheepishly. I felt a little bad about my lack of reciprocation, but tonight, I had planned to more than make up for it.

"He's down so bad." Harper laughs in delight, looking toward the ice to search for him.

"No," I argue quickly. "It's not like that."

We're both looking for a little fun. No strings. Right?

Avery quirks her eyebrow. "Post orgasm pizza and couch cuddling while watching soccer sounds a little more than casual."

This. This is exactly what I'm worried about. I'm rusty with this kind of thing and too close to this to know what the hell is happening.

The fans in front of us start screaming and gathering around the glass.

"No strings, huh?" Avery smirks, gaze shifting to the chaos in front of us.

I follow her gaze, seeing Nathan, helmet under one arm, standing at the glass, looking up at me. My heart stumbles in the way that is becoming familiar but no less terrifying. He motions for me to come down.

I shake my head no, but he's persistent. He leans against the boards casually, prepared to hold up warm-ups and the game if I don't go to him. It's a shame that this arrogance is part of what makes him so damn attractive. My body moves without my permission because apparently, I can't say no to him. At least not when he looks like that.

Once I get close enough, I can see that he hasn't shaved in a couple of days, instead letting his stubble cast a shadow on his face. He mouths, *Hi,* but I can't hear him over the swarm of fans around us. They've given us some space, but still form a tight semi-circle behind me.

My eyes shoot daggers at him, though I smile to keep up the act for anyone watching. And they are all watching. Instead of backing off, he smiles wider, acting innocent.

My skin is on fire with his sole attention on me mere minutes before he's expected to play three periods of elite hockey. He holds up a puck, tossing it up and over the glass. I catch it, pushing it into my pocket, without looking at it, desperate to get out of the public eye. The cameras have zoomed in on us, putting us on the big screens above the ice.

I tilt my head to where his team is gliding to the bench, and he reluctantly skates backwards following them. He watches me the entire way across the ice, smirking. His eyes burn with a promise of later. My heart is beating uncontrollably.

No, I won't be canceling on him at all.

When I get back to my seat, I pull the puck out and see a slip of paper taped to it. His messy handwriting is scribbled across it.

I've been waiting all day to see you.

I flip it over.

And even longer to get my hands on you.

I suck in a breath as heat crawls up my spine. He shouldn't be saying things like this. And I shouldn't be counting down the minutes until the game is over. But if I'm honest, I can't wait to see him either. Two weeks is a long time for me to sit with my own thoughts about what we're doing.

I like spending time with him.

I don't know if that's a good thing. Or the worst thing.

I tuck the paper back into my pocket, ignoring the questioning glances from my friends, and focus on the ice.

I'm the one in too deep, and I'm not sure how to get back out.

25

Nathan

The game is a blur of white ice and red Chicago jerseys. Even as the scoreboard glows 3-0 above center ice, no one is playing like the job is finished. Every player still has work to do, and every shift on the ice is a chance to ensure that we close this game as a shutout.

One of the three goals is mine. In the second period, Grayson slid the puck up my line. I pushed it deep, despite their defenseman trying to pin me along the boards. I rolled off the contact, my shoulder low, and slipped the puck back down the wall to Liam as he crashed the net.

His shot went wide, ricocheting hard off the end boards and popping out into chaos. I drove in, jammed my stick through the traffic, and finished it in the lower left corner before the goalie ever saw it coming.

It was my best play this season.

When it happened, I looked up without meaning to, scanning instinctively to find Wesley in the stands.

She'd been on her feet with her Blades cropped sweatshirt riding up, making me think about everything it still covered.

I should've looked away to get my head back in the game, but instead, my finger cut through the air, forming a straight line from me to her. I'd barely noticed the crowd exploding around her, or my teammates crashing into me, smacking my helmet.

There are always people in the stands cheering for my performance on the ice as Nathan Wilder, but it's different with her here. Wesley is just cheering for me. Nathan. I know better than to get used to it, but I'm reveling in it for the night.

Now late in the third, Chicago is desperate. You can feel it in the way their sticks start lingering a second too long. Their shoulders lean into contact that rides the line between aggressive and stupid.

My lungs burn as I hop the boards for another shift. The building is loud as the ice hums beneath my skates, the crowd feeding off every clean breakout and blocked shot. The Blades are rolling, lines tight, passes crisp, and legs fresh. We're playing like a team that has a chance at something bigger this season. It helps that I'm actually contributing on the ice.

I circle back through the neutral zone, staying wide on the left, reading the play as it develops. This position still feels new sometimes, like wearing someone else's gloves.

Tonight, though, it feels easy.

Things are getting uglier as they start tossing out late hits. One of their defensemen slams into me from behind.

He glances up at Wesley in the stands and smirks. "Your little girlfriend looks good cheering for you. I bet she'd be really good for me."

Something sharp and hot snaps in my chest.

The whistle hasn't blown yet. The puck is still live, but I don't fucking care. I drop my shoulder and drive him into the boards hard enough to rattle the glass. The impact thunders through my arms and skates.

He crumples, sliding down the wall with a grunt.

The ref's arm goes up, but it's worth it.

As I skate to the penalty box, he smirks at me, trying to play it off. "Touchy," he says.

I meet his eyes through the glass. "Keep your eyes off my fucking girlfriend."

I spend my time in the sin bin, ignoring the jealousy coursing through me at the idea of anyone other than me eyeing up Wesley. She is gorgeous. Anyone with eyes notices, but I still didn't like his tone.

Fuck.

I have no right to feel this way.

Luckily, we're still leading when my time is up, Chicago failing to capitalize on my penalty.

The ice opens up in front of me right as the puck hits my stick. The crowd rises, and a familiar surge of adrenaline floods my veins. I angle in, pulling the puck out of reach of the trailing defender.

The goalie squares up, trying to read me, but he's slow.

The puck hits the back of the net with a sound I'll never get tired of.

4-0.

I don't point this time, but I do look for her. She's laughing, her head tilted back and eyes bright as Harper says something to her. Even in the midst of her conversation, her eyes lock on mine as if she felt me watching her.

Something settles in my chest that has nothing to do with the score.

Our coach taps shoulders with three minutes left, sending the third line and fourth line over the boards, letting the younger guys soak it in.

I lean forward on the bench, elbows on my knees, as sweat cools on my neck. The noise of the game fades enough for me to notice my breathing, the ache in my thighs, and the way my heart is still racing even though I'm done for the night.

Coach Rylan stops behind me, his voice low so only I can hear him.

"See me after."

My chest feels too tight for a normal breath.

I nod, pretending it's nothing, but my thoughts spiral immediately. Is it about the game? The position? The contract? I replay the last few weeks in my head. It's been good. I've been good.

Better than I was a month ago.

The final horn sounds, and the crowd gives us a standing ovation. We line up for the handshake we don't really want as Chicago players skate past with tight jaws and forced nods.

In the tunnel, it's quieter. The adrenaline starts to ebb, replaced by a post-game buzz that makes everything feel a little exciting. As we peel off gear in the locker room, guys are still chirping, replaying goals and hits.

"Two tonight," Liam says, clapping me on the back. "You're unstoppable right now."

I shrug, but I can't wipe the smile off my face. My phone buzzes in my locker, probably my sister, considering she's the only one who watches my games. Except for Wesley, she watches too, now. Somehow, without even trying, she is working her way onto the list of people where that kind of thing matters.

Coach catches my eye from across the room and jerks his head toward his office.

Here we go.

I grab my towel and head for the door, ready for whatever comes next.

I knock once before stepping into his office, closing the door behind me. It smells like stale coffee and dry-erase markers, the same as it always does. It's the same cramped space where careers get nudged forward or quietly stalled. He's already sitting, his glasses low on his nose, and his tablet open on the desk.

"Sit," he orders.

I do, towel draped around my neck, catching the sweat still dripping from my hair. He studies me for a moment, the way he does when he's deciding how much to say and how much to hold back.

"Hell of a night," he starts. "You were everywhere. Smart reads and strong on the wall. You look comfortable on the left."

"Thanks, Coach."

He nods, then taps the tablet with his finger. "I talked to the front office this afternoon and again during the second intermission."

My pulse jumps.

"They're happy," he continues. "Very happy. Your improvements are obvious, but it's more than that. You're driving the plays and elevating every teammate on your line. The switch is working."

"That's good to hear." Relief douses the nervous flames that were burning in my chest.

"It is." He leans back in his chair. "Nothing is signed yet, so don't get ahead of yourself, but if you keep this up, you're putting yourself in a very strong position."

I nod slowly, absorbing it, letting myself feel the weight of his words. All the phrases my agent has been dancing around are confirmed by someone who actually has the power to sway the decision.

Then Coach sighs, and I know there's more.

"There is something else," he says.

Of course there is.

He folds his hands together on the desk. "I'm going to be straight with you. I noticed the timing of this turnaround."

I stay quiet.

"You were pressing earlier in the season. Then suddenly, things click. Your excitement on the ice is back. And at the same time, you show up to a couple of events with a girlfriend."

Something inside me sinks, and I shift in my seat. This is not something I want to be discussing with him.

"I don't love that," he says bluntly. "Historically, when guys in your position start dating seriously, it's a distraction. Especially when contracts are on the line."

"I hear you," I say, even though my jaw tightens.

Had he seen me toss the puck to her during warm-ups? It had been a spur-of-the-moment decision. I saw her in the stands and couldn't wait until after the game to talk to her. It seemed harmless at the time, but if they're worried about me getting distracted, it's not a great look.

"I'm not saying she's a problem," he adds. "I'm saying perception matters. And so does focus."

He looks at me hard now. "If you keep playing like this, your contract should take care of itself. But if that relationship starts affecting your game, or if it ends and you spiral, that's on you. The office won't be patient."

The words sit heavy in the room.

"Understood," I say.

"Good." He softens slightly. "You're playing the best hockey you've played in years. Don't lose sight of what matters."

I stand, nod once more, and leave before I say something I'll regret, like how Wesley is absolutely none of his business. She's not the office's business either. For the hundredth time today, I'm reminded how watched I am at all times. Exhaustion settles heavily onto my shoulders.

The locker room feels different now. It's quieter, even with the guys still changing and joking. The echo of the game fades into routine. I sit back down at my stall, staring at my skates without really seeing them.

Either everyone thinks Wesley is a distraction, or they think she's the only reason I'm playing well.

I hate both of those theories.

Sure, I started training with her because I thought mixing up my exercises would bring some excitement back into things, but that can't be the only reason I'm performing better. Can it?

The thought worms its way in anyway, unwelcome and persistent.

My head feels clearer when she's around, whether we're doing ladder drills, ice skating in a dim rink, or eating pizza on my couch. It's nice when there's someone waiting for me outside of this place besides my empty apartment.

Is that because of Wesley, or my own self-doubt and loneliness? Do I really feel anything for her, or is my excitement for hockey blurring lines that are too crossed to decipher?

Silent curses ring out in my head, directed at my coach for planting seeds of doubt that I don't want to face.

I think about her in the stands, about the way she looked when I scored, the way she ranted about soccer on my couch as if it mattered more than anything. The way she pushes me, challenges me, and has no expectations.

It doesn't feel fake when she laughs with me. It doesn't feel like a distraction when I'm thinking about her between shifts. If anything, it feels grounding.

And yet.

This will end. She's made it abundantly clear. Even if she hadn't, whatever this is doesn't align with either of our lives.

I finish changing slowly, thoughts looping and doubts creeping in where confidence used to sit. I remind myself that I've worked for this. I earned this position through decades of effort. No one can take credit for my performance other than me.

Still, the questions linger.

I grab my bag and head toward the exit. The warm air of the hallway hits me as soon as the door swings open. Players gather around with their families. Normally, I rush through this space, knowing that my family is at home thirty minutes away and not here. Never here.

This time, my eyes scan the area until I find her.

Wesley is leaning against the wall in her painted-on jeans with her hair cascading down past her shoulders. She looks up when she sees me, nerves flickering across her face before she smiles.

All of my doubts go quiet.

For a moment, everything steadies. The contract. The game. The future. It's all out of my control. I performed on the ice tonight. That's what counts. Well, that and that she's here, waiting for me.

Whether that's good for my hockey game or not is something I can't quite bring myself to care about, not when she's walking toward me.

26

Wesley

I'll never admit it out loud, but going out with Nathan's team is fun. The Blue Line is loud with everyone celebrating the Blades' win. Too many bodies are packed together, and the undercurrent of adrenaline hasn't burned off yet.

The whole team is still buzzing from the shutout, and it shows. Jerseys have been traded for button-downs and hoodies, but it's still obvious who the players are.

Nathan's teammates have taken over two couches and a standing table near the back, beer bottles lining the edge like trophies. Someone is replaying highlights on a phone. Someone else is shouting about missed calls that don't even matter because they won.

I'm wedged between Nathan and Avery on one of the couches. Harpers perched on the armrest, typing away on her phone, annoyance etched into every inch of her body.

Liam is sucking face with a girl I've never seen before on the couch across from us, her legs draped over his lap like she's claimed territory. He hasn't come up for air in ten minutes.

"Jesus," Avery mutters. "Does he even know her name?"

Harper doesn't look up from her phone. "Bold of you to assume he cares."

"That's just Liam," Nathan says, as if that sums everything up.

It's no wonder Nathan has earned a bit of a reputation for dating around when Liam is his best friend.

Nathan's thigh is pressed against mine. Not aggressively, but not accidentally either. Just there. Every time he shifts, I feel it. Every time I breathe, I'm aware of him.

I tell myself it's for show.

He is my fake boyfriend. We're in a public setting for a team outing, so it's all part of the arrangement.

My body does not care about logic.

Someone bumps into our table, sloshing my drink. Nathan's hand comes out automatically, steadying my glass before it tips. His fingers linger a little too long around mine.

"Careful," he whispers close to my ear.

My pulse reacts, remembering how his breath felt as it danced across every part of me, only two weeks ago. Would we go there again tonight? Should we?

Harper sighs loudly and finally locks her phone.

Avery turns to her immediately. "Where's James?"

I widen my eyes. Avery always teeters the line between straight to the point and flat-out rude, but this time, she's asking the same thing I've been wondering.

Harper shrugs, a little too quickly. "Home. Busy."

"Busy doing what?" Avery presses.

Harper lifts her drink and finishes it in one long pull. "Being tired."

I catch Avery's eye to confirm that she's as worried as I am. James has never been our cup of tea, but he's never been this MIA either. They've only been married for seven months, but Harper doesn't seem as happy as she should be.

Nathan's hand slides from my shoulder to my knee, and though I'm wearing jeans, the contact is distracting. I resist the urge to lean into it.

"Hey," I say, turning toward Harper, forcing a topic change. "How's school going?"

Harper takes the bait, launching into a hilarious story about the kids in her class. The mood lightens again instantly.

Time stretches. Drinks appear and disappear. Someone puts money into the jukebox, and something loud and nostalgic starts playing through the speakers. Liam and his mystery blonde stumble toward the dance floor. Others start crowding it, too.

Nathan doesn't leave my side.

Every time I stand to grab another drink, he stands with me. When someone tries to squeeze past, his hand finds my waist. When a guy from another table glances my way a little too long, Nathan shifts closer, shoulder brushing mine, his presence unmistakable.

It feels like foreplay disguised as optics.

I'm very aware of it. Of him.

Becca and Haley show up halfway through the night in Blades gear, their cheeks flushed from the cold.

"Wes!" Becca squeals, throwing her arms around me. "We saw you on the screen!"

Haley grins. "You're basically famous now."

I laugh, a little breathless. "Trust me, I'm not."

I've never really spent time with either of them until the past month, but I regret not having done it sooner. They're nice and fun. It's exactly what Coach Bennett was trying to get me to understand when she pointed out how my isolation hurts the team.

Grayson slides into the empty space Harper left when she went to the bathroom, flashing what I'm sure he thinks is a charming smile at Avery.

"So," he says. "You come here often?"

Avery glances up, grabs her coat, and mumbles, "Nope." Then she breezes past him and out the front door.

Grayson watches her go, then exhales.

"Don't take it personally," I say.

"Well, in that case…" Grayson stands and trails after her.

I shake my head. That's not what I meant. Avery won't change her mind no matter how much Grayson pesters her.

"Does he stand a chance?" Nathan asks, thumb stroking circles on my waist

"Not a chance in hell." I find myself leaning in. "She dated a hockey player before. Damon Woods. He plays for New York."

"That guy is an asshole."

"Yeah, which is why she's not interested in anyone from that world."

"What about you?" He leans in, smirking.

"I'm not interested in anything with anyone." The words stick in my throat, and his grin widens.

The group starts to fracture after that. People peel off in twos and threes. Wyatt pulls an Irish goodbye around the same time we watch Liam take off with a redhead that looks nothing like the blonde he started the night with. My teammates have all scattered, too, leaving us alone on the couch.

"You want to get out of here?" Nathan finishes off his beer.

The relief is immediate. "Yes."

We grab our coats quietly, slipping out without announcements. The cold hits hard when we step outside, the noise of the bar muffled behind us.

I shove my hands into my pockets. "I can walk home from here."

Nathan raises an eyebrow. "Then I'll walk with you."

"You don't have to."

"I want to."

He leaves his car where it is. I know immediately that I'll be inviting him inside. My skin prickles with anticipation.

We start down the street together, our steps syncing effortlessly. Our shoulders brush. His hand keeps finding mine, then letting go, then finding it again.

"This is still fake," I say lightly. A reminder for us both.

"Of course," he says. "Keeping up appearances."

I laugh. "For who?"

He glances at me, eyes teasing and warm. "Anyone who might be watching."

Finally, when his hand finds mine, he keeps it there. The warmth of his palm presses against my own. I should pull away. There are no cameras or teammates. We have no reason to keep up the act.

But we do.

My pulse starts to skitter, anxiety tapping at the edges of my chest. I focus on the cold air in my lungs, the sound of our footsteps on the sidewalk, and anything else that will keep me grounded.

"Your game was insane tonight." I tap my free hand against my jeans. "Chicago had nothing on you guys."

He chuckles softly. "They got scrappy there at the end."

"Scrappy is generous. And then you slammed that guy so hard, he's probably still seeing two of you."

Nathan glances sideways at me. "Worth the penalty."

I shake my head, smiling despite myself. "Two goals. You looked unstoppable."

There's a pause before he speaks again, like he's deciding something. "Coach Rylan pulled me into his office after."

My heart jumps. "And?"

"Good things," he says. "Nothing official yet, but positive. The front office is happy. He said if I keep playing like this, I'm in a strong spot."

"What?" I turn toward him, excitement bursting through my chest before I can stop it. "Nathan, that's huge." He stops too, surprise flickering across his face as I launch into his arms without thinking. "That's everything you've been working for."

His ears go a little pink. "Yeah. I guess it is."

"I'm proud of you," I say, without hesitation.

My words hang between us, his face a flurry of emotions before settling on something heavier than I expect.

He ducks his head. "Thanks."

We start walking again, hands still linked and our bodies closer than before.

"I appreciate you coming tonight," he adds after a moment. "Would've been even better if you wore my jersey."

I laugh. "Absolutely not. I won't feed into that misogyny."

He raises an eyebrow. "Harsh."

"No, think about it," I insist. "You don't see guys wearing their girlfriends' names. No one's walking around with 'Wesley Miller' stitched across their shoulders."

He hums thoughtfully.

The conversation drifts, the way it does when you're distracting yourself from the elephant in the room. Our elephant is the sexual tension that seems to be burning my lungs the closer we get to my apartment.

"Your family wasn't here tonight." I've been wanting to ask about them more and more lately, always chickening out. Something about the night makes me brave enough to press. "Do they come to games much?"

"No," he admits. "They're local, but they've never been to a game. Hockey isn't their thing."

My brows furrow. My dad would love to be close enough to come to my games regularly. Even if he hated the sport, he'd be there to support me. It's what parents should do.

"My sister, Delaney, comes occasionally, though," he continues, a smile creeping in. "She's in college. When she's in the stands, she's the loudest person in the building. You'd like her."

"You say that like I'm meeting her."

"I mean," he shrugs. "You probably will. At some point."

That feels like crossing a line into something more real than we've agreed on. There are only a few more weeks until we stage our fake breakup and move on.

"And your family?" he asks. "You must be close if you go back home often."

"Yeah. My dad and sister are both really important to me."

"What about your mom?" he asks, not realizing the landmines he detonated.

"She's dead." I chew on my lip.

He doesn't flinch or rush to fill the silence, instead squeezing my hand gently.

"That sucks. That kind of loss doesn't go away."

Something in my chest loosens at the way he says it. There's no pity in his words. No apology or promise that it gets better. Just understanding.

"It's been a long time since it happened, but my family really relies on me to be the glue that she was."

I'm not sure I've ever said those thoughts out loud. I know Avery and Harper have an idea, but that's after years of bits and pieces.

"That's a lot of pressure on you."

I swallow, nodding. "Yeah. Sometimes it feels like if I stop moving, everything will fall apart."

His thumb brushes over my knuckles. "You're allowed to be more than just the glue. Even the people who sacrifice the most sometimes have to pick themselves."

"I don't really have that choice."

He studies me for a second, like he's trying to decide something. "Or you just don't let yourself."

My breath catches.

"I'm serious," he says, softer now. "Why shouldn't you want something for yourself?"

"Taking risks is a luxury. Wanting things is a luxury. I won't let the people I love down over things like that."

"But what about you? When do you get what you want?"

I don't answer. I can't. I wouldn't even know where to begin. Just thinking about it almost undoes me, but I focus on the sidewalk until the tears that I refuse to let fall go back to wherever the hell they tried to escape from.

We shouldn't be talking like this. We should be keeping things light. Yet, somehow, I always find myself opening up to him. I know better, but it happens again and again anyway.

Nathan doesn't acknowledge it, instead keeping his hand firm in mine, grounding me back to the night.

By the time we reach my building, the silence has washed away the existential crisis in my head. Now, my head spins for new reasons.

I've never had a guy in my place. I've never wanted to.

As if sensing my hesitation, Nathan speaks up, "Did you get my note?"

I smile, warmth blooming low in my stomach, squashing my uncertainty entirely. "Yeah."

"And?"

I pull him up the stairs behind me, unlocking my door and stepping inside.

I meet his eyes. "Come in."

27

Wesley

The door clicks shut behind us, the sound louder than it should be in the quiet of my apartment. For a second, I stand there, keys still in my hand, hyperaware of the scuffed hardwood and the homemade throw blanket folded over the arm of the couch.

Nathan doesn't say anything. Instead, he moves slowly through the space while his eyes take everything in.

My apartment is clean, but not polished. The couch is a hand-me-down with cushions soft from years of love. The bookshelf is crammed with a mix of textbooks, old mail, and paperbacks with cracked spines. It's cluttered, but it's my clutter.

I've never brought a guy here before.

He stops in front of the framed photos lining the wall of the hall. His shoulders shift as he leans in, close enough that I can see the way his eyes track across the frames. They pause on a shot from my first professional game. My jersey was too big, and my hair was cropped short. It feels like a lifetime ago.

"This is not like your place." I try to get ahead of whatever he might be thinking.

He doesn't answer, instead reaching out to brush his fingers along the edge of the frame.

"I like it," he says quietly.

The knot I didn't know I was bracing against eases.

When he turns, the shift is immediate. The warmth in his expression darkens, his gaze dragging slowly from my eyes to my mouth.

He crosses the distance in two steps.

His hands come up to my face, thumbs brushing my jaw as his mouth crashes into mine.

The kiss is all urgency and heat, drowning out the noise in my head. I make a soft sound before I can stop myself, fingers curling into the front of his jacket as I melt into him.

When he finally pulls back, just enough for us both to breathe, his forehead rests against mine. My pulse is racing, but my concerns are blissfully silent.

"I thought your place would be more impersonal," he murmurs.

I pull back to look at him. "Impersonal how?"

He shrugs slightly. "Cleaner lines. Less history on the walls."

I shift to step back, but he moves with me.

"Why would you think that?"

"Because you're really good at taking care of everyone else and even better at keeping your own stuff locked down."

My fingers slide up to rest against his chest. "You make it sound like you've got me all figured out."

"Not quite."

I tilt my head, brushing my nose against his. "I'm not that predictable."

His lips curve. "No, but I'll still figure you out eventually."

"It's good to have goals," I nip at his lip. "Even when they're unattainable."

"C'mon, Wesley, it's just us here. Let me in."

"I don't know what you're talking about."

I don't understand why I feel so comfortable with him. So seen. But, I'm not sure I want to create boundaries tonight. I don't have it in me.

"Be selfish. Lose a little of that quiet control. Let yourself want something. Anything. Just for tonight." His breath is hot against my lips.

The air feels heavy with possibility.

"Tonight," I say softly, "I want you."

His jaw tightens, something predatory flickering there, but I still take my time leading him down the hall. The light from the living room fades as we go, replaced by softer shadows.

Nathan pauses inside my bedroom, turning to look at me like he is giving me one last chance to change my mind.

I step closer instead.

The door barely finishes closing before he's on me, hand framing my face as his kiss steals my breath.

The sound I make is surprised and hungry all at once, and he takes it as encouragement. His grip tightens, fingers sliding into my hair as he backs me toward the bed, kissing me like he's been holding back all night. Whatever patience he had has burned off.

There is something surreal about him wanting me, even if it's only for tonight or a couple of weeks. A man like Nathan Wilder wanting me so wholeheartedly is not something I ever expected. Not because he's a famous hockey player, but because of who he is.

He's sexy and carries himself with a kind of confidence I can only fake. He's kind and generous, despite what the media might say. He's everything I've never let myself have.

I fall onto the mattress with a soft bounce, and he follows immediately, weight settling between my legs. His mouth gets more desperate as if he's trying to devour me before I change my mind.

No part of me wants to stop this. I want this. With him.

My hands are everywhere as I tug off his shirt, scraping my fingers down his back. His abs look like they are carved from stone, and I think I audibly whimper.

No man should look this good. His body is toned perfection earned through years of dedicated focus, which makes it even sexier.

Every time he shifts against my body, heat pulses low in my belly.

"Fuck Wesley," he breathes against my mouth, the words torn out of him. "I've been waiting for two weeks to have you under me again."

I hook a leg around his hip, dragging him in, and the sound he makes this time is rougher. His mouth moves to my neck, sucking like he wants to mark the moment into my skin. My head tilts back, letting him.

Every shift of his weight and every brush of his hands makes my body chase more. He grinds into me, and I can feel how hard he is against my thigh.

"Last time, we were cut short." I almost don't recognize the breathy sound that slips out as I continue grinding against him.

"The worst interruption of my life," he teases, his mouth brushing against my ear before nipping at it.

My hands roam over his chest. "Poor pizza delivery guy got an earful."

His eyes darken. "I hope he enjoyed it while he could, because now, I'm the only one who gets to hear you moan like that, Wes."

I should point out that that's not the deal, but dammit if possessive Nathan doesn't have my mouth dry and my panties wet.

He shifts, pressing his cock against my pussy, and even with the layers of material between us, I can feel how big he is.

Tonight, there won't be anything stopping me from exploring that particular part of his body.

My shirt and bra are yanked off without ceremony, just hands and urgency. The bed creaks beneath us as he crowds me back into the mattress, his gaze heady as he takes in my body. His eyes take their time scanning from my face down to my chest, reaching out to graze his hands across my breasts. By the time he looks back up, his pupils are blown wide.

Leaning back in, his mouth trails down my chest, closing around my nipple. His tongue swirls around the peak while his hand toys with the other. My breath is sharp as my body arches off the mattress. He smirks against my skin.

There's something attractive and daunting about how he moves as if he knows exactly what he wants from me. It's like he's more in tune with my body than I am, meeting every desperate sigh and plea before they fall off my lips.

I meet him with the same hunger, nails biting into his shoulders so hard they'll leave marks.

My hand trails down his back before reaching around to palm his cock through his jeans, forcing a groan from deep in his chest. The sound spurs me on, so I do it again and again, until he looks up at me, eyes pleading.

"Don't make me come yet, baby, not before I've been inside you." His voice is a whisper against my skin, causing goosebumps to form.

It's an enticing idea, making Nathan Wilder come in his pants with only my hand, but it'll have to wait.

Everything on his face says he wants me to keep touching him, but he pulls himself out of my grasp and slides down my body, tugging my jeans and panties down with him.

"Then get inside me." It's practically begging, but I can't bring myself to care.

I'm aching for him.

I squirm under his hands as he finishes stripping me. My thighs squeeze together, but he uses one hand to push them open. When he glides a finger across my slit, I can hear how wet I already am for him. His eyes watch me carefully as he sucks my clit into his mouth, groaning as he grinds himself against my bed.

I've never been into foreplay. Before Nathan, I would've said it was wasted time before the good stuff. But watching him toy with my clit while he grinds himself into my bed is the sexiest thing I've ever seen. There is nothing about this that's wasted time. All I can do is picture how good it'll feel when he's thrusting into me instead of against my sheets.

He licks directly up my slit, breathing a sigh of relief. "I've been dying to taste you for weeks."

"Nathan," I beg when he licks me slower.

He pulls away, a smile breaking across his face, "Say my name again."

I glare down at him, hips raising to seek him out. My body knows how much pleasure he could give me if he'd only lean back in.

Instead, he gently blows across my clit, teasing me mercilessly. "Say it again."

Wesley Miller, the one in control, would argue. She'd be annoyed and frustrated by his teasing. Whoever the hell I am right now doesn't think twice, caving to his request desperately.

"Nathan, please." My voice doesn't sound like my own; it's breathy and shaky.

"Please what?"

He blows again.

"Please make me come."

"That's my good girl." He traces me with his tongue, slowly. "I'll make sure you come, Wes. Just let me enjoy myself a little first."

Nathan calling me his girl sets off alarm bells, but they disappear entirely when he sucks my clit into his mouth again, bringing me dangerously close to the edge. He slides not one, but two fingers into me, and I'm half delirious chasing the orgasm that feels just out of reach.

My hands find the way to the back of his head, tangling in his hair while he takes his time tasting me.

"You take my fingers even better than I remember, baby." His voice is gravelly as he watches his fingers move in and out of me. "I can't wait to see you take every inch of my cock."

He places a sloppy kiss against my thigh, then dives back in, tongue flicking across me at the right time. I cry out his name as the orgasm crests, my body tightening around his fingers in pulsing waves that steal the air from my lungs.

He slows his pace, working me through it, until I've experienced every ounce of pleasure. Then, he sits up and slides away from me. The cold air chills me instantly without his body heat against me.

It's not enough. I need more. I'm entirely too close to begging for it when I realize what he's doing.

Thank god he's on the same page. At the edge of the bed, he slowly slides his pants and boxers down while keeping his eyes on me. His cock springs free, and my pussy clenches with anticipation.

He's bigger than the toys that I've considered good enough for years. Hell, he's bigger than the guys before that, too.

Nerves skitter across my skin. He might know exactly what he's doing, but it's been so long for me. He plays in sold-out arenas. Women with perfect hair and curated lives probably throw themselves at him every day. And here he is, in my too-small bedroom, wanting me.

His eyes soften as if reading the anxiety on my face. Climbing back onto the bed, he turns onto his side to face me.

"Where'd you go just now?" His fingers trace my arm as if unable to resist having physical contact with me.

"Nowhere."

"I'm not going to fuck you when you're lying to me." He smirks when my cheeks flush. "So, do us both a favor and stop lying because I really, really want to fuck you tonight."

"I just," I trail off, the blush on my cheeks turning a darker shade of red. "It's been a while. And I know it hasn't been for you. Which is totally fine. But you're also really big." I look away. "I'm not sure."

"Look at me, baby," He holds my chin between his pointer finger and thumb, raising my face until I'm eye level with him. "If you don't want to do anything, we don't have to. There's no expectation here."

I cringe, hating everything about that option.

"But, if you're nervous because you think it won't be good for me. Or you. Then I need you to trust me. I haven't wanted anyone like I want you. It's going to be good for me."

He raises his eyebrows, flashing his arrogant smile. "And if you're worried about my size. I've already felt how wet you are. You're going to take me so fucking perfectly."

My thighs clench together. Nathan might not be the playboy that the tabloids paint him out to be, but he has the dirtiest mouth I've ever heard. It is unbelievably hot.

I lean forward, giving him a quick kiss as my answer. "Condom?"

He holds one up in his hand that he must've gotten before ever climbing up here to talk me out of my head. "Wishful thinking."

I laugh, but it's cut off by a kiss that's messy and urgent. The kind of heat that doesn't linger in the head but burns straight through the body. The condom package crinkles as he tears it open, his hands sliding it onto his length. I'm too lost in his mouth on my neck to focus on it.

"Ready?" His breath is hot on my ear.

I nod quickly, my arms sliding around to his back and digging into his skin as he slides into me.

It's deliciously slow, every inch stretching me and teetering the line of pleasure and pain. Once he's in, he slides out slowly and thrusts back in all at once.

I cry out as my body adjusts to the size of him.

He freezes. "Shit, are you okay?"

I wrap my legs around him, pulling him closer. "I'm so fucking okay." My hips move in a silent plea for him to keep going.

His hand loops behind my head, pulling me up until our eyes meet. He moves at a perfect rhythm, controlling the pace until I'm desperate. Our eyes stay on each other in a way that feels too intimate for what we've agreed to be.

When he leans in and kisses me, it's fast and filled with passion. Our mouths move in the same rhythm as our bodies, bringing us to the brink.

The bed rocks beneath us, the room filling with the wrecked sounds we cannot seem to stop making. His voice is in my ear, murmuring about how good I feel and how perfect I am, and that alone is almost enough to send me spiraling out.

When he finally reaches in and brushes circles across my clit, the tension snaps, sharp and overwhelming. I cling to him as my orgasm erupts through my body. He doesn't slow his pace, thrusting into me steadily while I ride it out.

"God, Wesley. You look so pretty when you come around my cock." He groans while following right behind me, his cock pulsing inside me as he comes.

"You don't look half bad either," I tease, placing a quick kiss against his lips before he buries his face in my hair.

My body feels deliciously wrecked, and my muscles are completely weightless.

He doesn't move right away, even though he should. I don't push him off me, even though I should. We're both breathing hard, our limbs still tangled around each other.

How the fuck did I go four years without that?

Nevermind. I know how.

Sex has never been like that, even when I was regularly having it. If it had been half that good, I would have never sworn it off in the first place.

Finally, he rolls off me, sliding the condom off, tying it, and tossing it into the trash. For a minute, neither of us says anything.

"So that was—" I start.

"Amazing." He finishes, eyes glinting.

I fail to fight the smile off my face. "Yeah, it really was."

It was amazing. But as reality sets in and the sated, sex-happy trance wears off, I remember what this is. A sex fling that will be over after my team party in January.

I will not confuse chemistry with commitment.

This is sex. Ground-breaking, earth-shaking, ruin-me-for-anyone-else sex. But it's still only sex.

My head starts to methodically build back up the boundaries that I'm usually careful to keep between us.

"Do you want to watch a movie?" He asks, there's something hopeful about his expression that has me shutting down.

He's probably had arrangements like this on and off for years, mastering the art of sliding from sex to small talk without letting it mean anything.

I'm not sure I can. I don't know how to go from this to hanging out in my living room without feeling things. Things we've both agreed to check at the door.

"You should probably go." I stand up, sliding on an oversized shirt.

For a second, disappointment flashes across his face, but he masks it quickly. This is why we shouldn't have done this. It's already too complicated.

"Yeah," He pulls on his clothes quickly, but I'm already heading for the hall. "That's probably for the best."

"Benefits, right. No strings." My words are clipped. "We shouldn't let the line get too blurry."

"Absolutely." He smiles, but it doesn't reach his eyes.

My chest tightens painfully, but I smile through it. I don't break for things like this. I don't break at all.

"See you Tuesday for training?" I ask, holding the front door open. I can't quite meet his gaze.

"Sounds good." He pauses as if to say something else, but nods his head instead, walking down my steps.

I walk back inside and look around. My apartment has always felt homey. Just me in the warmth and comfort I've created. I've never minded having this space all to myself.

But as I watch him walk down the sidewalk from the window, the space feels a bit empty.

28

Nathan

Lunch with my agent, Ryan Elliott, is supposed to be routine. It's something that happens every few weeks, whether I need it or not. A standing appointment disguised as a meal. We always go to the same downtown spot with exposed brick and too much natural light. We sit at the same corner table where the noise dulls, giving the illusion of privacy while we have the same conversation that always starts with small talk and ends with business.

Ryan is mid-sentence, hands moving as he talks, fork abandoned on the edge of his plate as if his food is an afterthought compared to this discussion.

"Eight wins out of the last ten," he says, checking his phone. "Second in the conference and first in the division. Nobody had you guys pegged for this back in October, but here we are. Everything is finally clicking, the defensive pairings are solid, and the fans are eating it up."

I nod along, mechanically, lifting my fork and lowering it again without actually taking a bite. He's right. The season is good. Better than good. The wins are stacking, the city is buzzing again, and for the first time in a long time, it feels like we're building something instead of surviving week to week.

I should feel lighter.

Instead, my brain keeps dragging me backward to an apartment that smelled faintly of laundry detergent and coffee, to her familiar clutter, and to the moment her walls slipped back into place as she shut the door behind me.

You should probably go.

She wasn't angry or dramatic. It was less emotional than that, just painfully careful. My stomach's been in knots for the past two days, wondering if she regretted it.

I'd walked back to my car afterward, hands shoved into my jacket pockets while the cold did nothing to clear my head. No matter how many times I replayed the night, I couldn't quite figure out where it all went sideways.

It was the best sex of my life. No hesitation or competition.

That thought alone should scare me more than it does. I'm starting to accept that she does it for me in a way no one else has.

But she sets the rules and boundaries, and I'm expected to follow them. I understand why, it's just really starting to piss me off. That woman has gotten under my skin and planted roots, but she won't even let me scratch the surface.

Now it's Monday. Tomorrow I'll see her again for our workout under fluorescent lights and professional expectations. Somehow, I'm supposed to pretend like nothing has shifted when everything has. I have no idea how to look at her. No idea how to speak to her without crossing the lines she drew for a reason.

Ryan clears his throat.

"Nathan."

I blink, realizing I haven't processed a single word he's said in at least a minute. "Sorry," I say. "What?"

He studies me for a moment, sharp eyes narrowing slightly. "You good?"

"Just tired," I say automatically, even though exhaustion has nothing to do with it.

He lets it pass, but his tone changes, becoming more professional. The real conversation is starting.

"Here's the thing," he says, leaning back in his chair. "As good as the last couple of weeks have been, we need to stay realistic."

My shoulders tense.

His phone slides across the table with the contract notes pulled up. Numbers and bullet points stare back at me as a reminder that nothing is ever as simple as it feels in the moment.

"The front office is happy," he continues. "They like your bounce back. They like your effort, but the last few seasons still matter. It's your inconsistency they're worried about. The narrative around you doesn't disappear overnight."

I stare at the screen without really seeing it.

"You need a damn near perfect rest of the season. No stretches where you disappear. You do that, and we have leverage. You don't, and we're talking short-term deals again. Prove-it contracts."

Something sharp twists in my chest, annoyance flaring up my spine.

"Of course. I'm only worth something if I'm flawless."

It always comes down to this. I'm a caged animal that can be shipped off at a moment's notice. I'm only useful if they decide I am.

Ryan's eyebrows lift. "That's not what I said."

"It's what it sounds like."

The edge in my tone surprises even me. This isn't how I talk to Ryan. He's been with me since before my rookie season, through injuries, rehab, and late-night doubts I barely admit to myself. He's never sugarcoated things, but he has always been on my side.

He exhales slowly, sliding his phone back into his pocket. "Hey. What's going on with you?"

The answer piles up all at once. The contract. The future. The woman I cannot stop thinking about, who made it very clear she doesn't want complications, even as she let me into her bed.

Everything feels out of my control. My career. Whatever is happening with Wesley.

It feels like I'm walking a tightrope with no net, aware that one misstep could send everything crashing down, while someone unseen waits below with a blade, ready to cut the line to see what happens.

"I'm sorry," I say quickly, forcing myself to breathe. "That was out of line."

Ryan watches me for a beat longer, then nods. "Yeah. It was. And that's not like you."

"I know."

"I'm not trying to scare you," he says more gently. "I'm telling you this so you understand the stakes. You're playing great. Keep doing that. Control what you can control."

Control.

The word sticks with me long after lunch ends, mostly because it's starting to feel like I have none.

The city noise hums around me as I head straight to the rink from the restaurant.

I contemplate texting Wesley, something casual that acknowledges our night together while taking the pressure off, but I chicken out.

I don't know which version of me she wants tomorrow or if she wants me at all.

The parking lot looks gross with gas streaking through the puddles of melted snow, and piles of icy, black sludge along the edges despite the sun. I click the engine off but stay in the car. The arena looms in front of me like a concrete reminder of everything I'm supposed to be prioritizing.

Players drift in and out through the side entrance with their heads down, each of them wrapped up in their own rituals. Normally, I'd already be inside, carrying out my own routine. Today, my body feels stalled, like my brain forgot to send the signal.

My phone buzzes against my thigh, the vibration sharp in the quiet of the car. I don't look at it right away. There's a small, stupid part of me that hopes it's her, even though I know better. I'm not sure what I'd even say if it were.

I finally glance down at the screen.

My sister.

It rings once more than necessary before I answer. "You have a sixth sense, you know that?"

Delaney laughs immediately. "I do. It tingles every time you're brooding somewhere with bad lighting."

"I'm not brooding." I stare straight ahead at the concrete and glass. "I'm thinking."

"That's worse," she replies. "Thinking never goes well for you."

I shake my head, a smile tugging at my mouth despite myself. "What do you want?"

"Well," she says lightly, "I was going to ask how lunch with Ryan went, but then I opened my phone and saw that little press clip from a couple weeks ago. You know the one where you announced your girlfriend. You've been avoiding me since then, so I figured I'd start there."

My grip tightens on the phone. "It's nothing."

"Oh, that's why you've been sending me to voicemail," she teases. "Mom and Dad are hassling me for details. It was adorable for about thirty seconds, but after weeks it's become deeply annoying."

I sigh. "You can tell them you don't know anything."

"I have," she says. "That hasn't stopped them. They've upgraded from curious to invested, which means they're asking me when you're bringing her home for dinner so they can interrogate you directly."

"I'm not bringing her home." Nausea churns in my gut.

"Mmhmm," my sister hums. "You could come alone then."

"You know we don't get along," I add, the words automatic and well-worn.

There's a reason I don't go home as often as I should. A reason why dinners feel more like obligations than comfort.

"I know," she says carefully. "But at some point, you're going to have to deal with that. All of it. You can't keep circling around it forever."

I stare out the windshield, jaw tight. "This is not the time."

"When is? Because from where I'm standing, you having a girlfriend might actually help. At the very least, it'll force everyone to stop dancing around it all."

I almost tell her that it's fake and nothing more than an arrangement that ends in January. It's rules and an end date with no real future in sight, which means telling my parents about her would only serve to make things worse.

Most people assume that my parents are proud. After all, parents should want their kids to reach their dreams. And what parents wouldn't support their son playing a professional sport if they were good enough to do it and loved it enough to commit?

Well, mine.

They expected me to be married, settled with kids, and in the family business by now. As if I could ever love insurance the way I love hockey. If they knew my contract was on the ropes, they'd throw a party.

Don't get me wrong. They love me. They care about me. They just think I chose something silly to spend my life doing. This silly little game prevents me from finding true fulfillment, which for them is a family, kids, and a life without press coverage.

It's a fundamental and age-old argument that's driven the wedge so deep I'm not sure it's possible to bridge the gap. I do hate that Delaney is stuck in the middle, though.

The words sit right there, ready. Tell her it's fake.

Instead, I say, "I might've blown it."

Her tone shifts immediately. "Okay. That's different."

"She doesn't want anything serious." I struggle to explain while staying vague about the details. "She was clear about that from the start. And I agreed. But now…"

"But now you caught feelings," she finishes.

"I didn't say that."

"You didn't have to."

I rub a hand over my face. "She wants no strings. That's it."

"And can you handle that?"

I picture Wesley standing in her apartment, composed and careful, even when everything between us felt anything but. Her words had been restrained, but her eyes had been filled with emotion. In my gut, I knew she shut it down not because she didn't feel it, but because she felt too much.

"If I want her at all, I have to," I say finally. "That's all she wants."

There's a beat of silence.

"Then take it," my sister says. "But don't ask for more than that. Let her come to you if she's going to."

"And if she doesn't?" An ache tugs at my chest.

"Then you find someone who wants you more than they want anything else," she says. "You deserve that. You can find that."

I'm not so sure I can, but I don't say that. Every single person I've dated always wants something more than me. My money. My fame. Hell, most people in my life always want something more than just me, too.

Even Wesley wanted nothing to do with me until she needed help. It makes my feelings for her more pathetic. I run my hand through my hair and rub the back of my neck. I need to get over this little crush. So what if she's attractive and athletic and driven? We're fooling around. I can do that without letting myself get carried away.

"I still think you should come home for the holiday," Delaney's voice rings through the phone, jolting me back to the present. "Mom's already planning something passive-aggressive, so you might as well be there to absorb it."

I huff out a laugh. "I'll think about it."

"That's not a yes."

"It's the best you're getting." Going home for Christmas sounds awful, but I can't avoid my parents forever.

"Fine," she says. "But I'm holding you to it."

We hang up a minute later. I don't move, tossing around Delaney's advice in my head.

Take whatever Wesley gives and don't ask for more.

If she wants me, she'll prove it.

It sounds so simple. Except not asking for more is getting harder, and Wesley doesn't allow herself to want anything outside of soccer.

She belongs only to herself and soccer. The problem is that even though she's made it clear she's not mine, I'm starting to think I might already be hers.

29

Wesley

By the time we hit mile one, my lungs are burning, and I'm entirely in my head. My calves ache in a familiar, almost comforting way. The burn that usually quiets my mind sharpens every thought I'm trying not to have.

We're jogging along the harbor path outside the stadium. It's cold, but warmer than it has been, thawing the last remaining frost on the ground, at least for now. The trees around us make me feel claustrophobic.

I'm running ahead of Nathan, close enough that I can feel him there without looking. Every instinct in my body is aware of his stride, his breath, and the way he matches his steps to mine. It's as if he can anticipate every step I take.

He's acting normal. He walked right in today with his usual coffee for both of us and jumped straight to business, asking for a longer jog in anticipation of the shorter endurance drills he'd be running at practice this week.

For the past three days, I've thought about how this morning would go. It would be awkward and embarrassing. There'd be a conversation to address what happened in my apartment, on my bed. We'd both chalk it up to a one-time thing, and I'd carefully step back inside the boundaries we should've stayed within in the first place.

Instead, he's all business as if nothing happened at all. It's what I wanted. At least, what I thought I wanted.

Except, after having the kind of sex that rewired something fundamental in my brain, I'm not sure it's what I want at all.

I'm confused.

At two miles in, we make the turn, crossing over the bridge that will circle us back around to the stadium. The path narrows, and his arm brushes against mine accidentally, but it makes my pulse trip anyway.

I hate that I notice. I hate that my skin burns long after he's moved in front of me. Normally, I lead, pushing us at a pace that I decide, but today, I let him stay in front. Instead, I let myself watch him, lingering on his hair that's damp with sweat and the side of his face, chiseled and covered in the kind of stubble that happens after a day or two without shaving.

I swallow, my body taking in how good he looks while remembering how perfectly our bodies fit together. It isn't the sex that scares me. It's how easily I can imagine letting it become routine, letting him take up space I've been guarding for years.

If things were different or if the timing were better, maybe I'd let that happen. But now, with where I'm at in my career, with my captaincy on the line and an invite to the Futures Camp at risk, there's no way I'll let him get that close.

My legs stretch out in front of me as if I can outrun the memory of how right it had felt to have him inside me.

You should probably go.

I'd meant it when I said it. The words had masked the panic crawling up my spine. The lines had blurred, the air shifting from something casual to something full of implications. Kicking him out had been the only move left that still felt like mine. So, I'd sent him into the cold before I could want more than I was willing to risk.

Nathan slows, matching my stride easily. "What are you doing back here?"

"It's scrimmage week," I say, keeping my eyes forward. "We have practice too, so I'm taking it easy." It was a plausible excuse, far better than saying I was checking out his ass.

Which, well, who wouldn't?

"San Francisco, right?" he asks.

"Thursday," I confirm. "They're fast and young. We didn't play them last season, so they're coming in annoyingly confident."

He laughs under his breath. "I'm sure you'll fix that."

I glance at him and immediately regret it. His expression is open and relaxed without any sign of conflict. It's as if this isn't complicated for him at all. For him, maybe it's not.

Just because the sex was earth-shattering for me doesn't mean it was anything out of the ordinary for him. He wasn't the one who'd gone over four years without sex. Surely, he had an endless list of amazing nights with beautiful women to compare me to. If I compared at all. I cut off that train of thought before it gets too self-deprecating.

"You're in New York this week?" I ask because talking about schedules is safe. Schedules don't have feelings.

"Yeah," he says. "Away game. They always have a big crowd, and they hate us. The usual."

"If you keep playing how you have been, you'll take them easily."

"My agent thinks so too." His smile drops an inch.

I'm tempted to dig in and figure out why, but that's a line I shouldn't be crossing. Instead, we fall into an easy silence, the kind that would feel comfortable if I weren't hyperaware of him. Every thought circles back to the one very specific night I have no intention of repeating.

I tell myself that again. Firmly.

We work through our standard mobility drills, both used to the routine and oddly in sync. We're taking it easy. He's in the thick of his season, and with any luck, I'll be trying out for the National Team soon. Neither of us wants to end up with an injury.

My focus is on muscle memory, precision, and the satisfaction of getting things right when everything else feels dangerously close to unraveling. I take the movements slowly, ensuring that every step is perfect. The repetitive motions bring a steady calm to my head.

I catch Nathan watching me more than once. Not openly, but curiously. My palms sweat as my mind tries to piece together what it could mean.

Probably nothing.

After our cooldown, we stretch at the end of the field, the late morning sun warming my back as I lean into the grass. I can't wait until it's warmer all the time. One nice day is not enough.

I focus on stretching every muscle in my leg, isolated and then with movement.

"Are you heading home for the holidays this weekend?" Nathan asks as we pack up, slinging his bag over his shoulder.

"Not this year." I mimic his actions. "I'm flying my family out, instead."

His eyebrows lift. "Your dad and your sister, right?"

"Yeah," I admit. "They don't make it out here often, but since I just went there, it seemed like a good time to change that."

"That's really nice." There's a soft edge to his voice, teetering between jealousy and kindness.

"Your family lives around here. Are you spending the holiday with them?" I ask.

He's never told me much about his parents, but I know he adores his sister.

His toe digs into the dirt as he nods. "Yeah. Figured I'd show my face."

The words sit between us, heavier than they should be for this conversation.

"You don't sound too excited." It's not a question, but an opportunity for him to elaborate if he wants. I know firsthand that not everything's easy to talk about.

We make our way down the tunnel to the exit, passing by groundskeepers who are heading to freshen up our paint lines before the scrimmage later this week.

"Why don't you want to go home?" I can't seem to mind my own business.

He exhales slowly, eyes flicking toward the ground before meeting mine again. "It's not that I don't want to," he says carefully. "It's just complicated."

I wait, refusing to pry the details out of him.

"They've never really been on board with this," he adds. "Hockey. The career. The whole thing. Of course, they encouraged me to play when I was a kid. Then, I ended up being really gifted. I got scouted and committed to it. They've never been able to get on board with me doing this for a living."

He shrugs. The gesture looks learned, like armor he's been wearing since he was too young to know he needed it. "It's hard to enjoy being around people who are perpetually disappointed in you."

Something twists in my chest. It sounds like a script he's practiced until it sounds like indifference instead of disappointment.

"They should be proud of the effort you put in."

My dad would never miss a game he could physically attend. My sister wears my jersey on game days, even if she can't watch. Despite the pressure to provide for them financially, we are close. Their belief in me has never wavered, and the thought of Nathan not having that is depressing.

He let out a dry laugh. "The effort I put in doesn't matter to anyone."

My heart clenches, and I find myself disliking people I've never met simply on his behalf. He's one of the most decorated NHL players of this generation. He makes small talk with the arena custodial staff. He agreed to help me save my captaincy without hesitation. Aside from the effort he puts in on the ice, which is extensive, he manages to put that same effort into caring about everything and everyone around him. How could anyone not see how amazing he is?

"I'm sorry." My words are laced with sadness. Mostly for him, but I'd be lying if I said it wasn't also for me. Because he's exactly the kind of person I'd be with if it were an option for me.

He gives a small smile. "Don't be. I'd rather run another four miles right now than go home for the holidays, but Delaney asked. I can't say no to her."

"Little sisters can be bossy." I tease, lightening the mood. "Emma is only eighteen, but she scares me."

"Ha." His eyes light up as he looks at me. "I can't picture anyone or anything scaring you."

We reach our cars and finally slow, the moment stretching thin. Our eyes stay locked on each other, and I wish things were different. This is the moment where we part cleanly, and I do the sensible thing. I have always been good at being sensible.

"A lot of things scare me, Nathan." My voice is breathy, a confession wrapped in subtlety. The corner of his mouth tilts up in a sad half-smile as if he knows exactly what I'm referring to.

"After the holiday this weekend, can we meet up Monday for training?"

My smile sharpens, even though my chest aches. The lines I've drawn simultaneously keep me from letting go with him, while tearing me in half over it. "Sounds like a plan."

We hesitate, then step apart, the spell breaking as I turn toward my car. My keys are already in my hand when I hear it.

A low, frustrated sound under his breath. My name is barely audible off his lips.

Before I can turn fully, his hand wraps around my arm, tugging me to him. I gasp as he spins me, my back hitting the side of my car. Then, his mouth is on mine.

It's hard and desperate. The metal of the car is cold through my jacket, a sharp contrast to the heat building everywhere else.

All thought evaporates.

I launch myself into him without hesitation, fingers fisting in his hair, kissing him back like I've been starving and just remembered what food tastes like. He presses closer, crowding my space, the solid heat of him grounding and unraveling me all at once.

I don't know why I ever thought I could stop touching him.

I never want to stop touching him.

My hands crawl under his sweatshirt and along his back as I grip him tighter. A soft moan escapes from somewhere deep in my throat. His hips pin me in place the same way he'd pinned me to the mattress. My thighs clench together as if remembering exactly what might come next.

Fuck, this man can kiss.

His hands are pressed against the car at the side of my head, caging me in. I'd gladly stay locked in between them forever if it meant reality didn't exist.

Instead, a car door sounds across the parking lot, snapping us back to ourselves.

My cheeks turn crimson. We were practically mauling each other in public. He pulls back. Our breath comes hard, foreheads nearly pressed together as we regain our bearings.

Almost as soon as his lips leave mine, my mind starts working.

As if he can read it on my face, his thumb traces my jaw. "Hey," he says softly. "No worries. There is no pressure here. Not from me. As you said, it's just some fun."

The words should calm me.

They almost do.

Except something in his eyes doesn't match them. Something unsteady, as if he's trying to convince himself as much as me.

I nod anyway. "Right. I know."

He steps back before I can say anything else. "Merry Christmas, Wesley." He gives me one last look, then turns and walks to his car.

A moment later, he's gone.

30

Nathan

I stand on the front porch longer than I need to.

The house looks exactly the same as it always has, though the white siding is in desperate need of a power wash. A wreath is on the door. The same one that mom insists on hanging every year, its pinecones and bows have faded to dull, pastel greens and reds. Warm light spills through the front windows, silhouettes moving inside.

It took me twenty-seven minutes to get here. After circling the block for fifteen minutes, I was officially late. I raise my hand to knock, hesitate, then consider the very real option of turning around and walking back to my car.

No one is physically stopping me.

Before I can go through with it, the door swings open.

"Nathan," Delaney says brightly, already grinning. "You made it. Congratulations. You're officially trapped."

She grabs my arm and drags me inside before I can protest, the door closing behind me with a loud bang.

"Delaney," I mumble, laughing despite myself. "I still had a chance to make a break for it."

She gasps dramatically. "You wouldn't dare leave your little sister on a holiday." She yanks my coat off my body as if stealing it will make me stay. "Welcome home."

The house smells like rosemary, like it did growing up. The only addition is the dessert baking in the oven. It smells like a memory, the scent settling onto my skin like a permanent reminder of how I've never quite fit here.

I follow Delaney toward the kitchen, every step feeling heavier than the last.

Mom is at the stove, wooden spoon in hand, and her hair is pulled back the way she always does when she cooks. Dad stands at the counter chopping vegetables with quiet precision, his sleeves rolled up.

They both look up when we enter, but neither one stops what they're doing. It's been six months since we've seen each other. Sure, we've had phone conversations, but considering we live in the same city, six months should seem too long. Instead, it's already starting to feel like not long enough.

"There he is," my mom says. "You found the place after all."

Let the passive-aggressive bullshit begin.

"I did grow up here." I force my voice to remain neutral. "Luckily, it's been warm this week. Getting up your driveway would've been tough if the snow had stuck."

Dad nods once. "Traffic wasn't bad?"

"Pretty clear actually."

That is the extent of my welcome home. No hugs or smiles, just small talk. The weather. The drive. Safe neutral ground.

My mom turns back to the stove, then glances over her shoulder. "We were hoping you'd bring your girlfriend."

She stirs the soup as if we haven't already had this conversation. Which we have, when I repeatedly told them that Wesley would not be coming. Yet again, they only hear what they want to hear.

"I told you she wouldn't be." I smile to hide my annoyance. "She's with her family."

She hums, clicking her tongue. "That's a shame."

I picture Wesley standing here with her hand brushing mine. The room would feel less suffocating just by virtue of her being in it. I always feel steadier when she's close, like my edges smooth out without effort.

It hits me hard enough that I have to swallow.

That is not a casual thought. That is not a fling thought. That is a boyfriend's thought.

I run my hand along my jaw. Ever since training on Tuesday, I've been thinking about her nonstop, no longer trying to stop myself from wanting her. Our kiss replays on a constant loop in my head, thinking about what we could've done if it hadn't been broad daylight in a public parking lot. My mind flashes with images of her on her knees or me on mine. The possibilities would've been endless.

Shit. I can't get hard in the kitchen with my parents. What is wrong with me?

I clear my throat and turn to Delaney. "How are classes going?"

Her face lights up immediately. "Oh my god. Do you want the short version or the one where you get trapped into listening to me talk for ten minutes?"

"Hit me with the long one." Maybe her ramblings will make this day go faster.

She launches into a story about her sophomore year and a professor who refuses to use email, sending out actual letters instead. She's had a group project that nearly ruined a friendship. She is completely at ease as she discusses her late nights fueled by bad coffee and worse decisions.

Mom laughs, and Dad shakes his head with a smile.

I stand there, nodding along, laughing at the right moments, feeling like I'm watching through glass.

Delaney belongs here in a way I never quite have.

She finishes her story with a dramatic sigh. "Anyway. I survive. Barely."

"You always do," Dad says.

Delaney glances at me. "So, New York. I saw you score and know you won. How's that adding to the season?"

"It's good," I say, looking between the three of them. "If we keep it up, we'll be playoff-bound."

Before I even finish my sentence, Mom turns back to the stove, and Dad resumes chopping, neither one saying a word. The moment closes as quickly as it opened.

"Oh," Delaney says. "That's great."

I nod and let the topic drop. There is no point. I've learned the rhythm. When the conversation turns to hockey, it's all veiled disappointment and silence.

Delaney shoots me an apologetic look. I shrug in return.

"I'm going to use the bathroom." I push off the counter and hurry out of the room.

No one stops me.

I shut the door behind me and lean against it for a second, breathing out slowly. The house is quiet in a way that presses in, every sound amplified by the overwhelming unwelcomeness of it all.

I pull my phone out of my pocket, fingers flying across the screen.

Me: Merry Christmas.

I hesitate for a second, then hit send before I can overthink it.

Wesley: Merry Christmas, Wilder. I hope you're surviving.

The tension in my chest eases a fraction as I laugh softly.

Me: How's it going with your family?

Time ticks more slowly as I stare at the screen, before tucking it back into my pocket without waiting for a response. I can't hide here forever, and dinner will be ready soon. Delaney's voice is drifting down the hall as she talks about dessert.

I wash my hands, look at myself in the mirror, and try to pull it together.

My breath comes a little easier as I head toward the dining room. It's as if texting her bought me ten more minutes of patience.

We sit down at the table, plates already warm, and the spread is impressive in the way it always is here. Everything looks perfect, but tastes like an obligation.

"So," I say, breaking the quiet. "How are things going for you guys?"

Mom launches into a safe answer about the neighborhood and a charity committee she joined. Dad mentions work in vague terms, something about numbers and end-of-year planning.

I ask a few follow-up questions even though we all know that I don't care. I've given up the pettiness that used to be showing them the same kind of indifference that they show hockey. Now, I offer only enough to qualify as conversation.

My phone vibrates against my thigh.

I glance down without thinking, then immediately feel my mouth curve up.

Wesley: Really great. Nice having them in my space for once. Exactly what I needed. How's yours going?

The question lands at the exact wrong moment.

Dad clears his throat. "Have you thought any more about your contract? It ends this year."

I look up. "Of course I have. I'm planning to renew it."

The motion in the room stops as he sets his fork down carefully. He and Mom exchange some sort of silent conversation. Things are about to tip on their head, so I take a minute to respond to Wesley.

Me: It's been thirty minutes, and we're about to get to the part where they tell me to grow up and quit hockey.

My dad coughs, drawing my attention back to the argument that's about to ensue. "We were hoping," he says, choosing his words like chess pieces, "that having a serious girlfriend might mean you're ready to grow up."

There it is.

"I am grown up," I say. "I'm twenty-eight. I live on my own. I pay my bills. I have a career."

"A career," my mom repeats. "Or a phase that's gone on too long."

I laugh once, sharp and humorless. "You can't be serious."

Dad leans back in his chair. "We want you to think about the future. Stability. A real plan."

"This is my plan."

"It won't last forever," my mom says. "At some point, you have to decide what actually matters."

This is the problem. They think that because my career is a sport, something that is mostly for others' entertainment, that it is somehow less than. Mom's charity work and Dad's insurance firm are apparently far more prestigious. They don't get it. They don't even try to.

Delaney opens her mouth. "Okay," she says quickly. "Who wants more potatoes?"

No one glances her way.

"I like my life," I say. "I'm good at what I do."

"You could be doing more," Dad says.

"With what? Something you approve of? Just because it's not what you would do doesn't mean it's not a valid path."

The silence stretches as everyone moves the food around on their plate, never actually taking a bite. It seems that the appetites left the building at the same time civility did.

My phone buzzes again.

Wesley: Ouch. How long do you have to endure it?

For the rest of my life, I think. But before I can type it, my mom cuts in, talking over Delaney's bid for peace.

"We worry," she says. "You chase this game like it'll love you back. But one day it will end, and you'll have nothing if you don't start prioritizing what's important."

Something in me goes still. It's been ten years of reasoning and explanations, and it still falls on deaf ears. They will never understand that this is what's important to me. I don't have it in me to keep trying to get them to.

My chair scrapes softly against the floor as I stand.

"I'm sorry." I turn to Delaney. "I didn't mean to ruin dinner."

Her eyes widen. "Nathan, wait."

"I can't do this tonight." My voice sounds steadier than I feel. "I hope you all have a good Christmas."

Dad looks stunned, and Mom looks offended, but neither of them stops me. They don't want me here any more than I want to be here.

I grab my coat off the hook by the door and walk out, the cold air hitting my face and dulling the frustration that's been building since I stepped inside.

Delaney will give me hell for walking out, but I can't find it in myself to regret it. At some point, doing something I love needs to be enough. I need to be enough.

Once I'm in the car, my body melts into the seat. I turn it on, blasting the heat and waiting for it to warm. Mostly, I'm trying to calm down before I drive home to an empty penthouse that doesn't feel like mine. I should've taken Liam up on the invite to his parents' house.

I decide to text him and see if it's too late. They only live five minutes away. When I pull my phone out, Wesley's text that I haven't responded to sits on the screen.

Me: Don't have to endure it at all anymore. I left.

The reply comes fast.

Wesley: Jesus. I'm sorry. You okay?

I stare at the screen, heart still pounding. Does she really care? Or is she being polite? I hate that all I ever seem to do is doubt myself at every turn.

Me: Will be after a take-out burger and a good night's sleep.

There's a pause. I'm about to text Liam when the bubbles appear that let me know she's typing.

Wesley: You could come here. If you want. As friends.

My fingers tighten on the phone as my mind races through what this could mean.

I should say no.

I'm wound tight. I'm angry and one bad comment away from snapping.

But the image of Wesley in her element forms anyway. The opportunity to meet the people that she puts above herself. The people who love her without conditions.

The pull is too tempting to refuse.

I type before I can talk myself out of it.

Me: I'll be there in twenty.

31

Wesley

Christmas at my place is cozy in a way that makes me yearn for my family to live closer.

Growing up, Christmas always came with a shadow. Even years later, even after the casseroles and grief settled into something manageable, the ghost of my mother still seemed to linger whenever we were in the old house. She was tucked into the corners of the dining room and threaded through every recipe card written in her looping handwriting. There is always a sense that we are honoring something fragile there, protecting it, and measuring ourselves against it.

I don't know how they do it every single day.

But here, in my apartment, there is no shrine to memory, no careful choreography around absence. It's just us. My dad. Emma. Me. Loud and imperfect and alive in the present tense.

The kitchen is already too warm, the oven humming as pots crowd the stovetop and jockey for space. Steam is fogging the windows, carrying the smell of garlic and butter through the entire apartment.

My dad moves between the sink and the counter with comfortable efficiency, sleeves rolled up, washing dishes as I use them. Emma drifts in and out, stealing pieces of food and offering wildly unhelpful commentary.

They both look at home here, which does something strange to my chest. My apartment has felt lonely this past week, but right now it feels like a real home.

We did gifts this morning in pajamas, sitting cross-legged on the rug. We don't exchange anything expensive, just small, deliberate things that say I saw this and thought of you. A framed photo of the three of us from a summer trip years ago. A mug in Emma's favorite ridiculous color. A cookbook for Dad with handwritten notes tucked inside.

A few years ago, we stopped doing big gifts after it started feeling like a performance review instead of a holiday. Without that pressure hanging over it, the day has become lighter and more centered on time together instead of transactions.

I cannot imagine choosing to be alone on a day like this, which is probably why I invited Nathan without thinking through the very obvious emotional landmines attached. It's not my job to rescue him. It's not my responsibility to patch the cracks in his family or make up for their lack of support. But the idea of him sitting somewhere by himself, feeling unwanted on Christmas, lodged under my ribs and refused to budge until I did something about it. So I did. Impulsively.

A month and a half ago, I would've said there was nothing impulsive about me, but now I'm not so sure. When it comes to Nathan, it seems reason evades me every damn time.

Now, I'm at the counter chopping vegetables with more force than necessary, trying to keep my hands from shaking. In two weeks, we break up and go our separate ways. Introducing him to my family makes the line harder to walk.

Emma is perched across from me at the bar, chin in her hand, watching me with the delighted curiosity of someone who smells gossip.

"Hey," she says. "Those carrots didn't do anything to you."

"I'm just focused." I don't look up.

"Focused," she repeats, eyes dropping pointedly to my bouncing foot. "Is this about Nathan?"

"Why would it be about Nathan?"

"Because five minutes ago you announced that your extremely hot boyfriend is coming over for Christmas dinner and now you look like you're about to either pass out or commit a felony with a vegetable peeler."

I plant my foot flat on the floor and will it to behave. "He's just coming by."

Her grin widens. "Just coming by. On Christmas. To dinner. With your family."

Before I can build a defense, Dad looks up from the table he's in the process of setting. "Boyfriend?"

"No," I say loudly enough that they both flinch. "There is no boyfriend."

Emma doesn't even try to hide her amusement. "That's not what's trending in the gossip columns."

"We are not dating," I say, heat crawling up my neck. "The media connects dots with crayons."

Dad turns fully now, interest engaged. "Why would it be in the media?"

Emma raises an eyebrow. "It's Nathan Wilder, Dad."

"You're dating Nathan Wilder?" He blinks. "Why didn't you tell me?"

Dad's a hockey fan. He isn't a die-hard fan or obsessed, but even a casual viewer has heard of Nathan. The reminder of how well-known Nathan is causes heat to rush to my cheeks. Why is he humoring me with all of this when he has to have more important things going on?

"We're not dating." I sigh and set the knife down.

Dad's expression shifts into a slow, knowing smile. "Then why is he coming to Christmas dinner?"

"Because his family situation is complicated," I say, defensive even to my own ears. "And no one should spend Christmas alone if they don't want to. That's it."

Emma makes a humming sound that means she believes absolutely none of that.

"Sounds like you know him pretty well." Dad grabs the silverware out of the drawer, making a show out of getting an extra fork for our incoming guest.

"Drop it," I tell them both.

They mostly do, at least out loud.

A few minutes later, I catch my reflection in the bathroom mirror, quickly putting on mascara and tinted lip balm for absolutely no practical reason whatsoever. I'm in the middle of debating whether I'm pathetic when Emma appears in the doorway.

"You don't put on makeup for friends." She picks up the blush brush, dusting it across my cheeks.

"I put on makeup because I look tired and it's Christmas."

"Okay." She turns to leave, but pauses at the last second. "I think it's good. For you, I mean. You had to grow up too fast. To take care of me. Of dad. It'd be nice if you had someone to take care of you."

She walks away, leaving me to watch myself in the mirror. My breath comes faster, fighting through the bundle of nerves growing beneath my ribs. She's wrong. That's not what this is. I don't need someone that way. I never have.

The doorbell rings, the sound causing a prickle at the back of my neck. I breathe deep for a count of five, then push my way to the front of the apartment.

"I've got it," Dad calls.

I step into the hall as he opens the door.

Nathan stands on the porch with snow dusting his shoulders and a small cluster of poinsettias in his hands. He looks out of place in the most disarming way, his eyes flickering between us as if he doesn't want to take up more room than he's offered.

Dad smiles and welcomes him immediately. Emma leans around the corner to stare without shame.

Any illusion that this was a simple, harmless idea evaporates on the spot. Nothing is simple when it comes to him.

Dinner smells incredible by the time we all sit down. The table is crowded with dishes and far too much food. Nathan takes the seat I gesture to without hesitation, setting the poinsettias on the sideboard.

A pang of jealousy courses through me at the way that nothing seems to rattle him, at least not visibly. Meanwhile, around him, I'm constantly rattled.

My dad wastes no time.

"So," he says, passing the potatoes. "Where's your family from?"

Nathan straightens a little. "Here originally. They still live about twenty minutes away."

"And you're not joining them tonight?" Dad asks, tone casual but eyes sharp.

If I could get away with it, I'd kick him under the table.

Nathan shakes his head, fiddling with his napkin. "No, sir. They had other plans."

"Work-related?" Dad presses.

Nathan hesitates briefly before taking the rolls from Emma. "Something like that."

I shoot my dad a look, but Nathan doesn't seem bothered. If anything, he answers every question calmly. When did he start skating? How long has he been with the Blades? What has his season been like so far?

My dad must know the answers to some of these questions, but he asks anyway. I soften at the way he lets Nathan explain who he is instead of believing what he's certainly seen on TV. Nathan is so much more than people realize.

Finally, after twenty minutes of grueling interrogation, my dad finally leans back in his chair, fork resting on his plate. "You've built an impressive career. That takes discipline and commitment. You should be proud of that."

Nathan goes quiet. His ears turn a faint shade of pink as his gaze drops to his plate. When he finally nods, it's small.

"Thank you," he says. "That means a lot."

I swallow the lump in my throat, wondering, not for the first time, if his parents have ever said that to him. Deep down, I know they haven't. And suddenly a lot of things make more sense. The pressure he carries. The way he doubts himself even when he's playing out of his mind. The fear that no matter how well he does, it will never quite be enough.

Irritation simmers beneath my skin on his behalf. It doesn't last, though, because Nathan smiles, shifting the conversation effortlessly, and I'm swept away with it. I'm determined to keep him smiling for the rest of the night.

Dinner rolls on with stories from Emma about her freshman year and from Dad about his physical therapy. I've never filled Nathan in fully about my family, but he doesn't show an ounce of surprise, rolling with the conversation comfortably. Instead of the anxiety that usually strikes when I think about Dad's health, I listen without spiraling.

Nathan fits into the rhythm without forcing it, answering when asked, listening more than he talks, and making Emma laugh hard enough to snort at least once.

After we clear the table, Emma disappears and comes back with the Taboo box like she's been waiting for this moment all day.

"Teams," she declares. "Wesley and Nathan versus Dad and me."

Nathan looks at the box skeptically. "I should warn you, my family never really played games."

Emma grins, tossing her long hair dramatically. "Perfect. Fresh meat."

I take the box from her and explain the rules, leaning closer than necessary to point at the cards and whisper examples. Nathan listens intently, brows furrowing with focus.

Our first round starts, and something clicks immediately.

We are good. Annoyingly good.

He gets my clues without hesitation. I know exactly how to pivot when he gets stuck. We high-five without thinking, laugh when we mess up, and talk over each other in an easy, overlapping way. Emma groans from across the room.

At one point, I catch my dad watching us, a small smile on his face.

The realization hits me quietly. I like this too much.

Nathan is on my couch, shouting guesses, and leaning into me like this is where he fits. He blends into my life, my family, and my space without effort. It's as if he belongs here in a way that is both comforting and deeply dangerous.

I shove the thought away.

Tonight is not about implications. It's about fun. About letting myself enjoy this without pulling it apart piece by piece.

Eventually, my dad yawns and stands, stretching. "I'm calling it. You two cheated somehow."

Emma laughs, gathering the cards. "They definitely did."

"Nice meeting you, Nathan," he says, before kissing my head and heading down the hall. Emma follows not long after, shooting me a knowing look that I absolutely refuse to interpret.

The house goes quiet.

Nathan and I are left alone in the living room, the remnants of a very full, very loud evening still hanging in the air.

"Thanks for inviting me." He shifts, his knee brushing against mine.

"It's no big deal."

"It was to me." He stands, rubbing his palms against his jeans.

"You don't deserve to be alone."

"Neither do you, Wesley," He murmurs.

The air leaves my lungs.

The meaning behind his words is clear. He's not talking about tonight. He's talking about all of it. I chew on my bottom lip, watching him.

"I've dedicated my whole life to soccer. To being the best."

"At what cost?" There is no judgment in his words, just a sadness that even his smile can't mask.

The truth is, it's cost me a whole hell of a lot. But to change things after coming this far would make the past years of missing out on things all for nothing. My chest tightens just thinking about it. Everything I've sacrificed can't be for nothing.

The evening full of fun becomes loaded with things we both want to say but won't.

"I'll walk you outside." I don't know what else to say.

I don't know how to address it. Whatever this is. Fake. Real. Convenient. It's all blurred, and tonight's not the night to figure it out.

The cold air outside is disorienting after the warm evening. Our breath is visible between us as we reach his car. He unlocks it, climbing into the driver's seat. This is the part where I should say goodnight and go back inside.

Instead, I open the passenger door and slide in.

He pauses, eyes searching my face carefully, as if trying to figure out if this is real and not another line I'm about to redraw. I don't give my anxiety time to speak. I lean across the console and kiss him.

Surprise turns to heat in an instant. His hand comes to my jaw, thumb brushing my cheek with a tenderness that nearly undoes me. The car is freezing, until it's not. The world narrows to breath and the familiar pull between us that's been building since the last time I had his mouth on me. It was only days ago, but it feels like forever.

When he draws me over the center console, settling me partly onto his lap with unspoken care, I go willingly, heart racing. The windows slowly fog as the space fills with warmth and want.

Our hands roam, tangling in hair and clothes, in the pursuit of skin. Time loses all meaning as he kisses his way down my neck, his breath hot against my ear. Eventually, his lips find mine again, and our kissing slows from hungry to something more lingering. A gentle exploration of how deep our connection may go.

All too soon, I ease back, resting my forehead against his, both of us breathing hard.

"I should go back inside," I murmur.

"Okay," he says, but there's caution there, a quiet uncertainty left over from the last time I hit the brakes.

Knowing that I've made him doubt himself more than he already does sends an ache crashing through my chest.

"When can I see you again?" I ask.

"We're training on Monday."

"Not for training."

His mouth curves. "Another public date?"

"What I have in mind," I say, voice low, "is not really public-friendly."

Understanding flashes instantly. "Tomorrow." The words tumble out in a rush. "After your dad and Emma leave. Come over."

I nod in response. Tomorrow.

Reluctantly, we separate. I step out into the cold, legs unsteady as I climb my steps. His headlights don't disappear down the street until my front door closes with me safely inside. My head feels light as I step into the hallway.

Emma is waiting with a cup of water and a look of vindicated satisfaction.

"Just friends," she says dryly. "My ass."

I laugh instead of panicking, the sound light and disbelieving. As I head down the hall, certainty settles into me.

I can't throw caution to the wind forever, but maybe I can for a little while.

I will let myself have this. Have him. For the next couple of weeks, I'll be selfish and lean into this no matter how temporary it is.

I know it's not built to last. Neither of us has a lifestyle that will support anything serious. Neither one of us should be willing to bet our careers on chemistry alone.

So, I set aside the part of me that knows better. I can enjoy this and still walk away. It's what we agreed to, and I'll do it, even if it might break me in two.

32

Nathan

It's nice being invisible.

We've been walking for thirty minutes, and not a single person has recognized me so far. It might be a record. The nighttime helps, along with the coat and beanie pulled low over my ears. But I also like to think it's because I've never walked around downtown, holding hands with a woman in public before. Whatever the reason, people pass us by without looking twice.

The early evening cold presses against my cheeks, sharp enough to keep me alert but not uncomfortable.

Last night keeps replaying in my head in flashes.

Christmas at her apartment with her family. They were great. Seeing how much love and appreciation flowed between them twisted the knife of my own family issues a little deeper. But after the initial ache, it was nice being a part of it. Whether it was dinner conversation or the games afterward, I'd felt like I belonged in a way I don't with my own family.

And then there was the car. The kiss.

I've kissed more women than I remember. I'm not proud of it, but it's nothing I can change now. Until Wesley, I would've told you that kissing is nice. Good foreplay for the better things to come. But I never knew what I was missing.

Kissing Wesley is like coming up for air after being underwater for years. It's like folding into warmth after walking through an endless winter storm. It's like a match striking in dry grass, the flames burning fast and uncontrollable.

It's not nice. It's not good. It's everything. And it's also really fucking with my head.

Which is why when she showed up at my doorstep earlier, after her family left, I took her out to dinner instead of inviting her in. All I wanted was to throw her over my shoulder, carry her straight to my bedroom, and spend the next few hours learning every single reaction she has to my hands, my mouth, and my cock.

That's what we're supposed to be doing. That's what 'benefits' means. Instead, we keep fucking kissing, which feels more intimate and dangerous.

This all started because I played better after working out with her. Sure, I also thought hooking up with her would be great. I'd have to be blind not to think that. But Christmas with her family, romantic nights like this, and the very real feelings I'm starting to have for her, were never part of the plan.

All I want to do is figure out if she feels it too, but I'm not sure I can take it if she doesn't. She's said it's a fling until her team party. I'm determined to respect that boundary even if I'm starting to want something more.

"I haven't walked through these lights in a couple of years," Wesley says, her head turning as she takes in each new display with childlike wonder.

"Me neither," I confess. "I forgot how many there were."

She walks close enough that our shoulders brush every few steps, close enough that I can feel her warmth through both our coats. Her fingers stay threaded through mine.

Her breath fogs in front of her as she exhales, white mist disappearing into the glow of the streetlights. Hair falls loose around her shoulders, slightly messy from her hat. Her cheeks are pink from the cold.

"Do you want to stay in Boston long-term?" I ask. I've been wondering since I saw her with Emma yesterday. It must be hard being across the country from them.

"Yeah, I really do." She waves back at a baby who keeps staring at her. "I can't really see myself anywhere else. As much as I hate being away from my dad and Emma, I might hate where they live even more."

"Why?"

"That house and town remind me of my mom. I was fourteen when she died, and it's like I have too many memories of her there. I can't go anywhere without being reminded."

Her eyes widen slightly. "That makes me sound awful."

"No." I squeeze her hand gently. "It sounds honest. I get how it would be hard to be reminded of your darkest experiences every day."

She nods. "Yes. Exactly that."

Then she shifts the conversation, and I let her.

"I've tried talking them into moving out here."

"If that's what you want, I'm sure it's only a matter of time," I say, grinning and bumping my shoulder into hers.

"Are you saying I'm bossy?" She blows out a breath, pushing her hair out of her face.

"Are you saying you aren't?" I raise an eyebrow.

"It's not my fault that I'm usually right."

"Except when you said you weren't a fan of hockey players."

"What makes you think my opinion has changed?"

"Just a feeling." My lips tilt up.

"Yeah, well…" She bites her lower lip like she's thinking about what she wants to say next. "Maybe sometimes I'm wrong too."

We turn with the path, so that we can keep watching the twinkling lights of the city's Christmas tree. We've circled it three times already, but neither of us makes a move to stop.

"What are we doing?" It's a whisper, her lips barely moving to form the words.

"Walking." I keep my tone playful, even though I know that's not what she's really asking.

"When I showed up at your door tonight, I expected sex." She laughs.

"Wow. That's a pretty big assumption. What would've given you that idea?" I swing our arms slightly.

"Seriously, Nathan." She stops walking. "I don't do this kind of thing. This whole fake-dating, friends-with-benefits shit. I don't know the rules."

Friends-with-benefits. Hearing the words makes my stomach turn over.

"Trust me, you do the benefits part just fine." I wink, but she doesn't laugh, and I know I've dodged the question long enough. "It doesn't feel right to have you show up, have sex, then have you leave."

Her eyebrows scrunch. "Isn't that what this is supposed to be?"

It is. That's exactly what this is supposed to be.

"You're forgetting the friends part of that arrangement."

"So, that's what tonight is?" Her lips tilt up. "Just friends?"

She doesn't even realize the words sting.

"Yes, Wesley. I like hanging out. We're already working out together, going on fake dates, and enjoying some very nice benefits." I nudge her. "Why not add some actual friendship to the list?"

There is no part of me that wants to be her friend.

She nudges me back. "I like being your friend."

My heart swells at her confession, until…

"I'm glad you can separate the two. And that you understand why it can't be anything more than that."

My heart deflates just as quickly.

We make it another half block before she slows.

I follow her gaze to the bakery on the corner. Warm golden light spills through the windows, making the snow-dusted sidewalk glow faintly. The smell of sugar and baked bread drifts through the cold air every time the door opens.

I glance at her. "You want something from there?"

She hesitates like she's deciding whether wanting something is allowed.

"I haven't had one of their chocolate croissants in forever," she says. "They're really good."

"Why not get one?"

She shrugs. That's not really an answer, but it's enough.

I tug on her hand. "Come on."

"Wait, I didn't say I wanted one."

"You did." I guide her toward the door. "You said they were good. I'm acting accordingly."

She laughs under her breath. "You are ridiculous."

The bell above the bakery door jingles when we walk in. Warm air hits my face immediately, carrying cinnamon, chocolate, and butter. My stomach forgets that I just had dinner an hour ago.

Wesley is already at the display case, eyes scanning while trying not to look too excited.

I lean against the counter beside her.

"Which one?" I ask.

She points at the croissant without touching the glass. "That one."

"Only one?"

She glances at me. "Yes. Only one."

I order two because I want to taste the pastry that makes her eyes light up like that.

We step back out into the cold with the paper bag between us, steam still faintly rising from inside.

She doesn't wait more than thirty seconds before pulling the croissant out.

She takes a bite.

And then she makes a noise that should be illegal in public.

It's low and soft. Completely unguarded. My body reacts immediately, cock straining against my zipper. Wesley shouldn't make that sound for anyone, but me. Ever.

"Jesus," I mutter.

She glances at me. "What?"

"You can't make that noise when we're surrounded by people."

"Why not?" She grins, clearly pleased with herself.

"Because it makes me want to take you around the corner, into that alley, and draw that sound out of you with my tongue."

Her cheeks flush. "Oh."

"Yeah. So, unless that's what you want, stop it."

She takes another bite, looking me directly in the eye as she makes the sound again.

"You're trouble." I step toward her and cage her gently against the brick wall.

"Not usually." Her voice comes out breathy.

I reach up slowly, giving her time to stop me, and brush my thumb across the corner of her mouth, catching the smear of chocolate she left there.

Instead of pulling away, I slide my thumb to the center of her lips. She parts them just enough to suck it into her mouth.

Her pupils blow wide as she swirls her tongue around my thumb.

I instantly regret not doing what I wanted to when she first showed up at my door. If I had, I'd be buried inside her right now instead of fighting off a public erection.

"How's it taste?" My voice is gravel.

"Find out for yourself."

The words are full of suggestion. I have a second croissant in the bag, but there's only one way I want a taste.

I lean in, pressing her more firmly against the wall, and kiss her.

It's slow and languid. The taste of chocolate and her is immediate and overwhelming.

There's no way that two more weeks are enough. I could kiss her forever, and it would never be enough.

Maybe it's because of how she supports me and jokes with me. Maybe it's because she's focused and committed in a way that inspires me. Or maybe it's because the past three times we've been together, we've only kissed, and it's been better than anything I've experienced with anyone else. Whatever it is, I know now that I've been lying to myself. There is no way that she's a fling for me.

Her fingers curl into my coat, tugging me closer until I am very aware of how little distance exists between us and how badly I want to erase it completely.

The street is still moving around us. People walk past. Someone laughs loudly farther down the sidewalk. Cars pass, tires hissing against wet pavement. Nobody pays attention to us.

It's dangerous because it makes me feel like we're completely alone. It's why I push my leg between her thighs, parting them to feel her heat.

Her hands slide up under my coat, fingers pressing into my sweater. I can't tell if she's grounding herself in me or pulling me closer.

My pulse is loud in my ears.

I break the kiss to breathe, but I don't move away. My forehead rests against hers while I try to remember how to act like a normal person in public.

"Chocolate croissants were a good decision," I murmur.

She laughs quietly. "You're only saying that because you're currently high on pastry and inappropriate PDA."

"Incorrect," I say. "I'm currently high on you."

It feels like more of a confession than I should make. Something more than the boundaries she keeps setting. But I don't take it back.

She swallows hard, but she doesn't look away.

Instead, she kisses me once more. This time it's quick and sweet.

We stand there for a little longer, pressed against the wall, breathing each other's air while the Christmas lights from the storefront across the street reflect in the dark windows around us.

This might be a fling for her, but she has to know it's different for me. Doesn't she?

33

Wesley

By the time Avery starts counting my touches out loud, I know I'm in trouble.

"One," she says as she jogs alongside me, watching my feet instead of the ball. "Two. Three. Wow. You're playing like you're either extremely well-rested or got laid."

"Can you not narrate my life?" I mutter, pushing the ball forward and threading a pass to Becca on the sideline.

Becca traps it cleanly, shoots me a grin, and immediately betrays me. "She's glowing," she says. "It's unsettling."

Haley, already jogging back into position, snorts. "I'd say her boyfriend is treating her very right."

"He must be." Avery nods for me to follow her to the corner. Once she's got me alone, she starts again. "What's with the post-holiday, post-fake-boyfriend, post-whatever the hell has been happening for the last week, glow? And why haven't I heard about it already?"

I wink, then send the ball back to Becca down the sideline harder than necessary and take off downfield. My lungs fill with cold air as my body falls into a steady rhythm. It's only a matter of time before Avery follows me over here.

We're running passing drills with quick touches. It's meant to keep us sharp since we have a break before our next scrimmage. It's working. My muscles feel loose and responsive. Everything is clicking perfectly, and we're moving as a unit.

I don't think it's a coincidence.

I can map this past week by moments instead of days. The sound of Nathan's laugh as it echoed through his parking garage when I tripped over my own bag. The way he leans against door frames like he has nowhere else he needs to be, even when I know his schedule is tighter than mine. The strange calm that settles in my chest when his hand finds the back of my neck as if it belongs there. The steadiness under the heat keeps catching me off guard.

Nathan's had home games this week, so we haven't been separated by distance. And without a plane ride keeping us apart, we've found a way to get to each other every single day since Christmas. Sometimes it's after our workouts, or late at night, or in the middle of the damn day. We've squeezed each other into whatever space we could find. It's an uncontrollable need masked by the unspoken agreement that we won't examine it too closely.

I've lost my mind. I'm not the Wesley Miller whose singular focus is soccer. That Wesley would never sneak into the custodial closet at the stadium after training with a professional hockey player. She'd never let him push her against the door and sink to his knees in front of her. She'd never let him put his head between her legs, using his tongue until she collapsed against him.

But I had, and I couldn't bring myself to regret it.

I was simultaneously making up for the time we lost fighting against this and making the most of the little time we had left.

It's New Year's Eve tomorrow. Nathan won both of his games this week and is leading his team in goals, all but cementing his spot on the team. My coach is thoroughly convinced that I have balance, because I do. It started as a charade, but getting out of my comfort zone with Nathan has made it real. I've made more friends on the team, and I plan to keep fostering those relationships.

After the party next week, we have no reason to keep this arrangement. I don't like to think about it. Then, I don't like to think about why I don't like to think about it.

Tomorrow, we are going out together. It's our last public date aside from the party.

Considering how well the Blades are playing and the fact that it'll be New Year's Eve, I know the paparazzi will be out in full force. But I hadn't thought about that at all. I was really only thinking about how much fun we'd have. Because if one thing was guaranteed when I was with Nathan, it was having fun.

Two months ago, I thought Nathan Wilder was overrated, over-hyped, and arrogant. Now, I know him well enough to know that the hype is warranted. He's got more stress in his life than anyone would ever realize because he somehow manages to smile through it. He is confident and charming, but not in an arrogant way. It's in a way that is totally deserved because his every action backs it up.

"Wes," Avery says, out of breath as she makes her way to me across the field. "You're ignoring me, which means I'm right."

"I'm literally in the middle of a drill." I try to refocus, checking my shoulder and laying the ball off to Haley before cutting inside.

"Multitasking is a thing," she fires back. "Now. Details. Are we talking about good sex or life-altering sex?"

I groan. "You're insufferable."

Becca jogs closer, lowering her voice like we're not all still very much within earshot. "Is it true that hockey guys are packing?"

Haley perks up immediately. "Oh my god, yes. Please confirm."

I shake my head, laughing despite myself as we reset at midfield. "I'm not talking about this."

"That's a yes," Avery says smugly.

"Oh, captain. My captain!" Becca teases, in a breathy fake moan.

Avery snorts, and my cheeks go molten.

Luckily, Coach blows her whistle, saving me from more embarrassment. We transition into shooting drills. I line up at the top of the box, take a touch, and strike. The ball snaps into the right corner of the net.

We rotate through another round. Pass, move, shoot. The repetitive motion should clear my head. Usually it does. But today, my thoughts keep drifting, circling the same truth I've been carefully avoiding.

The way his hands have learned my body in such a short amount of time. His confidence when we're together grounds me, even when my anxiety threatens to pull me under.

Sure, we don't talk about the future, and we don't pretend this is anything more than what it is. But my body doesn't care about rules, and my heart is starting to forget them entirely.

"So," Becca says lightly, as if we're discussing practice instead of my impending emotional demise. "You guys are coming tomorrow, right?"

"Yes, after dinner."

Coach calls time, and we jog toward the sideline, breath fogging in the air.

Avery bumps her shoulder into mine, so I hang back with her. "You look happy," she says, softer now.

She's seen every version of me that exists on and off the field. The ruthless one. The locked in one. The one who plays through pain and refuses help. She is one of the few people who also recognizes the difference between focused and hiding, and lately, I suspect she knows I have been doing a little of both.

"I'm good." I don't let myself smile.

"I know I was the one who suggested you go for it." She bites her lip nervously. "But be careful getting invested, Wesley. Hockey players, especially ones that get his kind of attention. They don't settle down."

"I'm not attached." Even as I say it, I know I'm lying.

I'm really fucking attached. But that doesn't mean I won't end it. I'm nothing if not exceptional at cutting my feelings off when I need to and ignoring the pain.

"I don't want you to get hurt." Avery leans over, giving me a side hug that doesn't draw too much attention.

"You know me," I tease. "Poster child for self-control."

She smiles, then walks away, leaving me standing, wondering whether it's even possible to avoid getting hurt when Nathan's already carved himself into me so deeply.

I grab my water bottle and take a long drink, eyes drifting to my phone on the bench, already knowing there will be a message waiting from him. There always is.

Tomorrow, we'll count down together. We'll laugh. We'll ignore the expiration date. We'll do what we do best. Fake it. I'm just not faking the same things anymore.

Coach catches me as I'm shoving my shin guards into my bag, the cold finally settling into my fingers now that the adrenaline is fading.

"Wesley," she says, hand light on my arm. "Got a minute?"

My pulse drums in my ears. It always does, no matter how old I get, no matter how many seasons I've played under her. I nod, following her a few steps away from the rest of the team, toward the far sideline where the noise thins out, and the field feels wider.

She crosses her arms, studying me.

"I wanted to talk to you before we break until the party," she says. "It's about the Future's Camp at the end of January."

My heart stutters. "The camp for the National Team?"

She smiles. "Yes, that's the one."

For a second, the world goes oddly quiet, like someone turned the volume down on everything except her voice. My chest feels tight, not in a bad way, just full.

"They've got a spot for you," she says finally. "If you still want it."

I suck in a breath, then another, trying to keep my voice steady. "If I want it? It's all I've ever wanted. Thank you."

I see flashes of every early morning alarm, every extra sprint, every night I sat alone rewatching game film while everyone else went out. The sacrifices never feel dramatic while you're making them. They feel normal, like part of the job. Hearing this now turns them into proof and direction. A door that was theoretical yesterday is suddenly wide open today.

She nods. "You've made huge strides this year, not just technically. You're seeing the field better, communicating more, pulling people up instead of carrying everything yourself. That matters."

The last eight weeks of team bonding have allowed me to understand my teammates in ways I never have before. Leadership has started to feel less like pressure and more natural.

"I'm proud of you," she says, meeting my eyes. "You're becoming a true leader on this team, Wesley. It's nice to see you making the changes I asked for."

Something warm blooms behind my ribs.

"I won't waste it." I know she can hear how much I mean it.

"Good. Because if you perform well at camp, you'll be on a very real path toward the National Team. This isn't a courtesy invite. This is an opportunity knocking."

When I was nine, I used to fall asleep in my National Team jersey even when it needed to be washed, convinced that proximity counted for something. I memorized roster lists like other kids memorized song lyrics.

Back then, the dream felt huge, like something that belonged to a future version of me who was braver and faster. Standing here now, hearing her say it out loud, I realize that the future version has been quietly building herself for years.

My pulse is racing. The end of January suddenly feels impossibly close and thrilling all at once.

"And," she adds, shifting her weight like she's about to pivot topics, "I'm looking forward to meeting Nathan properly at the team party next week."

I laugh, caught off guard. "He's great. You'll like him."

"I'm sure, but I want you to hear this clearly. Even without him, the work you're doing is obvious. You're not improving because of who you're with, you're improving because you've decided to."

Her words confirm that we don't need to keep pretending. I'm back in her good graces even without our arrangement. There is no need for Nathan to be my fake boyfriend. I hate it.

"I need you focused at camp," she finishes. "Play like you know you can. The rest will take care of itself."

"I will." I nod quickly.

She squeezes my shoulder once before turning back toward the field, leaving me standing there with cold fingers and a buzzing heart.

The Future's camp. The next step is to the National Team and eventually, the World Cup.

I should call my dad or Emma to tell them the news. Or maybe run to catch up with Avery. But the only person I'm dying to tell is the one whose name is lighting up my phone.

I sling my bag over my shoulder, smiling at Nathan's text.

Nathan: You left early this morning, and now, the bed's too cold.

His name on my screen has started to feel like exhaling after holding my breath. I don't overthink it when my finger hovers over the call button. Or when it rings twice before he answers. Or when the excitement of the camp spills out of my lips as I explain it all at a neck-breaking pace.

I only start to overthink it when we hang up, and I'm already wishing I could call him back.

34

Nathan

The bar is packed to the brim, but it's New Year's Eve, so no one seems to mind. Bodies press shoulder to shoulder, laughter stacking on top of music that is already too loud. The air smells like citrus peels, spilled champagne, and overheated speakers.

Someone has dragged in cheap metallic decorations that catch the rotating lights and throw them across the ceiling like restless stars. Every few seconds, another cork pops somewhere in the room, and people cheer.

The best part?

Wesley is tucked into my side. Her hip fits against mine, her arm sliding around me when someone bumps into us. Every time she laughs, she turns slightly toward me, as if I'm the anchor point that she checks in with before she floats away again.

I catch myself watching her more than I should, wondering if things have changed for her the way they have for me. She doesn't seem to realize that she smiles differently now or that she laughs louder and more carefree. I like to pretend it's because of me.

Both teams are here again, hers and mine mixing comfortably. A month ago, it would have been weird. Now, it feels normal. Becca is already halfway onto the dance floor, dragging Avery and one of our rookies with her. Wyatt is arguing with one of Wesley's defenders about which sport requires more conditioning and is losing badly. Someone from our second line is teaching Haley a terrible chant that is definitely going to get us fined if it ever makes it near a microphone.

I should feel watched, the way I usually do when I'm out in public. People have their phones out, sneaking pictures of us, and paparazzi linger outside waiting for us to leave. We're on display. Except I can't bring myself to care, not when Wesley's thumb keeps brushing the inside of my wrist.

It's a distracted habit of hers. She probably doesn't even know she's doing it. I do. I notice everything about her. The small habits and unconscious touches. The difference between her public smile and the one she reserves for me.

The last week runs through my head in snapshots instead of a timeline.

Memories of her laughing against my throat when we forgot the pasta boiling over or her body pinned between me and the door after our workout, while she's grinning as if she scored a game-winner, haunt me at all times. My personal favorites are the quiet moments after, when she goes soft and traces circles on my arm as if charting new territory on a map.

We've told our friends it's chemistry and convenience, but I stopped believing that after the third morning of waking up in each other's arms.

Avery steals Wesley away, but she looks back once and points at me like a warning to behave. I salute her with my drink. She laughs and disappears into the lights.

"You're gone," Grayson says beside me.

I glance over. "I'm right here."

He shakes his head. "No. You're physically present. Mentally, you're writing poetry about your fake girlfriend."

"I don't write poetry."

"Thank fuck" Wyatt says, clapping my shoulder. "It'd be awful. But you do have that look."

"What look?" I take a long pull from my beer.

"The one when your eyes track her even when you think you aren't."

I shove him lightly. "You're drunk."

"Working on it," he says proudly, then points toward the dance floor. "She's got moves, by the way. You're going to have to fight off half this bar at midnight."

The thought stops me cold. A knot coiling tighter in my chest as I watch a man work up the nerve to approach her on the dance floor. My feet start to move before I can stop myself, but I only make it two steps before Wesley shakes her head and turns back to Avery. He gets the message and walks back to the edge of the dance floor, scoping out someone else to hit on.

Good.

I notice Liam smirk, but thankfully, he doesn't say a word about it, instead letting the conversation shift to hockey.

We're on a hot streak, having won every game in the past three weeks. I've been playing better, sure, but it's not only me. Grayson has been steady on defense, and Liam has been on fire at center. Wyatt's also heading towards the team record for most shutouts in a single season. If we keep it up, we'll be a shoo-in to win the Cup.

The conversation is comforting, as we gossip about the other teams in our conference and the trades that will or won't happen. It's the first time all season that we can talk about trades without me feeling like I'll be one. The relief has the weight lifting off my shoulders a bit.

With my contract looking better and her team's party next week, I have no excuse to continue things with Wesley. Except that I just want to.

I lose track of the conversation, eyes scanning the bar until Wesley's dark top and bright smile come into view.

"She's good for you," Liam says suddenly, voice quiet enough that only I can hear.

I look at him, setting my beer down on the table. "You base that on what?"

"You're happy. Not in the bullshit way you've been the past couple of years, but actually."

I don't respond at first, trying to come up with a way to talk around it. I come up empty, and honestly, I really don't want to talk my way out of it. Liam's my oldest friend. If he can see it, maybe I should let myself be honest.

"I've already told you that next week, after her party, it's over." I force the words out as much for myself as for him.

"Why does it have to be?" He asks, turning his body to cut anyone else out of the conversation. "You both agreed to that almost two months ago. You can change your mind."

"I have changed my mind," I admit, running my hand through my hair. "That doesn't mean she has."

"How do you know?"

"Dude, you don't know her like I do." I pause, forcing my voice lower. "She doesn't do relationships for a reason. Her family counts on her success. She has so much pressure on her to stay focused. Even if I don't agree with it, I won't be the one to distract her from her goals. I would never ask her to do that."

"Being with someone you care about doesn't have to be a distraction."

"Says the guy who fucks around with any girl that asks," I snap, instantly regretting it.

To his credit, Liam masks the hurt only seconds later. "Yeah, I do, but you don't. You've never taken that shit lightly."

I pick up my beer, draining its contents. "I still don't."

"You're playing better than ever. You've got the girl. There's no reason to call it."

"That's the thing. Even if I've changed my mind, our sports are too tangled up in this."

He scrunches his eyebrows.

"I want her. Okay. You're right." I lay my head back onto the back of the couch. "And I am playing the best hockey of my life. Is that because of me or because of her?"

"Does it matter?" Liam leans forward, his arm draped across his knee.

"I need to be good enough on my own. She can't be the only reason I'm better now. Every time I decide I want to be with her, there's this nagging part of me wondering if it's because I'm afraid I'll lose my contract without her."

He watches me, waiting for me to continue.

"It's so fucked up. She doesn't deserve someone who only wants her out of selfishness and fear. Even if she wanted me, which she doesn't, I can't live with myself not knowing if I can do this on my own."

I'm a coward. At least, that's the conclusion I come to after saying it all out loud. I want her. But I'm too afraid that my success is tied to her to even try to make it happen. I'm too scared to ask if she wants me for real. I'm worried that everyone else won't think I'm enough on my own. Bullshit, bullshit, and more bullshit.

Liam's eyes dart behind me. He shakes his head slightly as Wesley comes up behind me, sliding back into my space. She's flushed from dancing, and her eyes are bright. Her fingers hook casually into my belt loop. My brain short-circuits for half a second at how easily she claims the spot.

"Miss me?" she asks.

"Constantly," I say, not entirely pretending.

That earns me a softer look than I deserve.

Eventually, Liam gets pulled away into a loud debate about power play structure. It leaves me, Wesley, and Avery on the couch that the staff roped off for us.

Avery watches us with her usual skepticism. She's annoyingly perceptive. I don't miss the way Grayson keeps glancing her way. He can't seem to take a hint, even when the hint is Avery quite literally telling him he has no chance.

"You two look really comfortable," she finally says.

"Avery," Wesley warns.

"For people who are fake dating," she adds, sticking her tongue out at Wesley.

There is a half beat where the air shifts.

Wesley lifts one shoulder. "Repetition builds skill."

"We're elite performers," I add, shifting Wesley closer on my lap. "Very committed to the craft."

Avery rolls her eyes. "Hey, I'm not judging. It's working. Both of your coaches are off your backs. You're both getting what you wanted." She lifts her glass. "And next week you're free."

Free.

That word lands like a puck to the ribs.

I nod because the script says nod. Free sounds a lot like done and back to before.

We both know it's the plan, but I'm sick of everyone around us pointing it out. All week, Wesley and I have let this be whatever it is. We've soaked up every fucking second and have managed to avoid the topic entirely. Now, our friends want to consistently remind us of it.

Wesley may not mind, but I do. It's like they're pre-drilling the hole for the knife Wesley is going to stab through my heart.

Now that the words are floating out there, Wesley seems distant. She's still here, hand in mine, but she's also in her head. I wish I knew what thoughts are swirling there.

When she sits up out of my grasp this time, I let her go. People move to the side as she carves out a path to the bar to get us all another round. I watch her go.

Avery waits until she is out of earshot. "Does my best friend know that this is real for you?"

"What?" I glance over at Avery, who sips her champagne casually.

"You heard me." She smirks.

"You and Liam should get together. Maybe then you could interrogate each other instead of me." I sigh, letting my breath out slowly.

"Way to dodge the question, Wilder."

"She's your best friend. Ask her." My lips thin into a line. "She doesn't want anything past next week."

"Bullshit."

"Not bullshit."

"I know what she says, but I also know that she's lying to herself as much as you."

"Didn't know you were a mind reader, Avery." I tilt my head, raising my eyebrows.

Avery flings her red curls over her shoulder. "I'm not. But I am her best friend. And contrary to everything you might think you know about her, I know more." She smiles and waves to Haley, who's yelling her name from the dance floor. "And unless you do something, I'll always know more."

A world where Wesley slowly becomes a stranger to me sounds depressing and desolate.

"Tell her how you feel, Nathan," Avery tosses the rest of her drink down, in preparation to take the next one from Wesley. "Prove to me that not all hockey players are idiots."

My heart picks up pace at the possibility that Wesley might really want me the way I want her.

Avery's up and moving, and my teammates fill her spot on the couch. Wesley passes a shot to Avery, who disappears toward the bar. My hand clings to the beer that Wesley hands me, while my other arm circles her waist, pulling her onto my lap.

I don't miss the way that she sits carefully, as if to maintain the distance that Avery's words created.

We have a little over half an hour until midnight, but the excitement has people talking louder. She leans into me so we can hear each other over it all.

"You okay?" She asks.

"Got evaluated by the panel," I answer, nodding toward Liam sitting at the table behind us and then toward Avery chatting up some guy at the bar.

"Let's hope they never get together. They'd be insufferable."

"You think they'll get together?" Grayson leans over, his eyes locked on Avery.

Wesley laughs. I try not to stare at her mouth when she does.

"Avery has sworn off hockey players, and she has damn good fol-low-through."

The words don't seem to settle Grayson at all. He mutters under his breath and walks off, but I don't pay him any attention. My sole focus is on the woman who is sliding her arms around my neck.

We sit comfortably, watching the chaos unfold around us, stealing glances at each other and exchanging grins that make me feel like a kid with a crush.

When the noise swells and the lights dim for the countdown, she finally speaks.

"I'm happy you said yes to this arrangement," she whisper-yells into my ear over the music.

I blink. "Yeah?"

"Yeah. I know it's almost over, but I've had more fun than I've had in a long time."

For a second, the bar drops away. She's on a bigger field. Bigger stage. Everything she's been grinding toward. And I'm supporting her from the stands.

The fantasy cracks when I remember that I won't be there to see it.

"Wes," I say, and it comes out shaky. "I..."

"No, please don't feel like you have to say anything." Her smile breaks open. She has no idea what I want to say to her.

At the last second, I chicken out. "I'm having fun too." I pull her into a hug without thinking.

She exhales against me, tension leaving her shoulders. Then she drops her arms, her careful distance returning. It's not rejection, but it still stings.

I understand it. I hate it a little anyway.

I know what this costs her. I've seen the pressure in her house and in the way her father watches her as if every game is a verdict. I will not be the one to ask her to choose me anyway.

The countdown starts. The whole bar turns toward the screens, and the DJ starts shouting numbers like a general calling troops.

Ten.

This feels like a clock running down on more than a year.

Nine.

My mind nags on the staged breakup and going back to separate routines.

Eight.

I try to picture not texting her first after a game. It's hollow.

Seven.

I try to think of having my freedom back and doing whatever I want.

Six.

She steps closer on her own.

Five.

Her palm rests flat against my chest. She can definitely feel my heart hammering.

Four.

I touch her jaw, slow enough that she can pull away. She doesn't

Three.

Her eyes are soft and a little scared, but she smiles.

Two.

Fuck my freedom. Fuck the pressure. I just want her.

One.

The room detonates into cheers and horns and falling glitter. I kiss her like the noise doesn't exist. I kiss her, trying to memorize the feeling of her against me. For after. For when I'm on my own again.

"Happy New Year," I murmur against her mouth. It sounds like a plea and a goodbye at the same time.

35

Nathan

I usually hate team events.

They're loud, performative, and full of people who want something from me or want to be seen with me. Usually, there are cameras hovering outside the door or phones pointed directly at my face. I don't enjoy them. Hell, most of the time, I'm on high alert with my every move monitored.

Tonight is different.

Wesley's team party is tucked into a private room above a restaurant that smells like fresh bread and wood polish. There's music playing, but it's background noise, with the conversation buzzing in all corners of the room. The lighting is dim, not designed for photo ops, but for comfort. Most importantly, there are no cameras.

When we arrived, it took only a second to notice there was no media anywhere.

That should not feel as novel as it does.

It is bullshit, really. Wesley is as much an athlete as I am. She's more disciplined than most people I know. Her training schedule makes mine look indulgent. Her body takes just as much punishment. Her career has just as much at stake.

And yet, because it's women's soccer and not a men's league that TV networks trip over themselves to televise, we get this one small mercy. A night where she can celebrate with her team without a swarm of paparazzi. A night where I can stand next to her without feeling like I am bracing for impact.

Selfishly, I love it.

Especially because it's the last time. After tonight, my brief journey into Wesley's world is over. We'll let the gossip fade, and in a couple of weeks, we'll release a statement saying it was mutual. It'll all be chalked up to busy schedules or some other excuse that doesn't make either of us look bad.

The thought presses in quietly, the way it has all week.

I've slept at her place almost every night. I like it more than mine. It has character and personality. It also smells like her.

Yesterday, I woke up alone and wandered the entire apartment looking for her until I remembered she had a meeting with her coach to discuss their lineup for the upcoming season.

When she had told me about it, I'd assumed she would wake me, so that I could leave when she did. But she hadn't, and being in her space by myself was surreal. It made my mind run a little wild, picturing a world where that was the norm. A world where we both focused on our careers, making sure to give them our all, and then returned to each other's sides each night.

Then my fantasy blurred with reality when she really had come home with coffee for both of us. She ordered mine exactly how I would've ordered it myself. Then we spent the rest of the morning in bed together. The only reason we finally dragged ourselves out of the apartment was to squeeze in an actual workout because even though she's let her guard down, she's still Wesley fucking Miller. And I wouldn't change a thing.

But underneath it all, tonight has been looming in the background, like a clock I can hear ticking even when no one else seems aware it exists.

I nurse a beer near the edge of the room while the team mills around talking to coaches, donors, and support staff. Avery is laughing loudly near the bar, and Haley is already halfway through a story that involves a referee and a missed call. Someone has pushed two tables together to make space for plates of food that are being steadily demolished.

For the first time, I realize it won't only be Wesley that I miss, it'll be all of this. Her friends and the comfortable way everyone interacts. A part of me wants to suggest that we all still hang out, but the thought of seeing her and not being able to hold her makes me nauseous.

A clean break. That's what it needs to be. It's the only way I'll be able to get over it.

"You're Nathan, right?"

I blink and look up to find a guy standing in front of me, holding a drink and wearing the slightly panicked expression of someone who is a fan.

"Yeah," I say easily.

"Trevor, Becca's date." He jerks his thumb vaguely across the room. "I wanted to say, uh, great season. You guys are killing it."

"Thanks," I reply, polite and automatic. "Appreciate it."

He asks a couple more questions about our playoff chances and strategy. It's all the usual script. I give the usual answers on autopilot, nodding in the right places and offering safe, practiced responses.

My attention drifts across the room.

It always does.

Wesley is there, pulled into a conversation with Coach Bennett and the Tempest team owner, Todd Sawyer. I notice her posture immediately. She's standing a little taller, smiling brightly. She wants to impress him.

I don't know how anyone could not be impressed by her. Aside from her dedication and success on the field, she looks like a dream tonight. I was speechless when she answered the door, and I'm not much better off now, hours later.

She's wearing a dark purple dress that has a slit up to her mid-thigh. It's elegant and tight against her toned stomach. Her hair cascades over her shoulders, brushing her collarbone when she laughs.

The blush on her cheeks is barely there, and the rest of her makeup is natural.

At the gala, she'd seemed miserable, like she couldn't wait to get away, but tonight, she doesn't seem to mind the show. Her shoulders are relaxed, and her eyes gleam while listening to her coach tell a story that I'm too far away to hear.

My chest aches a little. She belongs here, in this room, with these people, on the verge of something bigger.

Coach Bennett says something that makes Wesley laugh, her head tipping back slightly. The owner nods along. I watch the exchange play out and feel something warm and complicated settle beneath my ribs.

She's going to be extraordinary.

She already is.

The guy in front of me finishes his sentence and trails off, realizing he has lost me entirely. I offer a quick smile, clap him lightly on the shoulder, and excuse myself before he can restart the conversation.

I make the decision without thinking too hard about it.

If this is my last night with her, I'm not spending it standing across the room.

I weave through clusters of teammates and their dates. As I get closer, I catch snippets of their conversation about the Futures Camp and her thoughts on the upcoming season. Wesley answers his questions with confidence while still managing to sound humble.

She notices me as I reach her side.

Her expression softens immediately, something private flickering across her face before she reins it back in. She shifts slightly, creating space without looking, and I slide into it using muscle memory, my arm sliding around her waist out of habit.

Her coach glances between us and smiles knowingly.

"We were telling Wesley how proud we are of her," she says. "Her growth this year has been incredible."

Wesley ducks her head, embarrassed but pleased. "Thank you."

The owner nods. "She's a cornerstone for us. On and off the field."

I smile, pride filling my chest as I squeeze my arm a little tighter around her. This is what she's been working toward.

"She is incredible," I say, letting them continue with soccer while hoping she knows I meant far more than just on the field.

"The coach of this year's camp, Brian Folley, happens to be in town tomorrow," Coach Bennett says, pausing dramatically when Wesley's eyes widen. "He'd love to meet you and maybe do a quick one-on-one session?"

Wesley's surprise is written all over her face. "Really? Yes, I mean, of course. That would be great."

"Plan for early around seven. He has to hit the road mid-morning."

Wesley nods firmly. "I'll be there." She turns toward me and smiles brightly. Her body presses closer to mine in a silent conversation between the two of us.

I've never been a fan of soccer, not for any particular reason other than not having a lot of exposure to it, but I've started paying attention. I know what teams will be a challenge for the Tempest this year and most of Wesley's stats. The bones of soccer aren't too different from hockey, and I find myself turning it on during my free evenings.

It's because of this newfound familiarity that I understand how big a deal it is that the coach running the Futures Camp is willing to set aside time to meet with her early.

Their conversation moves on to the upcoming season and other plans I'm not going to be part of.

I stand there anyway, memorizing the feel of her next to me.

Tomorrow, this ends.

Tomorrow, I'm supposed to go back to being who I was two months ago. Star athlete. In the limelight. Light-hearted bachelor. Alone.

My stomach hollows out.

The three of them keep talking. I nod in the right places and smile when expected.

Wesley listens with her whole body. Her chin is lifted, and she has one hand wrapped around her glass, the other gesturing while she talks. It's confident without being loud. Every once in a while, she glances at me, like she is checking that I'm still with her, and every time she does, something tight in my chest eases.

I don't realize I've checked out completely until her elbow nudges into my side. It's not a hard nudge, just enough to bring me back to the present. I look down at her, startled, and she's grinning at me, eyes bright with amusement.

"You okay over there?" she murmurs.

Before I can answer, Todd Sawyer clears his throat.

"Nathan," he says, smiling easily. "Sorry, I was asking you something."

Heat crawls up the back of my neck. "Yeah. Sorry."

He waves it off. "I was curious. You're having one hell of a season. What do you think clicked for you this year?"

This is familiar territory, even if it sucks. To everyone, I'm just hockey. Becca's date, the owner of the team, my teammates, and even my own parents all look at me and see the hockey player. The only person who hasn't asked me some variation of this question is the woman currently pressed into my side.

I go with it anyway.

"It's been a mix of things. Consistency, but I've also spent a lot of extra time working on my conditioning and decision making."

Todd nods approvingly. "It shows on the wing."

"Thank you," I say, meaning it.

Then he tilts his head, expression shifting slightly. "And do you think any of that has to do with Wesley?"

The room does not go silent, but it might as well have.

My chest locks up. It's not panic exactly, but something close. This is the train of thought I've been avoiding, knowing that it doesn't lead anywhere productive. Still, it's been circling the edges of my thoughts for weeks.

I open my mouth, but nothing comes out.

Because how do I answer that without confirming the fear that's been eating at me? People only think I'm playing well again because of her, and when she walks away, whatever version of me they are praising goes with her.

My jaw tightens. I keep my expression neutral, but inside, everything is stalling out.

Wesley feels it immediately.

She shifts closer, hand lacing with mine easily, and speaks before the silence stretches too far.

"I don't think that's fair." She looks the owner of her team directly in the eyes.

Todd looks surprised, then amused. "Oh?"

She smiles, but there's steel under it.

"I mean, obviously I support him," she continues. "But I've never met someone more dedicated to their team and their performance than Nathan. He puts in the work whether anyone is watching or not. It's who he is, and that has nothing to do with me."

Coach Bennett's smile deepens.

"If anyone knows anything about dedication," she joins in, motioning at Wesley, "it would be you."

The tension loosens, the conversation shifting to Wesley's suggestions for off-season training, but my thoughts circle.

My fear of the future strangles me quietly. Without her, I might slide back into the version of myself that was on his way to becoming a free agent at the end of the season.

Maybe it's what I deserve.

Music swells suddenly, the tempo slowing, and the room adjusts as couples begin to move closer together. Conversations begin to trail off naturally as people drift toward the small open space that has become a dance floor.

Wesley turns to me, studying my face. "You're somewhere else."

I shake my head automatically. "I'm fine."

"You don't like that he implied that your success has something to do with me." It's not an accusation, just an observation.

"Would you like it if they said that about you?" I ask, tilting my head. It comes out icy, but I actually want to know.

She's silent for a minute, as if thinking it through. "No, I wouldn't."

It doesn't even matter anymore because she reaches for my hand. "Dance with me."

Out on the dance floor, the lights are lower, and the noise fades into the background. She loops her arms around my neck. I settle my hands at her waist, careful at first, then less so when she presses closer.

We sway. The two of us move slowly, her head tipping forward until her forehead rests against my collarbone.

I breathe her in.

For a few minutes, I let myself forget everything other than the warmth of her body, the steady rhythm of the music, and the quiet hope that maybe this moment can exist without costing either of us something later.

36

Wesley

The song is slow, but not sad.

It's the kind of song that fills space rather than demands attention with low bass and a steady rhythm. Nathan's hands rest at my waist, his thumbs tracing the fabric of my dress mindlessly. Anyone watching us would think we're comfortable.

I feel the difference, though.

He's here, but part of him is somewhere else.

I noticed it earlier, the moment Todd asked his question. Nathan's entire body had locked up. It was subtle, but I didn't miss it. I don't miss anything about him. I watched his shoulders tighten, while the easy confidence he wears so well slipped for a second.

I'd stepped in without thinking, not because he needed me to, but because I hated the implication that his success belonged to me in some way.

Nathan doesn't need anyone to make him better. He might've agreed to this whole charade for my help with cross-training, but I'm not foolish enough to think that he couldn't have gone on long runs and done new agility workouts on his own. He didn't need me. He still doesn't. If anything, I've only made his life more complicated.

Now, on the dance floor, his grip is steady but careful. I rest my cheek against his chest, listening to his heartbeat under the music. The rhythm of it is sure to play on repeat long after tonight ends, so I let it imprint on me. It's fast, too fast for someone who looks this calm.

I'm not sure how many songs play, but we dance through them all until last call sounds from the bar, and people start to peel out.

I miss this already.

The thought presses in, unwelcome but persistent. We both know tonight is the end. We've avoided talking about it all week, which was surprisingly easy since our mouths were usually preoccupied. But avoiding it doesn't mean anything has changed. We both have too much at risk to keep doing whatever we've been doing.

Coach Bennett and Todd Sawyer's conversation about Future's Camp echoes in my head. This is the moment I've been working toward for years. It's the edge of something bigger for me and for my family.

I wouldn't forgive myself if I let anything derail it. Especially if it's a man who warned me that he doesn't date seriously.

Another song starts, but instead of leaning into him like my body longs to, I pull back. "Let's make the rounds before everyone leaves."

He studies my face for a second, but gives up when he doesn't seem to find what he was hoping to. "Yeah. Okay."

We drift back toward my teammates as they start collecting coats and saying their goodbyes. The party has thinned out, and the lights are turned on a little brighter to signify the end of the event.

Haley hugs me hard and tells me she's proud of me for reasons she doesn't explain. Avery gives Nathan a look that's too knowing and promises to text me tomorrow, which I refuse to acknowledge. Becca waves from across the room, already halfway out the door with her heels in her hand and her date trailing after her.

"Don't be strangers," Coach Bennett calls over to us, her voice warm as she leaves.

Nathan promises he won't be, even though I know better. Strangers is all I was ever meant to be with Nathan. Two months of playing pretend doesn't change that.

Nathan and I linger, talking to the stragglers, helping stack chairs, and thanking the staff. It feels like we're both hoping the night will stretch on forever, until the ending we both know is coming gets lost somewhere along the way.

Eventually, even the staff starts to leave.

We grab our coats wordlessly, and my heart twists when he doesn't reach for my hand the way he has been for weeks.

Outside, the air is cold, sobering the moment into something painful. The street glows with traffic lights and passing headlights.

Nathan stands beside me, hands shoved into his jacket pockets, shoulders hunched slightly against the cold.

We drove separately when we found out he had a late practice.

The reality of it settles heavily between us as we step onto the sidewalk. This is the part where we split. This is the part where this ends the way we planned it.

I've always wanted to make the National Team. To get to the World Cup. It's what I've worked toward my entire life. Standing here with him, it feels like what I want and what I've worked for are standing on opposite sides of the street, daring me to choose.

Nathan turns toward me, his expression already serious.

"So, I guess this is…" he starts.

I cut him off. "It's not midnight."

My words are rushed and half incoherent. They slip out without rational thought holding them back.

He blinks. "Wes—"

"It's not midnight yet," I say, firmer this time. "The day's not over."

For a second, he looks at me as if trying to decide if I'm serious or if this is a cruel joke. Then his mouth curves into a small, surprised smile.

"So, what should we do for the last hour of our fake relationship?" His lips tilt up mischievously as he steps closer to me. He's not even touching me, but my body reacts anyway.

This. This is what I needed.

I nod toward the hotel across the street. It's not fancy, but it's right here, towering over us. The windows glow warmly against the dark like a beacon.

"Come on," I say.

His eyes darken, and his shoulders relax. "I'd follow you anywhere."

I don't wait for him to change his mind. I don't let myself think about the promise in those words. I grab his hand and take off, laughing as we dodge between cars and jog across the street like teenagers. A horn blares. Someone yells something we ignore. The cold air burns my lungs, and my heart feels like it's trying to escape my chest.

By the time we reach the other side, we're both breathless and grinning, the tension cracked open by adrenaline and anticipation.

Nathan squeezes my hand, his thumb brushing over my knuckles. "Are you sure?" He asks.

"Certain."

And for the first time all night, it feels like we're moving toward something instead of away from it.

The hotel room door barely clicks shut before Nathan's hands are on me. It's not urgent, but lingering. His hands trail lightly across my skin, causing goosebumps to follow in his wake. I let myself focus on his calloused fingertips as he slides the straps of my dress off my shoulders.

His mouth finds mine as if he's been searching for it forever. I let my tongue trace over his teeth as I moan against him. We're both taking our time, as if learning the shape of each other all over again, even though we already know every inch.

The door is cold against my back, but I warm instantly when he presses against me. I squirm against him, my body as desperate for him as ever. His forehead rests against mine for a second, our breath tangling.

"It's never going to be enough," he murmurs, voice low.

My eyes open wide to find him watching me. I nod furiously in agreement. My hands slip into his jacket as my fingers trace familiar lines, knowing that I'll never trace them again.

It will never be enough. There is no such thing as enough of Nathan. There's only the desperate need for more. It's terrifying and all-consuming and impossible.

Sure, we could keep doing this temporarily, but we're not compatible long-term, not with the goals we have. The longer we drag it on, the more it'll hurt when it all inevitably ends.

But, god, I need it to be real. For tonight, I don't want to pretend that this is just pretend anymore. It's not, and maybe it never was.

"Nathan," I whisper against his ear, while he trails open-mouth kisses along my collarbone. "I know this is the last time and that it's over. I know why it needs to be..." I trail off, nerves coiled around the confession on the tip of my tongue.

He pulls away, eyes focused on my face, hands steady holding my own, as he waits for me to say something I should absolutely not say. Something that only makes everything more painful.

"Wesley." It's a plea that's so full of hope my chest cracks open.

"I need this to end tomorrow." I close my eyes and breathe out, trying to ignore the sadness in his eyes. "But tonight, I don't want to pretend this is fake. I don't want benefits. I just want you. For real. Not as part of some deal and not to get our coaches off our backs, but because I want you. One last time."

His eyes search my face, blazing with words unspoken, but he clenches his jaw, biting them back. Instead, he nods and presses a slow kiss to my lips.

"Real. Just for us," he finally says, before tugging at the zipper on the back of my dress.

We take our time shedding layers, kicking off our shoes without care. Every movement feels intentional, stretched thin by the knowledge that there's no rush and no tomorrow attached.

He backs me toward the bed, kissing me the whole way. His hands map me like he's committing every inch to memory. When we fall onto the mattress, it's with a soft laugh and a tangle of limbs, warmth bleeding between us.

His head is between my legs instantly, his tongue teasing me in endlessly slow circles. I weave my hands into his hair, losing myself in the feel of his tongue and the sounds that he makes as he brings me to the edge.

Having him like this still feels surreal. Every flick of his tongue against my clit is better than the one before. He's not only amazing in bed; he's generous. I can't think of a single time in the past couple of weeks that I haven't gotten off first on his mouth, his fingers, or his cock. Most of the time, more than once.

He teases that getting me off is one of the sexiest things he's ever seen. Considering how enthusiastically he's moving right now, I'm inclined to believe him.

His fingers slide into me, curling up at the perfect angle. I gasp, and he repeats the motion over and over.

My back arches off the bed as the orgasm rocks through me. He slides his tongue along my slit, guiding me through it until I'm weightless.

"That's right. Come for me, Wesley," he murmurs against my thigh.

Only once he's wrung every ounce of pleasure out of my orgasm does he slide up my body, pausing along the way to tease each nipple into points. My nails scrape along his back, pulling him higher until I can kiss him. When our mouths finally meet, I exhale against him, losing myself in the kiss with the taste of myself still on his tongue.

We make out for a while, hungry yet patient, both of us wanting to make this last. It's not like the passionate, quick fuck against his door when I get to his apartment after practice. Or the needy, quiet sex in the dark when we both wake up wanting each other.

This is different. This is something we are both savoring with a desperate need to memorize every single second. Every touch. Every sigh.

He rips the condom packet open and shifts to slide it on. Once he has, I find myself pushing him onto his back until I'm sitting on top of him.

He's sprawled across the bed, while I straddle him. A wicked grin crosses his face as I lean over him, kissing his neck. His cock brushes my clit when I shift. I repeat the motion until we're both breathless.

I line him up and slowly slide down onto his cock until he's seated fully inside me.

"You feel so good." My voice is shaky as I slide up and down on his cock.

He closes his grip around my hips, his hooded eyes looking up at me with reverence while I ride him.

Will this be the last time he looks at me like this?

"That's it, baby, take what you need," he groans, leaning up to suck my nipple into his mouth. The sensation is overwhelming, and I pick up my pace.

Then, he slides his thumb over my clit in slow, teasing circles. I forget everything other than the feel of him on me and in me.

I shift down, my mouth finding its way to his own as our tongues tangle until I don't know where he ends and I begin.

We left the lights on, bright and fluorescent, giving me the chance to watch every single reaction on his face. He watches me just as closely, like I'm something precious and fleeting all at once.

He takes over, wrapping one hand around my back while the other grabs my ass. He thrusts up into me at the same time I move down to meet him.

Every move feels like a sentence left unfinished. Every touch says what neither of us has been brave enough to voice. It's devastating, full of pauses where we look at each other, foreheads pressed together as if we're trying to stretch time by sheer will.

Normally, our desire would take over until we're chasing the heat and each other, desperate for release.

But tonight, we stay present, letting it burn us alive.

I wonder if he'll think of me weeks from now when my nail marks on his back are long gone. I know I'll think of him even after the aches of what his body does to me are only a memory. I'm certain that I'll think of this night far too much to be considered healthy.

The room is quiet except for the soft sounds we make together, the bed creaking faintly beneath us, and the city humming outside the window.

Our kisses grow messy and desperate. His pace picks up, cock sliding into me faster while I meet him every step of the way. When he reaches between us, fingers toying with my clit, I spin out, falling over the edge and pulling him right along with me. Our orgasms feed each other until it's a blur of sensation and perfection.

We stay tangled together, skin warm and hearts racing. Nathan presses a kiss to my temple, then my cheek.

"Wes," he whispers.

He stays with his forehead tucked against my shoulder, fingers tracing slow, absent patterns along my arm like he's afraid stillness will break whatever this is. When he finally speaks, his voice is stripped bare.

"I don't want this to end. I don't want to wake up tomorrow and pretend like these two months haven't changed something for me."

My skin tingles where we touch as his voice slides down my spine. I shift to look at him, really look at him, the vulnerability he never lets anyone see sitting right there in his eyes.

Nathan Wilder, the man who doesn't settle down, might be willing to settle down with me.

"It's changed something for me too," I say softly.

His breath catches, and he presses a slow kiss to my mouth, different from before. A question and an answer all in one, like he's sealing something fragile and sacred between us.

We don't say anything else, the tiredness from the party and the past hour, lulling us into the quiet place before sleep. As I drift off, I let the seed of hope grow.

Maybe we can have it all.

I curl into him, wondering if he'll feel the same way tomorrow.

Will our hushed confessions get a chance to see the light of day?

37

Wesley

I wake up warm. Nathan is behind me with his arm slung over my waist and his face tucked into the space between my shoulder blades. His breath is slow and even, brushing my skin every time he exhales.

It's the kind of peaceful moment that makes you want to stay still so you don't disturb it. I let myself settle into him, the blanket acting as a cocoon hiding us from the world.

For one dangerous, perfect second, I let myself believe this could last.

The room is quiet and peaceful. Our heartbeats are pounding in a synchronized rhythm. My muscles ache in the best way, and my mind is soft around the edges, still wrapped up in last night. We said and did things that went far past whatever our arrangement was meant to be. Today, we would have to figure out if we want to keep this going. I don't know what the right answer is.

I almost close my eyes again.

Then the sunlight hits.

It's bright, not the gentle gray light of early morning, but golden, slicing through a gap in the curtains and landing directly across the bed. My stomach drops before my brain catches up.

No.

I twist to see the bedside clock.

8:02 a.m.

The warmth evaporates instantly, replaced by pure, white-hot panic.

"Shit," I gasp, already throwing the covers off myself.

Nathan stirs behind me, groaning softly. "Mmm… five more minutes," he murmurs, his voice thick with sleep and affection, making my skin prickle even as I spiral.

"I'm late," I choke out, scrambling off the bed.

My feet hit the carpet, and I nearly trip over myself, wrapping the sheet around my body as if modesty matters when my entire future is collapsing in on itself. My heart is in my throat.

Where is my phone?

I spin in place, scanning the room. Nothing.

"No, no, no," I mutter, yanking on my underwear, then my dress, hopping on one foot as I shove each leg through the opening. My hands are shaking. "Where is it?"

"What?" Nathan asks, sitting up abruptly now. He blinks at me, still half asleep, a lazy smile pulling at his mouth when his eyes land on me. "Hey. Morning."

I don't return the smile.

That's when he knows something is wrong.

"Wes?" He rubs a hand over his face, frowning. "What's going on?"

"I was supposed to meet him," I say, voice already climbing toward hysteria. "I was supposed to meet the head coach for the Futures Camp at seven for a one-on-one session. Seven."

Nathan's expression changes immediately, sleep burning off as reality snaps into place. "What time is it?" he asks, already swinging his legs out of bed.

"Eight." I toss the pillows off the couch, my phone still missing.

"Oh, fuck."

"Yeah." I shove my feet into my shoes without bothering to sit down. "I overslept. I missed it. I fucking missed it. How could I let this happen?"

"Okay. It's okay." He's moving fast now. "We'll figure it out."

"Nothing about this is fucking okay." I whip my head toward him, panic etched into every muscle on my face.

"You're right." He nods, standing up off the bed.

"This isn't a workout, Nathan. This is… this is everything." My voice cracks.

"I know." There's no hesitation in his voice. He's already pulling on his jeans, searching the room. "Where's your phone?"

"I don't know." Tears are dangerously close to spilling over, but I block them out. "I can't find it. It must've died last night."

He crosses the room in two strides and bends down by the nightstand. "Found it."

He holds up the black screen. "Dead," he confirms.

I press my palms into my eyes for a second, wishing I could rewind time. This is my worst nightmare.

Nathan's hands land on my shoulders, but they don't settle me the way they normally would.

"Hey. It's not over yet." His voice is soft, but tight as if he's already drawing conclusions in his head. "Where's the session?"

"The field across town." I meet his eyes, only to find too many questions hiding in their depths. This isn't the time.

"Then we go," he says simply, pulling open the hotel door. "Now."

We're out the door seconds later. My dress is half-zipped, and my fingers fumble with my car keys. The adrenaline buzzing between us could start a fire. The hotel hallway rushes past as we jog toward the elevator, neither of us saying what we're both thinking.

Last night was supposed to be the end. This was never supposed to happen. I'd been a fool to think there would be any outcome other than this.

Now, morning has come crashing in, loud and unforgiving, demanding everything from me all over again.

I don't know what it's going to cost when it comes to my career, but I already know it'll cost me him. I can't have that and him too. It was stupid to think I ever could.

We hit the garage at a near run, footsteps echoing off concrete. The air is cold and damp compared to the warmth we left behind upstairs. Rows of parked cars blur together until mine comes into view.

Nathan slows first.

"Let me drive you." He's already reaching for my door. "You're shaking."

I stop short, keys clenched in my fist so tight it hurts.

"No," I snap.

The word comes out harsher than I mean it to, sharp enough that his hand freezes midair.

"I need to drive myself," I add quickly, but the damage is already done. My chest is tight, and my breath shallow. "I can't show up with you. Not late. It looks bad enough without you there."

The underlying implication passes between us. His presence makes this worse.

He blinks. "Wes, I just meant I can get you there faster."

"This is the reason I'm late in the first place." I motion between us.

The second the words leave my mouth, I want them back.

It's not his fault. I know that. Rationally, I know this is on me. I didn't set an alarm. I didn't charge my phone. I let myself forget who I'm supposed to be. But panic has taken the wheel, and it's not interested in fairness.

Nathan's face falls, and I ignore the way my heart squeezes in my chest. He doesn't bother to mask the hurt in his eyes, and I wish I could be the one to fix it. I wish I could go back two hours and make sure I didn't screw everything up. It's too late for all of it.

He straightens, shoulders squaring. It takes him a second, but then he nods once.

"Okay," he says quietly. "Yeah. Okay."

I fumble with my door, hands unsteady. He steps back, giving me the space that I asked for, but it feels wrong.

"Good luck," he adds. "Let me know how it goes."

I nod, unable to trust my voice.

We both know I won't.

This is it. Missing this session is exactly why I never wanted this to become more than an arrangement. This is what happens when I let myself get distracted and forget that everything I want is one mistake away from slipping out of reach.

I slide into the driver's seat, slamming the door a little harder than necessary. My hands are still shaking as I start the car. The engine roars to life, and I pull out of the space, tires crunching softly against the concrete.

At the ramp, I glance up into the rearview mirror.

Nathan is still standing there watching me leave. My throat tightens, but I don't stop.

I drive out into the morning light, heart pounding, knowing with painful clarity that last night was real. It was the most real thing I've ever felt, but it might've cost me everything I've never been able to afford to lose.

I make it to Harborlight Stadium in fifteen minutes.

I don't remember most of the drive, other than the gas station two blocks from the stadium, where I climbed into the backseat, shedding my dress to pull on my backup gear.

By the time I pull into the stadium lot, my hands are sweating on the steering wheel. As I pull into a parking space, I see them.

Coach Folley is walking out of the stadium doors, coat already on, with his phone in his hand. Coach Bennett is beside him, mid-sentence, both of them slowing when they spot me sprinting across the lot.

"Coach," I call, breathless. "Coach, I'm so sorry."

They stop.

I skid to a halt in front of them, words spilling out before I can slow them down or make them sound composed.

"My phone died. I swear it was charged when I went to bed, but then my alarm didn't go off. I know that sounds like an excuse, but it's not. I've never missed a session. I take full responsibility."

Coach Folley looks at me. His expression is calm, but his mouth is pressed into a thin line that tells me he's already decided how he feels. He glances at his watch, and my chest hollows out.

"That may be," he says evenly. "But this was important."

"I know, and I'm ready now. I will take any time you have. Ten minutes. Fifteen. Anything."

Coach Bennett stays quiet beside him, her presence suddenly heavy.

He exhales through his nose and shakes his head once. "I have a flight to catch. I can't stay."

Dizziness clouds my vision, and my hands tremble at my side.

"I understand." My voice is tight, and I barely hear it over the roaring in my ears. "I want you to know how seriously I take this camp. This opportunity means everything to me. I assure you that despite today, I'm locked in."

His arms cross over his chest as he studies me for a moment longer.

"I hope so, because focus and preparation are not optional at this level. Come camp time, I expect better."

That's it. He's made up his mind about me, and it's not positive.

He nods once to Coach Bennett and turns toward his rental car, suitcase rolling behind him.

I stand there and watch him go.

My hands curl into fists at my sides, nails biting into my palms. I'm still going to camp, which is a small mercy, but the one person I need to impress already thinks I don't belong there. He thinks I'm unreliable, and unreliable people don't make it onto the National Team.

Coach Bennett doesn't speak right away.

She waits until his car disappears from the lot before turning back to me, her gaze sharp but not unkind.

"Are you okay?" She asks.

I swallow, pulling at my sleeve.

"No," I say honestly. "But I will be."

She watches me for another second, like she's deciding how much weight to put behind what she says next.

"This isn't like you. You're one of the most disciplined players I have."

I nod, swallowing past the tightness in my throat.

"When I told you it's healthy to have a life outside of soccer. I meant it." She pauses, choosing her words carefully. "But you are the last person I thought I'd have to remind that it can't come at the expense of this. Soccer still has to be the priority."

My heart might've broken into pieces when I drove away from Nathan, but now, those pieces cut into every part of me, leaving nothing whole in their wake.

I nod again because it's all I can do. My mind is spiraling, replaying the night in brutal, perfect detail. We'd taken our time, neither of us wanting to let go. It hadn't occurred to me once to check the clock or set an alarm. I was too lost in him.

And just like that, I'd forgotten the very thing I swore to never put second.

If I had walked away when I was supposed to, I'd have been early and prepared. I would've been exactly who they expected me to be.

Instead, I let myself want something other than this. I take a deep breath, resigning myself to the fact that I don't have that luxury. Maybe someday, but not now.

"I won't let it happen again," I say, forcing the words out with conviction. "Ever."

Coach Bennett searches my face. "Good."

Then she turns and heads back into the stadium, leaving me alone in the parking lot with the consequences of my own choices.

I get into my car and shut the door, the silence pressing in on me immediately. My phone lights up as I plug it into the charger.

One new message.

Nathan: I hope it went okay. Please let me know if you're alright.

Tears prick at my eyes, and for the first time in as long as I can remember, I don't fight them off. They trail down my cheeks in a stream that picks up speed the longer I let it happen. My head falls to my steering wheel as the sobs rack my body, wringing me dry until there is nothing left.

I'm not sure how long I let them fall, but eventually, the tears dry against my skin, making it tight.

For a second, my thumbs hover over his message, muscle memory begging me to respond. To let myself have one more moment. I could give us a soft ending instead of the sharp one from before.

But I don't.

I lock the phone and drop it face down in the console.

A clean break.

That's what this has to be.

Missing this session is exactly why we had an expiration date in the first place. We each got what we set out to get. Even without my response, he knows as well as I do what comes next. Distance. Space.

My future is fragile, and I will not gamble it away on feelings, no matter how real they felt in the dark.

I start the car and pull out of the lot, leaving whatever is left of us where it belongs. Behind me.

38

Nathan

I'm in Seattle, three floors up in a hotel that smells like lemon cleaner and recycled air. I already know how this night is going to go.

We won the game. The guys are loud down the hall as someone knocks on the doors, while someone else yells into the rooms. I scored the winning goal, so I should be out there. I shut myself in anyway. They pestered me on the bus ride back to the hotel, but I said I was tired. Which is true, just not in the way they think.

I check my phone out of habit more than hope.

No new messages.

There's a stupid part of me that keeps expecting her name to be there. But Wesley isn't the type to wake up and undo this. She isn't someone who would let her feelings get in the way of her plans, even if I wish she were.

I knew the second she got into her car that it was over.

I'd seen it in her eyes. It was the kind of resolve that's useless to argue against. The decision was made, and now, a week and a half later, I still don't know how to feel about it.

My mind does cartwheels trying to reason through it. It'd be easier if she felt nothing, then I could move on knowing that it was never supposed to be anything anyway. But, she did feel something for me. It just wasn't enough to change anything.

It didn't matter that it was real or felt good. It didn't matter that she wanted it.

What mattered was that whatever was between us had put her dreams at risk, and that was one thing she'd never compromise on. It was also the one thing I'd promised myself not to get in the way of.

I've been sick thinking about it.

The morning replayed in my head more than any bad shift on the ice ever had. Her voice had been sharp with panic. Her face was hollow when she told me she was late, like the ground was about to swallow her whole, and she was waiting for it to happen.

I didn't make her miss it.

I didn't turn off her alarm or ask her to stay.

But I was there. I was a part of it, and that was enough.

I strip out of my suit and stand under the shower longer than necessary, letting the water run hot until my skin turns red, and my thoughts blur at the edges. It doesn't help. Nothing does. Not the noise of the water, not the quiet afterward, not the game film looping through my head instead of her smile.

I dry off, pull on sweats, sit on the edge of the bed, and check my phone again.

Still nothing.

Two days ago, I finally pestered Liam to ask Avery for information. He clocked me immediately, but did it anyway.

She was still going to camp in a couple of days.

My chest loosened at that. Relief and guilt tangled together so tight it made me nauseous. Relief because she hadn't lost the thing she's been building toward her entire life. Guilt because I knew exactly what it had cost her to make sure of that.

Me.

Takeout should be here any minute, but I'm not hungry. I ordered out of habit from the same burger place we always order from here. Ordering in was an excuse to not be around the team. I don't have it in me to sit at a table pretending to care about the game or the gossip. Though sitting alone with the truth I can't say out loud, isn't much better.

It's taken everything in me not to text her or show up at the stadium. I woke up before seven every day this week. It was the universe's cruel way of reminding me that I no longer have anywhere I need to be at that time. I don't even know when it became so natural, but it had.

What kills me is that I'd already started planning. I'd thought about how we could make it work around flights, camps, and games. My mind got caught up in it all as if I hadn't known from the beginning exactly how it would end.

I check my phone one last time before tossing it on the bed in frustration.

This is fucking embarrassing.

I don't blame her for the silence. If anything, I respect it. She's doing exactly what she said she would. Choosing the thing that matters most. Cutting clean instead of letting it bleed out slowly. I should be doing the same.

Hell, I played great tonight. I've played great all week. I should go out to celebrate, but I can't stomach it.

Instead, I lie back on the bed and stare at the ceiling, the city humming faintly through the window.

There's a knock at my door, and I assume it's dinner, until the whispers on the other side grow louder. Wyatt laughs about something, and Liam argues with him about where they're going. Without hearing his voice, I know Grayson is there, too.

The knock comes again, louder this time, as if to emphasize they won't be leaving unless I answer. So, I push the door open, already halfway back to my bed by the time it hits the wall.

Wyatt is dressed in his usual laid-back, dark colors. Liam follows, jacket slung over his shoulder, tapping something into his phone. Grayson brings up the rear, eyes sweeping the room in one slow, assessing pass.

They all stop when they see me in my sweats, barefoot with my hair unbrushed. I ignore the stares, yanking my food out of Wyatt's hands.

He just blinks. "Wow. This is bleak."

"Jesus," Liam says. "Did we lose? Why do you look like we lost?"

"We won." I pull a fry out of the bag and pop it into my mouth. Maybe if I'm quiet, they'll leave.

Liam squints at me. "You sure?"

"I'm not going out," I add before they even ask.

Wyatt scoffs. "Didn't ask."

"Yes, you did. With your eyes."

"I didn't ask you shit with my eyes."

"You two done flirting?" Grayson eyes the two of us, ever the mediator.

Liam drops onto the chair by the desk. "Come on, man. You need to get out of your head."

"I'm fine."

"No, you're not." Wyatt rolls his eyes. "You look like a man who's about to watch three straight hours of SportsCenter and pine after a girl that didn't choose you."

"Dude, what the fuck?" Liam slaps his arm.

"I'm just saying he's not fine." Wyatt shrugs, clueless and careless as always.

"I ordered food," I say, as if that settles the matter.

Liam snorts.

They start talking over each other then, but I get the gist. I'm Nathan Wilder. I'm on a hot streak. I should be celebrating. It is all true and totally irrelevant.

"Get a drink," Wyatt says. "Get two."

Liam grins. "Get a rebound."

My stomach twists so hard it actually pisses me off.

"Don't."

He raises his hands. "What? I'm being supportive."

"I said don't."

Wyatt's grin falters. "Okay, damn."

"I don't need a rebound, I don't need a drink, and I don't need to pretend I'm having a good time, just so you guys feel better about me."

The room goes quiet.

I immediately regret the edge in my voice, but not enough to take it back.

Liam exhales slowly. "We're trying to help."

"Then help by leaving," I snap.

Wyatt mutters, "You were with her to improve your game. It worked. Even with it over, you still crushed it this week. Wasn't that the whole point?"

He's not wrong. I should be thrilled. I'd been terrified that she was the only reason my play had improved, but here I was, almost two weeks later, kicking ass and as miserable and alone as ever.

"Yeah, it was." I click through the TV channels. "Now, go."

Grayson hasn't said a word. He's watching me, head tilted slightly, looking past what I'm saying to the thing underneath it. He always does that. It's annoying as hell.

He finally speaks. "You guys go."

Wyatt turns to him. "What?"

"I'll stay," Grayson says calmly. "You two go."

Liam frowns. "You don't have to babysit him."

There's a beat of hesitation. Then Wyatt shrugs. "Suit yourselves. Text us when you decide to stop being an ass."

Liam looks like he wants to say something else, but Grayson shoots him a look, and he drops it.

The door closes behind them, the hallway noise swallowing them up.

Grayson sits on the edge of the other bed, elbows on his knees. "You want to talk about it?"

"No."

"Fine by me."

I stare at the takeout bag before pulling out the food inside. The smell hits, and I realize I am hungry after all.

Grayson watches me with real concern.

I ignore it. Suffering alone would be preferable to his hovering, but I don't tell him to go either.

Once the room smells like fried food and the takeout containers are stacked empty on the desk, he finally pushes.

I should've known he would eventually.

I'm propped up against the pillows at the top of the bed, my phone resting loosely in my hand.

"You've checked that thing a thousand times." Grayson points to my phone.

I don't look at him. "No, I haven't."

He huffs a quiet laugh. "You have."

Silence settles again with the hum of the mini fridge and the distant traffic outside, slowly driving me insane.

"What happened?" He asks.

"Nothing happened. It was always fake. It was always supposed to end."

Grayson turns on the bed so he's facing me fully. "That's all it was?"

I swallow because it feels wrong to lie about what it meant to me.

"We got a little too involved, but that doesn't mean the plan ever changed."

"You're not acting like any of it was fake."

The words are on the tip of my tongue, but convincing him it was nothing would be as impossible as convincing myself of it.

"It wasn't. At least, not to me. And not to her, not really. But now, I guess none of that matters."

He doesn't interrupt, so I keep going. I shouldn't, but the pressure has been building for days, and he's always been good at finding the cracks.

"She made her choice. Soccer was always going to be her choice. It was never going to be me." I finally look at him. "And it's for the best."

Grayson raises an eyebrow.

"I wasn't even sure how much I wanted her." The lie tastes thin as it rolls off my tongue. "Or if I was just scared that I couldn't play as well without her. I mean, I only pursued her so she'd help me cross-train in the first place."

Grayson stares at me for a second before laughing right in my face. It's loud and immediately grates on my nerves.

"Are you shitting me right now?" I glare at him.

"That's such bullshit," he says between breaths.

"You don't know that."

"I absolutely do," he replies calmly. "You've played your entire life. You were elite before Wesley. You never needed her to train with you, you dumbass. You wanted an excuse to spend time with her."

I open my mouth to argue, but he keeps going.

"And if it being over was for the best," he adds, holding his hand up to keep me from speaking, "you wouldn't be this miserable."

That shuts me up entirely.

I played damn good tonight. My body moved instinctually out there. My mind never drifted towards her. I was focused and unstoppable. It was only after the whistle blew that she consumed my thoughts.

I've been telling myself that I needed her help because it's easier than admitting the truth that it was never about need. It was about want. I wanted her. Want her.

But what good does that do now? Denial hurts less. At least then I can protect myself from wanting someone who doesn't want me enough.

"I'm not enough." The words are barely audible and more to myself than to him. "I never am. Not for her. Not for…" I let the words trail off and stand up, turning off one of the lights.

Thankfully, Grayson gets the hint, grabbing his jacket off the chair. "Seems to me it was never about if you can still perform without her, but more about if she can still perform with you." He pulls the door open. "And if you let her go without a fight, neither of you will ever really know about any of it."

The door clicks shut behind him.

I pace the room, my frustration growing to a new high as Grayson's words replay in my head. She ended this. She didn't even want to try. I'd have chosen her if I could have.

It wasn't my choice. Letting her go was the only thing I could think to do. I loved her too much to put myself in the race against her dreams.

Shit.

I love her.

I love her, and it's over.

I love her, and she doesn't love me.

39

Wesley

By the end of the week, everyone at camp has learned my routine. I'm early to the locker room and last to leave the field. I take extra laps when the sun is already sinking and ice baths that do nothing to dull the ache that's carved far deeper than my muscles. I watch game film twice if the schedule allows and stretch until my legs shake. I don't need to do any of it; they're already working us hard enough, but stopping feels worse.

It's easier when my body hurts, when the tiredness runs so bone deep that I have no choice but to fall asleep the second I lie down. Better that than staring at the ceiling, wondering if I've made a mistake.

The locker room hums with pre-scrimmage energy. It's our last chance to impress the coaches, and I plan to do exactly that.

Someone's speaker is playing the same hype playlist we've all heard since college. The air smells like grass and sweat as everyone slides on the gear that's been practically glued to us all week.

I sit on the bench and thread my laces through my cleats, slow and methodical. Right foot first. Pull tight. Loop. Cross. My eyes stay down because looking around means seeing faces that still laugh, joke, and have space in their lives for things that aren't soccer.

I don't.

Jess drops onto the bench next to me. Her ponytail is already damp even though we haven't stepped outside yet. She's good, and I'm relieved we're not competing for the same position. She's fast and smart; the kind of player who makes herself useful everywhere. The kind of player the National Team likes.

"You ready?" she asks, braiding her pony without looking.

I nod. "Always."

"After the scrimmage, a bunch of us are going out. It'll be low-key, just some dinner and maybe a drink. You should come."

I pull my left lace tight, harder than necessary. "I'm good."

Jess tilts her head. "You sure? It's our last night. It might be good to blow off some steam."

She's offered all week. Other players have too, but after consistently turning them down, most got the hint. Jess, though, offers persistently every day anyway.

"I'm sure. I need to stretch and get some rest. It's a long plane ride back tomorrow."

She laughs softly, tilting her head as if studying me. "You're intense, you know that?"

I look up, meet her eyes, and give her something that probably resembles a smile. "That's why I'm here."

She shrugs, standing up off the bench. "Suit yourself, but the offer stands."

Staying focused is a choice I make every morning. It's discipline. You wake up and decide what matters, then you build your day around that decision so there's no room for anything else to sneak in.

I have spent my life perfecting this, until him. But I've since course-corrected and won't be letting myself slip again.

Training is twice a day instead of once. Gym sessions after dinner instead of team outings. My phone is off whenever I can manage. My lights are out early. If there's a version of me that existed outside of soccer, she is archived, put away where she can't interfere.

The coaches love it.

They call me reliable and consistent. This version of me is the one who makes it to the World Cup. This is the version that provides financially for my family. There is no room for a different version, not anymore.

I jog out onto the field with the rest of the group, the Florida heat already pressing down on my shoulders. The grass is immaculate, cut short enough to be fast. If I've learned anything this past week, it's that everything about this camp is designed to make you sharper, faster, and better.

I'm thriving. I've played the best soccer of my life this week. It should make me happy.

This scrimmage is the last real evaluation. Ninety minutes of full-out play, nothing held back. I line up at midfield and bounce lightly on my toes, the familiar pregame buzz settling into my bones. Once the whistle blows, the world narrows.

Every touch feels intentional. I find space before it's open, sending balls through seams that most people hesitate to even look at. My legs burn from tracking back hard, pressing when I need to, and finishing anytime the chance comes. At one point, I catch Coach Folley's eye as he gives me the smallest nod, like he'd been hoping I'd play like this.

By the time the scrimmage ends, my lungs burn, and sweat has soaked my hair through. Regardless, I jog off the field, refusing to show how tired I am.

In the locker room, the energy is looser now. Everyone is thrumming with the adrenaline that comes after laying it all out on the line and knowing there is nothing left we can do.

Jess catches my eye across the room and lifts her brows in a silent question. I shake my head once. She rolls her eyes but waves as she leaves.

I peel off my socks so that I can slide my shin guards off, forearms resting on my thighs. My phone buzzes in my bag, but I don't check it. It's probably Avery pestering me about how the scrimmage went or Harper asking me how I'm doing. I don't feel like dealing with any of it, because it always leads to more questions. Questions that I don't want to answer.

When the room starts to clear, I sit on the bench contemplating my evening. It's only seven, and there's too much day left to go sit in my hotel room. I retape my ankle, fingers moving automatically. The joint aches, but it's a clean pain. Earned. I pull my cleats back on instead of putting them in my bag, grab my water bottle, and head back out.

The field looks different when it's empty.

The sun has dipped enough that the light is golden, stretching long across the field. I jog the perimeter slowly at first. A cool down to keep my muscles loose, while I reminisce on the past week.

This is it.

This is everything I ever wanted.

Futures Camp. The National Team. The success I've always dreamed of.

I jog another lap. Another lap in, and I'm still waiting for the excitement to hit. When it doesn't, my pace picks up. My strides lengthen, breathing growing more ragged. I cut across the field and push harder, legs burning as I break into a run, then faster, chasing something I can't quite name.

The ache is still there.

I sprint until my lungs scream and my vision blurs. Moving until there's nothing left in my head but the sound of my own breathing and the thud of my feet. When I finally slow, it's at midfield. I bend over, hands on my knees, sweat dripping onto the white line.

It doesn't go away.

My legs give out, and I drop onto my back, arms spread, staring up at the sky. The grass is warm beneath me. I stretch my calves and hamstrings on autopilot. This is what I've always dreamed of.

I keep repeating it, thinking that if I do it enough, it won't feel so empty.

A door slams somewhere behind me.

I sit up as Coach Folley comes onto the field with his hands in his pockets. His posture is relaxed, but somehow, he's still intimidating.

He stops a few feet away, eyes scanning me with the quiet assessment I've come to recognize.

"You were excellent today," he says.

"Thank you, sir."

"This is who I expected to meet at that one-on-one."

My stomach tightens. "I'm sorry about that. Again. I know apologies don't fix it, but…"

He lifts a hand. "Not needed." His mouth curves slightly. "You've more than proved yourself this week. I'm glad it was only a mistake."

I swallow.

Mistake.

The word settles uncomfortably in my chest. My gaze drifts back up to the sky, clouds barely moving. It's like I'm bleeding out slowly from a self-inflicted wound.

Because it didn't feel like a mistake.

It still doesn't.

That night, I felt alive in a way that even this doesn't touch. Happy in a way that isn't earned or ranked. There was no pressure, just wanting and something real enough to hold on to.

Except, I hadn't held on to it at all.

Coach Folley claps his hands once. "Get some rest. You've got a future ahead of you."

"Yes, sir."

He leaves me there, alone again, the field stretching wide and quiet around me.

I lie back down, the grass brushing my shoulders, and close my eyes. This was the right choice. The pain is temporary, and sacrifice is part of the deal.

I don't know how long it's supposed to hurt before it stops feeling like I gave everything up instead of choosing it.

40

Nathan

Liam is worried about me. He didn't say it outright, but he's insisted on hanging out every night this week. It was fine when that involved staying home and ordering something greasy, but now I wish he'd just leave me alone.

The pitying look in his eyes is the only reason I agreed to go tonight. It's Becca's birthday, and she wants the boys there. It's my fault, really. Wesley and I let our teams get too friendly, and now, I'm paying the price.

I've already tried to get out of it twice. I would've tried again, but Liam told me that Wesley is completely fine with me being there.

It shouldn't matter, but it does. Because if she's fine with it, if it doesn't matter to her, then I'm sure as hell not going to let it matter to me.

I can't say I'm surprised. Being okay is Wesley to a T. That woman could block out any emotion without blinking. I was a problem but ghosting me solved it. She's probably moved on and classified me as a two-month mistake. Nothing more.

Getting ready took longer than necessary because I couldn't stop standing in front of my closet, trying to find the right shirt. I hate that I cared. I hate that I even registered which shirt looked better, but I put on the black button-down anyway. It's just a shirt, but sitting in Liam's car outside the bar, I smooth it down too many times for it to be casual.

We make our way inside, finding it packed. Becca has gotten the bar to rope off a section in the back for her, and most of my teammates are already here. Music is thumping through the walls, bass rattling the windows.

Becca said it would be a small get-together, which apparently means the whole damn city. Wyatt is slumped down in the corner, sipping on what I'm sure is not his first beer. Over by the bar, Avery and Haley chatter away with a couple of guys I don't recognize.

I clock the exits and the time, wondering how long I have to stay before Liam will detach himself from my side so I can go home.

"Relax," Liam says, bumping my shoulder. "You should be having fun."

"I am relaxed."

"Sure you are."

Wyatt grins as he saunters up to us. "I'm surprised you showed up. I thought this might cut into your self-scheduled wallowing time."

I glare at him as he flashes a sarcastic smile and pats my shoulder.

We push toward the bar. I order a beer I don't want and take a sip that tastes like nothing. My grin feels forced, because it is, but dammit if I'm not trying to be the version of me that existed before her.

It works for about thirty seconds.

Until I see Wesley.

So, this is what fine looks like.

She's near the back, half-turned toward one of her teammates, laughing at something I can't hear. Her hair is pulled back, and she's tanner, probably from spending all of last week in the sun. I picture her at Future's Camp, hoping she did well. I wish I were still the person she'd call to talk to about it.

My chest tightens before I can stop it.

She doesn't see me at first, or maybe she does and pretends not to. Either way, the effect is the same. I stand there, beer sweating in my hand, feeling like I've been dropped into the wrong scene of my own life.

Liam follows my gaze. "She doesn't seem bothered."

"Thanks," I mutter.

"Maybe tonight will be like closure or something," he adds, taking a swig of his beer.

My stomach churns because closure means settled. It means it's over for good. She looks like she's already gotten whatever closure she needs. She's clearly not stuck in the part of this that I am.

Grayson whistles low. "You could go say 'Hi.'"

I shoot him a look that manages to shut him up for once. The last thing I want right now is his responsible, wise perspective.

The space between Wesley and me feels intentional. She's not avoiding me exactly. She's just existing in a way that doesn't account for me at all, even though I'm aware of her every move.

Becca squeals when she sees Liam and me, launching herself into a group hug that smells like tequila and perfume. She thanks everyone for coming. Someone buys shots, and the party commences.

At some point, it becomes unavoidable.

We end up in the same loose circle, friends overlapping, conversations bleeding into each other. I'm suddenly very aware of where my hands are and how close I'm standing to her. My heart rate has picked up as if I'm finishing a shift on the ice.

She notices me at the same moment I stop pretending I haven't been looking.

Her smile falters a fraction before she smooths it back into place and turns toward me. My hands start sweating.

"Hi," she says.

"Hey."

There's a beat where neither of us speaks. Music thumps behind us, the bass vibrating through my ribs. Avery says something to Becca that makes her laugh, but the sound feels like it's coming from another room.

I clear my throat. "Uh. Sorry if… if me being here is awkward."

The words taste like pride swallowed sideways.

Her eyebrows lift slightly. "What? No," she says easily. "Of course not."

Of course not. Great.

Maybe she really did pretend the entire time.

"How was the camp last week?" I ask because silence feels worse. "Did Florida treat you okay?"

"It was good. Really good, actually."

I nod, even though I'm numb. "Yeah?"

She nods back, a little more animated now. "I played well. The feedback was solid." A pause. Then, quieter, like she's letting herself have it for half a second. "I've got a real shot."

There it is. The thing that mattered more than us.

I should be proud of her. I am proud of her. That's the problem. Pride mixes with something bitter and ugly before I can stop it.

"Glad you got what you wanted."

The second the words leave my mouth, I know they're wrong.

They're sharp and laced with something I'd been trying to bury deep. But the words are already out there, implying everything we've left unsaid.

Glad you got what you wanted, and it wasn't me.

Her face stills, and I'm surprised by the hurt that crosses it. It's blatant but quiet, as if my words cut deeper than either of us knew was possible.

The music surges, someone shouting for shots, and suddenly I can't stand here another second without saying something worse.

"Anyway," I mutter, already stepping back. "I'm going to grab a drink."

She nods once, reflexive. "Yeah. Sure."

I don't wait. I don't look back. I cut toward the bar like it's a lifeline, elbowing through bodies, my pulse roaring in my ears. I grip the edge of the counter harder than necessary and signal to the bartender, jaw tight.

Smooth, Wilder. Real smooth.

I stare at the bottles lined up behind the bar and try to swallow past my heart in my throat while I wait for my drink. Once I have it, I down the first sip fast, welcoming the burn.

I hate that I said it.

I hate more that some part of me meant it exactly the way it sounded.

It makes me feel like an asshole I don't recognize.

I tell myself I'm not watching her, but even from across the room, I can feel her presence.

From the bar, over the rim of my glass, I find her easily. I'm pretending to listen to Liam argue with the bartender about tequila brands, while I watch Wesley laugh in a loose circle with her teammates. Her shoulders are relaxed in a way they weren't when she talked to me.

That's the part that gets me.

I drink faster after that. One beer turns into two, which turns into me losing track somewhere around the third round of shots to celebrate the birthday girl. The edges of the room soften. The noise gets louder and farther away at the same time.

At some point, I end up back at their table.

I don't remember deciding to go there. I just… am.

I drop into an empty chair with unsteady and careless movements. My lips tilt up in a grin as if I'm not totally aware that Wesley is close enough to touch.

Liam looks up immediately, eyes narrowing. "Hey, you good?"

"Never better," I reply, reaching for a beer that isn't mine.

That's when she appears. Some blonde that I'm sure we've seen here before. Her dress is short, and her makeup is dark. I hardly notice anything else about her before she takes it upon herself to slide onto my lap as if it were reserved for her. She has full confidence and zero hesitation.

I almost slide her off me. It's a knee-jerk response to the feeling that I belong to someone else, but I don't.

I never really did either.

It stings sharply enough that I decide to let her stay.

Her arm loops around my neck. "Well, hello."

Liam's hand clamps down on my shoulder hard enough to register through the alcohol. "Nathan," he says sharply. "Get up."

"Relax," I mutter, waving him off. "It's fine."

"It's not. Don't do this."

I turn my head, glaring at him. "Fuck off."

The words are louder than I mean them to be. People glance over, and the whispers start. I can almost track the murmurs as they make their way to Wesley.

The girl in my lap laughs. My hands stay pinned to my side while she wraps herself around me. The idea of touching her makes me sick to my stomach. But...

I sit there and let it look bad.

I let it look like I don't care.

Across the table, Wesley's smile is gone.

She doesn't say anything, no, she's far too controlled for that. Instead, she leans in, whispering something into Becca's ear. Becca's eyes flick to me, then back to Wesley, concern written all over her face.

After they talk for a few minutes, Wesley grabs her jacket and takes off.

That's when the fog in my head clears enough to feel my stomach drop. What the fuck am I doing?

I shove the girl gently but firmly off my lap, standing so fast my chair tips back. Liam says my name again, a warning this time, but I'm already pushing through the crowd, following her out the door.

Cold air slams into me when I burst outside. My head scans the street until I find her halfway down the block.

My strides swallow the distance until she's only a few steps ahead, arms crossed tight over her chest, heels clicking angrily against the sidewalk. I grab her shoulder without thinking.

"Don't," she snaps, yanking her arm free. "Don't you dare touch me." She turns on me, eyes blazing.

I drop her arm instantly, hands falling to my side.

She motions back to the bar. "What the hell was that?"

Oh.

She's mad.

While I've been miserable, she's been off at camp, happy with her friends, and doing who knows what else. At least now she's feeling something for me. I'll take this over her cold indifference every time.

A bitter laugh slips from my lips. "You're mad at me?"

"Yes," she yells, incredulous. "You let some girl climb all over you right in front of me. What are you trying to prove?"

Her voice carries loud enough that a couple of people look our way. I turn slightly, hoping they didn't recognize me. The last thing I need is the paparazzi seeing me lose Wesley for a second time.

I spread my hands, lowering my voice. "Why does it matter? Why do you care?"

She stares at me. "Excuse me?"

"You heard me. Why does it matter who's in my lap when none of this was real, right?"

She exhales slowly, like I'm a child throwing a tantrum. "Nathan, please don't be like this."

That tone flips something ugly in my chest.

"Like what? Like I'm hurt? Like I'm pissed? At least I'm not lying to myself."

"Neither am I."

"No?" I rub my jaw, taking a breath. "You're the one who said you didn't want to pretend anymore. You said it changed something for you. Then, you walked away like it was nothing."

Her jaw tightens, hands tapping against her thighs. "I didn't walk away like it was nothing."

"You're right. You drove away. I mean, fuck, Wesley, you didn't even text me back."

A part of me wants her to argue back. As if her yelling at me is proof she felt even a fraction of what I did. Of what I do.

Instead, she lets out a slow breath. "We both know why."

It's like I'm looking at a stranger. This isn't the Wesley who went ice skating with me. The one who danced with me. She isn't the person who opened up about her family and the pressure that she struggles to deal with.

This Wesley turns it all off.

"Yeah. We do."

"That doesn't mean it was easy." Her eyes shift from the cars passing by to the sidewalk, never glancing my way.

"Look at me, Wes." My voice cracks, and I swallow. "Please just fucking look at me while you break my heart."

Her eyes flash to mine, glistening with unshed tears.

"You didn't choose me." The words tumble out of me, fueled by alcohol and weeks of swallowing everything down. "You chose soccer. You chose the thing you always choose. And you know what? That's fine." I run my hand through my hair. "I get it. But don't stand there and act like I'm the asshole for being hurt."

"I couldn't risk everything I've worked for."

"You weren't the only one risking something."

She opens her mouth, then closes it.

I barrel on before she can stop me.

"You don't get to tell me it was real, make me collateral damage when you end it anyway, and then be mad that someone else touches me. You made it clear I'm not what you want."

"God, Nathan. I do want you. Every fucking part of me wants you. Every part of me wishes things were different. But they're not." A tear falls down her cheek. "Is that what you want to hear?"

"That just makes it worse." All the fight drains out of my voice. "Because you didn't want me enough." I blow out my breath, letting it cloud in the air. "We weren't worth taking a chance on. You didn't even bother to try. And you were never going to."

Silence drops between us, thick and brutal.

Her eyes shine, but her spine stays straight. The same way it was the morning she drove away.

I hate it.

I hate that I still love her, and she's standing here destroying me all over again.

"I didn't mean to hurt you." Her voice is barely audible over the traffic driving by.

"Kinda like how I didn't mean to fall in love with you. Looks like we both fucked up."

Her eyes widen, and I realize what I've said only after the words leave my lips. It's an embarrassing admission, but I can't bring myself to care. It's been eating me alive for far too long.

"Good luck," I say, jaw tightening as the words scrape on the way out. "With everything."

I turn before she can answer or say something that might make me stay. I flag down the first rideshare I can find without looking back.

Through the window, I catch one last glimpse of her standing there alone on the sidewalk, arms wrapped around herself like she's holding something together.

Then the city swallows her whole.

And I let it.

41

Wesley

When I was sixteen, I tried to have it all.

A few girls from school had this standing tradition of going to the diner down the street between the final bell and practice. It was never anything big or complicated, just fries and milkshakes, piling into a booth and talking about whatever crossed their minds. They asked me every time.

And every time, I said no.

Usually, that hour was spoken for before it even started. I used it to run to the grocery store, or head home to switch over the laundry, or start dinner if it was one of those days. The kind of quiet, necessary things that kept everything moving. The kind of things my dad never had time to get to, no matter how hard he tried.

He never asked me to do it. Not once. Hell, he never even hinted.

But by sixteen, I'd already been filling in the gaps for two years, and somewhere along the way, it stopped feeling like a choice. It was routine. For all of us.

That day, though, when they asked, I said yes.

I remember how it felt, too. Sitting there in that cracked vinyl booth, laughing so hard my stomach hurt, my head tipping back like

I didn't have a single thing waiting on me. For that hour, it felt like I got to be sixteen in the way everyone else was.

It was only an hour. It wasn't a big deal. I told myself I could do all three. I could show up for my family, keep up with soccer, and still carve out space for something as small and harmless as hanging out with friends.

It worked.

Right up until my phone buzzed halfway through my milkshake.

It was my dad asking me where I was. His voice had been tight, not angry, but stretched thin with panic.

The shift in my chest was immediate, like a switch flipping as I told him I was out with friends.

I remember him cutting me off impatiently. Emma's field trip form was still sitting on the counter. I'd forgotten to make sure she took it to school that morning. He had work, and the school office was closing in less than half an hour.

They wouldn't let her go if it wasn't turned in.

Emma had been talking about that field trip for weeks.

I've never forgotten the frustration that bled into my dad's voice when he reminded me that I was supposed to turn it in, and it was almost too late. Because I'd forgotten.

I pushed to my feet without a second thought, my chair scraping loudly against the tile as I bolted for home. It was a long shot, but I wanted to fix it.

The whole way home, I kept thinking about how I should've never gone in the first place.

When I got there, Emma was sitting at the kitchen table, her eyes red and her hands curled around the edges of the form like it might vanish if she let go. My dad kissed my forehead on his way out, already halfway out the door before I could say anything.

We made it.

I got her to the school with minutes to spare, breathless and flushed, the secretary clearly annoyed as she took the paper from my hand. But Emma would go. Back then, that was the only thing that mattered.

The relief barely had time to settle before I saw the clock and felt something entirely different take its place.

I was late for practice. Not slightly late. Really fucking late.

By the time I got to the field and got Emma settled into the stands with a juice box and a smile, practice was already in full swing. Coach didn't say anything when I slid in, just blew the whistle and pointed for me to join the drills.

But I remember the flash of disappointment on his face.

It was quick, almost gone before it even fully landed, but it was there. It was the same tight edge I'd heard in my dad's voice on the phone.

I ran harder than I ever had that day.

Hell, I'm still running nearly ten years later, and it never fully goes away.

I remember tucking Emma into bed that night, her hugging me like turning in that form was the difference between everything and nothing.

She told me she thought she wasn't going to get to go.

"You will always get to go," I told her.

And I meant it.

That was the moment everything clicked into place.

That one hour of fun hadn't been worth what came with it. Not the panic, not the scrambling, not the feeling of almost letting more important things slip through my hands.

I couldn't balance it the way I wanted to believe I could.

Something always gives.

So I decided, right then and there, that it wouldn't be my family. It wouldn't be soccer.

I stopped choosing anything that could put either of them at risk.

After that, every decision got easier.

I knew what mattered. I knew what didn't.

And when I started to forget that in college, I was reminded just as harshly.

When I'd told Nathan about that, I'd said it wasn't a big deal. And it wasn't. On its own, that situation was nothing. Neither was that day when I was sixteen. But stacked together with a hundred other moments like it, there isn't a version of my life where I get to have it all.

I'm well aware that it's bullshit. I know it's not fair. I even know that I could say fuck it and do what I want anyway. But what's the point when taking what I want could cost me everything I'm on the brink of?

So, I make the hard choices. I walk away from things that matter, even when I don't want to. I shut down feelings before they can take root and remind myself of the only two things that I will not compromise.

Family.

Soccer.

But standing on this sidewalk now, watching Nathan's rideshare disappear into traffic, it doesn't feel the same.

The city moves around me in a blur of headlights and noise, people passing by without a second glance, and all I can see is the back of his car driving away from me.

My arms wrap tightly around myself, fingers digging into my sleeves like I can hold everything in place if I don't loosen my grip.

I take a step forward without meaning to, like some part of me still thinks I can stop him, as if he isn't already gone.

His taillights vanish.

Something in my chest caves in.

Every other time I've made the right choice, I've been able to stand in it and breathe through it until it settled into something manageable.

This time, it feels like I'm carving something out of myself and leaving it behind.

I don't even know how Nathan got under my skin like this. I tried to keep my distance, to hold my boundaries where they were safe and clear, but he slipped past every single one of them until he became one of the best parts of my day without me even realizing when it happened.

My breath comes in short, uneven bursts. My throat tightens, and I swallow hard against it, blinking quickly as the pressure builds behind my eyes.

No. Not here. Not like this.

"Wesley?"

Harper's voice cuts through the noise behind me.

"I'm fine," I say automatically, the words out before I even think about them. "I didn't know you were coming."

"I just got here. I was heading in, but I saw you." She pauses, her voice softening. "Are you okay?"

"I'm fine."

The lie breaks me in two.

She doesn't respond right away.

I feel her step closer, the warmth of her presence settling at my side while she watches me carefully. I don't know what my face looks like, but it's enough that she knows. She knows without me saying a word.

"Oh, Wesley."

That's all it takes.

Everything I've been holding in snaps.

I turn into her without thinking, my hands fisting in the back of her jacket as I press my face into her shoulder, and then I'm gone.

My body shakes with it, every breath is uneven and shaking like I've forgotten how to do it right. Harper's steady arms come around me instantly, holding me together while I come apart.

The first sob tears out of me so hard it steals the air from my lungs, my body folding in on itself as everything I've been holding back crashes down all at once.

There's nothing but her arms around me and the sound of my own breaking.

I cry for me. For Nathan. For the years that I've carefully set myself on the back burner, focusing only on what needs to happen for everyone else.

I cry until it burns. Until my chest aches and my throat is raw.

Only once I run out of tears do the sharp edges of it all dull into something exhausted and hollow.

Harper doesn't rush me. She silently rubs circles on my back, like I'm a little kid.

In a way, I am because I've never learned how to get through something like this. My mom never got a chance to hold me while my heart broke.

After her death, I never let anyone close enough to break it.

But fuck, this isn't breaking.

It's shattering.

And I don't know how to put myself back together.

Eventually, still pressed into her shoulder, my voice comes out rough and unsteady. "He said he loved me." I let out a hollow, disbelieving laugh. "And then basically told me he wished he didn't."

I feel her body tense beneath my hands. Out of everyone I know, she's the most rational, but she's also loyal enough that she'd hunt him down without hesitation if I asked her to.

But I don't.

Because he didn't do this to us.

I did.

I pull back, meeting her eyes, finding nothing there but concern.

"You want him. Why won't you let yourself have this?" She asks gently.

"You should understand," I say, shaking my head. "You gave up soccer to be with James. I can't do that. Not just because I love it, but because I can't afford to let it go."

Her expression shifts, something lingering under the surface.

"James isn't Nathan," she says quietly. "If anyone would understand your career choice, it's him." She holds my gaze. "And you're not me."

I blink, pulling a strand of my hair that had dried against my cheek back away from my face.

"And not all love requires that kind of sacrifice," she continues. "Not the kind you're talking about."

"I didn't know he loved me," I admit, swiping at my face even though it doesn't do much. "When he said it changed for him, I didn't realize how much it had."

"Wesley," she says, softer now, "you know I've always got your back, but that man looks at you like you're the only thing worth his attention. Did you really not know that was love?"

She pauses, just long enough for it to settle.

"Or did you just not let yourself believe it?"

My breath hitches as memories flash through my mind, one after another, right up to our last night together. I squeeze my eyes shut, trying to push them back before they can drag me under again.

I don't answer because the truth hurts too much to say out loud. The truth that I knew.

I saw what it was becoming, but I ignored it, desperate to let myself have something. Desperate to hide behind our stupid, fake boundaries and benefits, even when we both knew they didn't mean shit.

I wanted him to want me for real. And I let him want me, knowing exactly how it would end.

My skin crawls, and if I could escape myself, I would.

He should hate me.

"We were always going to end like this," I say, trying to stomach it. "I couldn't risk it."

I need her to understand. I need someone to tell me I didn't just make the biggest mistake of my life.

She doesn't do that. Instead, she lets me keep going.

"I can't lose everything I've worked for," I say, my voice steadier now, even if it feels like I'm forcing it. "My family, my career, everything depends on me staying focused. I don't get to choose me. Not right now."

Harper tucks a piece of hair behind my ear, her thumb brushing under my eye in a failed attempt to fix my smudged mascara before she gives a small, resigned shrug.

"Just a few more years," I add, pulling back slightly, nodding like I can convince both of us. "That's all I need. A few more years of being all in, and then maybe…"

I trail off.

Maybe what?

Maybe Nathan will still love me?

The thought feels ridiculous even as it crosses my mind. I could never ask him to wait. I'd never want him to.

He deserves someone who chooses him every time and without hesitation.

Harper is quiet for a moment, letting everything settle.

"You're sure about this?" she asks finally.

No.

I want to knock on his door and take it all back. I want to be wrapped up in his arms, to laugh with him, to eat pizza on his couch doing nothing, to run the bleachers with him until we're both breathless and grinning.

But responsibility matters. Consistency matters. And I've spent more than ten years putting myself last. I don't know how to do anything different.

"Yes," I say.

And this time, the lie can't break me. I'm already in pieces.

42

Nathan

The arena stinks like varnish and sweat, but it comforts me. I'm sitting on the edge of the locker room bench, gloves in my lap, and helmet tucked under one arm.

I woke up at noon and skipped my morning lift. It's the routine that usually steadies me before a game, but I didn't feel like being on the receiving end of the skeptical glances from my friends.

I'm ninety-nine percent sure that my skull will split in two if I tilt my head the wrong way. I'd deserve it if it did. Bile rises in my throat, but I force it back. Going out last night, after almost a week in a row, was an awful decision.

The practice squad guys were desperate to hit a bar before the game, and for whatever reason, I went. They won't see the ice today, but I will. Normally, I'd never do this before a game, despite what the paparazzi likes to publish. Now, I'm paying for it.

No one has said anything. Not Liam, Wyatt, or even Grayson. Maybe because I've been pulling it together on the ice despite it all. I've been on fire, even if my off-ice attitude has been hard to deal with. As long as I'm not collapsing in the middle of a shift, they don't have much room to complain. That doesn't help me feel less guilty or less terrible, though.

Liam sidles up next to me, silently dropping a couple of Tylenol into my palm, along with a bottle of water. He tilts his head at me, his silent way of saying: chug, idiot. I do. The cold water slides down my throat, dulling the edges of the pounding.

Grayson's glare catches me across the room. He's leaning against the locker room wall with his arms crossed. It's his job as captain to be concerned about my performance, and his judgment is pressing down on me. I nod in his direction, but he just turns towards his locker.

Wyatt appears beside me with a smug half-grin plastered on his face. "Better pull it together come game time, Wilder," he warns, voice loud enough that a few heads turn and mine throbs. I almost tell him to shut up, but only manage another nod.

Then Coach Rylan's office door opens, the black of his silhouette framed by the fluorescent hallway light. He calls my name, and the room empties a little as I head in his direction.

Aside from his desk and the dry-erase board, the room is empty. Coach leans back in his chair. The intensity of his gaze leads me to believe that he knows exactly what I did last night.

Great.

"Sit," he orders, motioning to the chair next to me. I drop into it, still gripping my helmet like it's a lifeline.

I've been a jackass this week. Drinking before game day would be careless for anyone, but considering my contract is up, it's incredibly stupid.

"Do you know why I called you in?" He folds his hands on top of his desk.

This is it. I've officially blown it.

An apology is on the tip of my tongue when he adds, "It has nothing to do with the hangover. I've heard plenty of rumblings about you this week. I trust you'll get it under control."

"Yes, sir," I mutter, rubbing my forehead, trying to massage away the pain.

He leans forward slightly, eyes softening, though not entirely. "I've been watching all season. Even this week, even with your...

extracurriculars, you've been delivering. You've been reliable. On the ice, you've been exactly who we need."

I blink, trying to figure out where he's going with this.

"And there's more," he says, a small smirk twitching at the corner of his mouth. "The organization has decided to renew your contract. It's not signed yet, but they're willing to take another chance on you. You're getting another shot, Wilder."

I swallow hard, the tension in my shoulders melting away in an instant. For the first time in a month, a genuine smile flashes across my face, relief coursing through me.

My mind immediately races, almost irresponsibly, to the thought of telling Wesley, before I remember everything.

A bitter thought creeps in. Everything with Wesley started as a means to an end. For her and for me. I'm getting exactly what I wanted when I'd asked for her help. And yet…

I nod once, voice full of gratitude. "Thank you, Coach. I won't let you, or the team, down."

He leans back, satisfied. "Good. Now get out there. And Wilder? If you ever show up hungover again, you'll be skating sprints until you puke. You're better than that."

I nod quickly, the pounding in my skull returning with a vengeance. But beneath it all, I'm too excited to be miserable. Another contract. Another season. And maybe, just maybe, the spark for my sport that I thought I needed Wesley for is keeping aflame all on its own.

There's a spring in my step as I reenter the locker room. That same enthusiasm is conveyed in my voice as I tell the guys. They all can't help but be happy for me despite how annoyed they are with how I'm acting lately.

By the time we head to the ice, the water and Tylenol are doing what they do best, and I am focused on one thing: winning this game.

Warmups are already underway. The rink buzzes with the sound of blades scraping ice, pucks clattering, and teammates calling plays over the noise of the PA. I tie my laces, adjusting my pads and gloves methodically, trying to let the routine ground me. On the ice, I have a role. A purpose. A contract that's essentially guaranteed. After weeks of feeling broken, I suddenly feel invincible.

I glide toward the boards for warmups, the puck snapping off my stick, drowning out everything else. I catch a pass and wind up for a shot. I lift the stick, aim, and miss. The puck slides way too wide, clattering against the boards.

"Get in the fucking game, Wilder," Grayson shouts, his eyes cutting into me like lasers. His patience for me has run out, and I don't blame him. None of my bullshit has a place here.

I skate back to position, muscles coming to life the more I move. Warmups blur together as a sequence of passes, slap shots, and defensive drills, each one pushing me deeper into the zone. My head might be pounding, my stomach queasy, but my body knows what to do.

Next is the flashy team introductions. The crowd is loud. The announcer's voice booms over the speakers, each player's name drawing cheers from the stands. I skate to center ice, stick in hand, feeling the weight of the pads and the familiarity of the jersey against my skin. The lights glare down. This is where I belong.

Right before the whistle blows, I let my mind wander one last time, before I lock in completely. My eyes scan the crowd, searching for the one person I know I won't find.

Wesley's the invisible constant in the background. She's the silent motivator and complication all at once. Every decision, every push, and every extra drill started with her. And now? My contract's renewing, the team has decided to take another chance on me, and she won't even know.

I'd like to think she'd be happy for me. If anyone understands how much hockey means to me, it's her. She gets it because soccer means just as much to her.

That's why I can't blame her for her choice. I can be mad. I can be hurt. I wish things were different constantly, but I can't blame her. Because the commitment and drive she has to ensure she reaches her goals is what drew me to her from the get-go. She wouldn't be Wesley without it. I just wish she could be that Wesley with me.

I skate to the circle, my legs coiled and ready. When the puck drops, we win it clean. I pass to the center and immediately start tracking back on defense. The game breathes around me, the rush of the crowd and the slap of sticks setting every nerve ending on fire.

I move like I always do when I'm locked in, reading the play before it unfolds and anticipating passes. There's a streak of adrenaline that runs from my shoulders down my legs. It's a brutal joy that nothing else compares to. I make a give-and-go at the blue line, backhand a rebound to the slot, and see Liam slam it in. The bench erupts. I smile, just for a second, because the satisfaction is immediate.

The opposing team's center comes in fast. I square up, anticipating a pass, and force him wide. My skates carve arcs in the ice. Every hit I take, every puck I block, fuels me further. The pounding in my head from last night recedes into the background.

Fifteen minutes in, we're trading chances with the other team, neither side giving ground. I've already logged more minutes than usual, pushing to show Coach I'm deserving of the chance he's giving me.

I get the puck in neutral ice, see a gap, and surge forward. There's an opening near the slot. I rush forward with speed, ice flying beneath my blades. My heart races in a satisfying rhythm. I lift my stick, ready to snap it toward the net, but from the corner of my eye, a shoulder comes in too hard. And too damn fast.

The collision hits me like a freight train. Air leaves my lungs in a sharp, punishing exhale I can't control. The world tilts violently. My knees buckle, my stick slams against the ice, useless. Pain flashes across my shoulder, exploding into my skull. I try to brace or push myself upright, but gravity has other plans.

The lights above blur, the crowd noise distorts, and a high-pitched ringing takes over everything. My vision narrows and then fades. The cold ice bites at me through my pads. My helmet digs into the surface.

I'm aware of the whistle, players yelling, and skates skidding to a halt nearby. A voice shouts something, maybe Grayson or maybe the ref, but it's distant.

Then it all goes black.

43

Wesley

The locker room is loud, a combination of anticipation for our last scrimmage before the season starts and excitement over the warmer weather. I'm perched on the edge of the bench with a towel draped across my shoulders. Avery's voice cuts through the room like it always does, impossible to ignore.

"I'm not seeing anyone," she says, rolling her eyes. "I swear."

Becca snorts. "You? The queen of debriefing us on your sexual exploits, suddenly has none?"

Haley laughs, leaning against the lockers with arms crossed. "Suspicious. What are you hiding, Avery?"

"I'm not hiding anything." Avery protests, flopping back onto the bench. "It's not my fault that there are no guys in all of Boston that can keep me entertained."

Haley and Becca laugh, but there is a glint of something in Avery's eyes. There is a twitch in her voice that masks something she doesn't want to say.

I want to say something, push her the way Harper would if she were here, but I keep my mouth shut. Pushing her will prompt her to push me right back, pulling on the thread that is still too painful to address.

So, I nod along politely listening. My fingers fidget with the wrap that I use to keep my shin guards on, wrapping it tightly around my leg.

They all wonder what happened outside the bar during Becca's birthday, but I can't bring myself to say a word about it.

I'd spent the entire night pretending to be unaffected by Nathan's presence. It wasn't until I was faced with the reality that he could be with someone else that I broke. Nothing about the night was as painful as the look on his face.

He said he fell in love with me, and then, he said it was a mistake. I deserved it. He should never forgive me. Hell, I wasn't sure I'd ever forgive myself.

My thoughts are interrupted by a voice I don't immediately recognize. A rookie from the third line perches on the edge of the bench next to mine, curling her legs under her like she's not sure she's allowed to be here.

She's only nineteen, having skipped college to be here, still so green and hungry for the kind of success that I'm now finding myself. There's healthy envy and desire in her eyes as she watches me.

"Is it true?" she asks, voice cutting through the gossip. "Is one of the National Team coaches here to watch you tonight?"

I pause, pulling my socks up into place at my knee. A small smile tugs at the corner of my mouth. "Yeah," I say. "It's true."

The room gets a little quieter. Avery frowns, eyebrows drawn together. "Wow. That's… big."

I didn't tell her. Actually, I didn't tell anyone.

"Yes, it's big," Becca adds, voice low and conspiratorial. "Shouldn't you be like excited? Jumping up and down, screaming, texting everyone, or posting it on Instagram."

I shrug, shoulders heavy, trying to hide the fact that nothing seems to light me up lately.

"It is a big deal." My words sound hollow, even to me.

Haley cocks her head, giving me a sideways look like she's trying to figure me out. "You okay?"

I force a small laugh. "I am. Really. Just focused, you know?"

It's what everyone wants from me, and it's what I've always delivered. How can I admit that the part of me that should care, that should feel pride, is strangely absent?

Avery nudges me with her elbow, playful but sharp.

I shoot her a look while I finish the braid I wear for all my games.

Becca leans in, resting her chin on her hand. "Well, that's good. You've earned it. You've worked your ass off. You're going to kill it out there."

The rookie fidgets again, glancing at me and trying to gauge whether to ask me whatever is on her mind. "Any tips for someone who wants to be where you are?" She asks, softly.

My head jerks in her direction. She's chewing on her bottom lip, foot tapping a mile a minute.

I toy with the question for a second before I answer. "Be prepared to give everything you have. And then be prepared to give even more."

My throat tightens, words cracking, but I force them out anyway. I should be a better captain and give her advice that isn't an extension of my own pain, but I don't have it in me. Instead, I ignore the stress on her face and the concerned looks from my friends, turning back toward my locker.

I don't need anything out of it, but fidgeting with my bag buys me the time I need to get myself in check. When I finally turn back, only Avery is left watching me.

"You're terrible at this. Pretending like you're not thinking about him is worse than admitting it."

I manage a smile this time, tighter than it should be. "I'm fine. Just ready to play."

The locker room begins to buzz with movement as some of the team files back in after visiting the athletic trainer for treatment. The goalie coach is instructing in the corner, and the assistant coach has some of the rookies pulled aside. Noise fills the space and pushes the thoughts away for a moment.

I stand and walk toward the corner we usually sit in, trailing behind Avery. My hands tighten around my water. Tonight could change everything for me professionally.

The thought nags, uninvited: this should matter more. I should care more. All the things I've sacrificed for soccer. Him. All for a shot at what I'm so close to accomplishing.

Avery grabs my arm, her grip firm enough to make me stop in my tracks. "Hey," she says, voice low, pulling me aside away from everyone. "We need to talk. Now."

"What's up?" I murmur, though my voice sounds more tired than usual.

"You. You're miserable, and it's so damn frustrating because you don't have to be, Wesley."

I bite the inside of my cheek. "It's nothing."

"Nothing?" She repeats, eyebrows raised. "I'm your best friend. You think I can't tell that this is eating you alive?"

"It's empty, okay?"

She blinks at me impatiently. "Because you love him."

I frown. "No."

"You love him." She says again, nodding her head at me.

"I can't. It wasn't supposed to be anything." I can feel the tears forming and close my eyes, forcing them back.

"Maybe it wasn't supposed to be anything, but that doesn't mean it wasn't." Avery grabs my shoulder. "Why did you push him away?"

"I can't risk this. Not right now. Not with everything on the line. Everyone needs me." My breath starts to come faster.

Fuck.

Luckily, Avery recognizes the signs of my anxiety spirals, having helped me through them before. She moves me to the bench and pushes my head down to my knees.

"My schedule. The team. My dream. I can't—"

"You can't what?" Avery asks, her voice sharper now, though still concerned. "Love someone? Be happy?"

I shake my head. "It's not that simple. I missed my one-on-one session because of him. I overslept."

Avery raises an eyebrow.

"I was with him. I got distracted. I…"

She cuts me off with a soft laugh, sitting down next to me. "Wes, shit happens. It's not the end of the world."

I look at her, swallowing the lump in my throat. "You don't get it. I've spent twenty-two years dreaming of this. I've only known him since November. That can't be worth losing out on the National Team, not when I've worked my entire life for this. My family counts on me. The team counts on me. I don't get to," I trail off, frustrated.

Avery grips my shoulders now, forcing me to meet her gaze. "Your team doesn't need you perfect. We need you human. We need someone who can show us how to live on and off the field, not grind endlessly until everything else dies."

I blink, absorbing her words, the truth sticking like ice in my chest.

"And your family is proud of you," she continues, voice softening. "They'll be proud of you even if you aren't on the U.S. Women's National Team. It's not your responsibility to be a martyr, sacrificing every ounce of happiness for a dream you had as a kid. You're allowed to want both. You're allowed to want more."

She shakes her head slowly, as if trying to knock some sense into me. "Dreams change, Wes. Sometimes they change altogether. Sometimes they just expand. Why can't your dream be the World Cup with Nathan in the stands supporting you? Why does it have to be all or nothing?"

Her words hang in the air. The picture she's painted settles somewhere deep.

I nod slowly, because I know she's right.

I pushed Nathan away because I was worried he would get in the way of my dreams, only to realize too late that he was already a part of the very dreams I was desperately trying to save.

"Maybe you're right, but it's too late." My voice is barely above a whisper. "I hurt him."

Avery smiles, just the faintest upturn of lips. "If anyone can fix it, it's you. So go out there tonight, and show the coaches what you've got. You can win Nathan back tomorrow."

I take a deep breath, shoulders loosening. She lets go of me, and I feel lighter. Maybe the field isn't the only place where I can chase what I want.

Until the whispers start.

"Oh, shit."

Becca's and Haley's voices are low, but not low enough. They murmur Nathan's name and something about a video. I freeze.

My head snaps toward them. "What the hell is going on?" I ask, voice sharp, heart already picking up pace.

They exchange a glance and hesitate, like they don't know if they're supposed to tell me. Their faces stop me in my tracks.

Haley presses a button on her phone, turning it toward me. It's glowing, catching the fluorescent light.

The video starts.

Nathan is moving fast on the ice, chasing the puck. Then, he's hit from the side. It must've caught him off guard because he doesn't brace for it. The hair on the back of my neck stands up as I watch him fall. His body collapses, helmet slamming into the ice as his stick skitters away.

My hands tremble, bile rising in my throat. His body twitches, but he doesn't get up. He's out cold.

The world tilts and my heart thunders in my ears. The video restarts, but I look away, unable to watch it a second time. Nathan. My Nathan. He's completely unconscious on the ice. I sink onto the bench, not even aware of doing it.

Coach Bennett's voice cuts in, like a distant echo. "Okay, team, eyes up. Warmups are almost…"

I don't hear the rest. Everything is Nathan. His face, the way he used to hold me, and the sound of his helmet hitting ice. The panic in my chest claws through me until it's all I am.

My body is fighting to stay calm, but my mind is hazy with only one thought breaking through the fog. I love him. I've been trying to bury it, ignore it, rationalize it away with training and focus, but seeing him there, helpless and out cold, it's like a punch through the center of my chest.

He may not ever forgive me. I could never expect him to after hurting him the way I did. But now, right this second, I'm not sure how I could ever forgive myself if I don't go to him.

Something clicks into place. I jump to my feet, keys in hand, and my cleats forgotten on the bench. "I have to go," I interrupt, voice sharp enough to make every head turn toward me.

Coach Bennett freezes mid-sentence, eyebrows raising. "Wesley, sit down. We're about to play a game here. This is important."

"I can't," I breathe, my keys shaking faintly in my grasp.

Her gaze is calm, even as she tries to stop me. "National Team coaches are in the stands. This is your moment, Wesley. Don't throw it away."

"I know," I say, my voice shaking. "I know. But..."

Coach's eyes narrow as she steps closer, voice quiet but intense. "Is it worth it?"

I pause, heart hammering, eyes flicking toward every face in the room, knowing that the only face I need to see isn't here.

"He's worth it."

She scrunches her eyebrows in confusion. Avery jumps in explaining Nathan's injury, but I only hear bits and pieces, the picture of him hitting the ice replaying in my head.

Coach Bennett nods at me, her expression softer. "I'll take care of it, Wesley. Go."

Without another word, I turn, racing past my startled teammates toward the parking lot. My fingers tap against the steering wheel, but adrenaline pushes me forward as the car peels away from the stadium.

I don't look back. I don't let myself worry about what I might've given up. I choose him.

44

Nathan

The light in here drills straight through my skull. A low groan barely makes it past my throat, and I immediately regret it when pain blooms behind my eyes. My head feels thick, stuffed with cotton and glass that pulses every time my heart beats.

I try to move and realize I can't. Or maybe I can, but my body is slow to respond, as if there's a delay between the thought and the action. My right shoulder aches in its sling, so I hold it as still as possible.

"Hey," a voice says. "You're awake."

I blink, squinting against the light as shapes start to form. The hospital room is bright and sterile. My eyes dart from the chair across the room to the bed rail at my side, trying to identify the voice.

"Easy," the voice says, softer now. "They said you'd be groggy as the pain meds wore off."

"Delaney?" My voice comes out hoarse, like I've been screaming all night instead of sleeping.

Her face swims into focus, curly hair pulled back in a messy knot. Her eyes are glossy and red-rimmed, making my chest sink.

"Yeah," she says, breathless. "We came as soon as we could."

It's only flashes, but the memories come flooding back. The ice and the pain. The stretcher that I'd woken up on. The hospital lights marked the path to this room, before I dozed off into a pain medicine-induced sleep. I swallow.

"How bad is it?" I ask, though part of me already knows. I'm in a fucking sling after all.

Delaney lets out a shaky laugh, holding back tears. "Not nearly as bad as it could've been."

Before I can push her for more, two more figures move into my line of sight, one from either side of the bed.

My mom's hand is already on my arm, fingers curling into the sleeve of the hospital gown as if she's afraid I'll disappear if she lets go. My dad stands closer than he ever does.

"We got here while you were sleeping." My mom's voice breaks as she speaks. "Nathan, you scared us."

It's not meant to grate on my nerves, but it does. I scared them. As if I chose to be knocked unconscious on the ice.

She leans down and hugs me carefully, like she's not sure where she's allowed to touch. I can smell her perfume, the same floral scent she's worn since I was a kid. For a second, I relax into her, forgetting the strain in our relationship.

"Hey," I murmur. "I'm okay."

My right arm is immobilized in the sling, strapped against my chest, but I test out moving it anyway. Huge mistake. The sharp stab of pain spreads across my chest.

Fuck.

I definitely broke something.

My dad clears his throat. "How are you feeling?"

I shrug, or try to. The movement sends a jolt through my shoulder, and I hiss, biting back a curse. "Like I got hit by a truck."

My mom presses her lips together, brushing a piece of my hair, stiff from sweat, away from my face. "They said it was a clean hit, but since you didn't see it coming, you didn't brace for it."

She recites what someone else told her, because of course, they weren't watching my game themselves. They never have.

"How bad is it?"

My dad chimes in. "You broke your collarbone on impact and sustained a mild concussion when your head hit the ice."

"Mild?" I repeat. Being knocked out cold surely had to mean that it was more severe than mild.

"You lost consciousness briefly, but they said your scans look good. No bleeding or swelling as of now. They want to keep you overnight for observation, but expect a full recovery."

My chest loosens a fraction. "So, I'll be okay."

A broken collarbone and a concussion are serious injuries, sure, but they aren't career-ending injuries. I can heal from them and not lose too much ice time.

Being off the ice for any length of time is a risk this season. Just because the team decided to renew my contract before this, doesn't mean they can't change their mind.

Delaney steps to my side and squeezes my left hand. "I'm really glad you're okay."

My parents exchange a look I don't like. I've seen it before, usually when they think they're about to say something reasonable and necessary that I'm going to hate.

My mom sits down on the edge of the chair. "Nathan, this could have been so much worse."

"I know."

Her hand tightens on my arm. "We can't help but think this might be a sign."

A spark of irritation flares to life behind my ribs.

"A sign of what?" I ask.

"That it's time to be done with hockey."

The word lands like ice water along my spine.

I stare at her, waiting for the punchline, but her expression doesn't change.

"Mom," I say, willing myself to stay reasonable. "Things like this happen in hockey."

"That's exactly the point. You've given everything to this sport. How hurt do you have to get before enough is enough?"

My dad steps in. "You've already broken records. It's been a decade. You have nothing left to prove."

"That's not true," I snap, sharp enough to make my head throb.

Delaney stiffens beside me. "Maybe we should all let Nathan rest. This isn't the time."

"I am resting." I try to push myself up. The movement sends pain screaming through my shoulder, but I grit my teeth and keep going, propping myself up against the pillows. "I'm not quitting."

My mom's eyes fill with tears. "Nathan, please. You deserve more than some game."

And there it is. It's not about the injury at all.

"It's not just a game to me." I pause, taking as deep a breath as I can. "Yes, I got hurt, and that sucks, but it happens. I love what I do."

"That's exactly what scares us." My dad waves his hands through the air before letting them drop to his sides. "You talk about all of this as if ending up in the hospital is normal."

"You don't get to decide this for me."

My mom flinches. "We're not deciding. We're asking you to think about your life. About what comes next."

My shoulders feel tight, frustration bleeding into something hotter. I swing my legs slightly, trying to sit up straighter, needing the space and distance.

Delaney puts a hand on my arm. "Slow down."

"I'm fine," I say, though my vision blurs in protest. "I need you to hear me. Hockey isn't just a game I play. It's who I am."

They've never understood how ingrained hockey is in every fiber of my being. The only one who ever had understood was Wesley. It's some kind of cruel irony that the person who held no judgment against me for my passion left me for hers.

My mom wipes her eyes. "We want more for you because we love you."

My dad sighs, rubbing a hand over his face. "Let's revisit this later when you're feeling better."

There's nothing to revisit.

"Fine," I say. "But the answer's not going to change."

The argument is still hanging in the air when the door bursts open.

"Nathan." Wesley's voice cracks as the door slams behind her.

I jerk my head too fast and regret it instantly, pain flaring along my collarbone and up into my skull.

She's here. Standing inside the doorway, with her soccer uniform on and her hair braided. Her eyes are wide and a little wild, like she ran the entire way.

For a second, we stare at each other.

She takes a step closer, stopping at the side of my bed. Her hands hold onto the bed railing so tightly that her knuckles turn white.

"Hi," she says, face going soft when she sees me sitting upright. "You're okay."

I nod once, because if I open my mouth, I'm not sure what will come out. Her gaze flicks to the room around me, and her eyes widen when she notices my family standing in the corner.

"Oh," she says, straightening immediately, professionalism snapping into place even as her eyes stay warm. "I'm sorry, I didn't realize… I'm Wesley. Wesley Miller."

My mom lights up as if she's meeting a celebrity. I add it to the list of things that annoy me when it comes to my parents.

"His girlfriend." My mom smiles widely. "We've been hoping to meet you."

I drop my head, jaw ticking at her seemingly innocent words. I haven't talked to my parents since Christmas, which means I never told them we broke up. Or weren't real. Or whatever the hell happened.

I brace myself for Wesley's correction. The one where she explains that I'm nothing to her. It doesn't come.

Instead, Wesley's smile is polite. "Nice to meet you." She sticks out her hand, shaking both of my parents' hands in turn.

"You too." My dad claps his hands together once. "He's lucky he's okay. Which is what we were just saying. Sometimes these things are signs."

Here we fucking go again.

I groan. "Dad, stop."

My mom waves me off and turns fully toward Wesley. "We were telling him that maybe this is the universe saying it's time to step away." She trails off meaningfully. "Maybe you can help him see that."

Wesley blinks once, then her expression turns to stone.

"I'm sorry." Her tone is calm but sharpened underneath. "You want me to help him see what, exactly?"

My mom hesitates. "That it might be time to move on and think about the future. Grow up."

"With respect," Wesley says, standing taller, "Nathan is a grown man and a hell of a hockey player. He has one of the most impressive hockey careers ever, and it'll be solely his choice when that career ends."

My heart stutters, and I swallow. I almost reach for her hand on the rail, my fingers twitching at how close she is, but I stop myself. I don't know why she's here, but she's not mine to hold, even if she's defending me in a way no one ever has.

"We want him to consider our perspective on this." My dad says, still holding firm on the topic.

Wesley's eyes flare, and for the briefest of seconds, I find myself feeling sorry for my dad. It passes quickly, excitement taking its place the way it always does when watching Wesley put a grown man in his place.

"No one," she says with authority, "gets to decide when someone else's dream is over. Especially not people who, as far as I can tell, haven't supported that dream or their own son for way too damn long."

Wesley's eyes glance toward me briefly before locking back in on my parents.

My mom opens her mouth to speak. Wesley doesn't let her.

"You have an amazing son. He's a good person, and you get credit for some of that because you raised him. But who he is on the ice, he is, despite you. If anything, you've been another obstacle in his way, making his success that much more impressive. Asking him to give it up proves how little you know him. Because if you knew him at all, you would stop trying to take away something that makes him who he is."

"That's not what we're trying to do." My mom's voice comes out small.

"Well, it's what you're doing. And I will not be contributing to it," Wesley adds firmly. "Loving him doesn't give me the right to do anything other than be here for him."

My breath catches as I process her words. *Loving him.* My heart skips a beat as the words settle into me, comforting and terrifying all at once. Is it true? I almost blurt out the question, but stop myself before embarrassing both of us in front of my family.

My dad exhales slowly, the fight draining from his posture. My mom presses her lips together, embarrassment etched into her expression.

Delaney clears her throat. "Well, I think that's our cue to give them a minute."

She steers our parents toward the door before they can argue. Before shutting the door, she shoots Wesley a look that's equal parts impressed and grateful, then winks at me.

I let out a breath I didn't realize I was holding.

Wesley finally looks at me again, eyes flicking over the sling, IV, and the monitors. Her expression softens, all that fire folding into vulnerability.

"You're okay." Wesley's entire body relaxes as if she's been strung up for hours worrying about me.

Her eyes hold nothing but relieved honesty, and yet, I'm more confused than ever.

"You're dressed for a game." I motion with my good arm to her uniform. "Did you guys win?"

She huffs out a breath, then shakes her head. "I wouldn't know."

"What do you mean?"

"I left before the scrimmage started, as soon as I saw what happened."

I watch her as she glances down at the shin guards she's still wearing. She's shifting from one foot to another, her nervous energy looking for a way to escape.

"You left your game," I repeat, still trying to wrap my head around it. Wesley doesn't miss games or scrimmages. She puts soccer over everything.

Her eyes latch onto mine, as if she can see through me to all of the unasked questions underneath that one. "Yes, Nathan. I left my game. You were hurt, and I needed to be here."

Something in me thaws. She needed to see me. It's a small victory, knowing that I still mean something to her.

"Thank you for what you said to my parents." It's my turn to feel nervous.

She shrugs, but there's a tremor underneath it. "Someone needed to say it. I meant every single word." Her eyes bore into me with the kind of reassurance I expected her to shy away from.

Loving him. She'd said it. She meant it. But why now? Something bitter dampens the part of me thrilled to hear those words.

"Why are you here?" I ask, the words clipped.

"I just told you." Her brows furrow at the change in my tone.

"Yeah, because I'm hurt." I motion to the sling. "But Wes, I've been hurt for a month. Hell, you're the one who hurt me. You didn't care then. So, why now? Is it guilt? Really, what is this?"

I shift, wincing at the ache, but refusing to flinch fully.

It's been a month, and she hasn't shown an ounce of regret for her choice. I don't want to win by consolation. I don't want my broken collarbone to be what finally changes her mind. I want her to want me as much as I want her.

"No, it's not like that." She reaches out, grabbing my hand. "I've been miserable. I went to Future's Camp and damn near killed myself exercising, trying to distract myself from how much I missed you."

She laces her fingers through mine, and we both watch the motion.

"I panicked when I missed the one-on-one session. Soccer has been my only priority for so long, but then that night, I didn't think about it once. It scared me."

"I get it." And I do. I know how terrifying it is to think you might lose the sport you love.

"Then I was at camp with everything I thought I ever wanted, and I couldn't even bring myself to be happy. And today, for our scrimmage, I had National Team coaches in the stands, but when I saw you were hurt, it didn't even seem like a choice. This is where I wanted to be."

I meet her eyes. "National Team coaches in the stands?"

She arches an eyebrow. "You were unconscious on the ice."

And just like that, I know.

Whatever this is between us, whatever we broke or ran from or pretended wasn't real, it's still here. Bruised and complicated, but here.

45

Wesley

I didn't go to the hospital expecting forgiveness. I didn't give myself time to have any expectations at all. I just went, letting myself follow the gut feeling that I needed to be at Nathan's side. No plan. No clue what I wanted. Until I saw him, sitting in a hospital bed with his dark hair messy and his eyes locked on mine.

The emptiness that had been plaguing me for the past month dissolved in an instant. The sight of him with his guard down brought every single emotion I've been hiding from back to the forefront.

Relief came first, because he was awake and smiling. Then, there was the sharp stab of self-hatred after seeing how surprised he was to see me. As if my showing up for him had been the last thing he'd thought would happen.

I'd spent a month trying to convince myself that I'd made the right choice, despite how much it hurt. Apparently, while I never fully managed to convince myself, Nathan had believed it wholeheartedly. It didn't sit right with me, especially after meeting his parents.

They've been telling him to be different for years, and then I came in and reaffirmed his self-doubt by not choosing him. Making Nathan believe that he wasn't enough for me and that I wanted something else more than him was haunting me at every turn. Not only because it's completely false, but also because he deserved someone to choose him without hesitation. I wanted to be that person.

That's why I snapped at them, ranting on about how I loved him when I'd never even admitted it out loud.

We've both said it at this point, once in anger and once in desperation, but neither of those confessions held weight when they weren't said with intent. Instead, they floated awkwardly between us, neither of us willing to lay it all out on the table for real.

I told Avery and Harper about my visit to the hospital. It was the exact reason why the three of us now sat around Avery's couch watching some action movie, with bowls full of ice cream. I wasn't being so strict about my diet plan these days, part of my attempt to maintain a healthy balance on and off the field.

"You look like you're thinking about it again." Harper pauses the movie, looking over at me.

She's referring to the fact that I embarrassed myself, showing up to the hospital, just to be turned down.

Well, I hadn't been turned down, but not quite forgiven either.

"I am," I groan, sliding further down into Avery's ridiculously oversized couch.

Avery's apartment looks exactly like you'd expect a single, thriving, late twenties' apartment to look like. It's full of velvet textures and golden accents and a ridiculous neon sign over the bar cart that says *good decisions later*. There's a faint citrus candle burning somewhere, and the smell of the Mexican takeout we'd ordered still lingers in the air.

"He hasn't forgiven you yet? You made a stupid rash decision in the name of pursuing your dreams. That should get a free pass." Avery takes another bite of her cookies and cream ice cream.

A stupid rash decision. Yeah, that about sums it up.

I narrow my eyes at her. "Tell me how you really feel." The sarcasm rolls off my tongue.

"Oh, c'mon. We all know it was stupid."

Harper snorts. "True."

"Yeah. Yeah. I hate you both."

They both watch me with expectant eyes.

"He forgave me, I think. It's complicated." I twirl the spoon deeper into my ice cream. "He says he understands, but that he doesn't want to rush back into anything. Besides, it's only been two days."

"You two make things so much harder than they need to be." Avery shakes her head.

"Then let's talk about you," I give her a smug look. "Who are you sleeping with?"

"No one." The answer is far too quick.

"We're supposed to believe that Avery Holt, self-proclaimed sex enthusiast, is celibate?"

Harper gives up on the movie, turning it completely off, as she smiles at Avery.

"Yes. Because I am." The words are sure, but she doesn't look at either of us.

"It's not your ex, is it?" I press.

"No. Absolutely not. No chance in hell." Now, she looks at us, a silent plea in her eyes. "Can we not talk about him? Please."

Harper lets her off the hook. "Fine. We can talk about your mom coming to town in a couple of days."

"Ugh. That's just as bad. You know how that goes. It'll be the Shonda show." Avery rolls her eyes, taking a bite of her ice cream. "That's why I told her I only have time for dinner."

"We can grab drinks after so you can vent about it," Harper offers.

I nod in agreement. They shift topics to the movie we'd given up trying to watch, but my phone dings, stealing my attention.

Nathan: How's movie night?

I smile before I can stop myself.

Me: We ditched the movie. Girl talk.

Nathan: About what?

Me: As if I'd tell you.

We have been like this since the hospital, circling each other with half jokes and careful check-ins. No declarations.

"He's afraid I'll run again," I say aloud, letting the smile slip from my lips. "He hasn't said it, but he is."

"Will you?" There is no judgment in Harper's question.

"No." My lips tilt up. "I love him."

It feels good to let myself feel this. It would feel even better if he felt it back.

They look at each other and laugh. I pretend to scowl.

"Duh!" Avery teases, "I tried to tell you."

"But the last time we got together, it was pretend. It was an act to help us both with our coaches. He doesn't want us to jump back in, just because he's injured or because I regret my decision to call it off."

It makes sense. It's the logical, rational choice.

It also sucks.

I've been holding myself back for so long that, now that I know I want him, I want to jump back in with both feet, no safety net. But I hurt him. I left him. So, the ball is in his court, and I have to accept his terms. Showing up at the hospital didn't magically undo what I did, no matter how much I wish it had.

So, I text him. A lot. About nothing. About everything. About how the weather sucks and how his sister has followed me on Instagram. I show him, quietly and consistently, that I'm here and not bolting this time.

It's the least I can do to try to make up for hurting him. I will do it for as long as it takes for him to trust me.

As if sensing my frustration, Harper puts her hand on my arm. "He loves you too, you know."

In theory, I know that. He said it. He also said it was a mistake, so until those words come from his lips a second time, I won't let myself believe them fully.

"I hope it's enough."

"Patience has never been your virtue, not once you've decided what you want."

She's right. I am always the one in control. Leaving the future of us in Nathan's hands is killing me, but I'm also hoping it shows him how serious I am.

Nathan: Your season opener is next week, right?

Me: Sort of. The season will kick off in March, but since we are last year's champs, we'll play in the Annual Cup Game first. It kicks off the season.

Nathan: Have you heard from the National Team coaches?

He knows what I risked to be at his side. I don't regret it. There was no part of me that could play a soccer game knowing he was in the hospital. But I still hope it doesn't cost me my future.

Me: Nah, but there is still plenty of time before the deadline.

I bite my lip and let out a sigh, trying to convince myself of what I'm telling Nathan. I wait for the anxious spiral and racing heart that normally accompany the idea of not making the National Team, but they don't come. Could it really be this simple?

Harper glances at Avery and me. "The cup is next week. Are you guys feeling ready?"

"It's just another game." Avery shrugs, her usual nonchalance in full force. I nod in agreement.

The pre-game jitters, the endless worry over the scouts, and the pressure to perform all feel manageable. The image of the ball against my cleats has anticipation humming beneath my skin. I'm excited to play.

"And?" Harper prompts.

"I'm trying not to let myself get too fixated." I hesitate, then add, "Coach Bennett wasn't as mad as I thought she'd be about me leaving the scrimmage."

Avery turns toward me. "Really?"

We'd lost the scrimmage. While I am not egotistical enough to think it was solely because of my absence, I am realistic enough to know it played a role.

"Yeah. Once everyone realized Nathan was hurt, she didn't blame me for needing to be there, especially because it was just a scrimmage. If anything, she's been more solid about me being captain this season."

Harper smiles softly. "I'm proud of you."

"She told me that it makes me human, which is exactly the type of person who should be leading the team."

Avery lifts her glass. "Here! Here!"

"The National Team coaches still haven't called," I admit. "Which is fine. I mean, not fine, but I'm still hopeful."

Harper nudges my knee. "They'll call."

"And if they don't, I still get to play. I still get to lead my team. There are worse things."

Avery studies me for a second. "You sound different."

"Good different?"

She smiles. "Yeah, good different."

I lean back into the couch, letting the noise of the cars driving by settle into me. Knowing my friends see the changes I'm making means the world to me. Hopefully, Nathan sees the changes, too.

My phone buzzes.

Nathan: They'd be insane not to pick you.

I don't know what comes over me, other than that Nathan makes me want to feel the things I've shied away from for years. He makes me honest about what I want in a way I never have been.

Me: There's only one person I care about picking me these days.

The next move is his.

46

Nathan

Grayson's house smells like pizza grease and stale beer. Normally, he has a girlfriend, but he's on some sort of dating hiatus, and the smell shows it.

I'm sunk into the far end of the couch, my right arm locked in its sling, useless and heavy against my chest. Every time I shift, my collarbone reminds me that I am very much not healed.

Instead of moping, I'm watching game replays on ESPN while we all tear into a second box of pizza like last night's loss didn't kick everyone in the teeth.

"Tell me again why you couldn't play last night?" Wyatt flops into the armchair across from me.

"Because science," I say. "And bones."

Liam snorts from the floor. "Selfish. Truly."

Our game from last night flickers across the TV. The game I should have been playing in. I look away right as we miss a clean chance in the second period, the kind of play I know exactly how to finish. I grit my teeth and flinch at another awful attempt on goal.

Grayson kills the replay and turns to face us, arms crossed, captain mode fully engaged even in sweatpants. "We shouldn't have lost that fucking game."

Wyatt takes a swig of his beer. "It was a mess."

"We had chances," Liam adds, "but nothing flowed."

Grayson nods once. "No rhythm."

I stay quiet because there's a line between reality and enjoying it too much, and I'm dangerously close to it.

Wyatt nods at me. "Without Wilder on the ice, we didn't click. The power play stalled, the transitions were slow, and practice this morning wasn't any better."

"Even practice?" I ask.

Liam nods. "Yeah. Drills were clunky. Everyone was thinking too hard."

Grayson exhales through his nose, looking at me. "I might be captain, but you set the pace. When you're not there, we hesitate."

The words settle in my chest. A tiny, selfish part of me feels good hearing it. I hate that it does, but I won't pretend otherwise. It means I matter. It means my absence is loud. It means that even injured and stuck on the bench with my arm strapped to my body, my value to this team is obvious.

That's important considering my contract is up. As far as I know, they are still planning to resign me, but a little extra evidence of my value to the team doesn't hurt since I can't prove it on the ice myself.

I flex my fingers in the sling, testing sensation. "Did Coach say anything?" My mouth closes around another slice of pizza. Wesley has ruined pizza for me, apparently, because I can't eat it without thinking about her in my shirt, on my couch, eating it with me.

I shake it off.

Grayson studies me for a beat. "He asked how you're doing."

"And?"

"And he said the locker room feels it when you're not there," he replies. "Didn't sound like someone planning to cut you loose."

Relief slides through me. Good.

I knew it, rationally. I knew getting a relatively minor injury after they'd already decided to renew my contract shouldn't change the plan. But hockey is a brutal business, and nothing is guaranteed until ink hits paper.

Wyatt grabs another slice. "Honestly, if you were worried about your contract, last night probably helped."

I laugh. "That's a fucked up thing to say."

"Yeah, but you're already thinking it."

He's not wrong. A slow smirk crosses my face, drawing curses from all three of them.

Liam nods to the sling. "So, what's the timeline?"

"Two months minimum," I say. "More if they're being cautious."

Grayson grimaces. "You're going to lose your mind."

"I already am."

Wyatt grins. "At least you get to watch us suffer."

"I'd rather be suffering with you."

And I mean it. The ice is where my thoughts shut up. My body knows exactly what to do without asking permission. Sitting still feels wrong.

Grayson leans against the counter, arms folded. "You'll be back. Until then, we will adjust."

"You better," I say. "I don't want to come back to a dumpster fire."

The guys drift into easier conversation after that, trash talk, upcoming road games, and which rookie needs to stop overthinking everything. I half listen, my thoughts circling elsewhere, whether I want them to or not.

Wesley. Always back to Wesley.

My phone buzzes in my pocket. I know it's her, but I don't move to check it right away. I've been waiting a few minutes before responding, not to play games, but to make sure I'm not rushing things.

Last time I was all in, she wasn't. This time, I want to give her time to figure out if it's really me that she wants.

Wyatt notices. "Are you going to answer that or stare into space?"

"Shut up," I say, but I pull my phone out.

It's her.

Wesley: How's the shoulder today?

There's a familiar pull in my chest that hasn't gone away since the hospital, since she walked in and lit my parents on fire with nothing but calm conviction.

Me: Sore, but still attached to my body.

Wesley: Hang in there.

Me: I will. Good luck tomorrow.

I don't add anything else, even though all I want to do is talk to her. I want to tell her that watching my team play without me was worse than the pain. I want to tell her that my contract is still solid. I want to tell her that this injury didn't take anything from me the way I feared.

Mostly, I want to tell her that I still want her. That I still love her. But I don't.

Because that's not what we talked about. When I mentioned starting things back up slowly, she jumped at the chance. I'd be lying if I said it didn't have me worried she'd change her mind again.

Despite the increase in flirting the past week, we're still going slow. We need to choose each other because we want to, not because we're sad, or lonely, or because I'm hurt and she's scared.

Grayson clears his throat. "You good?"

I look up. "Yeah."

He nods, satisfied.

I tuck my phone back into my pocket and lean into the couch, just in time to see Liam step out of Grayson's bathroom with a black lace bra pinched between two fingers.

The room goes dead silent.

Wyatt is the first to recover. "Oh *shit.*"

Grayson closes his eyes slowly, pretending that if he doesn't look at us, we'll disappear.

Liam smirks. "Found it hanging on the towel rack."

I snort before I can stop myself, which sends a sharp reminder through my shoulder. Worth it.

Grayson opens one eye. "Can we not?"

"No," Wyatt and Liam say in unison.

Wyatt leans forward, elbows on his knees. "Okay, but like whose is it?"

Grayson exhales. "I don't see how that's relevant."

"Nice try," Liam says smugly.

"Grayson has a secret girlfriend," Wyatt sings. "Grayson has a secret girlfriend."

"I don't have a girlfriend." Grayson stands, slapping Wyatt in the back of the head and grabbing the bra from Liam. "And she's not a secret."

Wyatt blinks. "Then why don't we know about her?"

"Because this isn't a group project," Grayson replies evenly while tossing the bra into the closest closet.

I shake my head, smiling. He's always been like this. Loyal. Private. A terrible liar, but incredible at redirecting.

Which is exactly what he does next.

"Speaking of girlfriends." He turns to me. "How's Wesley?"

The air shifts instantly.

Liam drops into the chair beside me, while Wyatt shifts his entire body toward me, widening his eyes like a teenage girl gossiping.

"You've been suspiciously quiet about that," Liam says.

I sigh. "She's fine."

Grayson tilts his head, studying me. "You're keeping her at arm's length."

I stiffen. "I'm not."

"You are," Liam says. "And it's stupid."

I run my left hand through my hair. "I'm being careful."

Wyatt scoffs. "Careful how?"

"She didn't pick me. Sure, she might want to now, but what's stopping her from running again?" The words sound more insecure out loud. "I don't want to rush back into something just because I got injured and everything went sideways."

There's a beat.

Then Liam groans. "God, you're being stupid."

"Thank you," I mutter.

Wyatt points at me. "She left her game, from what I heard, to sit next to your dramatic ass in a hospital bed."

"That was a scrimmage," I argue weakly.

"She had National Team coaches in the stands," Grayson adds.

I freeze. "You knew that?"

He shrugs. "People talk."

Wyatt leans back, incredulous. "So, let me get this straight. She chose you over the biggest opportunity of her career, defended you to your parents like she was ready to throw hands, and you're... what? Testing her?"

"I'm not testing her," I snap. "I'm giving us space."

"For what?" Liam asks. "To overthink yourselves back into misery?"

My jaw works. God, they are fucking persistent.

"She didn't pick me at first."

"And she owned it," Wyatt says. "Then showed up anyway."

Grayson's voice is quieter now. "Nathan, you're going to blow it playing scared."

If it were Liam, I could shake it off, but despite his current single status, Grayson knows more about stable relationships than anyone else in this room. His last one lasted two years before they called it off.

I look down at the sling and the way my fingers flex uselessly against the fabric. "She has her first game of the season tomorrow. It's like a cup game for last year's top two teams."

Wyatt's head whips up. "Are you going?"

"No."

"You're so fucking dumb," Liam says through his mouthful of pizza.

Grayson frowns. "You're seriously not planning to be there?"

I don't answer fast enough.

Wyatt throws his hands up. "Unbelievable. You want her to prove she won't run, but you won't even show up when it actually matters."

"That's different," I argue.

"How?" Liam presses. "Wesley doesn't seem like the type to wait around forever. She chose you. Choose her back or be done with it."

Grayson crosses his arms. "Do the damn thing, Wilder."

Silence stretches.

They're all looking at me like they already know the answer and are waiting for me to catch up.

I swallow, then slowly lift my head.

"Fuck, okay." I sit up, sliding the plate off my lap. "I have an idea."

47

Wesley

By the time the whistle blows for halftime, my lungs are burning, and my legs feel like they're humming. I'm balanced in the sweet spot where exhaustion and adrenaline overlap and everything sharpens instead of dulls.

We're only up by a goal, but she was a beauty.

Avery put it in the top corner with my assist.

We jog toward the sideline as a unit, jerseys clinging to our bodies, which have long since forgotten the chill still in the air. The sweat is cooling fast against my skin.

Columbus came in swinging. It's the cup game that kicks off the season. It sets the tone, and we're the champions. They weren't going to come with anything other than their best. Still, their best is struggling to keep up with us, which has me standing a little straighter on the sideline.

I take a long pull from my water bottle, hands on my head with my chest heaving as the noise of the crowd fades into a dull roar. My head feels clear, and the excitement to be here, on the field, is thrumming through me. Every touch tonight has felt intentional, like the ball is an extension of my foot instead of something I have to think about controlling.

I'm on fire.

It's not arrogance, just a fact. I've been everywhere I need to be, dropping back when Columbus presses, creating space in the middle so that I can push the ball to the corners, right where my teammates are waiting. We're moving like a unit, and it makes the coming season seem like it's ours to lose.

Avery bumps her shoulder into mine as we pace on the sideline. "Hell of an assist, Cap."

I grin, breathless. "Hell of a finish."

She shrugs like it was nothing, but her eyes are bright. It's the first goal of the season, and it came off her foot. Sure, she might act like she couldn't care less, but she wouldn't be our best forward if that were true.

"See?" She wiggles her eyebrows. "You play better when you're not spiraling."

I snort. "Bold claim."

She opens her mouth to say something else, probably something about how much better I'd be playing if a certain hockey player were in the stands, but Coach Bennett's voice cuts through the noise before she can.

"Head to the locker room."

We gather in a circle around her, the air thick with sweat, shin guards clacking against the floor as we pull them from our socks, giving our shins a second to breathe. Coach Bennett stands in front of us, tablet tucked under her arm, eyes assessing like she's cataloging every movement we made in the first forty-five minutes.

"Good half," she says, and coming from her, that's high praise. "You're dictating pace, controlling possession, and making them chase."

She looks directly at our back line. "Columbus is going to come out harder. They'll press high. I want you to push the line. Let them be offside, trust each other to push them out or get the call."

Then her gaze shifts to the midfield, and finally, it lands on me.

"All of you are seeing the field beautifully. Keep doing exactly what you're doing."

Something warm settles in my chest at the approval. Maybe I won't get the call for the National Team, but I have a team here, and I won't let them down.

She finishes the talk with a few tactical adjustments and reminders to stay disciplined, finish chances, and not let one goal make us complacent.

The team starts to disperse, some heading for the benches, others stretching or re-taping. I'm halfway to grabbing another bottle of water when Coach Bennett's hand lifts slightly.

"Wesley. Hang back a second."

My stomach flips, just a little.

I wait while the rest of the team filters out, the room quieter now, the hum of the stadium bleeding faintly through the walls.

Coach Bennett studies me for a beat, her expression unreadable. Then she nods.

"You're more than making up for the missed scrimmage." She adjusts the deep purple Tempest hat on her head.

I let out a breath I didn't realize I'd been holding. "Thank you."

She tilts her head. "You look settled tonight. Confident."

"I feel good," I admit.

"Good. This is what leadership looks like. You set the tone, not with words, but with how you play."

I nod.

"They're here in the stands. Keep showing them what you've got."

I thought I'd caught a glimpse of Coach Folley, but hadn't been sure. I hadn't let myself hope. Coach's confirmation sends a jolt of excitement up my spine.

She claps her hands once, sharp and decisive. "Alright. Go warm up. There is still a lot of game left."

She doesn't wait for a response before turning away, already focused on something else. Her words stick with me as I head back out to the field.

I sink down onto the bench, towel draped around my neck, heart still racing as I replay the half in my mind. My pass to Avery had been damn near flawless despite the way Columbus's midfield kept trying to close me down. Confidence is humming under my skin.

This is what I've worked for.

And yet.

My eyes flick, involuntarily, toward the stands.

It's stupid. I know he's not there. I knew he wouldn't be. He's injured, and we're not anything. Not really. At least not yet.

The thought slips in anyway, uninvited.

What if he were?

I can almost see it, him somewhere in the lower bowl, one arm tucked awkwardly against his chest, his jaw set in that familiar way he gets when he's trying to read the game. I imagine the way his eyes would follow me and how he'd lean forward every time I pushed into space.

Avery nudges my knee with her cleat. "You good?"

"Yeah," I say quickly, tearing my gaze away from the empty section of seats. "Just catching my breath."

She gives me a knowing look. "You're kind of kicking ass. It would be fun if your favorite hockey idiot were here to see it."

I huff out a laugh. "Subtle."

She grins. "I try."

The thing is, she's right. And we both know it.

I wish I'd let myself want that before I hurt him, before I convinced myself that wanting more than one thing meant failing at both. Because right now, in this moment, the only thing that would make tonight better is knowing he was somewhere in the stands, watching me do exactly what I love.

I tighten my grip on the water bottle, knuckles whitening briefly before I force myself to relax.

Focus.

This is my job. My responsibility. My dream.

And I'm playing the game of my life.

The whistle blows again, and we rise as one, stepping back onto the field. The noise of the crowd swells, anticipation crackling in the air as we take our positions for the second half.

I take my position, bouncing lightly on the balls of my feet as Columbus lines up across from us, their body language more desperate now.

As the ball rolls back into play, everything else fades. There's only the grass under my cleats and the weight of the captain's armband on my bicep.

I lose track of time as plays bleed into one another without pause. Normally, Coach would sub me out, but tonight she lets me go as if she knows I need this more than I need a breather.

It's not until the final whistle cuts through the night like a release valve that my fatigue sets in.

We win. The sound of it crashing over us, as the crowd gets to their feet. We don't usually have a big crowd, but this game is packed with everyone wanting to see the first big game to kick off the new season. I bend at the waist for a second, hands on my knees as sweat drips down my spine.

Avery whoops somewhere behind me, Becca tackles Haley into a half hug, and I straighten, grinning as we jog toward the sideline. My legs feel heavy in the best way, like proof of work done right.

That's when the cameras start going off.

At first, I barely register them. The media is always around after a season opener, especially a cup game and a hometown win. This time, though, it seems louder and more frantic than usual. A staccato burst of flashes comes from one section instead of being spread evenly along the sideline.

I glance over.

There's a cluster near the tunnel entrance, a mess of bodies and lenses. Security is trying and failing to keep a perimeter. Whoever is in the center of it is obscured by shoulders and microphones, but it's clearly not one of us.

I watch for a beat, curiosity tugging, then shake it off and turn back toward my team. I start down the line, shaking hands with Columbus players, murmuring good game and nice effort to each and every one. My body moves on autopilot, muscle memory carrying me through.

Once we make it through the line, Becca grabs my arm.

"Wes," she squeals, voice pitched somewhere between disbelief and delight. "Wesley."

I glance at her. "Becca, I'm in the middle of something."

She ignores me and physically turns me, pointing so hard her finger nearly pokes my shoulder. "Look."

I follow the line of her arm.

And my heart forgets how to beat.

The cluster breaks apart enough for me to see the back of him. Nathan.

He's pushing through with his good arm, his sling strapped tight across his chest. His hair is slightly damp as if he rushed to get here. That view alone stops me cold, but my breath leaves me in one sharp, stunned exhale when I take in what he's wearing.

A Tempest jersey with the number ten across the back.

My jersey.

It's white and teal with my number on the back and my name stitched clean and bold across the shoulders. It hangs a little awkwardly on him because of the sling, the fabric bunching at his side, but somehow that makes it better.

The cameras go insane when he finally breaks free of the crowd, but they hang back to swarm Nathan's teammates, who are decked out in our gear.

Avery swears softly behind me.

"Oh my god," Becca whispers. "Is that…"

"That's the whole hockey team," Haley says, already laughing. "Holy shit."

My heart swoops so hard it feels like it drops straight into my stomach. He looks ridiculous and perfect and entirely too hot to be walking over to me.

I don't even think.

My feet move on their own.

The noise fades as I cross the grass, like my focus narrows down to him and only him. Nathan meets me halfway, eyes bright and a little apologetic as the flashes explode around us.

"I'm sorry," he says immediately, his voice low so only I can hear. "I swear I didn't plan the media thing. I don't know how they found out I'd be here, and then the jersey sent them into a frenzy."

I blink up at him, still trying to process the fact that he's here.

"You're here," I say stupidly.

He scrunches his eyebrows, doubt disrupting his smile. "I can go. Shit. I, um…'

I grab his hand, letting the electricity of his contact flow through me. He lets out a relieved sigh. I laugh, breathless, my gaze flicking down to the jersey again. "You're wearing my jersey."

"I am," he says, glancing down like he's just noticing it, too. "You mentioned once that boyfriends don't walk around wearing their girlfriends' jerseys. I wanted to prove you wrong."

Boyfriend.

He says it casually, but it feels anything but.

The cameras are still going. Reporters are shouting questions I can't make out, and security is looking wildly unprepared for whatever this has turned into. I barely register any of it.

"What does this mean?" I ask, quietly.

He doesn't hesitate. "Let me be your boyfriend for real, Wes. I already love you. I have for a while now. I don't want to pretend not to anymore."

My chest tightens, emotion rushing up so fast I get dizzy with it. "You're sure? I know I hurt you and…"

"You've spent so long proving you could do everything alone. But I don't want you to do everything alone. I want you to do it all with me."

The noise swells around us, the flashes relentless, but it doesn't feel invasive. It feels like background. Like static.

I smile, wide and unguarded. "Kiss me."

He looks startled for half a second, then reaches up with his good arm, cupping the side of my face. I grab the front of his jersey carefully, mindful of the sling, and pull him down to me. The second our lips meet, everything feels right in the world, like the last puzzle piece sliding into place.

It's the kind of kiss that says 'yes' and 'finally' and 'I'm here.'

His lips curve against mine as I push the kiss deeper, our tongues teasing each other.

We're not pretending this isn't real. We're not pretending that we don't love each other. Finally, we're not pretending at all.

Eventually, I pull back, forehead resting against his, laughing softly. "I can't believe we're going to be splashed all over the tabloids."

He laughs. "It comes with the territory."

"Well, worth it." I squeeze his hand, grounding myself in the solid truth of him standing here, choosing me in front of everyone. "I love you."

Then he kisses me again.

For the first time in a long time, there's no split or choice tearing me in two.

It's just us, and it feels exactly right.

Wesley's Epilogue

Five Months Later

We don't have time for this.

I'm very aware of that. The clock on the nightstand and the morning light creeping through the blinds are stark reminders that the world's still moving even when I want it to slow the hell down.

Nathan doesn't care.

He hooks a finger in the waistband of my sleep shorts and tugs me back against his chest before I can fully sit up.

"We've got ten minutes," he murmurs against my neck, voice still rough with sleep. "We can be quick."

I laugh, breathless, the sound dissolving the second his mouth follows the line of my shoulder. "You said that last time."

"And I was only slightly wrong." He grins into my skin.

I should get up and be the responsible one. I should remind him he's meeting his agent in less than an hour.

Instead, I cave.

Because even after five months, I want him as badly as he wants me, and because being tangled up in our sheets, all warmth and lazy touches, still feels too good to be true.

We don't rush. He rolls on top of me, his body weight pressing me into the mattress. My body aches with need at the contact. His hands know where to go, tugging my shorts down my legs until the only thing separating us is his boxers, which are gone just as fast.

His mouth trails down my neck, and I lose myself in the feel of his tongue against my skin. He continues south until he teases my nipple, toying with the sensitive bud. My back arches up into him, his length pressing hard against my thigh.

I push him over, rolling on top of him, letting my hair cascade around us as I kiss him deeply, our hands roaming.

I sink down his body, gripping his cock and moving up the length of it until his eyes darken. My grin is playful as I lower my mouth and wrap my lips around him, swirling my tongue across the tip.

His hand moves to my head, grip tightening on my hair, as I work him over with my mouth. I take my time working him over until he groans, a gravelly sound from deep in his throat.

Only then do I slide up, lifting up enough for him to slide on a condom and line himself up under me. When I sink down onto him, I gasp, getting lost in the feel of him stretching me so perfectly.

He doesn't give me more than a second of straddling him, hips moving with him deep inside of me, before he's back on top of me, setting the pace. Nathan loves it when I let go for him, when I let him have control. I love it, too. Inside this room, on this bed, is the only place that I don't overthink a single thing. His brown eyes meet mine as he thrusts deeper into me.

"God, you're fucking perfect, baby." He leans down, kissing me slowly.

I wrap my legs around his waist, opening myself wider so that each thrust of his cock feels deeper than the last.

"You said we'd be quick," I tease.

I'd known when he said it that it was a lie. We like to take our time.

"Forgive me, baby." He thrusts fast and hard. "I lied."

I moan against his neck.

He takes his time, fucking me at a slow and relentless pace. I can feel every nerve in my body tightening, my pussy clenching him tighter as I get close to the edge. Then, he brushes his thumb against my clit, sending me all the way over it. The orgasm stretches all the way down to my toes. He thrusts a few more times before coming and collapsing next to me.

I give myself two minutes, staring at the ceiling and catching my breath. There is nothing that compares to this with him. There never will be.

When my two minutes are up, reality taps me on the shoulder. Even amazing sex doesn't stop my sense of responsibility from pushing me forward.

I groan and roll out of bed, tugging one of his shirts over my head. "Okay. Up. You cannot be late today."

He props himself up on his elbows, watching me with that smug, lazy smile that still gives me butterflies. "You sure? Pretty sure my agent would understand."

"Your contract is getting signed," I say, pointing at him. "Today. You are not blowing that because you couldn't get out of bed."

He laughs. "Fair. But for the record, it'd be worth it." He heads to the closet, pulling on dress pants and a collared shirt. "Besides, it's only been a week since the season ended, so I'm sure ownership is still riding high."

"Losing in the championships is still losing." I grab my phone off the dresser.

He sneaks up behind me and nips at my ear. "It's so hot when you do that."

I giggle, turning to wrap my arms around him. "Do what?"

"Go all competitive athlete on me." He gives me a quick kiss, pushing me backwards toward the bed. "Makes me want to lay you back down and show you exactly…"

"Nope!" I cut him off, ducking under his arm and down the hall. "Now, we really don't have time. The moving truck is going to be here soon with my stuff."

He only had to ask twice before I agreed to move in with him. Maybe that's insane, but after spending almost every night together when we weren't on the road, it just made sense.

Our new place isn't flashy like his penthouse; there is no rooftop infinity pool or modern fixtures. It's a penthouse at an older complex. It has creaky hardwood floors, a weird built-in bookshelf, and actual art on the walls. It feels lived-in and permanent, like someone plans to stay.

And we both do.

"Leaving my place still feels weird," I admit.

Nathan stands and wraps his arms around me from behind, his chin resting on my shoulder. "You're not really leaving it. You left most of the furniture for your dad. And with your sister transferring to the university here, you're bound to have endless family dinners there."

I smile, warmth spreading through my chest. "I know. It feels like closing a chapter."

"Or starting another," he says quietly.

He has a way of calming my anxiety and quieting the pressure that used to overtake me. I sink into him, grinning.

My dad's going to be a fifteen-minute drive away, and my sister's starting fresh. For the first time in a long time, my family feels like it's moving toward something instead of being stuck in the past.

"I'm actually excited," I say. "I get to have them close without being stuck in all the hard memories."

He presses a kiss to my temple. "You deserve that."

I turn in his arms, looking up at him. At the man who chose me publicly, stubbornly, for real. At the life we're building without pretending it's temporary.

"And what about you?" I ask

"We'll see how lunch goes." He huffs out a laugh. "I can't believe my parents actually offered to take me out to celebrate my contract extension."

"I'm glad they are coming around," I say, nudging him toward the door.

"Only because of you." He gives me another kiss, our hands lingering on each other.

"Go sign your contract, superstar."

He grins.

My phone starts ringing. I see the screen and freeze.

Coach Folley.

Nathan notices immediately. "What's wrong?"

I don't respond, already having answered. "Hi, Coach."

Nathan hovers, suddenly very alert.

"Wesley," Coach Folley says, all business. "I'll get right to it. We finalized the roster this morning."

My throat goes dry. The hallway feels too narrow. I'd given up hope for this call. The roster is always finalized right around now, at the end of June, but I assumed most already knew if they made it.

I have mentally prepared myself for the disappointment. There are other years and opportunities. This won't make or break me.

"You've been selected for the National Team roster."

For a second, I don't breathe.

"Oh," I manage, which is wildly inadequate for the moment I've been working toward since I was a kid kicking a ball against a cracked driveway. "Thank you. I… Thank you. You won't regret this."

"I know I won't," he says. "Look, I have more of these calls to make. Someone will reach out for a more detailed conversation. Enjoy the moment. You've earned it."

The call ends just like that.

I stare at my phone as if it might explode.

Nathan's voice is careful now. "Wes?"

I look up at him and promptly lose my mind.

"I made it," I choke out, hands flying to my face. "I made the team. Oh my god. I fucking did it."

He crosses the space between us in two strides, pulling me into his arms like he's afraid I might float away. "You did it," he says, voice thick. "Holy shit, you did it."

I laugh and cry at the same time, words tumbling over each other. "I tried to stay calm and professional, but I blacked out a little and…"

He kisses my forehead, then my cheek, then my lips, grounding me. "I am so proud of you."

Emotion swells in my chest, too big to contain.

I picture little-girl me, dreaming of the U.S. Women's National Team as if it were something magical and far away. All of the sacrifices, the tunnel vision, and the belief that I had to do it alone or not at all brought me right here.

And then I look at Nathan.

At the man who chose me despite my mistakes. The man who chose me for me alone. He makes this feel bigger, brighter, sweeter.

Having him here doesn't take anything away from the dream. It completes it.

I lace my fingers through his. "On to the next big dream."

He grins. "Good thing I've had a lot of practice chasing after you.

Nathan's Epilogue

Three Years Later

There are very few places in the world where I feel out of my element. Between NHL arenas and press rooms, I've learned how to carry scrutiny and attention without letting it crush me. If anything, over the past three years, it's only gotten louder, more relentless, but even still, it doesn't rattle me anymore.

This, though, is something else entirely. I'm halfway across the world in one of the largest stadiums I've ever seen. It's completely sold out, with the kind of crowd that makes even my biggest games feel small by comparison. The roar is loud enough that it feels like it could carry for miles.

I tug at the hem of my jersey, trying to mask my nerves, reminding myself that it's Miller stretched across my shoulders, not Wilder. Somehow, that makes it worse, not better. I have no reason to be this anxious on her behalf, and yet, here I am anyway.

The roar of the fans in the stands pulses overhead as I creep through the tunnel Wesley pointed out to me yesterday. I'm not supposed to be here, but even the World Cup can't stand in the way of our pre-game traditions.

For the past three years, every game I've attended has started like this, with Wesley sneaking out of the locker room to find me. It started because we couldn't seem to keep our hands off each other, and if I'm being honest, not much has changed.

So, World Cup rules be damned.

I try to look like I belong as I pace the hallway. Just as I'm about to give up, thinking we've missed our window, the door finally opens.

My beautiful wife squeals and bolts straight into my arms. I don't hesitate, scooping her up and spinning her with equal enthusiasm.

It's the kind of excitement that refuses to be contained, which makes sense considering it's the World Cup Final and the U.S. is favored to bring home the win.

Once I get her feet back on the ground, I give her a slow once-over. Her hair is pulled into her signature game braid, her jersey already tucked in, shin guards strapped on and ready. Some people love it when their wives dress up, but I love mine like this.

There is nothing sexier than seeing Wesley ready to go kick ass on that field. It's a shame we're not at Harborlight Stadium, or I could try my luck sneaking her off to our custodial closet to remind her just how hot she is when she's focused.

"You're looking at me like I'm a snack," Wesley teases, her eyes bright with excitement.

"You're the whole damn meal." I wiggle my eyebrows playfully.

"You're ridiculous."

She wraps her arms around my neck, hugging me tight, and while she's at it, she taps my back right where her name sits. "My name looks good up here."

"Well, considering you wouldn't take mine when we got married, it'll have to do."

I'm just egging her on. I knew from the moment we started doing this thing for real that Wesley would always be her own person. Taking my last name, for a woman building her own legacy in her sport, was never in the cards. It's just one more reason I love her.

My hands find her waist as she pulls back to look at me.

Her voice drops to barely a whisper. "Can you believe this?" The words come quickly, tumbling out of her. "Like, actually, can you believe I'm here right now?"

I don't even hesitate.

"Yeah," I say, pressing a quick kiss to her cheek. "I can."

She rolls her eyes, but there's a softness there. "Of course you can."

"I've been telling you that since we met," I remind her. "You want something, Wes? You go get it. Every time."

Her expression shifts just slightly, something quieter threading through the excitement.

"We're both good at that, huh?" She says, nudging me. "Mr. Stanley Cup champion."

My chuckle is loud enough that a security guard glances our way, and we both instinctively step closer to the wall like that'll somehow make us less noticeable.

A month ago, the Blades brought home the Stanley Cup. I'd be lying if I said I wasn't still riding that high. When Wesley wins today, too, my ego might just explode.

She's shifting on her feet now, adrenaline and nerves fighting for control, both looking for somewhere to land.

I take her face in my hands. "You've got this."

Then I kiss her. She melts into me instantly, her arms wrapping around my neck as she pulls me closer. We move together like we always do, lips parting as we tease each other, the kiss playful and charged, mirroring the same excitement buzzing through both of us as we stand on the edge of everything she's dreamt of.

The kiss is too short, but considering she's already given me more time than she should, I force myself to pull back.

"Did our families find their seats okay?" She asks, adjusting the captain's band on her arm.

"Yeah. Emma and Delaney are what they're calling 'boy-hunting.'" I throw up air quotes and laugh.

"What does that even mean?"

"You're the woman. You tell me." I give her a pointed look.

"When I was twenty-two, I'd already sworn off men."

I smirk. "Must've taken a really hot, amazing guy to get you back in the game."

Instead of teasing me back, she leans in sincerely, placing one last quick kiss on my lips. "The hottest. Also, the best man I've ever met. I love you."

"I love you, Wes."

The crowd surges louder, signaling the start of something big and the end of our pre-game ritual.

Wesley turns toward the door, and I swat her ass as she goes, because some things never change. She still has the best ass I've ever seen.

I race back out to the stands, not wanting to miss a single second. Once I find our families, I slide into my seat.

It didn't take long after Wesley and I got together for my parents to come around. They still don't agree with all my choices, but they've learned to accept them. Wesley helped, but I think it had more to do with them finally seeing me happy in a way I never had been before.

I always thought hockey was enough. And for a while, it was. But having Wesley? That's what made everything brighter. Better.

They still wish we'd settle down and have kids. And we will, eventually. But neither of us is ready to walk away from our sports yet, so for now, it's just something we have tucked away for the future.

"How'd she seem?" Wesley's dad leans over, raising his voice over the noise.

Even with my parents around more, I'm closest to him. Once he moved to Boston, I found myself sitting beside him more often than not, watching games, grabbing beers, and filling the quiet when Wesley was away.

I've never had to earn his approval. He's never cared about anything I bring to the table except how I love his daughter.

"Like she's ready to win."

"That's our girl."

A grin pulls at my mouth as I watch her take her place on the field as if she owns it.

Because she does.

And if anyone out there still doesn't believe that?

They're about to learn.

For the next ninety minutes, I watch the love of my life take everything she's ever worked for and make it hers.

She's a World Cup champion and a damn good soccer player. A leader. A force. An inspiration. The best thing to ever happen to me. The brightest star wherever she goes.

A woman like her will always find a way to get everything she wants.

How lucky am I that she wanted me?

Keep reading for a sneak peek of
Avery and Grayson's love story.

Out in Fall 2026

1

Avery

If there's one thing I've learned about New Year's Eve, it's that men lose their minds around eleven-thirty. Something about the promise of a midnight kiss convinces them they're suddenly charming instead of desperate.

Newsflash, they're not.

But the bar's packed, the music's loud, and one of my teammates just shoved a tequila shot into my hand like it's water in the desert, so I've had worse starts to a night.

I down the shot, skipping the lime. I'm buzzed enough not to care that it burns while sliding down the back of my throat.

My elbow sticks to the countertop as I watch a guy get rejected for the third time in ten minutes. A different woman every single time. I admire his persistence. Though I prefer my bad decisions to be a little more efficient.

Right on cue, someone slides into the empty space next to me.

"Can I buy you a drink?" He asks, flashing a smile that probably works on most people.

I glance down at my empty shot glass. "I don't know. Can you?"

His lips quirk, a dimple flashing. Yep, this definitely works on most people.

"What's your poison?" He nods to the array of liquor behind the bar.

"Tequila sour." I'd really prefer another shot, but I need to slow down.

He leans into the bar, getting the bartender's attention. After ordering my drink and a beer for himself, he turns back to me.

"Here by yourself?" He asks, shifting closer to me in a way that I'm not particularly fond of.

"Nope. My friends are over there." I nod in their general direction, but don't point out specifics. The last thing I need is him trying to get autographs when he realizes the friends I'm referring to play for the Boston Blades, our local NHL team.

I shift away slightly. It's not enough to be rude, but it is enough to send a message.

A message that he ignores entirely when he leans right back into my space.

I glance at the clock. 11:40pm.

See?

Desperate.

"Is your boyfriend over there with them?" His breath is hot against my face.

Before I can answer, the bartender sets our drinks down.

I consider leaving it behind, already not liking this guy's inability to respect my personal space. But I do really want that drink. It would take a special kind of asshole to let someone buy them a drink and bolt with it in hand.

"Do I get a midnight kiss as a thank you?" His hand lands on my waist, grip firm and confident when it shouldn't be.

Just call me a special kind of asshole.

"Not a chance in hell." I pick up my glass with one hand while prying his hand off me with the other. "I'm going to head back over there. Thanks for the drink."

I hear him shout out after me, something about me being a bitch. It's lame and predictable, so I just hold up my hand, flashing him the finger while I walk away.

Everyone likes to make mistakes on New Year's, as if they all get wiped clean the second they wake up tomorrow. It's part of why I love this holiday so much. There's nothing quite like watching a crowd full of people embarrass themselves, then collectively agree that none of it counts in the morning.

I smile at my friend, Becca, on the dance floor. She tries to wave me over, but I shake my head. That girl hasn't stopped dancing all night, and while I went out there for a bit, I won't risk it this close to midnight.

Being trapped on a dance floor when that clock strikes twelve would be the worst possible way to ring in the new year. All hot and sweaty and crowded.

Instead, I slide into one of the two booths we've commandeered in the back. I spot Wesley at the next booth over and catch her eye, winking.

Wesley is one of my best friends and has been since we met through soccer our freshman year of college. Now that we play on the Boston Tempest together, we're closer than ever. Which means she should know better than to think I believe a second of her fake relationship with Nathan. He's a fan favorite on the Blades, and currently, the man with his hands all over her.

They're both fooling themselves, but I've already done my best friend duties trying to talk sense into them tonight, so now I'm off the clock.

Come to think of it, her fake relationship has really screwed up my life. I encouraged it because Wes absolutely needed to have some fun, but if I'd known that said fun would end with me spending New Year's crowded around a table with half of the Blade's first line, I would've told her to run. Far.

Seriously, if anyone told me three months ago that I'd be not only spending time with the city's hockey team, but also kind of enjoying it, I would've laughed in their face. Then, I would've maybe fled the state.

"Hey Aves, want to trade drinks?" Liam yells over the music, shaking a stray strand of his blond hair off his forehead. He motions to his empty glass.

I huff a laugh. "Get your own."

Liam is my favorite person on the team. I met him at an awards banquet a couple of months ago, and after making it very clear that I was not, and would never be, interested, he started growing on me. Mostly because he's fun, but also because he's essentially the male version of me.

At least the version of me that everyone thinks I still am.

The version I used to be.

"If I go now, I'll be swarmed with girls at midnight." He smirks and nods to the crowd surrounding the bar.

He's not exaggerating. I may play professional soccer, but no one recognizes anyone from my team off the field. The Blades, however, are another story entirely. If Liam tried to make it to the bar now, with ten minutes before the ball drops, he'd be swarmed with women vying for a chance to change his life with their lips at midnight.

"That sounds like heaven for you," I tease.

"Now that you mention it, why stop at just one kiss?"

I chuckle, taking another sip of my drink. "Giving all those women false hope that they might get you all to themselves."

He wiggles his eyebrows. "And what? I'm supposed to believe you bought that drink yourself?"

I scrunch my face because he's got a fucking point.

"You forget Aves," he says, plucking my glass from my hand and taking a swig. "You and I, we're the same."

I steal my cup back and roll my eyes. "Fucking soul sisters, alright."

"Hell yeah," He yells, having no sense of shame over the title.

So yeah, he's not so bad. Neither is most of the team, really. It's not their fault my ex-boyfriend is the devil reincarnate. Or that he happens to play for the New York Yeti, the next closest NHL team to us.

To say I have a skewed opinion of hockey players would be a vast understatement. No one would blame me if they knew the whole story, but I'd rather have them think I'm crazy than spill the details.

Though the more we hang out with the Blades, the more my grudge against all hockey players fades.

That is, until Grayson Shaw slides into the booth on my other side.

"What's so funny?" He asks, eyes bouncing between Liam and me.

The laughter dies in my throat the second I see him. I'm not exactly sure what it is about Grayson that gets under my skin. Maybe it's the whole nice guy act, or how he seems to show up everywhere, but whatever it is, he kills my vibe every single time.

"Nothing. Now." My tone is clipped and full of attitude.

Grayson just smiles easily.

Okay, I lied, I know exactly why he gets under my skin. It's because nothing gets under his. I'm fairly confident I could punch this guy in the face, and he wouldn't blink. I've tried insulting, ignoring, avoiding, and anything else I can think of to get him to realize I don't like him. And still, he slides up next to me in the booth like we're pals.

"Always so quick to inflate my ego." He shakes his head, a grin firmly in place.

"It's a thankless job, but someone has to do it."

"Poor thing, I know how exhausting it must be to try not to like me."

"Oh no." I take a sip of my drink, finishing it completely. "That part is the easiest thing in the world."

His eyes glint, and I'm furious to find not even the slightest bit of annoyance in them. He jokes about me inflating his ego, but his ego must be massive to be this unbothered all the time.

Maybe everyone else is falling for it, but no one is actually that nice. I know that first-hand.

"Alright, you two," Liam cuts in, motioning between us. "Go to your separate corners."

"Better yet, separate ends of the earth." I flash a tight-lipped smile.

"Seriously, I want to talk about them." Liam points over to Wesley and Nathan while I fight the urge to audibly groan.

"What about them?" Grayson asks.

"How are we going to get them to admit they actually like each other?"

"Oh no." I set my cup down hard against the table. "No. No. No. I've already told Nathan to quit being an idiot. Tonight, in fact. I will not be doing anything else. It's their life to fuck up. I'm plenty busy fucking up my own."

Both Liam and Grayson look at me like I'm crazy. Probably because I am.

They chat for another minute about the clueless couple while I plot my escape. If there's anywhere that I don't want to be when midnight hits, it's sandwiched between these two. Honestly, if I were smart, I'd be at home.

But like an idiot, I thought maybe tonight would be the night I finally broke my dry spell. The one that's lingered since the breakup.

Sure, I've resumed most of my pre-relationship habits. I flirt and dance, embrace an occasional steamy make-out session, and have even gone on a couple of awful dates. Despite all of that, I haven't been able to get out of my head long enough to close the deal since everything happened.

When I mentioned to my friends that I wasn't having any sex, I'm not even sure they believed me. Considering I've intentionally made sure it looks otherwise, I don't blame them.

Tonight, I came out determined to find a solid one-night stand. In theory, it should've been a perfect night for it. As soon as I got here, though, I knew it'd be another bust.

Instead, at midnight, I'll be safely tucked into a bathroom stall, locked away where no desperate man's lips can find me.

"Who are you looking for?" Grayson asks, noticing me glancing around the bar for an excuse to escape.

"Probably trying to find the man she conned into buying her that drink. Maybe she'll get a second one out of him." Liam smirks.

I glare at them both. "Better him than the guy who tried to buy me the one before that."

"Why's that?" Grayson takes a pull from his beer.

"Because that guy opened with a magic trick." I snort, remembering how awful it was.

"A magic trick?" Liam sits up, fully invested.

I nod. "With a coin."

"What'd he do? Try to pull it out of your shirt?" The fact that Liam is one hundred percent serious with that guess says everything about how his mind works.

I slap his arm. "Fuck no, that would be too creepy for anyone."

Liam smiles widely. "I bet it would work for me."

For once, Grayson and I agree, both shaking our heads in disappointment.

"He made it disappear," I finally say, shrugging, because after Liam's guess, it sounds pretty boring.

"And?" Grayson asks.

"I told him it was impressive and suggested he try the same thing with himself."

Liam howls with laughter, while Grayson watches me carefully.

His gaze feels a lot like judgment weighing on my skin. Good. Maybe if he thinks I'm awful, he'll finally leave me alone.

A girl ducks under the rail, sliding in next to Liam and wrapping an arm around him as if they go way back and she's not just a fan hoping for his tongue down her throat.

Liam, being Liam, smirks and lets her hang off of him.

Now. Now I need to go.

Just as I'm about to stand, the DJ pauses the music, announcing that it's one minute to midnight. The crowd turns frantic, everyone trying to make it back to the person they want to ring in the New Year with.

Fuck.

There is no way I can make it to the bathroom. I look around, and everyone is paired off. Even Liam is giving the brunette next to him his full attention. Everyone has someone to celebrate with.

I look to my left.

No.

Absolutely not.

Grayson's lips tilt up in a smirk, his eyes glinting with a curiosity that has my skin heating.

There is no way in hell that I'm kissing Grayson fucking Shaw at midnight.

I go to stand, but his hand lands on my arm. It's gentle, but I shrug it off anyway.

"Wait," he starts, but his words are drowned out by the yelling as everyone starts counting down from ten.

I try to watch his lips to see what he's saying, but all I can think while I look at them is what they'd feel like against my own.

Am I about to find out?

No. No, I am not.

When the countdown hits five, I sit back down, knowing there is literally nowhere for me to run to.

My palms start sweating, and I rub them against my thighs, noticing for the first time how close Grayson is to me in his stupid fitted jeans, watching me with his stupid blue eyes.

When the countdown hits two, I'm in full panic mode. My hand shoots out, grabbing Liam's arm and pulling him away from the girl whose name I'm confident he still doesn't know.

"What are you—" Liam doesn't get another word out.

As the clock hits twelve, I press my lips to his with all the confidence I can muster.

Luckily for me, Liam doesn't seem to mind. He opens his mouth and kisses me back. I close my eyes, leaning into it, trying to ignore the fact that Grayson is probably shooting daggers at me, the brunette is probably plotting my death, and Liam is probably getting all sorts of ideas that will never happen.

Don't get me wrong. The kiss is great. It's so great that I let it linger, even after the cheering stops. But there's no heat to it. There's no mind-numbing, skin-tingling, life-changing fireworks. It's just a great kiss.

Finally, I pull away, breaking the contact.

Liam's grin is as wide as possible. "Damn Aves, I might just get all the hype around you."

"You're not so bad either, lover boy," I tease.

He laughs, but it's all playful in his eyes. I exhale a sigh of relief, realizing he felt nothing, too. At least I won't have to figure out how to refriend-zone him.

"Soul sisters," he says, holding his empty cup out toward me.

I laugh. "Soul sisters." I pick mine up too and tap it against his.

When I turn back, I find Grayson watching me, one eyebrow quirked as if I'm a puzzle he's still trying to figure out.

I scan his face, trying to find an ounce of hurt or disappointment, finding only his controlled calm instead.

I'm still not buying it.

"You hate me that much, huh?" He asks.

It's a loaded question. Acknowledging it means admitting I only kissed Liam to avoid kissing him. Which is true, but not something I plan to admit. Especially because using the words kissing and Grayson in the same sentence makes me want to kill off whatever brain cells are curious about it.

"I don't know what you're talking about," I say, standing up now that the crowd has started to disperse. I turn toward Liam. "Thanks for the kiss."

He doesn't hear me, already back in a very close conversation with the brunette at his other side.

I silently curse him for not being the buffer he always is between Grayson and me.

Finally, I turn back toward Grayson, giving him a quick wave. "Bye, Grayson."

"See you around, Chaos." Grayson waves right back.

I feel his eyes on me long after I've walked away.

Nikki Reid

Acknowledgements

To my friends, thank you for letting me talk your ears off about this story and these characters during our many phone calls. Your constant encouragement means more than you know. Even with countless miles and busy lives between us, you have always been the support system I could lean on.

Thank you to my biggest fan and loudest cheerleader, Mom. Your excitement for my writing is the thing that keeps me going on the days when doubt creeps in. Knowing you believe in me makes all the difference.

Gisele G., thank you for the truly spectacular cover art and for answering my endless stream of questions. As a first-time author, seeing you bring my characters to life visually was surreal and helped me see their world in a completely new way.

My husband, thank you for supporting me through every late night spent in front of my computer, and every moment I disappeared into my writing cave. Your patience throughout the endless drafting and revision process meant everything. There is no one else I would want in my corner. I'm also incredibly grateful for your sports knowledge. Nathan would have been a far less believable NHL player if I had not been quizzing you along the way.

A huge thank you to my amazing beta readers, Amanda, Jasmin, Ellie, and Britnee, for your thoughtful, detailed feedback and for caring so deeply about these characters and their story.

And finally, to my readers. Thank you for taking the time to meet Nathan and Wesley. I hope their story made you laugh, ache, and fall in love along the way. I look forward to sharing Avery and Grayson's story with you next!

About the Author

Nikki writes romance novels that capture the kind of true, life-altering love everyone deserves. Her characters might play professional sports, but their lives and struggles are relatable to all.

Married to her high school sweetheart and mother to two energetic toddlers, Nikki embraces how loud, messy, and entertaining the everyday moments of life can be when spent with people you love.

Most days are spent chasing small humans, but once bedtime actually sticks, Nikki can usually be found reading or binge-watching reality competition shows.

Subscribe to her newsletter to be among the first to receive up-to-date information and sneak peeks about upcoming releases.

Subscribe to Newsletter

Follow me on Instagram, Threads, TikTok, or Amazon to stay in the know for all things Boston Playmakers. Any review is appreciated.

Instagram - @authornikkireid
TikTok - @authornikkireid
Threads - @authornikkireid
Amazon – Nikki Reid